"A serious, fascinating work, indeed a great novel, perhaps the author's masterpiece . . . Leaves its readers mesmerised"

RAFAEL CONTE, *ABC Literario*

"*Variable Cloud* is intensely serious, literary and wryly humorous, its mesmerising, labyrinthine sentences induce sense of wandering the corridors and topiaried gardens of Marienbad"

SHENA MACKAY, *Sunday Times*

"Excellently plotted and written with that perfect simplicity that tends to escape notice and which has characterised Gaite's novels from the start . . . She has once again made the difficult art of writing into easy reading. Here is a novel destined to enjoy a long and prosperous life" **GONZALO SANTONJA**, *El Mundo*

"This spirited novel . . . has a Madrid-in-the-nineties feel to it that is occasionally reminiscent of Almodovar's zany moments on screen" **LIZ HERON**, *Times Educational Supplement*

"Beyond any doubt the outstanding novel published this year. The reader will find it unforgettable" **CARLOS GALAN**, *Alerta*

CARMEN MARTÍN GAITE was born in Salamanca in 1925. She published her first novel at the age of 29, and won the Premio Gijón. Her subsequent novels have won many awards. The publication of *Variable Cloud*, her first novel after 14 years, was a considerable event in Spain where it headed the bestseller lists for several weeks. Two novels have followed: *La reina de la nieves*, which won the Spanish National Prize for literature, and *Raro es lo vivir*. Both of these will be published by Harvill.

MARGARET JULL COSTA is the translator of Javier Marías, Bernardo Atxaga and Juan José Saer. Portuguese writers she has translated include Eça de Queiroz, Mário de Sá-Carneiro and Fernando Pessoa, for the translation of whose masterpiece, *The Book of Disquiet*, she was joint-winner of the 1992 Portuguese translation prize.

Carmen Martín Gaite

VARIABLE CLOUD

*Translated from the Spanish
by Margaret Jull Costa*

THE HARVILL PRESS
LONDON

*The translator would like to thank Carmen Martín Gaite,
Annella McDermott, Antonio Martín and Ben Sherriff
for all their help and advice*

First published with the title *Nubosidad variable*
by Editorial Anagrama, Barcelona, 1992

First published in Great Britain in 1995
by The Harvill Press, 84 Thornhill Road, London N1 1RD

This paperback edition first published in 1997

This edition has been translated with the financial assistance of the
Spanish Dirección General del Libro y Bibliotecas, Ministerio de Cultura

1 3 5 7 9 8 6 4 2

A CIP catalogue record for this book is available from the British Library

ISBN 1 86046 347 9

Photoset in Fournier by Servis Filmsetting, Manchester

Half title illustration: by the author

The Random House Group Limited supports The Forest Stewardship
Council® (FSC®), the leading international forest-certification organisation.
Our books carrying the FSC label are printed on FSC®-certified paper.
FSC is the only forest-certification scheme supported by the leading
environmental organisations, including Greenpeace. Our
paper procurement policy can be found at
www.randomhouse.co.uk/environment

MIX
Paper from
responsible sources

FSC
www.fsc.org   FSC® C016897

Printed and bound in Great Britain by Clays Ltd, St Ives PLC

Whenever I write a novel, I always feel as if I were holding the shattered fragments of a mirror in my hands, and yet I'm always hopeful of being able to put the mirror together again. I never will manage it and, the longer I go on writing, the more remote the possibility seems. This time, I knew from the start that it was hopeless. The mirror was broken and I knew that I would never be able to put the pieces together again, that I was not skilled enough to recreate the whole mirror for myself.

Natalia Ginzburg in the introduction to *La città e la casa*

Contents

For the soul that she left on
constant guard, like a tiny light,
in my house, in my body and in the
name that she called me by.

I

Plumbing problems

Yesterday, after almost two months of changeable weather and intermittent downpours – which, it seems, have been a blessing for the farmers – spring finally burst forth and I could feel it bubbling provocatively on the other side of the window. The fleeting shadow of a pigeon revealed, as it vanished, the flood of light invading everything with its sudden, surprising clarion call, an anachronistic tug in the direction of now impossible adventures. I remembered that I'd been dreaming about Mariana León. We were lying in a field somewhere gazing up at the clouds; before that, rather less pleasant things had happened. I seem to recall that I was on the run because of my involvement in a murder and I may have been talking about it to Mariana as we lay there on the grass, although I can't be sure; I'm not even sure if she was with me when I was being pursued. You land from your dreams slightly stunned, and fundamental details are always lost in the process. The light coming in through the window, a similar light to that in my dream, found an echo only in my irregular breathing, like the flutter of dying butterflies.

Eduardo was already up. Still staring at the window, I lay for a while listening to the shower, which only increased my sense of unease as the sound slithered out from beneath the bathroom door.

The bathroom may look beautiful, but I hate it. Last autumn, we spent 3,000,000 pesetas doing it up in style, taking the opportunity to enlarge Lorenzo's old bedroom which we made into a dressing room with a mirrored wall. "It's best to make a really good job of it, because it will increase the value of the apartment if we ever sell it," said Eduardo who, for some time now, rarely talks about anything but money. "Do you know how much people these days are prepared to pay per square metre in this area?" In fact, we finally had to rip out all the old pipes and replace them with copper ones anyway in order to put a stop once and for all to our conflicts with our downstairs neighbours on the seventh floor, and that struck me as a much sounder reason for changing things. For years, they've been traipsing upstairs to complain about the damp stains that sporadically bloom on their ceiling and demanding from us both diagnosis and cure for what, in the end, turned out to be an incurable epidemic. I realize now that the symptoms of the problem, the unpredictable stains that kept appearing on the ceiling downstairs, marked a parallel process in my own erosion – the decline of my enthusiasm, hopes, willpower and of my more than questionable abilities as wife and mother.

When Eduardo began earning more money and we first moved here, our children were still quite young – Encarna was nine, Lorenzo was eight and Amelia was two, I think – and we nicknamed the people on the seventh floor "the Family of the Flute-playing Ass" because their eldest son spent every spare moment playing the clarinet in his bedroom. You could see him through the patio window, applying himself to his task with furrowed brow, although listening to him was hardly a delight to the senses. His parents didn't seem particularly bright either; in fact, they proved distinctly difficult and, quite apart from the tedious problems with the plumbing that forced us to have dealings with them, there was never even a hint of cordiality between us. To me, their existence was a torment. Every time there was a knock on the door and that woman appeared with her dyed hair and her thin lips, lips that struggled hard to disguise the reproach concealed beneath the courteous smile, I would be gripped by a treacherous, unmistakable feeling, familiar since childhood, one which overwhelms me when I least expect it, looming over my happiness like a great, black cloud: the need to justify myself to someone else for faults I cannot even remember having committed.

"Not again, surely. It's not possible, Señora Acosta. The plumber only came five months ago, don't you remember? And we paid for the redecoration. Besides ..."

2

"So what are you saying? That I'm making it up? Come down your-self and have a look."

I would follow her down the twenty-one marble steps that separate our apartments. The journey was usually made in silence. They had gold wallpaper in the hall with a raised pattern of seaside motifs and, as we advanced down the corridor, everything I saw through the doors oozed the same chilly ostentation and bad taste that reached its peak in the master bedroom – all satins and Pompeian furniture – through which I inevitably had to pass in order to reach the cause of the discord.

Those exploratory visits to the apartment downstairs, which always ended with a decision to recall the plumber, left a residue of disquiet in me that took time to heal over because I knew that, when I least expected it, the wound would open up again somewhere else. The damp stains, for which I felt obliged to take responsibility, never appeared in the same place twice, and the effort it took to match up the stain downstairs with the guilty spot upstairs demanded from me a degree of concentration I could not shirk, but against which my whole organism rebelled. The worst thing was that the woman on the seventh floor had realized – with a torturer's refined sense of cruelty – that she could wield some power over my vacillating moods by means of these domestic investigations and she clearly enjoyed cornering me with her questions.

"It must be the washbasin this time. You have got a washbasin in that corner, haven't you?"

"I don't really know, I can't quite orient myself."

Beneath the critical gaze of my neighbour's cold, blue eyes, I would look at the ceiling like someone studying an unfamiliar map on which you're going to have to take up positions in order to fight a pointless battle.

"I must be having a nightmare," I used to think, "I must be dreaming. I'm sure I'll wake up in a minute and the two of us will be sitting laugh-ing on the floor which is in the process of becoming grass, and the toilet will have turned into a leafy apple tree and the stains on the ceiling into drifting clouds and no one will be insisting that I account for their chang-ing shapes, unravelling clouds circling above our heads, evoking images

3

of freedom and adventure, of just living from day to day; I'm sure that the apartment upstairs and Eduardo and this woman's husband with his grey moustache will all have disappeared and that I'll look at her and she'll have turned into Mariana León and we'll wake up, safe from the future, two schoolfriends sitting on a spring-like carpet, laughing out loud and savouring the fact of having skipped class together, while they munch their sandwiches and talk about how stupid boys are."

Of course, that never happened, and the tense relationship which the endless plumbing problems had created between us and the Family of the Flute-playing Ass didn't get any easier later on either. Quite apart from the torments it caused me, there was the feeling obliged to take an interest in how the work was going, in the colour of the tiles and the size and shape of the new bath, in the recent megalomaniac refurbishment of our bathroom, designed by an architect friend of Eduardo's, which only increased hostilities with Señora Acosta who, it seems, is a martyr to her nerves and couldn't stand all that banging going on above her head for the best part of a month.

"Anyone would think you were building the Escorial," her husband said to mine one day when they met each other in the lift.

When he told me, Eduardo was indignant at such rudeness, but I found it funny and thought that our neighbours on the seventh floor were absolutely right; I was the first in line for a nervous breakdown, what with all the comings and goings of workmen and the shifting of rubble, but I didn't dare laugh in front of Eduardo, although at one time almost anything was enough to set us off; now he takes himself more seriously, and money even more so – it's his panacea for all ills and therefore should be mine as well.

He emerged from the bathroom already dressed and as he walked round the bed to open a drawer in the dressing-table he came between me and the light from the window. He looked to me like a complete stranger and when our eyes met, he must have sensed what I was feeling because I noticed that he seemed intimidated as he always is when he doesn't get the unconditional response he needs to endorse his new image. He's been buying a lot of new clothes lately, chic and casual, and I think he goes to

4

the sauna too and uses gel on his hair. The children don't talk about him much when I go to see them at their place but when they do, they refer to him as "the plaster wall", I don't know if that's because of the renovations he's always planning or because of his plastered-down hair or because he himself has become a kind of seamless wall that won't allow any problem to slip through that can't be solved with money. I don't know what to do when the children talk about Eduardo in that tone of voice; they're right in a way, but I find it hard to accept; my upbringing didn't prepare me for the fact that one day I might find myself in a situation like this. It's clear that for him the children are becoming less and less important, and that he just needs to know they're around somewhere at a safe distance; when the children and I are together, we hardly even mention his name. It must be my fault, I never find the right moment. But it's not a question of scapegoats, for things aren't that simple; there's a lot of underlying tension.

He had stopped by the bed and was looking at the ashtray full of cigarette ends, my clothes draped any-old-how over the armchair and my book lying on the floor. I still didn't move. I closed my eyes.

"Are you all right?" he asked. "You don't usually wake up this early."

"I had a very strange dream and I was trying to remember what it was. I've got a bit of a headache."

"You and your mania about not taking any pills!"

"If I started, I'd only have to break the habit some day. Anyway, my dreams aren't always unpleasant. The one I had today was really nice."

I tried to catch his eye but failed. I watched him standing in front of the mirror doing up his tie, but his voice belied his apparent impassivity when he asked me what time I'd finally got to sleep.

"I heard the clock strike three, I think. You still weren't back."

He changed the subject and deep down I felt grateful. Another of the things he's lost is the talent he used to have for inventing some attractive topic of conversation when he wanted to distract me from another that threatened to be rather less so. He could have sat down for a few moments on the bed and asked me what I'd dreamed about. I know that's asking too much, but I would have liked it and I felt sad for him too,

5

because we used to have a lot of fun interpreting each other's dreams in the days when we still used to do that.

As expected, he didn't ask. So the name of Mariana León wasn't mentioned between us that morning. Perhaps it was for the best, and even if it wasn't, it doesn't matter. As my son Lorenzo says, what happens happens and that's all there is to it, no point worrying about it.

Out of the corner of my eye I watched him lingering over the task of getting the knot in his tie just right and although he kept up a stream of talk, I suspected that his logorrhea was a symptom of his desire to ward off my silence. He told me not to expect him for lunch and that, later, he was going to have to go to an exhibition of paintings by his friend, Gregorio Termes. Gregorio Termes is the architect who masterminded the refurbishment of the bathroom, someone I've never got on with very well, although I've had to put up with him. I didn't know he was a painter as well. Eduardo got annoyed. It seems he's told me this several times and I've just never taken it in. That doesn't surprise me. I find him so stupid, so vain and, above all, so moneygrubbing that if Eduardo did tell me something about him, I would have responded in the same way I do with anything else that's of no interest to me: switch off. At first, he tried to put on the charm and dazzle me with an image of himself as the cultured executive, up-to-date on all the latest European trends, but subsequently, when I didn't take the bait, he began to treat me with haughty disdain; I don't know why, but he never seemed to notice that it made me laugh every time he unrolled his plans and stood there, rapt, as if in a trance. Señor Acosta was right about one thing: anyone would think he was the architect of the monastery of San Lorenzo de El Escorial. Anyway, he relegated me in his mind to the category of ordinary housewife, entirely lacking in any aesthetic sense. You get the picture. If he knew how I used to take him off for the children's benefit when I went round to see them, just to let off steam ... Encarna, especially, used to roll around laughing, and they don't even know Gregorio Termes or how good my impersonation of him is. So now it turns out that he's a painter too. A remarkable artist, a real original. I began to feel curious about these paintings; you shouldn't just dismiss as rubbish something you haven't seen. I felt suspicious of the adjectives used to describe his work, though. These days there are so many overnight successes described as being "real originals" that you can't help wondering if they are, in fact, that original, or if they're not simply artists with one eye on market forces pinpointed for them by a computer. A lot of important people were going to the exhibition, even the Prime Minister's wife. Of the other names Eduardo mentioned, some rang a bell and others didn't. According to him, I've lost all interest in modern culture lately.

He'd finished doing up his tie and with the tip of one Italian shoe he prodded the novel that had kept me company in my insomnia and had fallen open on the floor. I'd gone to sleep at the point where Mrs Dean was beginning to suspect that Heathcliff has begun prowling round Thrushcross Grange again like a threatening shadow.

Eduardo said: "You must be in a bad way if you're re-reading *Wuthering Heights* at your age."

The idea of having to defend Emily Brontë bored me and it seemed more prudent to say nothing, because I'd suddenly had a blinding revelation that verged on certainty: the landscape to which Mariana and I had escaped in the dream were the marshes at Gimmerton, and yet I couldn't reconstruct it, I couldn't put myself back in that situation. It had gone completely. Suddenly, by contrast with the spring sunlight pouring in through the window, the remaining part of the day seemed more opaque, the sunlight just reminded me of a series of errands to run and obligations to be met which displaced the memory of my dream once and for all. Some awakenings are like sulphuric acid.

Eduardo said goodbye. Without quite knowing why, I asked him where Gregorio Termes' exhibition was being held and what time the private view began, just in case I fancied going. He looked at me in surprise, as if slightly embarrassed. He wouldn't have time to come and pick me up, he said. I came out with a stream of that particular brand of insouciance that my daughter Encarna is always advising me to make more use of.

"What's it to you? D'you think I'm so far gone that I wouldn't know how to get to Calle Villanueva under my own steam? Bloody hell, Eddy, I find that positively insulting. Give me a bit of credit, please."

He tried to laugh and couldn't. It's awful, it's against his religion.

"I thought you didn't like exhibitions," he said, while he was putting on his jacket, "but if you want to come, fine, I'll see you there. Do smarten yourself up a bit, though, and don't turn up looking like a hobo."

I felt a strange jolt and our eyes met for a second, like startled birds. His warier eyes took flight at once. "Looking like a hobo" is one of those phrases that corresponds to what Natalia Ginzburg calls "the family lexicon". It was coined by Eduardo himself, in its early version, some thirty years ago; looking or dressing like a hobo equated with a certain independence of spirit; it wasn't in the least pejorative – on the contrary. He used to like the fact that I didn't wear make-up, that I could be ready at a moment's notice. He liked my way of dressing, of moving and of expressing unusual opinions. He used to say that I was a gipsy at heart and that I should never even consider being anything but a hobo; once, he told me, he was waiting for me and when he saw me in the distance, he said to himself: "There's my hobo lady." So dressing like a hobo became a kind of compliment; I was the hobo lady and more than pleased to play the role. The expression had now clearly lost that semantic slant.

"Don't worry," I said, "I'll find a disguise worthy of Gregorio Termes and Co."

I didn't go disguised as a hobo. At six I phoned Encarna to ask if I could borrow an Indian silk dress of hers that really suits me. Well, it used to be mine. She brought it over along with some make-up, but she couldn't stay, not even for a cup of tea; she was in a hurry. She seemed distracted and rather excitable; she didn't look well. She didn't like me asking her if anything was wrong. Well, I never used to like it when my mother asked me.

"Look, Mama, these things happen, but it really doesn't matter. You just get on with your life, please, that's what I always tell you, and don't worry about us. Have a good time, love. And don't worry. I'm just having a bit of a bad day."

When she left, the cleaning lady ironed the dress for me and at eight o'clock, after a few moments of indecision, I hailed a taxi and gave the address of the gallery where Gregorio Termes was holding his exhibition. There were still a few slight glimmers of spring light in the sky. "Surprise is like a hare: if you go out hunting for it, you won't find it sleeping in a field." I wrote that in one of my diaries in my youth. What I didn't know was that I wasn't the only one to remember that phrase and that, in a short while, someone would greet me by quoting it word for word back at me. Who could have imagined that after all this time, in that place bursting with celebrities, I would meet you, of all people, Mariana León in person.

Although now, as I write this, I wonder: Did I really meet you or just someone with your name?

(To be continued; Mariana, although I don't quite know how.)

II

The lion's den

Madrid, 30th April, night

Dear Sofía,

Despite all the years that have passed since I last wrote you a letter,
I haven't forgotten the ritual we always kept to. First, make sure
you're sitting comfortably and always choose a pleasant place,
whether it be indoors or out. Then, describe that place in some detail,
like setting the scene for a play: it's daytime, in the foreground there's
a sofa, on the right-hand side a door that opens on to the garden, or
whatever, just enough for the recipient of the letter to be able to
orient herself and know what the situation is right from the start.
Those are the rules that you suggested – I'm sure you remember –
just as you laid down the rules for nearly all our games, almost
without our realizing it.

Anyway, I am sitting comfortably and I've uncorked a bottle of
French champagne I've had in the fridge since Christmas. (When I
opened it, the cork hit the ceiling!) I had good reason to open it. If you
knew what a miracle it was for me to want to write a letter again and not
just a business letter, or a letter of complaint or advice, or in order to sort
something out, a letter for its own sake, without drafting it out in your
head first, because it comes straight from the heart, just because you feel
like writing it. I'd forgotten. It's the most urgent thing in the world, but
also the least pressing. As for the rest, well, it's eleven o'clock, I've got
the whole night ahead of me and I'll just see what happens, I'm not going
to check what I've got in my diary for tomorrow, the world can go hang
for all I care, I've got things of my own to be getting on with and I feel
sorry for all those people dining in five-star restaurants or who have just
sat down to watch television or to spend hours talking on the phone.

After all, that's the sort of thing I would usually be doing on Fridays at this hour.

I've just drunk the first glass of champagne, to your health; I drank it very slowly, looking at it against the light between sips, watching the way the bubbles rise, because that's the important thing about champagne; you drink it in with your eyes too and it collides with the imagination. It's delicious, so cool and fizzy. If you drink champagne without a good reason to, it doesn't taste of anything, it doesn't even look golden. Cat's piss.

Before pouring a second glass, I've got up to get my cigarettes and to switch on the answering machine. I have no intention of answering the phone, whoever it is. I've also been looking for this particular writing paper, the creamy-beige colour of chickpeas, which is why it took me a while; I'm using it for the first time to write this letter to you and I couldn't remember what I'd done with it. Just as well; if it hadn't turned up, I'd have thrown a fit. Nowadays, it's only stupid things that get me all worked up. I found the paper with its matching envelopes in a lovely little box with the Statue of Liberty on the lid. It was beginning to seem more like the lid of Sleeping Beauty's coffin. It hasn't been opened for ten years, imagine that; it's exactly as I saw it in a shopwindow on 14th Street during one of my first visits to New York. I don't know if you've ever been to New York. It always reminds me of you, mainly because of the stationer's shops.

Right, two reference points so that you can orient yourself, one to do with time and the other with light. A short while ago, the wall clock chimed half past eleven; it's the clock that used to be in my parents' apartment in Calle de Serrano, at the end of the corridor. There's no point describing it, because you once said that, for you, the notion of time would always be bound up with that clock. Of course, the passing of time can easily erase the very notion of time that we once believed to be immutable. Second reference point: I'm writing to you by the light of a lamp that you also know. It's the table lamp my grandfather had in his study, do you remember? The one with the gold stand and the glass shade – billiard-table green outside and white inside. I'm enclosing a map on

11

squared paper and I've written a "C" and an "L" in red to indicate the places occupied by these two old acquaintances of yours in the room where I now spend most of my life. The map is a bit of a mess, but then, as you know, drawing's not really my strong point. Anyway, it gives you a rough idea. As you can see, it's actually two large rooms separated by an arch with a velvet curtain across it which, at present, is drawn back. It's fifty-eight paces long (I count them when I walk from one end to the other) and there are four windows facing on to the street. The three marked with a "B" have balconies and the last, marked "W", is a large, magnificent window with a splendid view over the street. Seen through the arch, from my seat at the table, that window, wrapped in tenuous light, looks somewhat unreal at the moment. I'm looking at it in a strangely detached way, imagining that I'm showing it to you, that the two of us are twelve years old again and that we're both busily sketching it and that you're helping me to people it with fantastic objects – it's a sketch that is both transient and eternal and which the clouds carry with them towards the future. You used to see all kinds of things in the clouds: empty beaches, children's faces, dragons. I saw a house with a large window overlooking the street.

Look at the map. As you see, I'm sitting near the end wall, in the most protected place, because there's no door. There used to be one, but I had it bricked up. From the corridor you go straight into the part with the large window which I call "the lion's den". For, however pretty I've made it sound, that area frightens me a little, why deny it? Sometimes it gives me the creeps, the way a horror film might. It's where I see my clients and, at one time, I gave a lot of thought to the decor; it had to be both welcoming and relaxing. Given the results, I think I got it right. If my clients don't like it, they've never told me so. I do my best not to let them notice my fear. This is strictly between you and me; if you tell anyone, I'm done for.

I know you. I bet you've already added a couch. Well yes, my dear, there is one, immediately opposite me, that little rectangle marked with a small "c". It's exactly like the one you're imagining, with one arm and a headrest, that's right, exactly as a child would draw it, upholstered in green and black, a fantastic bargain, the sort of thing you used to be able to find in the Rastro. It was love at first sight. I think it was a deciding factor in my becoming a psychiatrist.

I changed quite a lot after buying it, when I began to get regular clients, in the late seventies. I'd just ended a relationship with a gentleman who frequently used to, and indeed still does, lead me down the street of sorrows. When I say "ended", that's just a manner of speaking. He's a writer who has problems with his sexuality, problems I tried unsuccessfully to resolve, first on the couch and later in bed. I might tell you the whole story one day. He didn't behave entirely badly. He lent me the money for the deposit on this apartment and for the work that needed doing at the outset. We're quits as regards money, but as regards other matters, that's not so clear.

The apartment is on the third floor, in an old house in the old part of Madrid. You know the address. If it weren't for seeing that address written in your unmistakable handwriting on the big envelope that you sent me the day before yesterday, the box containing the writing paper I bought in Manhattan would still be lying in Sleeping Beauty's coffin. I hope you'll come and see me one day, although it's best not to plan anything. For the moment, I reply to your letter with another letter. That was another of your golden rules and presumably still is, since you haven't told me your telephone number. Of course, I could find out and, in fact, I did look it up in the phone book. My first impulse was to call you and tell you to come over, but then I realized that I shouldn't, that the ground we're treading might still be fragile. The precaution of an initial exchange of letters seems a healthy one to me. There's still a lot of ice to break.

I was telling you that I live in an old house. The thing I really fell in love with, apart from the big window, were the high ceilings decorated with a moulding of acanthus flowers. I've always like lying down and staring up at the ceiling. That's how I prepare myself to dream, to regain my calm or to reach a decision. The larger the space between my eyes and the wall they're staring at, the freer my thoughts are to travel, the more surprises there might be. Needless to say, they're not always nice surprises. The upstairs apartment is an attic with, immediately above this room, an enormous roof garden on which a lot of the paving stones are uneven or cracked. Suddenly, when I least expect it, when I'm at my most distracted, staring at the ceiling, I suddenly notice a suspicious damp stain. As you see, I'm the Señora Acosta of my upstairs neighbours, an old couple who, to make matters worse, spend long periods in Alicante, so that I have to solve all my plumbing problems through the mediation of a bad-tempered, boozy, rheumaticky old porter. Sometimes water runs down the walls and some of my books get damaged. It's a well-known fact that everything in life is a question of plumbing, and you just have to accept it. Later on, I'll tell you how much your story made me laugh. For the moment, I'm just finishing off the prelude. And my third glass of champagne.

As I told you the other day when I saw you, I live alone. I have no children. I used to have a cat called Aitch who was very affectionate and had bags of personality, but I refused to have her spayed and she left me, one April night, when she was on heat. It sounds like the words to a tango, doesn't it? In fact, it did feel a bit like that, because I do have tendencies in that direction. I've never wanted to have another cat since then and sometimes, on moonlit nights, I call her name, knowing perfectly well that she'll never come back. However much I feel like crying when I remember how she used to curl up on my lap, I wish her all the happiness in the world and I like the fact that she chose her own destiny. That's the danger of giving someone plenty of freedom. The same thing has happened with a few men too, and I never learn.

You knew the first of those men, Sofía, but what you don't know, because it was then that I started drifting away from you, is how much that first painful love affair changed my life; I still bear the scars. By re-running the film over and over, I've come to understand that the reason it hurt me so much was because it was a double grief. The terrible thing wasn't that Guillermo left me from one day to the next without any explanation, but that you didn't give me any explanations either, and you knew all the answers. It took me a while to realize that, and in the end I didn't find out through you. It took me a long time to understand why

14

you were behaving so strangely towards me, why you looked away when you saw that I was sad, and for me to accept your silences. I suppose you were suffering too. Possibly even more than I was. I know now from my studies and from what my clients tell me that when problems aren't cleared up at the right time they start to form a wall of porous sludge that immediately begins to solidify until it's so hard you couldn't break through it with a pickaxe. Yes, the plaster wall, that's it. A dam forged out of the cement of cowardice and inertia that blocks the path to a relationship that was once utterly straightforward. The tubes get blocked up and a lot of crap gets stored up inside, although we're not aware of that, because it takes a long time before it starts to smell. Even worse, the plumbing of the soul is difficult to locate and you can't just use any old plumber, you have to get a specialist in.

Do you remember the quote (from *Ecclesiastes* I think it was) that we used to like so much: "How is the gold become dim! How is the most fine gold changed!" Those were questions I often asked myself throughout that spring when our fine gold first began to dim, but they were questions that had no answers; deep down, I didn't want to find one, I was afraid of rooting around in things that might produce an answer I didn't want to hear. So I contented myself with my role as the unfortunate victim of fate. Then, when I found out what was going on, my reaction was unexpected.

It was after an anatomy class; Julia Rodrigo told me that she'd seen you and Guillermo near the woods, kissing. What I felt has already been described by Bécquer and with such accuracy that I can never understand why people label him as kitsch: "When they told me, I felt the cold of a steel blade in my entrails." That only lasted a matter of seconds. My superego immediately took over, like an implacable lion tamer, and ordered me to adjust my mask, get control of my voice, and, allez hop!, jump through the ring of fire, and no snivelling. I told her that I knew all about it, that you'd told me yourself. Julia gave me an odd look. We were in the bar, we'd ordered some *tapas*. "And you're still friends?" she asked me. "Of course we are, why shouldn't we be? All this stuff with boys is just plain stupid. The only thing that gets me is that Sofía takes it so seriously and can't concentrate on anything else, right in the middle of exams too."

I wasn't entirely lying, because it did make me angry and it still does. It was our first year at university and you'd enrolled in the arts faculty mainly because I made you do it; you remember how keen your father was on your taking a secretarial course so that you could help him out in the office. I've been telling you ever since you were a child that you're enormously gifted when it comes to literature and I was quite right. Here's the proof: the party I'm celebrating tonight with champagne is in homage to your wise and skilfully woven words, to those eight pages that you half-jokingly entitled: "My homework", so you see I *was* right. It's infuriating that you have to put up with that fool Gregorio Termes treating you as if you were a conventional, unimaginative housewife; you don't seem to care, you even laugh about it, but it makes me angry, as does the way you live. You should have gone on studying and taken a competitive exam for some high-flying job in teaching or government, or else applied for a grant – something. Even though you were lazy at school, you could run rings round the swots. I know that after the first year at University you had to resit some exams in September, but so what? Did you have to throw in the towel when it came to the second year just because of that? It's something I've never really understood.

I didn't throw in the towel, in fact, I held on to it almost too obsessively. Yet, for what it's worth, my professional career had its beginnings in that first confrontation with calamity, of that there's no doubt. Sometimes when I attend some congress or other, or see myself talking on television, I think that the woman I see there – with whom I sometimes get on reasonably well and who at other times makes me sick – must have devoured the Mariana León who used to watch the changing shapes of the clouds with you, and that she's grown up at the expense of the fine gold of our adolescence. There's nothing to be done about it though. You can't have everything and there are always going to be losses, although some are more irreparable than others. In a way, I capitalized on your loss, I know that sounds horrible, but that was more or less what happened.

A few days later, on 28th May, you phoned me up to wish me happy birthday and I could tell by your voice, which sounded a bit depressed, that you wanted to see me. I don't know what was wrong with you, how your love affair was progressing or whether or not you were experiencing it as a guilty passion. I wonder about that now and I'd love to be able to travel back down the tunnel of time to help dispel that sense of guilt, if you had one, and perhaps help prevent things turning out so badly, as, I learned later, they did. I didn't even suggest meeting. You know how I am once I've decided something: I can't be budged and, at the time, I'd decided to do exactly as my lion tamer ordered, and he told me to have nothing more to do with Guillermo, you or with anything else that might be contrary to my status as tame lion. I'd thrown myself wholeheartedly into my studies, working furiously night after night, fuelled solely by coffee and dexadrine. I told you off you because you weren't doing the same. A perfect opportunity for you to ask if I'd got over Guillermo, or words to that effect. But how could you? After I put the phone down, I cried for a long time.

Then we saw each other one evening at the end of June, at your house, with a lot of other people. You were wearing a red dress I'd never seen before. Failing some of your exams didn't seem to have affected you much, but I didn't think you looked at all well and you seemed very tense. I went to help your mother who was preparing some canapés, and she mentioned that she was worried about you because you'd completely lost your appetite and she asked me if I knew what was wrong with you. At that moment you came into the kitchen. "She must be in love," I said. You just stood there looking at us. You'd heard what I said. Then I knew that you knew that I knew everything. But Guillermo wasn't there and his name didn't crop up all evening.

Not that there was any reason why it should. For a while now, I've been feeling increasingly uncomfortable, and I realize that I'm getting into the one area I wanted to avoid, the lion's den. A shadow has fallen across the clear, joyful prelude in which I simply wanted to thank you for the light that blazed forth from what you wrote and to reflect it back to you in mine, to celebrate the resurrection of Sleeping Beauty, to respond to this new game you've so unexpectedly proposed. I'm much more out of practice than you are and I've run out of steam already. I've spent two whole pages talking to you as if you were lying there in front of me on the couch. I've just drawn the velvet curtain so as not to see it, in order to forget about the lion's den. An occupational hazard. Forgive me.

Instead of asking your forgiveness for them, I could just tear up these last two pages, but then I remember the seventh and last of your epistolary rules: "Never cross out anything you've written except to make a correction to grammar or style." But that's not the case here. So I'll leave it as it is. I won't break the rules of the game just because this particular game has gone slightly wrong. We will try instead to put it right.

The same room as in the previous scene but, this time, with the curtain drawn. Floor-to-ceiling bookshelves with some library steps in order to be able to reach the books at the top. There's a mark in the middle of the ceiling made by the cork from the champagne bottle. Señora León lights a cigarette and pours herself one last glass of champagne. She raises it solemnly. Happy month of May, Sofía.

1st May, dawn

The clock's just struck one o'clock in the morning. It's May already, dear Sofía. Do you remember how much we liked the month of May? You said that when we were older and were earning a bit of money we would travel to Yorkshire together, in May, in order to visit the tomb of Emily Brontë, see the countryside described in *Wuthering Heights* and roll down a grassy slope. I'm touched to see that you're still reading that novel, you must know it by heart by now. You've made me feel like reading it again too; however, I'm not writing to you in order to discuss Emily Brontë's literary talent, but yours.

I've had two really busy days – people's problems always seem to get worse in the spring – and this is the first quiet moment I've had to read the eight typed pages you sent me the day before yesterday by messenger, together with a handwritten note. In it, you refer briefly to the suggestion I made the other day that you should write something, anything. How could I not make such a suggestion after your wonderful lecture on broken mirrors, the hare in the field and fried eggs? It was as if we'd never been apart. It just pours out of you, quite unconsciously, in the middle of a cocktail party, and you're not drunk or trying to put on some kind of pose, you don't even realize you're doing it. I've always known that what you need is stimulus and I get the impression that, at the moment, you don't get much stimulus at all. On the other hand, your capacity for response remains astonishing. Nothing anyone says to you ever goes to waste.

When I picked up the fat envelope and saw my name written in your handwriting, my heart leapt and I realized that you were giving me back something I'd forgotten about, something that rejuvenated me. I felt something similar the other night when I saw you standing with your back to everyone else, looking intently at Gregorio's paintings with that air, so peculiar to you, of a bird perched on a telegraph wire. It was a matter of seconds. Before I identified you, I was thinking: "Well, thank God there's one person declining to take part in all this hooha and not kissing everybody left, right and centre," then suddenly, you put your head on one side and bit your lip as if you were trying to puzzle something out, just the way you used to at school, and then I knew it was you.

From the age of thirty onwards, all traces of childhood are gradually erased from people's faces; it's a kind of atrophy of the spontaneity reflected in our behaviour and our expressions. There have been a lot of studies made of this and I notice it myself in my work every day. I can sense at once when it will be possible to salvage something of a person's childhood and when it won't. The people in the second group are the hardest nuts to crack.

But you're just the same as you were, Sofía, exactly the same, I mean it. The same voice, the same smile, the same gestures and that half-ingenuous, half-provocative curiosity of yours, and the way you ask questions, the way you look at things and comment afterwards on what you've seen with your own eyes, with no regard whatsoever for received opinion. And then there's that capacity of yours, which you've always had, for turning the most inhospitable places into pleasant corners for conversation, as if you touched them with a magic wand.

I was sorry I had to leave just when, thanks to you, we'd managed to find a bit of space to ourselves and had just begun to get along better, but I'd already told you that I'd arranged to have supper with a friend. Afterwards, I wondered why I didn't invite you to join us; with that surreal sense of humour of yours you'd have taken all the tension out of our supper and the three of us could have had a good time, certainly better than Raimundo and I would ever have on our own. That's his name, Raimundo. He's the writer I was telling you about before, the one who lent me the money for the deposit on this apartment. He's having a hellish time at the moment and he won't be happy until he's passed it on to me and he can see that I'm being dragged with him into his hell. And, of course, the worst thing is that I let myself be dragged in; I can't seem to detach him from my life. It's too tortuous a story for me to give you a summary; I'd have to lie down on the couch and have you sit behind me at the head. One night we'll do that, if you like. I don't want to talk about him just now. He wasn't at Gregorio's exhibition. He pokes even more fun at Gregorio than you do.

I don't want to talk to you about Gregorio either, although I know him quite well and I could tell you some amusing things about him and about his relationship with that twenty-something blonde who was glued to his side. Not that you were ever much interested in gossip. I noticed that you looked at them and at the other people who came to greet me, trying to cut in on our conversation, as if they were Martians. It was as if you were calling to me from some storybook garden. I sensed that, but I found it very difficult to get into the garden; I couldn't find the gate, I couldn't open it. "It's like in dreams," you said, "in which you keep getting minor characters from other stories butting in. They're put in to throw you off the scent. They make the most noise and fuss, but they're not vital to the plot. You must take no notice of them."

I was standing opposite you, and it seemed that I had to keep apologizing all the time for knowing so many people, for smiling at them, talking to them, responding to their salaams. I was furious that, after all these years, we had to meet in such an inappropriate place, and I said as much. You didn't agree. You looked at me, one finger raised in the air, and said: "I've caught you out, Mariana, remember what you said before: 'Surprise is like a hare: if you go out hunting for it, you won't find it sleeping in a field.' Isn't that what you said? Unless it's just a clever quote." And then you asked me in an amused tone: "Or did you come out to hunt tonight?" I felt disconcerted. As usual, you were in control of the game, you held the keys to the riddle. I looked at you and you were smiling. What did you mean? No, I hadn't come out to hunt. And it was so hard to get into the storybook garden, what with that constant stream of "minor characters" passing by, calling me by my name and kissing me. You were completely unfazed by it all. "If you weren't on the hunt for something, then it isn't a case of seeking, but finding. And this is where we found each other. It will disappear if we reject it. It's the right place, Mariana, because this is the place where the hare sleeps in the field, or rather, it's where surprise was crouching, waiting for us." Then you said how life is made up of the broken fragments of a mirror, but that we could see ourselves reflected in each fragment, and how you felt like dipping some bread in Gregorio's paintings because they looked just like fried eggs splattered across the canvas, and how the world is constantly transmitting messages that we don't even know how to pick up. That's when I realized that if I wanted to keep up with your verbal flow, I'd have to recover the childish faith that you haven't lost but which I have, and be able to believe in the possibility of transforming a place and allowing the poetic miracle of its new incarnation to take place. Towards the end, when it was time for me to go, I became aware that there was a kind of aura around us that separated us off from the other "characters", that distanced them from us, and that the place itself had become unbewitched; it had shuffled off its deceptive outer appearance and become the place where the hare sleeps; I could see it there in the middle of the room, in the middle of the storybook garden, like a still, white symbol. It was ten o'clock. I couldn't stay any longer. I realized that we'd barely scratched the surface of the chapter entitled "Our respective lives" and that the occasion of our reunion had flown past. I had to run away like

Cinderella. It was time for my date with Raimundo. That was when I asked you to write, about anything you wanted, but you must do it at once, that same night when you got home. I couldn't let you disappear without you promising me that. I have to confess with a certain embarrassment (more intense since I've read your eight pages) that I ask a lot of my clients to do the same thing, but I asked you with a different kind of urgency, I was staking a lot on it. You looked at me amazed. "You mean a composition?" "Yes, exactly, a composition." "It will have to be very simple, I haven't written a composition in ages, but I love the idea. If I write one, can I send it to you?" "Of course, that's what I'm asking you to do, I want you to send it to me." That was when you took out your address book and rested it against the wall in order to write down my address. I saw, as I see now on your envelope, that you still write with a fountain pen and still form your a's the same way, with rounded bellies.

I'm sorry, Sofía, but I can't keep up this pace. I genuinely am sorry, because I was beginning to get into the swing of things, your swing of things. I'm going to have to interrupt this letter and finish it tomorrow. Raimundo has just left me a very distressing message on the answering machine. I don't know what's wrong with him, but he sounded really bad. I could barely understand what he was saying. He wants me to go over and see him. I have no alternative but to go.

4th May

It has to be this afternoon. If I wait until I've got a free moment to finish the letter in the tone and rhythm with which I began it, God knows when I'll be able to send it to you. I haven't even had time to re-read it, although I usually carry it around in my handbag.

I've been in a terrible state these last few days. Raimundo tried to commit suicide and he's only being released from intensive care this afternoon. He survived by the skin of his teeth. I'm in a hospital waiting room, resting this letter on a copy of today's newspaper in which his photograph appears. As you can see, neither the paper I'm writing on nor my handwriting are up to the standard of the previous one. In this world of shattered mirrors, peace is an ephemeral luxury.

I'm replying, albeit in rather telegraphic form, to the note that accompanied your eight typed pages. "I'm sending you my homework," you said. "Thank you, Mariana. It's been a long time since anyone set me homework like this and I really enjoyed doing it. If you don't find it too boring, I can continue if you like." It isn't a matter of "can", you must. It is homework after all. More than that, it's fun and that's why I beg you not to cut off my supply, not now that I need it so much. Remember what Don Pedro Larroque used to say to you after reading your compositions, that if you enjoy writing something, then what you write is bound to be enjoyed by others; remember how his eyes used to shine behind his glasses when he patted you on the back: "Keep writing, Señorita Montalvo, always be a writer." Well, just for now, I am Don Pedro Larroque. Please, Sofía, keep writing and write about anything you want to, because you can squeeze the juice out of anything, you can turn the most sordid and routine things into literature. You lay down the two of spades on the table and it turns out to be the king of diamonds. You've no right to waste that gift.

Bored? I'm afraid my silence may have made you think that. Nothing could be further from the truth. I long for your next instalment, I await it impatiently, whatever the subject, whether it's in flashback, written in the first person or in hendecasyllables. Keep writing, Señorita Montalvo, always be a writer.

I have to leave you now. One of these days I'll phone you up and we'll arrange to meet, but not just now, I need to feel stronger. I really don't know how I've managed to keep going these last few days. I may leave Madrid for a week or so.

Goodbye and blessed be forever the hare in the field.

Lots of love,

Mariana

PS Just one suggestion for the next chapters: the character of Eduardo is of no interest to the reader. Could he not be removed from the action, given less to do?

PPS I'm enclosing a prescription for Loramet. I don't know if that's the sleeping pill you normally take, but if it isn't, I can recommend it. It doesn't leave you with a hangover.

III

The experiments with collage begin

It was half past five. Amelia arrived wearing her air hostess' uniform and carrying a small overnight bag. She'd just got back from Colombia. She'd had her hair cut. I wasn't expecting her and I didn't hear her come in, so I felt a bit embarrassed that she should find me closeted in the room that is still considered to be hers, however infrequently she sleeps here. It's my favourite room in the whole apartment and I sometimes think that perhaps she feels I'm taking it over. Not that she's ever said anything to me – on the contrary, she seems to find it natural. She came over to the table, smiling. I immediately took off my glasses. I don't enjoy being kissed if I've got my glasses on.

"What were you doing, Mama?"

"Nothing. Just doodling. I suddenly had the urge to paint, I felt like it the moment I woke up. Do you mind me using your box of water-colours?"

"No, please do. Things go rotten if they're left in a box, that's what you always say. And since the only thing I'm likely to paint at the moment are clouds ... But that's really nice, really different, what is it?"

"It's called 'People at a cocktail party'. It's a sort of collage. Now I'm going to stick little triangles of silver paper all over it, as if they were fragments of a mirror. Do you see? I was cutting them out from cigarette paper."

She was standing behind me and had placed one hand on my shoulder. I stroked it with mine.

"And what's that white rabbit doing in the middle? It looks a bit like the white rabbit in *Alice in Wonderland*."

"It might be, except that Alice's rabbit wore a waistcoat and a watch. That's a hare or rather it's supposed to be. It symbolizes surprises."

"What surprises?"

"I don't know, the surprise of you turning up now, for instance. Surprises in general. But it might also be a homage to Lewis Carroll. I hadn't thought of that. If you like, we can give him a waistcoat. Look, we could make it out of this red-and-white striped cardboard. What do you think? Shall we give him a waistcoat?"

Amelia burst out laughing and threw her arms around my neck.

"You're a scream, you really are. You don't know how nice it is to come home and find you here like this. Let me take a photo of you now, just as you are."

She started rummaging around inside her vast handbag, crammed with all kinds of disparate objects. She ended up tipping it out on to an armchair and once more I was amazed at the quantity of things Amelia manages to fit into her bag. It was a Polaroid camera, the sort that don't give you a chance to get impatient to see the result of the click. The recently captured image emerges slowly before your eyes, the way coloured transfers used to. The children are vastly amused by the mixture of fascination and awe I feel when confronted by any technical advance. For them, the Polaroid is no white hare. I wonder if they ever see white hares at all and where.

"Stranger bring glass bead necklaces to great Indian chief," said Amelia, noticing my concentration, waiting for the miracle to occur. "Big Chief no be afraid, this no work of Devil."

I watched myself emerge from the damp stain on the newly expelled rectangle, as if I were pushing my way through a mud-coloured mist, with my chin resting on my hands and a happy smile on my face – my reaction to looking at Amelia. The light from the smile grew stronger and stronger until it filled everything. Even the mess on the table looked nice, as each object became clearer and filled with colour: the open box of water colours, the scissors, my glasses, the red-and-white tube of glue, the cigarette packet, the pencil and the large hare grazing in the middle of the picture. I realized that you have to look at things from the outside if disorder is to become order and take on meaning. Then you understand and appreciate everything differently.

"It's come out really well, hasn't it?"

Amelia took off her shoes and lay down on the divan.

"Yes, Big Chief, but no touch yet. Fingers leave evil mark."

Then she yawned and said she was tired. She sounded slightly sorry for herself, as if she had the beginnings of a cold; it was the voice of a little girl who doesn't want to go to school and is playing for time.

Despite the fact that she's the only one of my children who earns a living – the other two show no signs of doing that – she's still the youngest and, in moments of weakness, she's not embarrassed to use that voice with me. I asked her if she was going to stay the night and she covered her face with her forearm. She said, in a discouraged tone suddenly tinged with impatience that firmly closed the door on any further questions, that she didn't know anything, that she didn't know anything about anything. Until recently, when she wasn't working, she lived in the Chamberí district in the flat of a friend of hers who works in films. I don't know him. Encarna says he's very handsome and that Amelia is madly in love with him, in the old-fashioned way. It seems, however, that they're not getting on very well at the moment, the usual thing, jealousy. Encarna told me that as well.

I started clearing up the mess on the table. I didn't want to lose the little triangles of mirror so I put them in an envelope.

"Is there anything to eat?" asked Amelia. "I'm a bit tired of plastic meals and synthetic orange juice."

"I'll go and see. You just stay here and relax and I'll call you when it's ready. It's really lovely to see you."

I went to the kitchen. Daría, the daily help, had had to go to the doctor because she was feeling a bit off-colour. I started heating up a saucepan of fish stew left over from yesterday and I was just beginning to get out the ingredients for an imaginative salad when I heard Amelia's footsteps in the corridor. She put her head round the door. She had some clothes slung over her shoulder.

"I'll eat in the kitchen, Mama. I'm going to have a shower and get changed and see if that wakes me up a bit. Can I use the Escorial?"

"Of course you can. There are clean towels in the dressing room, in a new chest of drawers you'll see on your right. And if you've got any dirty washing, leave it in the laundry room."

I realized at once that the most urgent reason for her excursion to the far end of the apartment had been to make a telephone call in private. The phone on the bedside table in our bedroom is connected to the one in the utility room and you can hear a dull tinkle as the person dials the numbers. Big Chief stops sorting out vegetables and stands listening. The beat of that particular drum came from very far off, interspersed by silence, reflecting the indecision of the finger doing the dialling. She dialled five numbers and then, after a brief pause, I heard a noise more like a click. She had hung up. She couldn't do it.

I abandoned my culinary tasks and sat down with my elbows on the table, in a state of total concentration, my eyes fixed on the white telephone hanging on the wall in the utility room. My heart had started beating faster, just as it does when I'm watching a film and there's one of those scenes coming up that encourages you to identify with the protagonist. I not only knew what was going to happen, I was orchestrating it from my chair, it depended on me, because I was her.

She needs to screw up her courage; she walks towards the wardrobe mirror which returns her sleepy gaze, full of desire. She starts taking off her dress, her tights, her shoes, all very slowly.

"I like watching you undress," says a voice behind her. The viewer knows that it's an off-screen voice because there's no one else there; she strokes her own shoulders and responds by uttering a secret, almost imperceptible name, which, of course, can be any name, depending on each viewer's individual response. Guillermo, Guillermo, Guillermo. She lies down on the bed and lights a cigarette. "Go on," I say to myself, "go on," and out of the attic of the memory surfaces an indestructible combination of seven numbers. Ever since I began to struggle against the temptation to use it, it has remained burned in my memory, so much so that each number, which before I would dial carelessly, naturally, became a scar, one step nearer the abyss. We don't know what it means to breathe until breathing becomes difficult. Go on, call him, go on.

She'd hung up again. This time the first six echoes of her dialling came more quickly. Then there was a pause, finished off by a final energetic tinkle which, to judge by the time it took, must have been a nine. I waited. Don't hang up. She didn't hang up. She'd done it. Now I could relax, the matter was out of my control.

I got up quickly, because a suspicious smell was coming from the cooker. The stew was sticking to the pan. I turned down the gas, added a bit of water and started stirring rather unenthusiastically with a wooden spoon, feeling suddenly quite faint.

The phone in the utility room was only five steps away, I could go over there, furtively pick it up and eavesdrop on that conversation. I wouldn't, though, and Amelia knew that I wouldn't. I started to hate my mother from the moment I knew that she used to read Guillermo's letters. When she died, ten years ago, I realized that I still hadn't been able to forgive her for that. I tried to concentrate on the salad and turned on the radio to pass the time.

Amelia didn't come back for a while. I'd already set the table some time before and was opening a bottle of wine. The corks always split, I know from the start that they're going to.

"Give it to me," said Amelia, "honestly, you're useless. You don't put the corkscrew in straight. Let me do it."

She was wearing jeans and a mauve T-shirt with the words "I'm free" emblazoned across the front in white. I don't know if she's as free as she says she is. No one is when they're in love. I noticed that she hadn't showered, because she never wears a shower cap and her hair was completely dry. She'd been talking on the phone all that time and it was evident that what was said hadn't pleased her.

"They're so ugly those uniforms they make you wear. You're much prettier like that, you look really lovely."

"Do you think so?"

She smiled wanly at the corkscrew, but the smile died halfway, as if

29

swallowed up by a well of darkness about which I know nothing. She probably knows a lot more about mine.

The voice of Georges Moustaki emerged from the radio:

> Votre fille a vingt ans,
> que le temps passe vite, madame!
> Hier encore elle était si petite …

Suddenly, I had a vision of myself standing on the edge of my own particular well of darkness and I didn't want to look into it. I tried to resist that unhealthy, insidious feeling of vertigo, but felt drawn to it too. The kitchen was the well and at the bottom of the well, like shifting ghosts, three childish faces were looking up, calling to me with siren voices, asking me for their tea, three silhouettes that merged into one, entwining and dancing around me to the sound of the clarinet played by the Flute-playing Ass downstairs, tossing exercise books and banana skins into the air. Mama, look what Lorenzo's doing, who broke the jam pot?, it wasn't me, listen, look at my exercise book, don't take any notice of him, Mama, look at me, look how well I can whistle, Daría, Daría, face like a tortilla, please, be quiet, all of you, look, Encarna's finger's bleeding, look-look-look-look. And my mirror spun around to take in everything, I was a full-length mirror that reflected them back when I looked at them, returning to them the image they needed in order to go on existing, absolved of guilt and fear, a mirror that could not crack or tarnish. Take no notice of them, Daría; come on, sit down and eat, Papa will be here soon, you've got five croquettes each, what do you mean, is that all, they're delicious, did you make them yourself?

Amelia had managed to remove the corkscrew without splitting the cork and had sat down. Her gaze was inert, impenetrable. It was clear that my mirror was of no use to her any more. She said she couldn't stand Moustaki and switched off the radio.

"Why have you set two plates?" she asked. "Are you going to eat as well?"

"Yes. I wasn't hungry before. It depresses me eating on my own. You'd think I'd have got used to it by now."

I immediately regretted having said that, because it isn't quite true; for example, I would have enjoyed the Moustaki song much more if I'd been on my own; sometimes I really enjoy not having to worry about other people's likes and dislikes. I'd said it now, though, and the pathetic jingle of my last words slithered round the kitchen walls like a black streamer.

Amelia looked down at her plate and started eating in silence, without even saying whether or not she liked what she was putting in her mouth. For many years, years now lost in the mist, my mental well-being was dependent on coming up with delicious recipes and on getting the approving comments of the little imps reflected in my mirror. Such vices can become chronic if you don't struggle against them. I refused to ask Amelia if she liked the stew, but the trouble was that all the other questions that occurred to me were rejected too. They all seemed like a clumsy darn over that great gaping silence which was now growing thicker and splitting off into two divergent streams, hers and mine, each one sweeping its own alluvion along with it, both affected by a shadow cast by the same black streamer.

The phone rang and I went to pick it up in the utility room.

"If it's for me, I'm not in," said Amelia.

It wasn't for her. It was Consuelo, Daría's daughter, another of the inhabitants at the bottom of the well, the cheekiest and the most rebellious, a redhead who started having periods when she was only ten. The children were fascinated by her vulgar self-confidence. Now she takes over from her mother when the latter isn't able to do the housework, and I pay her a certain amount every month to tidy up the apartment where Lorenzo and Encarna live; it's called, in the family lexicon, "the refuge for tortoises".

Consuelo speaks with a very strong Madrid accent, peppered with new words that she picks up every day out on the streets; according to her mother, if the house suddenly fell down, there was little chance that Consuelo would be found amongst the rubble. Her dream is to be in a rock group and the children encourage her, because they say she's got talent. Her main field of operations is Vallecas.

She was phoning me from the refuge or the "ref", as she calls it (she has a penchant for abbreviations). At first, I couldn't understand why she was phoning, but that was nothing new. She was in the habit – quite a common one as it happens – of launching into a conversation without filling you in on the background first, "the scattergun approach" Mariana and I used to call it, the kind of story for which you lack any point of reference or previous information about the subject, usually some knotty problem, and which is fired off at you without any preamble.

This time the crux of the matter seemed to be some vases which Consuelo assumed were mine.

"And like I said to the man who'd had to carry them all the way up from the third floor, those ought to go to the other apartment, they must be something to do with the Señora, but this is the address he was given along with Lorenzo's name, although underneath it says "for Antonio" and, of course, as there's nobody here, I can't ask, but they don't go with this place at all, and where are we going to put them, because they're huge, whatever made you buy such huge vases?, by the way, there should be two of them, but at the moment there's only one and the base of the other one, hang on a minute … What? Oh, right, the man here says that that's how they were handed to him and that it's not his problem."

"But who gave them to him? And when? For goodness' sake, Consuelo, explain yourself more clearly, I don't know anything about these vases."

"They're sort of Chinese-looking, with big flowers on them."

"But who is this man? No, Consuelo, listen, I don't mean I want to know his name, and no, I don't want to talk to him either. All I want to know is who sent him and where did the vases come from. Yes, OK, I'll wait."

Amelia had looked up from her plate and was watching me through the arch that separates the kitchen from the utility room.

"What's up?" she asked.

"I don't know, I can't work it out. Some baroque tale involving the inhabitants of the refuge, you know the kind of thing."

"Oh God," she said, "now what? If you're getting the news courtesy of Radio Consuelo, your lunch will have gone cold by the time she's finished."

"Never mind, I'll turn it into a funny anecdote for you afterwards."

"I'm sure you will," said Amelia, smiling for the first time since she'd come into the kitchen.

Then she went on eating, but she seemed less abstracted, less distant. When Consuelo started off again on her long explanations at the other end of the phone, I was much more interested in getting a smile out of Amelia with my comments on the whole confused story than I was in understanding it. I was speaking for her benefit, in order to catch her eye which met mine as if across a bridge in the process of being built.

"Right, come on then. Characters in the plot," she said as soon as I'd put down the phone and joined her at the table again.

"A truck driver called Cayetano Trueba, a gentleman who lives in Calle Covarrubias, a couple of Chinese vases and a certain Antonio who hangs out at the refuge and seems to be the intended recipient of this mysterious consignment. Only he's not there at the moment. That was about all I could find out. Consuelo is no Flaubert, hard rock's more her line. We'll have to trust in the narrative gifts of the truck driver who's on his way over here now, because it looks like I'll have to pay the freight charges for these two vases. Do you want a bit more salad?"

"Yes, it's delicious. But you are silly, Mama, don't pay anything, what's it got to do with you? They're conning you."

"Don't you believe it. They make me laugh too."

The rest of the meal passed in a much more relaxed atmosphere and twice Amelia laughed out loud. Stories about the refuge were always good for a laugh and she enjoys it when I tell them as if they were a sort of French farce which, I've discovered, is the right tone to tell them in. On the other hand, her relationship with her brother and sister – who, ever since they were children, have formed an exclusive block – has grown increasingly difficult with the passing of time; their disorderliness distresses her and she rarely goes to the refuge, although in fact it belongs to all three of them – their grandmother left it to them in her will – and there's more than enough room. When my mother lived there alone, after Papa died and the apartment was divided in two, we used to call it "4bL", 4b Calle de Lagasca; I think it was Lorenzo who called it that. Latterly, I had the Devil's own job rounding up all three of them to go and have lunch there and when one of them didn't turn up, Mama would be put out and she'd blame me, saying that I wasn't strict enough with them, that they didn't show me any respect. I can hardly believe it's the same apartment.

Memories of the move to the refuge surfaced, a move that represents an important landmark for me in what a sociologist would call "the family dynamic". However, all that upheaval becomes an amusing anecdote when revived for someone who can see its funny side. A kind of linguistic complicity had grown up between Amelia and me which freed us from our respective wells and, in the middle of the empty field, the hare had reappeared surrounded by fragmented mirrors. Loads of them. So many that you could't look at them all at once.

For example, the fragment showing the refuge where Encarna, Lorenzo and their occasional refugees hang out began to grow blurred, obscured by a cloud. What happened before that move? And the light glittered on another fragment of mirror corresponding to an earlier stratum of the story. I must remember that flashback, I have to add it to the collage, even if I have to use spit not glue.

The scene takes place in an airport. It's summer. I've gone there to say goodbye to two sixteen-year-old girls who are travelling abroad together for the first time. They whisper excitedly to each other, radiant, weightless, ignoring me completely, while I keep re-counting the suitcases, trying hard to identify myself with their adventure. I wish I was coming with you, I tell them. Soledad smiles dutifully, but Amelia hasn't even heard me. With a sudden flash of intuition, I realize that they have driven me out of paradise; it's not them who are saying goodbye, it's me.

"Oh, I forgot to tell you, the other day Soledad rang up asking for you."

Amelia's eyes lit up and her whole face was transfigured.

"But Mama, why didn't you tell me that straight away? I wrote to her a little while ago at an address I had for her in Paris and the letter was returned. Was she calling from Paris?"

"No, she's in Madrid."

Amelia stood up and threw her napkin in the air as if it were a winning card at bingo.

"I can't believe it!" she shouted. "I'm so happy! How long is she staying in Madrid? She can't have left already."

"I don't think so. She said she'd come and see me, she said she wanted to talk to me. Her parents have recently got divorced apparently, just like that, it was very sudden. Well, you know what Soledad is like; when you were both small, she always used to tell me her secrets. I think she loved me as much as you did."

Amelia wasn't listening to me.

"Really, Mama, it's like a miracle. I've been thinking about her constantly for months. You distance yourself from people who are fundamental to your life, and always for the most stupid reasons, that's what happened with Soledad and me; you lose track of their lives and suddenly you realize that it can't go on like that. When we landed at Barajas this afternoon I was thinking how I'm just dying to see Soledad again. Without her around I get all mixed up. You've no idea what a blow it was when that letter was returned to me, a really long letter telling her everything I've been doing these last few years. And now I'm going to see her, I'm really going to see her, that's better than any letter; I'll just have to hear her voice to feel I'm back on that plane carrying us to Brighton, that marvellous feeling of taking off together, looking out at the clouds, and you know how bored I get with flying now. I don't know if the same thing has ever happened to you, that suddenly when you most need it, something clicks, and it brings you back to life, do you know what I mean?"

I placed my hand on the hand she had placed on the table, and briefly stroked her cold, thin fingers. On her third finger she wears a slender ring encrusted with tiny diamonds that belonged to my mother and doesn't fit me any more. I was wearing it the first time Guillermo took my hand.

"Of course I do. The same thing happened to me. Two days ago."

She seemed to emerge from her daydream and she looked at me strangely.

"What happened to you?"

"One of those encounters with the white hare. Do you remember Mariana León? That friend of mine from school, I've often shown you photos of her."

Amelia put on a neutral face.

"No, I don't remember. Look, tell me about it later, all right? I'm going to call Soledad right this minute. I'm sorry. It's just that I'm so excited."

When she rather brusquely withdrew her hand from mine, she knocked over a glass of wine.

"It doesn't matter, don't worry. Go and see if she's in, go on."

I was left alone, looking at the red stain on the tablecloth. Almost at once I heard the dull tinkle of the phone in the utility room. I felt so indifferent, I didn't even stand the glass upright again. Suddenly, all I wanted was to leave the apartment. Even the idea of tidying the kitchen seemed to rise before me like a mountain and another even larger mountain loomed when Amelia came back and I would have to force myself to share her feelings. I needed to go out, to give myself a break.

I grabbed the notebook where Daría writes down anything we need to buy: milk, sugar, potatoes, and I tore out the second page, which was blank. "Big Chief she drown in domestic well, escape to street. Be happy", I wrote. Then I took the note to Amelia's room and left it on her bed.

I went out without even combing my hair or changing my trousers, without a handbag. I just picked up my keys and my purse, like when I nip down to the bar to buy cigarettes. I almost ran out of the front door.

"Will you be back soon?" asked the porter, who was talking to another man.

He wanted to ask me when would be a good time to give us the monthly maintenance bill. Of course, it's the beginning of May. I said brusquely that I was in a hurry and that he should ask my husband. A hysterical reaction. It was because, when I was coming down in the lift, I'd spotted Señora Acosta waiting on the seventh floor and the last thing in the world I wanted was to meet her – there's some bill outstanding for something or other. I didn't want to have to think about the well and its inhabitants. Although even as I said the words: "my husband", I'd already leaned over to peer into the well without even realizing it, and that fleeting glimpse of him paralyzed me. I looked at my watch. We'd arranged to go to the theatre with his brother and his sister-in-law; I'd have to go back upstairs to leave another note. Had I really not thought about Eduardo all day? And I realized something else that left me feeling even more disturbed: that Amelia hadn't even asked after him. Too many perplexing questions. One thing was certain, I needed to go out into the street and think about them. Big Chief not return to well just yet.

"Excuse me," said the porter, "I think this gentleman wants to see you."

I looked at him. He was a well-built man with receding hair and a very frank gaze. Did I know him from somewhere? He held out his hand with a certain familiarity.

"Cayetano Trueba, at your service," he said.

The lift had gone up and was starting to come down again. No, I really couldn't stand to see Señora Acosta just now.

"Oh, right, the deliveryman who was at my kids' place! Delighted to meet you. Would you mind coming with me to a bar so that I can get some change and pay you. Come on."

These last words were spoken as I was racing out towards the door, not even checking to see if he was following me until I reached the door of the bar and stopped. He was by my side. He was wearing a corduroy jacket.

"You're very light on your feet," he remarked, smiling.

It was a straightforward remark, amusing, objective, something that required no explanations. And it was nice to hear the voice of a stranger who from the very start seemed so trustworthy and companionable.

As soon as I pushed open the door of the bar and caught the smell of grilled prawns and coffee, I felt temporarily safe and my anxiety lifted. There were quite a lot of people there and you could hear fragments of conversations drowned out by the clatter of slot machines. Everyone there was seeking relief from something, nursing their mid-afternoon wounds. I observed them with calm curiosity, they didn't impinge on my mood nor I on theirs, we accepted each other's presence but demanded nothing.

Cayetano Trueba is from a village in Alcarria, from a family of beekeepers. He told me this while we were standing at the bar, drinking beer at my suggestion. He's very attached to his village and to his family and there's a terrible crisis at the moment because a plague called varroasis has spread throughout Spain and is infecting every bee in sight; whole families, not only his, were being reduced to poverty. In the Las Hurdes region, near Salamanca, people walk down the streets openly weeping. A tragedy.

"It's something you see, but at the same time don't see. You go along to visit the hives one day, a bit like going to see if a child is still asleep – because, as you probably know, bees hibernate in the winter – and there's nothing there, there are no bees. You look here, there and everywhere, how can they not be there?, it's not possible, but there's nothing, not a trace, not even the consolation of seeing them dead, because what happens is that when they get the disease they fly off and go and die in the countryside, away from the hive. What instinct can it be that drives them? Maybe they don't like funerals. They say it's some sort of acarid, whatever that is, but there's no cure, it's like a sort of AIDS, they say they're going to try and come up with a vaccine, but who ever heard of vaccinating bees, honestly, it's just not possible. The two dairies in my village look like pharmacies what with all the concoctions they use to keep the animals from falling sick and then there are the fish dying in the rivers and loads of animals in the nature reserve at Coto de Doñana, where, as it is, they keep the animals wrapped in cotton wool, you must have heard about it. And it's because everything is poisoned, the air, the water, everything. This varroasis business, I'd never heard of it in my life and then from one morning to the next, there it is, varroasis, it's a word you have to learn whether you want to or not, it's certainly stuck in my mind."

He told me that, before he got married, he was a beekeeper too. He came here because his wife wanted to come to the city. He worked as a truck driver until a few years ago, but it was a very hard life; he prefers removals and deliveries, at least that way you get to see different houses and meet all sorts of different people, and you get the chance of a chat, a bit of conversation. And there's no shortage of work, thank God, now that people move around so much, now nobody stops in the same place for long.

He gave me a card which read: "For lightning fast service call Transportes EL OSO". That's what he calls his truck, he usually parks it by the sports stadium. He's bought another one for his son now, a really nice lad, his only son. He still lives at home.

"How many children have you got?" he asked me.

"Me? Three, but they don't live at home any more."

"You look too young to have three children. What you need now is to see them happily married. Or is one of them married already?"

"No, young people today don't marry so easily. They're cleverer than we were."

"Well, yes, they do have more time, you're right there. And then there's unemployment, of course."

"Exactly."

I changed the 5,000 peseta note I had and paid him, but he wouldn't let me pay for the beers. Men in Alcarria aren't used to letting a woman pay; it might seem old-fashioned, but he thought it was rather nice. He said he'd really enjoyed himself. People who live in big cities are losing their taste for a chat, everyone just goes about their own business, but you can usually find someone. The girl with red hair said I was easy to talk to. A nice girl, by the way, though a bit of a scatterbrain. At first, he thought she was one of the family, the way she talked about us, with such familiarity.

"I know, but then, in a way, Consuelo grew up with us."

When we said goodbye, out in the street again, he asked me if Don Raimundo was also one of the family.

"Who's Don Raimundo?"

"The one who sent these vases. Now his house really is strange! Have you ever seen it?"

"No, I don't even know him. He must be a friend of my children."

"A very uptight gentleman," he said.

I didn't pursue the topic. I held out my hand and said I'd call him if I ever needed anything moving. I already had quite enough fragments of broken mirror. Too many.

I set off down the pavement at a brisk pace, not knowing where I was going. The afternoon had turned out very cold. I didn't have a coat on, so I stuck my hands in my trouser pockets, hobo-fashion, and I felt free.

I needed to think exclusively about Mariana León, at least for half an hour. I'd fled precisely in order to think about her, to try and recall her voice and remember her face. The other evening, there were moments when she seemed exactly the same as before, but I don't know, life changes us so much. When I remembered how confident she seemed and how many people she knew, I regretted having sent her my first batch of homework and I felt a stab of jealousy. I won't be able to rest until she writes to me.

IV

Heading south

Dear Sofía,

It's getting dark and I'm writing to you from a sleeping compartment on a train, whilst outside the window a succession of housing estates, scrapyards, allotments, factories, waste ground, rubbish tips and junkyards go by, as well as the shanty houses that extend further out each day, spreading like a sore, as the speculators and their excavators force the poverty of the outlying areas into retreat, as if they wanted to deny its existence by removing it from view. The sun was setting as I was leaving Atocha station and there are still a few brilliant bands of orange striping the dark clouds.

This train is going to Cádiz, but I'm getting off shortly before that, at Puerto Real, my final destination. I was there last year and I liked it. A friend of mine, a woman of sixty and a marchioness into the bargain, has got a big house there in Calle de la Amargura, yes, that's right, the Street of Sorrows, and she's given me a set of keys to the house. She's not often there because she doesn't have time, what with travelling all over the place making decisions about the many properties and businesses she's had to deal with since the death of her father, an Andalusian landowner straight out of a nineteenth-century novel; anyway, she's grateful to me for coming to Puerto Real every now and then when I need a rest. According to her, because my eyes perceive the empty house as a refuge, that somehow unbewitches it, cleanses it of ghosts and exorcises all the tedium and routine it's been host to. On one occasion, when she was rather the worse for drink, she even proposed giving it to me, and I think she was serious. I tried to make her understand – which she did at once, since she's highly intelligent, especially when drunk – that if she did that, the ghosts would start to enslave me too and that would be the end of my temporary refuge. I look at the paintings and the furniture and what I like about them is that they don't remind me of anything, and that it doesn't matter to me how much they cost or who they belonged to or what will happen to them when I pass on. Silvia burst out crying and said she envied me, that she'd love to be able to look at her own house like that. "To you, of course, the house is like a lover, but to me it's a sick husband and I can't even desire its death because that's a sin punishable by God." She loves the house, as she does all the property she owns, but it's a schizoid love, in conflict with the principles of loyalty to the family heritage that have been drummed into her ever since she was a child. That contradiction between rootedness and a desire to uproot herself forms the nucleus of the neurosis that brought her to my consulting room when she was left alone in the world. Sometimes, she decides that she's going to get rid of everything and at others that she can't get rid of anything at all; they're just phases she goes through and she knows it. I should tell you that most of the people I go around with nowadays are people I first met on the psychiatrist's couch, which, in the long run, is an impoverishing, wearisome or, rather, unharmonious way of living. But anyway, let's leave Silvia for the moment: I'm sure I'll have occasion to talk to you about her again when the time comes. Now what I need is for you to listen to me.

As I said, I'm going to ease my sorrows in that Street of Sorrows, a coincidence of names that also has its ironic side. Life, even when it seems blackest, does sometimes offer us these linguistic compensations that can still manage to wring a momentary smile from us.

I'm not so much leaving as running away. I just upped and went. For the moment I'm not thinking about the consequences, I'm just trying to squeeze what pleasure I can out of the sensation of flight. We'll see how long it lasts, not long, probably, because it was a decision made against my own better judgement. Every time I decide to go on a trip, I fit my plans around my free days, around outstanding appointments. In other words, common sense prevails. This, however, is more like a sudden fit, like the panic that seizes a bullfighter when he suddenly throws down his

42

sword and cape and runs away from the bull threatening to gore him to death. If you've read my previous letter, it won't take you long to realize that the bull in question is Raimundo.

The thing is, everything was going so well. It happened very suddenly. Less than seven hours ago I was in his house, ready to stay with him for as long as was necessary; I didn't mind if that was a week or my whole life, if that was what he wanted; I mean it, and you've no idea how odd that sounds now, even to me, but I was so happy.

It's just that, oh, I don't know, I wanted to give you a proper account of what happened, because if I don't, I won't understand it either. It's just as well I can write to you. So, please, be patient.

From the moment he came out of hospital yesterday morning, in a frame of mind completely different from the one I had envisaged (he specializes in the unexpected), from the moment he hailed a taxi and said to me: "Come on, get in, you're coming with me, aren't you?", I knew that I was letting him make all the decisions, that I didn't have the strength to take charge of anything. It had been like a week spent in hell. I felt like a convalescent child who will simply have to be taken care of by somebody; and Raimundo's calm voice, when he leaned forward and gave the taxi driver his address, radically reversed the roles of protector and protected as set out in the cast list up until then. What a relief! I leaned my head back against the seat and closed my eyes, sure that he had understood. His initial gesture of putting his left arm around my shoulders was a hopeful sign. Then, as we drove along – a prologue with more music than words – everything he did felt right.

I didn't speak, I hardly dared move, I just let myself be led, blindly, and every now and then he would stroke my hands or my hair with a delicacy charged with electricity. He put his lips to my ear and whispered: "Ferme tes jolis yeux, car tout n'est que mensonge", and that was when the tears I'd been struggling to hold back finally began to flow, because his voice came from the corner of the soul that people accustomed to pretence and to defending themselves always keep safely walled in. It was a very gentle order, exactly right for a little girl who's been suffering from a high fever and delirium. How could I not obey? So I kept my eyes closed and just let myself enjoy the nearness of this person who had picked me up and carried me off with him, to enjoy the smell of his clothes and the touch of his hands, concentrated now on slowly tracing with his thumbs the damp tracks left by the tears on my cheeks, until I vomited up all the fear and poison I'd been storing up in the depths of my eyes during the nights spent watching over him.

I've no idea how much time passed, but I didn't open my eyes until I heard him say to the taxi driver: "Would you mind stopping here a moment, my girlfriend loves lilacs." It was like emerging from a tunnel. We were in the Glorieta de Alonso Martínez, near his house; it was very sunny and a gypsy was standing by the pedestrian crossing selling flowers. Raimundo came back with a bunch of lilacs that still smell as sweet as they did that moment when I emerged from the tunnel, and I'll put them in water in a minute or two, so that they can preside over my journey south. They're the only thing I brought with me as a souvenir of the hours spent with him in his apartment, some thirty hours by the clock, not that I pay much attention to chronological time.

Raimundo lives in a chaotic apartment in Calle de Covarrubias. I've often slept there. Or rather, I've often stayed there in order to do battle with his insomnia, to expend vast amounts of energy trying to convince him that it's worth going on living, even at the risk of getting out of my depth and ending up believing quite the opposite, which used to happen fairly frequently. I usually left at dawn, with my morale at its lowest ebb, once he had finally managed to get to sleep. I'd leave him a note. Then days, weeks and even months could go by without my hearing from him, apart from through mutual friends, and the news I heard rarely reassured me and was never a matter of indifference to me.

When we walked into his apartment building and we were waiting for the lift, he smiled at me and said: "Promise me one thing, that you'll forget all about Dr León. Would you do that?" and I, still clutching my bunch of lilacs, pressing my face into them, spoke the first line of my new role: "Raymond, there's nothing in the world I'd like better." It probably sounds like a line from a trashy novel, just as it does to me now as I'm recounting it. And even then, as I dreamily listened to the lift coming down, it occurred to me that that Dr León sounded rather too like one of Carmen de Icaza's sentimental heroines and that we were both getting a bit old for that. Those, however, were my last flickers of lucidity until this afternoon. I'd decided to plunge wholeheartedly into my role.

The hours we spent together in his apartment, the two of us alone, not answering the phone or watching the clock, interspersing music, coffee and poems with sleep, always talking, laughing and touching each other, those hours are a creation of Raimundo's which only needed my consent in order to take shape and to bring new life to that faded backdrop. He was the one wielding the baton in that symphony of resurrection dedicated exclusively to me. He knew that I was utterly captivated, and that only spurred him on to deploy his not inconsiderable gifts for verbal improvisation. I forgot that he was seriously manic depressive, that little more than a week ago he'd decided to dispatch certain objects and bits of furniture to various friends as posthumous souvenirs, that he'd subsequently been admitted to hospital almost in a state of coma; I forgot that no one can stand him for long, that no one can bear to stay at his apartment and, of course, I forgot all about my appointments and my commitments. I hadn't seen him like that for years, entirely given over to pleasing me, giving me the old soft soap about love at first sight between two soulmates, so wise, so provocative and so dazzling that at one point I even said, quoting from a play by Valle-Inclán: "Now, Max, don't overdo it!" It was like rediscovering him, like getting to know him for the first time, only more so, an even more intense sensation than that because, although I was forgetting everything in order to surrender myself to that intoxication, however much a drunkard drinks, something always lingers in the innermost recesses of his memory. And the one thing I couldn't forget was precisely what raised that intoxication to a different level and made it unlike any other: the fact that Raimundo had been on the point of death, and that looking into his dark, shining eyes was like coming back to life with him.

I've always found rediscovery more exciting than discovery, although it's also a state more subject to illusion. And now that I'm writing this, I wonder too if it isn't just another illusion to imagine that I've rediscovered you. Anyway, Sofía, if it is, it's a delightful one. You don't know how good it makes me feel to think of you as the only possible recipient of this letter, which is, in turn, all I have to cling to. I'm in no hurry to finish it either; the same thing happened with the letter I wrote last week. I've got the whole night ahead of me, with the advantage that today there'll be no interruptions, because no one knows where I am at the moment. Not even you.

After two hours spent in the buffet car, I re-read what I wrote and continue. I'd started to get hungry and I realized too that I was getting confused and needed a break so that I could impose some order on the story I want to tell you. There are too many ramifications that you don't know about, and I don't want the story to fall victim to the "scattergun effect". I picked up a notebook and as I passed from carriage to carriage following the steward with his little bell, it occurred to me that I could write a kind of script in order to orient both myself and you. These are tricks I've picked up on my journeys to congresses and symposia, making use of the plane or train trip to make notes on a lecture I haven't quite finished preparing, still all held together with pins.

Then, while I was having supper and watching the night fall over the countryside, I did nothing but think about you, about how strange it is that you should reappear and about the unknown chance occurrences that have perhaps guided your thoughts and your steps throughout this week. And I was also thinking about the fact that the only viable alternative for us at the moment is for each of us to go our own way, not drift about dreaming that we're going to pool our respective losses, however much we tell each other about them. Your life, although I can only glimpse it through a crack in the wall, obviously moves to a different rhythm from mine, and the truth is that we've both grown up. To grow up, of course, means to begin to separate yourself from others, to recognize that distance and to accept it. The enthusiasm of our youthful encounters with people who aroused our interest was based on our assumption of a continuous permeability between their lives and ours, between our problems and theirs; then, that kind of annexation seemed perfectly possible. It's true that there still are moments when the illusion of permeability resurfaces, but they are brief, extraordinary moments that one should not expect to continue or to last. When I was a young girl – and I know the same thing happened to you – I was convinced that the people who loved me would never fall out with me, that my life was indispensable to theirs. Deep down, what I wanted was that they should never stop needing me. Of course. Later on, though, you see that things aren't like that and that it's better not to let anyone need you too much.

I was thinking nostalgically about how easy it used to be for me to write to you years ago when I didn't have to make a "summary of publications", when all that was necessary were a few simple allusions and the use of a common language that reflected tastes, jokes and feelings held in common. Now, apart from the fact that you have plumbing problems, three children and a husband who thinks yuppies are God's gift, I know very little about the last thirty years of your life. Besides, this journey puts on hold any possibility of our recovering a certain synchronicity between what you tell me and what I tell you because, by the time you receive this letter, who knows what direction your homework will have taken – assuming you decided to continue with it. I forgot to tell the porter to forward my mail to Puerto Real. Well, actually I didn't even see the porter. I went home to put a few things in a suitcase, get the keys for the house in Calle de la Amargura and order a ticket over the phone. I was almost out of the door when I had to go back and leave a hurried note for Josefina Carreras, the colleague who stands in for me. I didn't have time for anything else, I would have missed the train.

And here I am, drinking and thinking about you, leaning on a table in a buffet car while night falls outside. You were so funny when you were thirteen years old and you wore your hair in plaits on top of your head; on the nights they let you come and sleep over at my house in Calle de

47

Serrano, I used to undo them and brush your hair. "Don't stay up all night talking, because there'll be no getting you up in the morning if you do," my mother used to say when she came in to give us a kiss. We never took any notice of her, and she knew that we wouldn't. We used to talk endlessly, whispering in our beds, sometimes smothering our laughter beneath the covers and at other times noticing, despite the dark, that we were both crying at the same time. You did most of the talking, your words took off towards exotic fictional lands, you said the night loosened your tongue, and the night, like everything else you mentioned, became a character in a story. It was the goblin, Noc; you could hear him fluttering his dark, iridescent wings, flying gently down towards you, towards your open mouth, into your body; he untied the knots in your tongue, rushed inwards down the passageways of your lungs, your heart and your intestines, and you noticed that as he passed he switched off all the switches that gave you cramp and switched on the ones that provided moonlight. There was always moonlight in your stories. What you liked most was imagining future situations, embellished with so many details that listening to you was like reading a novel. A recurrent theme in those stories was our meeting again when we were older, having been separated for years by force of circumstance. Both the circumstances and the reunion took on the most unexpected variations, modelled on the Gothic or the chivalresque novel, which were the kind of novels that most attracted us at the time. My life had always been more dangerous and more romantic than yours and I was as likely to find myself trapped in a castle from which I could only escape with great difficulty as I was to find myself in the midst of a duel between two of my lovers or about to board a liner and leave the country for ever. There would always come a point when we would meet: the landscape varied but there was always moonlight, and I would tell you a very long story that you would subsequently set down in writing. "I'm your Per Abat," you would say, "the man who first transcribed the *Poem of the Cid*." It made me laugh the way you dropped your voice to make that shadowy personage from the past seem more dramatic, and it ended up becoming your nickname. "Come on then, Per Abat, tell me a story."

48

That was why I was smiling in the buffet car. I'm so glad you've been resuscitated, my good Per Abat! Do you realize that we used to dream about what's happening to us now; could there be any greater happiness? We only pay attention to what we've already experienced or to what we hope to experience; we hardly ever take any notice of what's happening to us now – we consider that normal. But it isn't normal, Sofía, it isn't in the least normal, what's happening to us. You would never have been able to invent a peculiar letter like this to adorn your versions of the future, but I bet you would love to have read it. So there you are. It's addressed, in fact, to the girl with the plaits, for her files.

From there I drifted off into thinking how complicated any writing task is that attempts to be coherent without being tied to linear time, and about what you said about broken mirrors, and about the relationship between the content of a message and the situation of the person who receives it, and about Roland Barthes – *Le plaisir du texte* – in short, a complete stream-of-consciousness trip that made me forget all about Raimundo.

And do you know, my good Per Abat, a little while ago we passed through Aranjuez! Could anyone ask for more? Suddenly, the trip we made together to Aranjuez the autumn before our gold grew dim became the magnetic pole for the whole of my progressively disintegrating inner discourse. What a moment to pass through Aranjuez, a specially arranged commemorative pilgrimage could not have been more opportune, more appropriate.

That was where I first spoke to you about Guillermo – do you remember? – where we first began to grow up, to be two and not one. The brilliance of that afternoon on the banks of the Tagus, after strolling about in the Royal Gardens, coincides with the last gleams of pure gold that surround our adolescent symbiosis, gold in the trees, gold in the clouds, gold in your hair, and a sharp, almost painful desire for time to stand still. You noticed I was different and you started pumping me for information. "Different, how?" "Just different, I don't know, as if you were stuck in a Flemish painting, with your hands tight shut, hiding something you didn't want to show me." No, I didn't want to show it to you. I was avoiding it. It seemed to me that something would be spoiled if I opened my hands and showed you. And when, at the end of the afternoon, having tea in La Rana Verde, I finally did open my hands and I pronounced Guillermo's name, I knew that my fears had been well founded. I didn't like saying his name; for a week I'd only said it to him in a low, secret voice, only to receive mine back in return, a non-transferable exchange of breath, administered mouth to mouth, and even you were excluded from that particular story. There was an awkward silence and the name "Guillermo" remained lodged there between us for ever. Up until then we'd always told each other about our romantic dabblings; it was natural, each of us conscious that the best part was sharing it with each other, and in a way those early love affairs became more real when we talked about them, more substantial. Not this time. You realized that this was different, just by the way I said Guillermo's name and the way I immediately withdrew. You went very quiet and sat staring out at the river. Then you asked me what he was like. "I don't know really, I've never known anyone like him. He's not particularly nice. There's something wolfish about his face." "I envy you," you said.

Isn't it odd how things turn out, Sofía? Raimundo has the same wolfish face. I meant to tell you that earlier and, would you believe it, without needing to make any preliminary notes, I'm back where I left off.

For a while now, I've been lying on the bunk bed with my knees up, resting this block of airmail paper on them, with the little light on and the curtain at the window open so that I can see the night outside and the fleeting shapes silhouetted against it. The goblin Noc is in my blood and the moon is in the first quarter. I abandon myself to the clackety-clack of the train rushing me through the night.

Yes, Raimundo does have a wolfish face. I think that's what happened yesterday. I've just realized it. I noticed his wolf's face for the first time and I completely lost my head. The strange thing is that I'd stopped feeling afraid of him, and even his den (about which I've so often grumbled and to which I've sworn so many times never to go back) drew me on like a glorious promise of passion and disorder, like

50

the cave of a wizard who's given you the elixir of youth to drink mixed in with a bitter potion. Yes, I lost my head. It was great! I'm fed up with keeping my head firmly on my shoulders in a state of unstable equilibrium; it rolled underneath the sofa, bounced off the walls, sat on top of the bookshelves and snuggled up between the paws of that wolf-man who was perfectly within his rights to destroy it or submit it to disquieting mutations; a crazy head, yes, excitable, yes, under the spell of a cruel, capricious creature. He could do what he liked with my head and my life just as long as he dedicated all his howls of both pain and pleasure to me, as long as he had eyes only for me, as long as I was his one prisoner, as long as he never needed anyone else but me ever again. As a flamenco song might put it: "If you were to ask me to throw myself into the fire, I would burn up just like wood. If you were to ask me to open my veins, a river of blood would splash you." Or, in the psychoanalytic jargon of Dr León: Sacrificing oneself for the sake of the dubious pleasure afforded to another by one's own disintegration. The trouble is, Sofía, it's no joke. What a burden all that rhetoric about self-denial is to us women; it grips us in our vitals, however much we try to laugh it off. I'm ashamed to say this, but I have to confess – because this letter is a kind of confession – that my most secret erotic fantasies burn with a desire to lose myself in another, to surrender myself to someone without reserve so that he may do with me what he will, a desire later pitilessly analyzed on sleepless nights and immediately suppressed, because I know what a slippery slope that is. I'm less frightened of actually sliding down it than I am of someone else finding me out.

Well, yesterday Raimundo did. I suppose that was what made him feel so happy, so excited and sure of himself. It was also what made him grow tired long before I had shown the slightest sign of tiredness. Stealing a march on me, great! After five o'clock in the afternoon, for no reason and without transition, the euphoria of being in charge of the situation began to channel itself along more tortuous paths.

First, there were two phone calls that occurred within a quarter of an hour of each other and neither of which he answered. Raimundo didn't react to them as he had to all the previous phone calls, which had elicited either no reaction at all or expressions of annoyance occasionally followed by the decision to leave the phone off the hook for a while. Then he replaced the receiver because he said that it only made matters worse, that the engaged tone was in itself an indication that he was in, which might encourage certain of his friends simply to turn up. He can't be persuaded to get an answering machine.

Although he didn't say anything, those two phone calls did affect him. They plunged him into a silence that presaged strange changes. The second time the phone rang, and continued ringing with unbearable tenacity, Raimundo jumped to his feet and started pacing about the room. He went over to the record player – we had Beethoven's Fifth on, conducted by Von Karajan – and he took the record off, without asking whether I minded or not. He remained standing by the phone, his hands in his pockets, looking at it, although still without picking it up. When, to my great relief, it stopped ringing, he pretended that he was looking for a book in that part of the room. He took a long time. I didn't dare ask him what was wrong. After a while, he came back and sat down in the armchair opposite mine. He kept stroking his hair luxuriously and looking distractedly over at the window. Raimundo's best feature is his hair: soft, wavy and almost completely white. He's proud of his hair. He knows that it's his main erotic attraction.

"I suppose we'll have to do something," he said suddenly. "We can't spend the rest of our lives like this."

It was a totally reasonable remark, but it caught me off guard. Besides, he said it without looking at me. He was still stroking his hair.

"Well, as you know, I've got loads of things I could be doing, but I don't want to be reminded of that just now."

He didn't reply. Then I went over to his armchair and knelt down on the carpet.

"Raimundo, what's wrong? And don't tell me there isn't anything wrong. Please, look at me."

He looked at me, clumsily concealing his impatience behind a smile worthy of a bad actor.

"There's nothing wrong with me. Don't spoil everything now, don't start one of your interrogations."

I looked down at the carpet. It was filthy, there were even cigarette ends trodden into it. God knows how long it can have been since he got anyone in to clean. I had a sudden, surprising image of myself wearing an apron and wielding a big broom, flinging wide the windows and singing jolly songs whilst the smell of homemade stew wafted in from the kitchen; I saw myself approaching Raimundo's large desk almost devoutly in order to tidy up his papers.

"No, I just got the feeling you were trying to get rid of me," I said rather coyly, not looking up from the carpet.

I was beginning to slide down the slippery slope and I knew it. It was his cue to say: "Look at me," but he forgot his lines. The room was stuffy, it smelled of cigarettes and sweat.

"I'm not trying to get rid of you, love, you can stay if you want to," he said nonchalantly. "I just fancy going out for a while. I'm starting to feel a bit claustrophobic and I need to go for a walk. You understand, don't you?"

"Yes, of course I do. Would you like me to come with you?"

"Not really, to be honest. You obviously haven't understood."

"Where will you go?"

"I don't know. I might drop in and see some of those people you don't like very much. No doubt lots of my friends have been phoning ... but since you didn't want us to pick up the phone."

I looked up and I realized that my face was burning. All my demons were suddenly unleashed.

"Me? You're the one who didn't want to talk to anyone! You said so yesterday, don't you remember? You said you didn't need anyone else but me. For God's sake, Raimundo, answer me. Did you or did you not say that?"

He burst out laughing.

"Come on, darling, don't make a scene now, it doesn't suit you. What if I did say it? Maybe I've changed my mind. Anyway, you're a fine one to talk. Or do you never change your mind?"

I lost control. I can see that now. I lost control of the argument. I know the phenomenon only too well. It consists in no longer listening to the other person, in charging up the batteries of one's own obsessions and, no longer capable of listening to reason, letting fly at a blank wall. I put my arms around his knees which, it seemed, had suddenly turned to stone. I begged him not to get sucked back into that spiral of seeking out the very people who use him and later abuse him, not to let himself be dragged into that quagmire of dependency; I reminded him that they were the same people who had destroyed his will and driven him over the edge into the black hole. I even spoke of tortuous intrigues, the kind of thing a castrating mother would say in order to put her son on his guard against bad company. And Raimundo, in a way understandably, fell back into old habits, shied away. Everyone defends themselves as best they can.

Quagmire? Intrigues? People using and abusing him? Please, I was making it sound like a soap opera. He proposed discussing the question on a more theoretical level, a discussion he looked likely to win for the simple reason that he was utterly calm and I, on the other hand, was hysterical. He accused me of subjectivity and lack of perspective, he rejected my metaphors, which struck him as too elementary, and got into a brilliant disquisition on the good and bad sides of that characteristic Spanish tendency to dramatize things which, in the end, leads to the belief that the human right to seek pleasure is a sin. Experiencing dangerous emotions didn't mean that one would necessarily fall down the black hole: one could simply explore it, fly over it. You could learn as much from exploring the shadows as you could from exploring the light. I found it very hard to follow him. I just noticed his arrogant tone and that frightened me. How long would it be before he turned that fragmented dialectic of the explorer of other people's ruins against himself?

"Besides," he concluded, "what do you know about black holes?"

Well, I knew a lot about them, actually; how could I not know about black holes and quagmires and subterranean channels?

"You get all that from books, of course," he said.

"From books and from what you lot tell me!"

The worst mistake you can make is to repeat out loud to a client the very arguments that he on some occasion might have employed to explain his own contradictions. A good psychiatrist has to behave as if she doesn't remember anything about the confessions that emerged in previous sessions, she has to pretend that they never existed. Sometimes, however, you can't. From who else but Raimundo would I have found out that he knowingly walks straight into cul-de-sacs, that he mixes with people who don't understand him and aren't worthy of him? Worse, he didn't always like what he saw reflected back at him in those rented mirrors, like the distorting mirrors at a funfair, those were his very words; that doesn't appear in any of the books I've studied. If he didn't want me to know all the details of this process that, time and again, left him a complete wreck, then he shouldn't have given me all those hundreds of different versions of it, and he shouldn't have asked for my help when he was at his lowest ebb. It's not my fault I've got a good memory.

All this gushed wildly and incoherently out of me, almost like a scream, as if the room were on fire and I was the only one capable of seeing the flames rising, the only one to call for help. I couldn't deal with all that in theoretical terms and he shouldn't expect me to do so.

Raimundo's eyes darkened, they looked almost fierce. It's a look that Dr León knows all too well and which at times, with tact and patience, she has managed to defuse. Unfortunately, Dr León wasn't there, she couldn't help me. She would have been ashamed to see me kneeling defeated on the carpet, launching into incoherent arguments, getting further and further out of my depth, with my arms clasped anxiously about the knees of the wolf-man.

"You'll revert to your old ways but, I'm warning you, Raimundo, don't come running to me when you do! You'll have to climb out of the pit on your own this time, I mean it. Or find some other psychiatrist to help you out, and that won't be easy!"

He pushed me away and stood up.

"That's enough, Mariana, that's enough! Just consider for a moment, when you've calmed down, and tell me who it is who needs the psychiatrist here, you or me?"

That was the last straw. That was really reaching rock bottom. I realized that I had to get up and make a decision, but I didn't have the strength. He'd come over to where I was kneeling. I was aware of his suede ankle boots as he stopped a short distance away; I looked at his tight grey velvet trousers and his long legs. He touched my hair with his finger tips.

"It's just that sometimes, my dear, you psychiatrists need someone a bit mentally unbalanced to open your eyes for you," he said in a lofty, condescending tone, quite different from the one he'd used in the taxi when he'd poetically asked me to close my eyes.

I hid my head in my arms and leaned on the seat he'd vacated, trying to evoke the warm breath of that voice that had whispered in my ear: "Ferme tes jolis yeux, car tout n'est que mensonge." Close your eyes. Sleep. It's all lies, all of it.

"You're obviously exhausted," said Raimundo. "The best thing for you would be to spend two whole days just sleeping. But it's up to you. I'm going to wash my hair, it's filthy."

I didn't answer. His feet again moved out of my field of vision. I heard the phone ring and he answered it at once. Then I looked up, pricked up my ears. A bookshelf acts as a divider and the telephone is on the other side so that I could listen to him without either of us being able to see the other's face. To judge by his tone of voice, the expression on his face must have been one of deep joy. He was speaking in a low voice.

"Hi! What's up? Me? No, I'm in better shape than ever ... in phoenix mode, rising from the ashes, yes, a change of skin. Really? Now you're pandering to my baser instincts, honey ... I'm on my own. Yes, really I am. Why? Ah, I see."

I got noiselessly to my feet, picked up my handbag and the bunch of lilacs and tiptoed towards the front door. I heard him say, almost in a whisper:

"Are you at home? No, it's just that you got me out of the shower, there's no great mystery about it. No, of course I haven't got any clothes on. Don't say things like that ... Look, I'll call you back in ten minutes. Honestly, word of honour. That's right, slut's honour. What?"

56

I left silently, without slamming the door, with the slow, carefully timed movements of a stage thief and, once out of the danger zone, I raced downstairs like a bat out of hell, my hair flying, my cheeks aflame.

I don't know what Raimundo must have thought when he came back and I wasn't there. I don't know what will have become of him, whether or not he's phoned me, or to whom he will be dedicating the glorious litany of his resurrection on this night of warm breezes. I have no idea and I don't even want to think about it.

It was a quarter past six and a beautiful afternoon. For a long while, I wandered aimlessly about the streets, bumping into people, unable to walk straight, the way you feel when you get off a roller coaster. Then I remembered that we'd hardly eaten anything and had done nothing but smoke and drink. The dizziness I felt might be due to that, as well as lack of sleep.

I went into a bar in the Plaza del Dos de Mayo and ordered a coffee at the bar, but no sooner had I drunk it than I broke out in a cold sweat, started retching and had to rush to the toilet, pressing a handkerchief to my mouth.

I'd left the the bunch of lilacs on the bar and when I breathed in their scent again after being sick, it gave me the illusion of feeling almost restored. In the mirror behind the bottles, however, I saw an ashen face; my legs felt like cotton wool and I could barely stand. I remembered that line of Poe's: Never more, never more.

"I'm going to sit down at that table for a moment," I said to the waiter.

"Shall I bring you another coffee?"

"No, just a glass of water, please."

When he brought it over, I was leaning my head against the wall and looking through half-closed eyes at the figures moving lazily about outside, on the other side of the window. I was trying to breathe deeply and to concentrate on my determination not to burst into tears, a fluctuating determination, just like all the humours and juices in my body at that moment. The waiter placed the glass of water on the table and nonchalantly sat down at my side. He was a slim young man, very handsome, with an afro hairstyle. He wore an earring in his left ear. From time to time I breathed in the scent of the lilacs.

"So, how are you?" he asked me, smiling. "You look awfully pale."

"It'll pass, thanks."

"Did you have a blackout or did you just feel dizzy?"

"Both … I don't know."

"And now you're tripping on lilac juice. Come on, don't cry. Drink some water, go on. Your pulse is all right."

He was holding my wrist and we sat like that for a while without talking. I didn't find it embarrassing either crying or having him sit so close to me, listening to my pulse. On the contrary, I liked it. Outside in the square, the afternoon seemed to have stood still.

"So what's wrong with you? You seem like you're in a bit of a dream."

"Why do you say that?"

"I don't know, the way you're crying. I watch you cry and, I don't know, it's just weird. Have you ever seen *Casablanca*?"

"Yes I have, but I don't remember anyone crying in that."

"Well, it doesn't matter, there's no piano here either; I just thought of it because you came in looking like Ingrid Bergman in search of Humphrey Bogart. Do you know what I mean? You're too much. I can just picture you in a black-and-white movie."

The place was almost empty, there were just three young men at the bar, but they weren't looking at us. With my free hand I wiped away my tears.

"Tino!" one of men shouted. "Another rum and coke."

Tino got up and gave me a friendly pat on the knee.

"I'll leave you to have a ponder, but don't do your head in with too much thinking. Now, you're sure you don't want another coffee?"

"No, thanks, really. I'll be going in a minute."

"Stay as long as you like. Don't you worry. And take my advice, don't think too much, it's not worth it."

"Thanks, you're right."

I stayed for a while under the protection of these strangers and slowly I began to feel better. Yes, it was like a scene from a black-and-white movie. Sometimes Tino would look over at me from the bar and I'd smile back. When I got up to pay him, he didn't want any money, he said that they didn't charge for vomiting. I broke off a sprig of lilac and held it out to him. He looked at me hard when he took it and, still looking at me, he bent towards me across the bar.

"Listen, weren't you on telly about a week ago, talking about junkies?"

The others had heard and were looking at me too.

"On telly? No. It must have been someone else."

"Well, she looked just like you," said one of the lads who was wearing a denim jacket with a tiger emblazoned on the back.

"Only you're much prettier," said Tino. "You're really something. I bet you have men falling over themselves to take you out."

"Yeah, and the lilacs are really cool," said the boy with the tiger on his back.

I left feeling much better and promised to go back another day. Bars in Madrid at mid-afternoon can be so nice.

When I left the bar and walked down Calle de Ruiz, I was saying to myself, as I recovered my usual rhythm of walking, that it wasn't worth being sick over anyone, not even Raimundo. People have to learn to look after themselves. It's his loss and he had no right to drag me with him down the street of sorrows. It was then that the idea of going to my friend Silvia's house in Puerto Real popped into my head, like a bubble in a cartoon. When I got to Glorieta de Bilbao, I hailed a taxi. Just to get as far away as possible, to escape, how wonderful! I'd had quite enough sorrow and bitterness for now.

And that's where I'm heading, to Calle de la Amargura, the Street of Sorrows, and we'll see what happens.

Raimundo was right about one thing, though, however much it hurt me to hear him say it – in fact it was what hurt me most. It was, I realized, high time that I got taken down a peg or two. I need a psychiatrist more than all my patients put together. And if I don't have one, then I'll talk to you, good Per Abat. It's just as well you turned up, just as well I can imagine you listening to me.

It's three o'clock in the morning and I'm getting tired. I'm going to turn out the light and pretend that you're sleeping in the bunk above. I feel very contented.

Good night, wherever you are.

I'll write to you again from Puerto Real.

All my love, Mariana

V

Octopuses in a garage

Since I've started writing again, my life has undergone a complete revolution. I thought it was something only apparent to me, but it must show on my face too.

"Something's happened to you, I can tell," Consuelo suddenly said to me this morning, by way of a greeting, when she saw me come into the kitchen, just fresh from the shower, to make myself some coffee.

Her mother has had a bad attack of lumbago so Consuelo's been working here for the last two days. She says that someone's obviously rattled the bars of her mother's cage because she's always trying to pick a fight and she's driving everyone mad, especially in the mornings.

"That's why I got out of there early today; you wouldn't believe how stroppy she gets, she's like a character in a Kung Fu movie; as if I were to blame for all her aches and pains. She's in what you might call an awkward mood."

"And I'm in an awkward mood too, is that what you mean?" I said, interrupting her, as I looked in vain for the tin of coffee.

"No, I don't mean that. Yours is a different case altogether. Either I'm explaining myself badly or you're deliberately missing the point. And if you're looking for the coffee, I saw it in the pantry, on top of a stool. I'll get it for you. Honestly, the state this kitchen's in. It's nearly as bad as the refuge. It's hard to know where to start."

"You can start by trying to explain yourself better and see if I get the point this time. What exactly is my case?"

"You're the only one who knows that. I don't mean to poke my nose in where it isn't wanted, it's just that you look more sort of laid back than you did a few days ago – I don't know – as if you couldn't give a damn.

Just now, when I heard you come down the corridor singing, I said to myself: 'That must be Amelia.' I mean, belting out 'Yellow Submarine' at this hour in the morning; enough said. It *was* 'Yellow Submarine', wasn't it? By the way, the way you sing is really cool, with a proper English accent and everything, great."

"I suppose you think you're the only one who knows how to sing."

"Good God no, I'm not the boastful sort and I wouldn't ever do down someone else's talents. If I could speak English as well as you, I'd be over the moon; I really envy you. It's like I was saying to Encarna and a friend of hers who's staying at the refuge, English is the in thing now. It's amazing. And you all tried so hard to teach me, but I was really stupid when I was a kid: my mother's quite right about that. Then, as you get older, you get a bit smarter – how can I put it? – you have to keep yourself up to date. You'll have to write out the words of some Beatles songs for me. It's just a question of patience, isn't it?"

"Yes, everything's a question of patience."

"Let me make you some coffee."

The kitchen was indeed a mess. Last night, when Eduardo and I got home, there was a note from Amelia in the hall saying that she'd brought Soledad back with her and they were sleeping in her room and please not to wake them until lunchtime because they were going to sleep in. We got back at half past three and when they heard the key in the front door they immediately switched off the light. Eduardo didn't notice and I didn't say anything, but we came upon the scene of destruction at once, because we both headed straight for the fridge to get a drink of water. They must have invited some other people back for supper with them in the kitchen, and they hadn't bothered to put anything away nor even to empty the ashtrays. This seemed to me like a good sign since this was Amelia, who, according to her sister, is well on her way to becoming a finicky old maid. I know her and I know that she only relaxes when she's having a good time, so I was pleased to think that perhaps she'd decided to bring her boyfriend back with her. Besides, I'm not opposed to untidiness in principle. It's a sign of life. Eduardo pulled a face, though, and it gave him the opportunity to go on about his current, predominating obsession: that this apartment isn't up to scratch. How would he know, I'd ask, he's hardly ever here? Anyway, it's his latest bugbear. In the car, he'd been going on at me about the same thing. I didn't say a word, because it's worse if you argue with him. That kind of remark always conceals a more or less veiled allusion to the fact that the person who isn't up to scratch as a housewife is me. It's a familiar subject and it arises more and more frequently now that I refuse to organize the kind of parties and suppers that his present-day friends are into. I just refuse to play the game, to play the part of the status wife who hides her tiredness behind a smile, who calmly takes the lead in trivial conversations, passes little trays around and finds sufficient reward for all her hard work in the words: "Darling, you were wonderful", spoken by her husband once the guests have departed, none of whom have enjoyed themselves in the least. Fortunately, he's given me up as a lost cause; at least I've managed that, which is no small thing. And it was all done through passive resistance.

"I bumped into Señor Eduardo in the hall when I was coming in," said Consuelo. "He was in a filthy mood. Or perhaps he's just got a down on me."

"No. It's just that he works a lot."

"Bloody hell, he earns enough money though. He obviously wants to have his cake and eat it too. His problem is he's too modern. He looks like your typical executive."

Then she asked me if there'd been a party here last night.

"No, but we went to a party at someone else's house, a really flash place. Do you remember that tall man who sorted out our bathroom? Well, the party was at his house."

"The one who built the Escorial? Of course I remember. He was a bit of all right, don't you think?"

"Not really, but there's no accounting for tastes."

The fridge was bare. I drank my coffee and left Consuelo some money to do a big load of shopping and prepare something nice for the girls who were bound to stay for lunch.

"What's up? Are you off now?"

63

"Yes, I'm off. It's the first day of May and I'm going out to celebrate it in my own particular way."

"Is it your wedding anniversary?"

"It's the anniversary of my wedding with May. Have you seen what a lovely day it is? I'm in your way here and May is outside waiting for me."

Consuelo stood looking at me, her eyes wide open.

"Incredible! May is outside waiting for me. Did you think that up by yourself?"

"I certainly did."

"Well, it would make a knockout title for a song, really ace, I mean it. Why don't you write it?"

"Perhaps I will, who knows. It depends which way the wind blows. The wind is the only thing I trust at the moment."

"You see what I mean? You see what I mean about you not giving a damn? And it really suits you. You even look prettier. You've got a secret. You're up to something."

"Well yes, I am up to something as it happens."

I went into Amelia's room to leave her a note. Soledad was asleep on the sofa bed, her arms around a teddy bear, just as when the two of them were small. The room stank of cigarette smoke and they hadn't lowered the blinds. The photo album lay open on the carpet. I knelt down to close it and the two of them, both in miniskirts, smiled up at me from a street in Brighton. I took that photo when I went to fetch them at the end of that special summer, the first time I'd travelled abroad on my own for years, the summer Guillermo suddenly reappeared in my life, just as Mariana had the other evening when I least expected it, like a hare in a field. I must write a composition about that Brighton trip, it could be entitled: "Reunion with Guillermo at Victoria Station"; on the other hand, I've got so many ideas jotted down for my homework they're coming out of my ears.

Neither of them woke up, although Amelia purred voluptuously when I bent over to kiss her on her forehead. Then I lowered the blinds trying hard not to make any noise. In the note I wrote: "It seems the muse is upon me. I'm going to the Ateneo because I can't concentrate at home.

If you need me for anything or if you want to drop by and see me, the number is 4194939. Consuelo's going to leave you something delicious for lunch. She'll wake you up at one o'clock. If you want to have a shower, you can use the Escorial. Lots of love, the Big Chief."

It's now four o'clock in the afternoon and one of the porters at the Ateneo, who's known me for ages, just came up to tell me that there was a phone call for me. It was Amelia. Her voice sounded very sweet and reassuring. Everything was fine. In order to make yourself unnecessary, there's nothing like simply removing yourself from the scene. Lunch was great. No, there were no messages. They'd had a good laugh with Consuelo. And how was I? Was I enjoying myself? Amelia is off tomorrow on another transoceanic flight and tonight she'd like to treat me to a Mastroianni film that's just been re-released. Soledad is coming too because she wants to see me. I've arranged to meet them at ten outside the cinema. I'm really looking forward to it, but what I'm looking forward to even more is that it's another six hours until then. Another six whole hours all to myself. It seems that May was indeed waiting for me.

I'm sitting at desk 22, which is the one I used to sit at when I was a student and, for a while now, I've been staring up at the ceiling – a rather grubby skylight – with the foolish smile of one trying to evoke whole stretches of time without quite knowing when they began or when they ended. I've always liked reading and writing in public libraries and, from time to time, I still take refuge in this old place which I love so much, although I don't know any of the people who come here now. I ate a sandwich at the bar and I feel free and glad to be starting my homework again. I'm beginning to take it seriously.

The last thing I wrote was about Cayetano Trueba, but since Mariana has still not written to me and I don't know where she is, when I woke up this morning I decided I would write out that last bit of homework neatly just in case I should lose the little scraps of paper I'd scribbled it all down on.

The time has simply flown by, because the pleasure of trying to understand my notes and unhurriedly write them out afresh in nice, clear handwriting forces me to edit them and add extra stories that before were only sketches. Like the story about Cayetano Trueba, which I've worked on a lot in this second version in the notebook just to make Mariana laugh when she reads it. I even made myself laugh too, because CT really was a most amusing character, even if he doesn't appear again. Mariana always loved the minor characters in American films. That was what she remembered best when we used to talk about the plot afterwards.

Suddenly, I fancy writing down whatever comes into my head, as she told me to do the other day at the cocktail party, as she used to say to me when we were small and she'd ask me to tell her stories: go on, just tell me the first thing that comes into your head. What I have to do now is to fill up this new notebook so that I can give it to her the next time I see her. "Look, I've brought you my homework as a present, do you like it?" I don't know when or where that will happen or what the expression on her face will be. It's enough just to imagine it. That's sufficient motivation in itself. It's enough for me to be sure that I will see her again. Before the Gregorio Termes exhibition, the idea of seeing Mariana again was an abstract hope, like a withered flower that has lost its perfume. Not now. Now I'm just waiting, sitting it out, lulled by the whisper of the fountain pen as it runs across the smooth pages. Sitting it out. That was the prevailing rhetoric of our youth: laying down the foundations of some desire and then feeding it to make it last. It seemed that happiness would melt away in our hands the moment we touched it. I have desired few things with the intensity with which I now long to see Mariana again, wherever, whenever (I know it will happen), and to be able to say to her: "Look, I've brought you my homework as a present"; so I enjoy slowly filling up this new notebook, taking care over my handwriting. It's like being with her already even as I write, an anticipation of happiness that wards off the death of time. It's a pleasure in itself, a rare pleasure based on an anachronism, because nowadays nobody begins a notebook with such loving care, not even children. I feel as if I were swimming against the tide in this age of computers and electronic typewriters, almost as if I were one of a dying race of artisans. And as well as the light of this first day of May filtering through the skylight, I seem to see the souls of those stubborn nineteenth-century members of the Ateneo, some of whose faces look down at me from the gallery of portraits that line the stairs. They too sat in this library, sitting it out, while they wrote in their notebooks.

My notebook is ringbound, A4, ruled, with a black cover. It was quite expensive because it's good quality paper. I bought it at Muñagorri's before coming here, along with an inkwell, glue and a file tied with pink ribbons. I haven't been to a stationer's in ages. On the first page I've stuck the white hare collage, although it still needs finishing. For the time being, I've added the little triangles of broken mirror that I cut out from the silver cigarette paper.

Speaking of broken mirrors, Gregorio Termes will have to be wheeled out again, because last night we were at his house. He was giving an informal supper to celebrate his exhibition which, it seems, has been a huge success. In less than a week he's offloaded every single one of those fried-egg bespattered canvases, even though they're priced at a million and a half pesetas or more. Or perhaps that's exactly why they have sold. These days nobody likes anything cheap, it automatically loses in prestige. Indeed, last night, I got the impression that in some circles it's even considered slightly offensive to speak of people, institutions or activities that don't make a lot of money, and not just a lot, we're talking money by the shovelful; they deal in figures beyond the imaginations of most ordinary people, it's ridiculous. They only deal in millions of pesetas.

Gregorio Termes lives in an enormous house complete with swimming pool that he's just had built in Puerta de Hierro, and from remarks made by some other guests at the party (which was also given to inaugurate this post-modern Escorial), I learned that all the objects, furniture and equipment that make up the decor and furnishings are top-flight, exclusive designs and that included in the furnishings is a very pale, blonde girl with a rather peeved expression on her face, wearing shot-silk harem pants. At first, I thought she must be our host's daughter, since she was the only one who seemed to be in control, albeit remote control, of that confused Babel. But no, it's clear that Gregorio has parked his children and his dear wife in another house in Argüelles where he used to live before he became so modern. As the night wore on, I learned this and other things; all you have to do is listen to other people's conversations and look as if you know it all already. Gregorio's wife is the daughter of a financier; she's five years older than him and people refer to her as "poor Fefa". They separated when he came back from New York where he'd spent a year broadening his experience more or less at his father-in-law's expense. Putting two and two together, I think that is when Eduardo must have met him, when people started talking about Spain entering the bloody Common Market. The date when the little blonde in the harem pants appeared is something of an unknown, but I imagine it must be fairly recent, because she doesn't look much more than nineteen, however hard she cultivates a certain likeness to Marlene Dietrich and other cinema *femmes fatales* of that era. Her name is Aglae and she's a dress designer with a great future. I don't know if she lives permanently in the house or if she's just here on half board. It's as if there were a thick pane of smoked glass between her and everything that surrounds her.

She looked almost shocked when I asked her for some talcum powder to sprinkle on the mayonnaise stain on my skirt. In fact, she burst out laughing, a stifled laugh submitted to a variety of special effects.

"Talcum powder?" she said, adding in English: "Are you kidding? There are no babies here, thank you very much."

Consuelo is right. English *is* the in thing. But I'd already had a bit to drink and I preferred to use the language of my elders, the language I know best.

"Listen, sweetheart, even if there aren't any babies here, any house without talcum powder, bicarbonate of soda and a darning mushroom is built on very shaky foundations indeed."

A lady wearing a sequined jacket, who had been circling me for a while now, laughed loudly at the joke, so loudly that some people turned round to look; but Aglae wasn't amused, she said what did I think dry cleaners were for and stalked off to the buffet table, gazing into the void. In the distance, I caught Eduardo looking at me with serious eyes and I waved to him, as if I were in an American comedy:

"I'll be right with you, Mr Frivoly!"

"Who are you talking to now?" asked the woman in the sequined jacket, who was clearly somewhat boozed.

"William Powell."

Eduardo responded with a tense smile, like the smile he'd worn in the car. My new attitude obviously disconcerts him. He was with a rather pretty redhead whom I'd also noticed on the day of the cocktail party because she presents a programme on television. The two of them had plates of food in their hands. They were leaving the buffet table and moving off towards the door that opened on to the terrace.

The buffet table, with its long table cloth and its array of technicolour foods, some cold and others hot, was situated to the left of the vast living room and was a place where people could rub shoulders with each other, like a drinking trough where people go to fill up on euphoria. Around midnight, people were quite unashamedly jockeying for position there. I asked the woman in the sequined jacket if it reminded her of the Metro in the rush hour and she laughed a lot – she laughed at almost anything I said – then admitted that she hasn't been in the Metro since the day they assassinated Carrero Blanco, it's one of those things you can't forget; she heard about it when she was in Calle de Velázquez and now she's just as terrified of riding above ground. That was more than fifteen years ago. The Metro's a frightening place, above ground and below, muggers everywhere! She had her hair plaited and done up in a very complicated bun and suffered from a rather disquieting tic in one of her eyelids. She wasn't ugly, though, far from it. I reckoned she was about fifty. I sensed that she didn't feel very comfortable there and was dying to talk to someone.

"I understand they're expecting even more people," she remarked. "Some are coming on from the theatre or some other engagement. The usual Madrid scene, hundreds of people; well, you know what Fridays are like."

People did indeed keep flocking in. Every time I saw Aglae walk by carrying overcoats and jackets to the rooms in the rear, I would scrutinize the new arrivals. Would Mariana be there? After all, a lot of those people knew her. They were the same minor characters from the other night, the fragments of mirror surrounding the great white hare.

However, miracles rarely happen twice. If you go out hunting for a hare, you'll never find it sleeping in a field; of course, how could I have forgotten when I'd gone on about it so much? The woman in the sequined jacket asked me why I kept looking at the door, was I expecting someone? I came to and told her with great conviction that I wasn't and I stopped watching, that is, I stopped waiting for Mariana. Instead, I would pay closer attention to everything else and thus be able to write amusing compositions about the minor characters. That was when I decided to start a new notebook. The more shocking the things one looks at the better. What about that painting? It was almost as big as Velázquez's *Las Meninas*, but what a waste of fried eggs!

"You are funny," the woman in the sequins said to me. "Now what are you laughing at?"

"I was just looking at that big painting and it started me thinking about the difference between doing something and not doing something. I mean, instead of saying: 'I feel about as out of place here as an octopus in a garage and what the hell am I doing here?' if you pay close attention to things, then you're actually doing much more than anyone else."

"What a riddle! Do you like that painting? I'll tell you for free that I don't like it at all. It's by Gregorio."

"You don't exactly have to be eagle-eyed to see that."

She put one hand on my shoulder and her laughter became more confiding.

"Everything he paints looks exactly the same, but if you go by the titles, you get thrown and you say to yourself: perhaps it's me who hasn't understood. Do you know what that one's called? *Geometric Transformation With Orgasm*; seriously, he told me so himself. He said it was his best painting and that he wouldn't part with it not even for three million pesetas. By the way, how do you know Gregorio?"

"He did up our bathroom. My children call it El Escorial, the bathroom, I mean. But you know, now I come to think of it, that painting

70

could just as easily have been called: *Geometric Transformation Without Orgasm*."

The lady creased up laughing and I was beginning to enjoy myself too. A waiter passed by carrying a tray full of drinks and we picked up two glasses of champagne.

"Listen," she said, "if you're not expecting anyone else, I came on my own. My name's Daniela. What's yours?"

"Sofia."

"I'm a bit pissed. You know, you're very pretty, why don't you wear make-up?"

"I just don't."

"Ever since Fernando left me, I slap it on like nobody's business, but I always end up crying and then my mascara runs. What shall we drink to? You think of something, since you're so clever."

"What about drinking to the minor characters at the party?"

"Excellent! Bottoms up!" exclaimed Daniela raising her glass.

She drank it down in one. Her tic became more pronounced. She told me that her life was a mess and I started to find her a bit tiresome.

People were still circulating, carrying plates of food. The room suddenly looked to me like an enormous hangar and I remembered Lorenzo telling me that in New York that's the latest craze. Trendy architects have started doing up factories and semi-derelict warehouses in the Soho district, and the fashion now is for acres of empty space with the occasional column in the middle of it all – minimalism, like living in a garage. Well, like an octopus in a garage. It occurred to me that that might be a nice idea for a collage. Gregorio Termes' garage full of little coloured octopuses, flanked by two larger ones at either end, one in silver with my face and the other in gold with Eduardo's. I could cut out the faces from the photos on old identity cards. It could be really lovely. "Octopuses in a Garage." The champagne was starting to go to my head and every so often Eduardo the Octopus would glance over at me from afar, intrigued, as if he wanted to keep tabs on me. He didn't come over though. He wouldn't dare.

He was very withdrawn in the car, silent, glancing at me out of the corner of his eye because for some days now he's been feeling the same as Consuelo, wondering what I'm up to. He was surprised when I jumped at his suggestion that I should go with him to Gregorio Termes' house, even showing signs of enthusiasm. I can understand his surprise. A few months ago, I wouldn't have been seen dead at a party like that. I would have made an excuse and he would certainly not have insisted. My depression, which had worsened as a result of the work carried out on the bathroom – although I'd been suffering from it for a long time before that in the form of a kind of generalized indifference – must have given him a pretext lately to refer to me as "poor Sofía", stressing that I was at a difficult age and describing my apparent inability to adapt to change. I don't know, the thing is that when people invite us out somewhere together it's just for form's sake; they must assume we live more or less separate lives. And although, of course, out of sheer apathy, I may have given some grounds for that interpretation, last night I felt that it was he who was spreading that view amongst his new friends. No one asked me anything, they just looked at me a lot. After all, the poor Fefas and poor Danielas of this world are ten a penny, and since introductions are no longer the norm, it depends on the individual how they react: if someone feels excluded, that's because they choose to. I noticed the same thing at the cocktail party, which also had a cast of thousands. Of course, I'd met Mariana there and didn't notice details that I do now. Everything's falling into place. Last night, to use Consuelo's expression, I was determined to make a splash.

According to Daniela, the supper had been ordered from a very famous restaurant which delivers the food to your home along with two waiters, one to serve at the buffet and the other to serve the drinks.

"Then they clear everything up afterwards too, however late the party finishes. They must charge a fortune. At least a million and a half pesetas – no, what am I saying, more than that. And poor Fefa stuck at home crying, I can see her now. As soon as they leave their dear wives, they go mad. He's certainly flying high."

The adjective "informal" when applied to this kind of supper party does not refer to any improvisational quality nor to any limitation on expenditure. If it refers to anything, I think it's the sheer discomfort. Everything they gave us was excellent as was the octagonal, black dinner service and the cutlery with opaque glass handles piled up on the buffet table, doubtless all exclusive designs. The worst thing, though, is that, once you've managed to fill your plate and avoided other people's elbows, you don't know whether to eat sitting down or standing up. "Informal" means that you're then condemned to wander about the garage, amongst other octopuses all beset by the same dilemma, looking furtively about for somewhere halfway comfortable to sit.

In Gregorio Termes' house, all the seats, which come in colours ranging from lilac to apple green, are placed rather far away from each other and are extremely low, the sort you disappear into when you sit on them. The tables – of which there are many, although you could easily fit in another dozen – are equally low, nowhere near any of the seats and are completely useless if you want to put anything down on them, because they're all crammed with magazines, collections of little boxes, framed photographs and heavy abstract sculptures. The waiter passes by picking up empty glasses and offering full ones, but no one tells you how to solve the problem of what to do with the plate and the glass. So a lot of people spill things. It's only natural.

I felt like asking if there was a phone so that I could call Encarna at the refuge, just to be able to say to her: "I'm in one of those houses full of little tables, the sort where, as you would say: 'There isn't room to put a book, a glass, an ashtray, or even lean one wretched elbow'," just to hear her laugh, because I felt the lack of some warm, shared laughter. But then I thought I'd probably find her in one of her down moods, or even more likely, since it was Friday night, I wouldn't find her at home at all, neither 'in nor out nor up nor down' which, by the way, is another of our surrealist tongue-twisters. Of all the things that one can do on one's own in life, laughing is the most difficult. Robinson Crusoe is always depicted as very serious until Friday arrives. "Right," I said to myself as I picked up another drink, "today is a very Robinsonian Friday." But I still didn't manage to make myself laugh.

ut one o'clock, I went out on to the terrace, fleeing from Daniela, who was pretty well out of it by then. She told me all kinds of gory details about the dirty tricks her ex-husband had played on her, about whom, on the other hand, she swore blind she didn't give a damn. Yet she felt insecure without him, she couldn't seem to enjoy herself anywhere. I asked her if she'd enjoyed herself before and she said she hadn't but that she'd had to put up with an awful lot, and that a happiness paid for with tears was better than no happiness at all. She sang that last bit to the tune of a *bolero*, rather off-key, because her tears made her voice falter. I'd made the mistake of sitting down next to her on one of those extremely low sofas and I couldn't get up again. That was complicated enough, but then Daniela's head, which had come to rest at last on my shoulder, made things even more difficult. As she herself had predicted, her mascara was beginning to leave black trails down her cheeks, her eyelid was twitching neurotically and her hair was beginning to collapse. She kept saying how kind and pretty I was and that we really ought see each other more often.

"Listen, are you one of Dr León's patients too?" she asked me suddenly.

"Me? No. Why?"

"Because the other day you were talking to her for ages."

"We used to go to school together."

She started talking about Mariana in contradictory terms. She needed her, she couldn't live without her, but she was hateful. Always so impassive, always so aloof, as cold as ice, she didn't know the meaning of passion. She was like that with Fefa too; Fefa said exactly the same.

I felt a sudden stab in my stomach remembering Mariana's reaction when I fell in love with Guillermo. I thought I'd buried those ancient wounds. The whole edifice of my life shook. Daniela was rambling on and stroking my shoulder with one hand while keeping a feeble grip with the other on the plate of leftovers on her lap. She was talking about love-hate relationships and about her honeymoon. I decided not to drink any more and to go for a walk on the terrace.

"Just stop for a moment, Daniela, please. Give me that plate and I'll take it over to the buffet. You're drunk," I said resolutely.

When I got up, I noticed that my legs felt numb and my head was spinning. At the same time, I felt as if I were climbing out of a black pit. Daniela was crying, sitting with her head resting on the back of the armchair.

"Forgive me, Sofía, you will come back, won't you? Don't leave me all alone," she said with her eyes closed. "Nobody loves me any more."

I passed Gregorio.

"What's up with Daniela?" he asked, looking over at the sofa. "Did she come on to you? She's into women at the moment."

"No, it's just that she's drunk too much. She must be having a hard time."

"I'll see if someone can give her a lift. Or else she can have a lie down. She always does the same thing. She's a bore. Are you looking for your husband?"

"Not especially."

Gregorio looked at me with a mixture of attention and intrigue.

"You know, you've improved a lot since I first met you," he said.

"In what way?"

"I don't know. You seem somehow freer."

"I am – free as a bird."

"Tell me more!"

"Some other time. See you later, maestro."

I went out on to the terrace, after depositing Daniela's plate on a tray and taking a turn about the garage. I couldn't see Eduardo anywhere. A few octopuses had started dancing to the beat of some strident music. Others, the majority, were still talking about money and which businesses were booming. The words you heard most were "theme", "issues", "price", "future prospects", "collateral" and "obsolete". But most of all, you heard the word "million". Not millions of steaks, not millions of gold bars, not millions of sheets of paper, but millions of nothing, a formless, sticky, brown mass in which people splashed compulsively about, in which they were immersed up to their eyeballs, millions of kilos of shit.

Some steps on the terrace led down to a garden area with a floodlit

75

swimming pool in the middle. It was a very pleasant night and a few thin clouds were sailing obliquely through the stars. I sighed deeply. Sometimes we forget how good it is to sigh. Something surfaces from beneath the make-up masking the soul. It's a physical need for a truce, like lowering the curtain before beginning another act; and suppressing a sigh can be bad for you.

The month of May was just beginning. I sat down by the swimming pool, remembered Mariana and burst into inconsolable tears.

VI

A prison with mirrors

Puerto Real, 11th May

Dear Sofía,

I knew that what is happening to me now was bound to happen one day, I just didn't think it would be so soon. I can't bear being alone, I can't bear it, it frightens me. I can feel Silvia's house closing in on me and when I leave it, despite the good weather we're having and despite my walks around the village and beyond, I'm incapable of enjoying anything, not even the spring, nature, other people. And the people here are really nice and always ready for a chat. You go into a bar or a small open-air restaurant and they give you some fried squid or some fried fish as an aperitif and, after a while, you realize that you could feel at home there and that no one's going to ask you any indiscreet questions, that they see you for what you are at that moment, a middle-aged woman sitting in the bar just as they are, it doesn't matter where I come from or the kind of life I led before. It's entirely my fault and that's what makes me so angry. It's as if I'd shot the bolt on the door keeping out any words and gestures that other people might speak or make to arouse my curiosity, to offer me a little human warmth.

To say that I miss Madrid and the life I could be leading there now would be one of those half-truths bristling with spines that one neither dares to pick up nor leave alone. One thing is sure, the phone would ring a lot, I'd be forever consulting my diary and I'd have no time to be alone with myself or to ask why I can't bear my own company. I'd be spending all my time giving advice on how to accept themselves to patients who come to me with precisely that complaint. I've written pages and pages on the subject and it's a lesson I know by heart, one that I'm always annotating with quotes from other publications and which I can recite faultlessly. The key is learning to face up to your free time, to stand your ground and fight it as if it were a bull, instead of simply running away. I use these sorts of similes a lot because many of my clients are keen followers of bullfighting, but I make use of other metaphors too; I have a fairly varied repertoire. If I wanted to impress you, I would simply have to pluck the most brilliant phrases out of that repertoire and unpack them, as I usually do, like a kind of armour behind which I can hide. I don't always do so with quite the necessary conviction, and some of my patients – almost always the women in this case – recognize that it is just armour, whether they actually say so or not. I can tell by the way they look at me and that's where I go wrong.

Yesterday, for example, I phoned my friend Silvia, the owner of the house, who is currently staying at a farm of hers in Carmona that was recently hit by storms – part of the roof has fallen in, several trees were uprooted, and there was all sorts of other damage too. It was late evening, I caught her in a moment of euphoria and her voice rang rather false to me because I suspected that she'd been drinking. I've been so corrupted by my egotistical habit of detecting other people's lies that it was a while before I understood that she, with her alcohol-enhanced intelligence, had in fact sensed my unease and was trying to throw me a lifeline. My phone call had rung false to her right from the start.

Speaking of beginnings, I'm telling you all this so badly, Sofía! Perhaps I should try again. So far in this letter, I haven't provided you with even a tiny crack for you to press one beady eye to and get some idea of what the place I'm staying in looks like. I can almost hear you saying: "Listen, either you keep to the rules of this epistolary game or you don't write to me at all, I don't want any botched jobs." All right, my good Per Abat, I'll stick to your golden rules. Maybe, once again, it will be rules that help me to put a brake on all this disorder, on the gradual collapse of my inner edifice, although I no longer know if it's just the roof falling in or if the actual foundations are crumbling. If my story stumbles a little, it's because I haven't got around to placing it in the frame of its surroundings.

Let's begin with the mirrors. There are a lot of mirrors in this house – too many. I didn't notice them so much when I came here before. I must have been in a different emotional state then and so they didn't make me feel uneasy. The worst thing is that they seem so solemn, almost tragic, and they ambush me (or is it that I go towards them as if drawn by a magnet?) at the precise moment when seeing my own image is as painful as being stabbed in the back, just when the struggle I'm engaged in – between accepting myself and fleeing from myself – is reaching a peak of unbearable tension. It never fails. It's always at such moments that a mirror appears before me or I find that I've been standing in front of one for a while without realizing it. There are four full-length mirrors, but the one that really freaks me out is the one with a carved black wooden frame, crowned by an allegory of death; the anonymous master carpenter who created such a piece, God knows when, must also have been endowed with a certain amount of Baroque imagination. I'd noticed it on other occasions – it's too ostentatious not to – but it's the sort of artefact about which you'd say: "God, Visconti would have loved that!" and just saying that is enough to imagine it incorporated instantly into a Visconti film rather than into the script of your own film that's being shot at that very moment even though there aren't any cameras; it's a way of fiction-alizing something that is in itself pure fiction. The mirror in question is in the drawing room downstairs, an enormous room papered in red and gold, with a greenish marble fireplace, velvet curtains, loads of armchairs with tassels on them, signed portraits of Silvia's ancestors and a distinctly musty smell.

What I don't understand is what impulse keeps making me want to come down to this room and walk around it, even though every time I put my hand on the door handle and push the door open I always feel afraid. To say nothing of going down there after sunset, when it's dark, because then, in order to turn on the light, you have to feel with your hand for the plump, golden, fluted switch which is placed high up to the left of the door. I swear that when I feel my way up the wall and my hand touches the hole just below the switch, it's all I can do not to cry out. You'd need to consult Freud to understand why I go into that room so often, so furtively and almost against my will, as if giving in to a spell cast by some wizard. But then, who am I going to tell about it, eh?

The temptation of the closed room, which has already appeared in certain fairy tales and in many others invented by you, will seem more obvious when I tell you that I don't live in the downstairs part of the house (which, if you don't mind, we'll call the hall of mirrors), but in one of the apartments reached by a spiral staircase that leads up from the hall. I live in the apartment to the left, which has an independent entrance that opens on to a large living room decorated in the very latest fashion, with kitchenette, bathroom and a bedroom with piped music. You go up the stairs and it's like leaping a century and a half, the way people do in science fiction movies. These two upstairs apartments, which Silvia had installed in one of her momentary fits of enthusiasm so that her friends could come to Puerto Real and feel at home, were only finished recently. You've no idea of the problems involved. It's been a mammoth task, not so much because of the final cost, although I suppose that comes into it too, but because it was always at the mercy of her mood swings, like every other plan Silvia has come up with since I've known her.

It was the first bit of serious refurbishment she'd got involved with since her father died and, shortly after starting it, she became horribly depressed; she couldn't be bothered to deal with the workmen and didn't want to see anyone. The maid didn't know what to do and so for several months there were bricks, planks, sacks and bidets piled up willy-nilly on the staircase, at the end of the corridor and in a lovely courtyard that had to be restored afterwards because some of the wall tiles got smashed, what with all the rubble being piled up there as well as the continual deliveries of furniture and newfangled gadgets that Silvia had ordered for upstairs. Anyway, it ended up looking like someone had burgled it. All this time, she was downstairs in the big bedroom where her father had died; she just lay in bed, not lifting a finger, drinking heavily, day after day. Every now and then, she'd manage to remove one hand from beneath the sheets in order to sign the occasional blank cheque. That was her only activity. It was around that time, about three years ago, that I began to treat her. Right, that's the frame, now I can begin the story.

It was summer and I was spending my holidays in Cádiz, half-pleasure, half-retreat. Believe it or not, the purpose of my retreat was to start writing a rather ambitious essay on eroticism that I've continued to work on with great difficulty ever since, but which is now near completion and which I've brought down with me again, this time with the aim of finishing it during my stay here. (It was, in fact, an idea I cooked up as I was packing my suitcase, to provide some logical explanation for this crazy journey.) So the index cards and the books that I took to the Hotel Atlántico in Cádiz that summer are more or less the same ones as those on the table here before me and which, out of sheer boredom, I've pushed to one side in order to write to you, since I wasn't making any headway with it. I'm afraid to say, Sofía, that in order to do battle with eroticism, even if it is only a battle based on index cards, you need to feel at one with the world.

I did at the time: my body had emerged from behind its walls and raised the flag of victory, first coming to an agreement with my soul rather than leading it, a prisoner in chains, to its encampment. That phrase about the body coming to an agreement with the soul came to me just like that and I wrote it down on a card that I pinned on the wall, the way you used to pin up encouraging quotes at exam time. In short, I copied you just as I did in so many other things. I laughed to myself thinking that you might like to make a collage of a winged body bearing a flag through the clouds, leading by the hand the soul dressed perfectly normally, perhaps even eating a sandwich. But since I'm useless at anything like that, I simply sellotaped a red rose to the wall – a rose sent by a young man, of course. It slowly withered during the month that I was there. I still have it. And when I went back to the hotel, on the nights that I did go back, I used to think how strange you would find it to have a rose pinned to the wall and to watch it growing older, the way you tear the leaves off a calendar. I often thought of you then – it'll be three years ago this summer – and I even began several letters that I knew from the

81

start I wouldn't send to you. Anyway, I was very happy. I was having a glorious love affair, the sort that just appear one day like a hare in a field, that provide you with a provisional hope of resurrection and manage to give the lie to even the most pitiless of mirrors. He was a painter from Cádiz and quite a lot younger than me. I'd met him there by chance at an exhibition of his water colours. It was one of those days when you've been taking a pleasant, solitary walk about a city not your own; it's getting dark, there are children playing in the square, you haven't spoken to anyone all day and suddenly you notice a crowd of people somewhere and, drawn by their chatter, you say to yourself: "I think I'll join them." I'd already noticed the water colours outside the gallery, they were very romantic paintings of boats. But I'm going to shelve this story for the moment. All I'll say is that during that summer, which I still remember as being surrounded by a nimbus of tiny, brilliant sparks, I felt not only beautiful but very bright too, and I was constantly coming up with new ideas for organizing that essay on eroticism which now feels more like a lead weight.

One evening, when I was sitting on the balcony making some notes, looking out over the sea, I got a call in my room. It was Raimundo phoning from Madrid. He was very worried about a friend of his in Puerto Real, whose father had died at the beginning of the year. He always does the same thing; he immediately starts talking about whatever is on his mind without even bothering to ask how you are, what mood you're in or if you're busy. We only saw each other very occasionally then, but we'd met shortly before my trip – having supper at the Hispano – and I'd spoken of my plans for the summer as a kind of retreat. Some actors who were with him at the table had remarked that it was a bad time to go to Cádiz because of the Trofeo Carranza, but I'd already reserved a room, and that was when I'd mentioned the Hotel Atlántico and Raimundo had asked if I had any friends in Cádiz; he likes to keep me under his thumb.

While I listened to him talk, I was looking at the rose, it was still quite fresh then, and I told him to get to the point because I was expecting another call. The truth is, though, that I was beginning to feel intrigued by the family he was telling me about. It was like when you half-heartedly begin reading a novel and then get so caught up in it you can't put it down. Silvia's father was a widower, a marquis with intellectual leanings, quite well known in certain circles in Madrid which he often visited, always accompanied by his only daughter who had never married. He had a suite permanently reserved for him at the Palace Hotel. Don Armando – for that was his name – had an undisputed reputation, even until he was quite advanced in years, as a seducer of women. He'd been a very close friend of Raimundo's mother with whom he had an affair when they were both young. A brother of Silvia's, a weak individual called Félix, died in a car accident leaving no heirs; his widow, one Mari Luz, had got married again to an extremely wealthy industrialist, and so Silvia had inherited all the marquis' wealth, a vast fortune tied up in land. She couldn't cope; the symbiosis with her father had been too complete. She used to do all his accounts for him, she had typed out a few very long poems he'd written, inspired by Góngora's *Soledades*, they went to concerts together, to parties and to the theatre, and whenever they travelled, they shared a room; there were rumours of an incestuous relationship. Now she was ill.

"What's wrong with her?" I asked.

"Mari Luz, who called to tell me about it, couldn't explain. Hardly surprising: she's not very objective, and she lays it on a bit because she's never particularly liked Silvia – you know, the usual relationship between sisters-in-law. Anyway, it's not a pretty picture. I was afraid this would happen. She's been lying in bed in the dark for months and the doctor says there's nothing wrong with her. I think what she needs is a psychiatrist."

He asked me to go and see her, since I was so close and therefore had a good excuse for visiting.

"You don't need to say anything, you just go there as if you didn't know anything about her situation. You tell her you happened to be passing through Puerto Real, that you're a friend of mine and that you've been dying to meet her for ages because I've told you so much about

83

her and I said that I thought you'd get on well together. I think you will actually."

"But, Raimundo," I said, interrupting him, "if you really thought that, surely you would have told me about her before? It's the first time I've ever heard you mention her."

"I must have mentioned her to you before; you've just forgotten."

"No, Raimundo. For good or ill, I always remember everything you tell me."

"All right, Mariana, but what does it matter? Must you always come on like some card-index system. All I'm saying is that you won't regret meeting her, quite apart from the fact that you can help her. Silvia's great, she's a wonderful singer and mimic and she'd do anything for her friends. Everyone thought that her father's death would be like a weight lifted from her shoulders but, of course, it may have happened a bit too late. The odd thing is that I saw her in February, shortly after the funeral, and she was fine, full of plans for the future. Perhaps she was a little too euphoric. I was a bit worried to be honest. Anyway, you can judge for yourself what's wrong with her, because you certainly do have a good eye for that. You simply go in and you say ..."

"Please, Raimundo, will you stop trying to boss me around," I protested. "I'll decide for myself what I say or don't say. Besides, I haven't even said I'll definitely go and visit her yet. If she's as bad as you say she is, she probably won't even want to see me."

"She's bound to want to see you when she knows you're a friend of mine. It'll be like a ray of sunshine coming in through the window. She's always been a bit in love with me, ever since we were children."

"Well, then, why don't you go and see her yourself and leave me to finish my holidays in peace?"

"Now don't be beastly, Mariana. That would be counter-productive. She's seen a bit too much of me."

I felt the first stab of jealousy and, I admit it, a kind of morbid curiosity began to grow in me – one that has only grown stronger since – a desire to peer into the secrets of that woman's soul. Until then, I'd thought I was Raimundo's closest woman friend, possibly his only one, and I was disconcerted by the sudden eruption on to the scene of this other female character. As you may recall, I've always been a rather impatient reader of novels. I'm the kind of reader who tends to skip pages – something you reproached me with severely – although with the years I have tried to correct that defect.

"Seen too much of you?" I asked Raimundo.

I could tell by his voice that he had registered the change in mine. He knows me too well.

"That's just a manner of speaking. I haven't slept with her if that's what you're asking."

"What gives you the idea I'd want to know that?"

"Okay, I'm sorry, let's not argue. I told you because I thought it might interest you, because I thought you were in a hurry to skip a few chapters. I meant that sometimes in these cases a stranger gets quicker results, especially if she's used to dealing with unstable people. Come on, Mariana, don't tell me that you're not already just a little bit curious to meet Silvia."

He had no idea how curious. I didn't respond though. I played the professional and told him I'd go over to Puerto Real the next day. Then he gave me Silvia's address and that was the first time I heard the name of that Street of Sorrows, Calle de la Amargura.

"It sounds like something out of a novel, doesn't it?" he said.

"Well, yes, it does a bit. But I'll have you know I'm living out my own novel at the moment. God, it's nine o'clock! I've got to go. Waiting for me at this very moment in Callejón del Tinte is Manolo Reina, an extremely handsome young man from Cádiz. He's always there from about eight o'clock onwards, just in case I turn up, and tonight I feel like seeing him."

He burst out laughing and I didn't like that at all.

"Don't tell me you've got a boyfriend called Manolo Reina, please! He sounds like a character in a popular ballad."

"I bet you'd give anything to meet him!"

I was furious with myself for even mentioning it and still more for having entered into the kind of tit-for-tat dialogue that amused him so much. I hung up as soon as I could, but the conversation had left a nasty taste in my mouth.

I didn't say anything to Manolo, who was in fact waiting for me in a café in Callejón del Tinte, because I felt it was a personal matter. And besides, since I'd arrived late, he was already with a group of friends of his who used to meet up there, and he didn't even ask me what had kept me; he was never one for asking questions. At one point, I told him that I wouldn't be able to see him the next day, because I had a patient in Puerto Real who needed my attention. That was when he first found out that I was a psychiatrist. He'd planned to make a trip with me to Arcos de la Frontera, but we left it for another day. He didn't seem to mind. The fact is that when there were other people there, he didn't act as if we were lovers. He was in one of his extrovert moods that night and we stayed until quite late with those noisy friends of his. Then they suggested going on for a drink in the Barrio de la Viña, but I wasn't in the mood. As soon as anything to do with Raimundo enters my life, I'm drawn back into his orbit. Every now and then Manolo would look at me across tables and bars, but I was distracted, and that night I didn't want to go back to his studio with him; I said I had a headache. I kept asking myself obsessively why Raimundo had never mentioned Silvia before if he really had known her all that time.

That was the beginning of my interest in her and also of one of the most unsettling patient-doctor relationships I've known throughout my whole career. I've never seen that quite so clearly as during these last few days, especially after last night, when I barely slept, and during which the letter I'm writing to you now began to take shape. The truth is that I've owed you this letter for a long, long time, ever since you first complained that it was always you who had to tell the long stories.

I broke off briefly to have a sandwich and I switched on the piped music in search of something soothing. They're playing Vivaldi. I'm in the upstairs apartment where I've been holed up for several hours, ever since I started writing to you. I've got the window wide open and the moon is in its first quarter. Look out of your window, Sofía, and look at the moon. I want you to know right now how much I need you and how important it is to me that you're there waiting for my letter. The moon will get the message to you somehow. Mariana is writing to you, don't move, can't you feel it? You're finally going to get your long story. You might well be looking out at it; you always were a great one for the moon and for the stories that get invented or remembered under its narcotic influence. Tonight I'm telling you things I've never told anyone, not even myself, at least not in quite this cold-blooded way. So you see, it's my turn to lie on the psychiatrist's couch. For the first time since I got to Puerto Real, I feel at peace, without that knot of anxiety that wouldn't let me sit still for more than half an hour at a time. Thank you, Sofía. I've re-read what I've written so far and I've tried to put myself in your shoes, tried to imagine what you would find interesting. I think the story is on the right track now and, although I may have to skip a few chapters, it's not turning out too badly. However, as a perspicacious reader of novels, it will not have escaped your notice, nor mine for that matter, that the character of Silvia has undergone a gradual change.

In the letter I wrote to you on the train she seemed like a character who was secondary to the main plot, someone I merely sketched in. Well, she's certainly not a minor character. And when I first mentioned her, I gave a distorted view of my relationship with the house in this bitter Calle de la Amargura. It's true that my relationship with it has never been quite as bitter as on this occasion, but there's always been a bitter undertow. A few days ago, when I was wandering the streets with my bunch of lilacs and had a sudden urge to leave Madrid, I was deceiving myself when I thought of this house as an oasis; I refused to see the darker motives behind my flight to Puerto Real rather than to one of the many other places I could have chosen, more suited than this one to rest and forgetting.

Now, while I listen to Vivaldi, I wonder why I've ended up here of all places, why I'm incapable of leaving, despite the fact that I'm not having a good time or getting very far with my work, especially since I succumbed to the temptation of phoning Silvia yesterday, knowing full well that Raimundo, the person I say I'm trying to get away from, was

crop up in the conversation. Underlying these questions is
...er that arose as soon as I hung up. Are Silvia and I really friends?
Do I care about her or don't I?

I'm not going to go into the fine detail of the ups and downs in my
relationship with her, at least not tonight. You'd have to be a Faulkner to
do that and have a few months to spare. It's taken me four sheets of
paper to put you in the picture about how I came to meet her which
meant that I could only give you a brief sketch of Manolo Reina, one of
the kindest men I've ever known and one of the few who's ever understood me, a really lovely man. A lost paradise, and I was the one who
lost it, since it was me who backed off after the unstoppable crescendo of
that summer. If it had been left to him, we would have embarked on a
longer relationship, despite the age difference. But I was afraid. Now he
lives in New York with the owner of an art gallery and he still writes to
me now and then, although, according to him, writing letters isn't his
strong point: he says he needs to meet people in the flesh, to look them in
the eye.

But returning to Silvia, what I do want to say is that on my first visit
here – when the furniture in this apartment was still all piled up downstairs – the foundations for what she considers the most significant of her
friendships with other women were already shaky. I have to recognize
that at first I gave her some reason to think that I felt the same as she did;
I deceived her, though whether I did so deliberately or not, who knows?
And yesterday when she accused me of doing that, I defended myself
with arguments so feeble that even someone less intelligent than Silvia
would have seen through them. I've never really trusted her, she's right
there. Part of me has always been on the defensive, watching.

To help you understand better, I should explain that a job like mine
requires a rare balance between curiosity and passivity. You have to listen
to what people tell you with interest, of course, but everything gets
distorted if the receiver of those confidences is impatient to worm out
more from the patient than they are prepared to tell you. That eagerness
prevents you from making a correct interpretation of the information
received; you listen badly. Ever since the first day we met, I've felt

uncomfortable with Silvia, and it's gradually got worse. I find the things she says about Raimundo so disturbing – and my attempts to hide that only make matters worse – that it gets in the way of my coming to grips with what is actually troubling her. She grew up with Raimundo, she knew his childhood friends, his mother, a sister who died young and whom he almost never mentions, and she even knows by heart some old poems he wrote that already hint at his repressed homosexuality. I don't quite know what to do with the images of him she's regaled me with throughout her analysis. They create a narrative that undermines my own version of events.

As soon as I undertook a more serious treatment of her case (she started making trips to Madrid especially to see me), I realized that she knew Raimundo better than I did, something that didn't sit well with my *amour propre*. However, it wasn't until last year that I made the most painful discovery: he confides in her about me. I kept an absolutely straight face when I found out – you know me – but I slept badly for several nights afterwards, as if I were standing at a crossroads unable to decide which way to go. A chink had opened, disquieting and tempting, which I didn't know whether to make use of or not, in order to find out how Raimundo really sees me. It's a dilemma I still haven't resolved, a constant source of torment to me. Feigning indifference, I almost always managed to get Silvia to change the subject and not pass on those confidences to me. On other occasions, however, I was the one who slyly encouraged her to do so, even though I would always curse myself afterwards. What never occurred to me, though, was to open my heart to her, to tell her my anxieties as I would to a true friend. I never allowed myself to ask her any direct questions and she, unaware of my unease, just said whatever rather extravagant thoughts occurred to her, thoughts that never quite fit the Freudian rules, with the mixture of bravado, humour and sweetness that is so characteristic of her.

Yesterday afternoon, before phoning her, I was talking to Brígida who inhabits the downstairs part of the house like a shadow and whom I always think of as Mrs Dean. I imagine that this reference to *Wuthering Heights* will suffice to put you in the picture. There's no getting away from Emily Brontë. I first made the comparison three years ago when she opened the door of this house to me and said, with tears in her eyes, that no one wanted to set foot in there any more, that Señorita Silvia was possessed by the Devil and that it was God himself who had sent me. This time, however, she received me coldly. I've noticed that she avoids me, that she doesn't want to talk to me, and the truth is I hardly ever see her. At first I thought this was a blessing, but as the days pass, I find her silent presence becoming almost unbearable. She's one of those old servants who's been in the family all her working life, the kind who carefully file away all the stories, the kind best equipped to write a novel about the family, because they've spent years and years just looking and saying nothing, they've taken note of everything and discarded what is superfluous in order to arrive at the essence.

Yesterday I didn't see her all day. I woke up very early and caught the bus to Cádiz. I wandered along La Caleta, through the district of La Viña and through various other streets and squares all evocative of idealized memories of Manolo. I stood for a while at the Mirador de Santa Elena, leaning on the balustrade, looking down at the trains, at that intersecting labyrinth of lines with the bay in the background. It has a kind of desolate beauty, like an old postcard. "It's a place I've always come to, ever since I was a child, whenever I felt in need of crying," Manolo confessed to me on the last walk we took together that summer, shortly before my train left. We hadn't talked much. We'd agreed that he would come and visit me in Madrid, but I knew that everything would be different from then on, that the unrepeatable summer was slowly burning itself out. "Off you go," I said to him when we got to the station where we'd arrived far too early. "I hate goodbyes. I never know what to say." He didn't say anything. He helped me lift my luggage up on to the rack in my sleeping compartment and we just sat there, on the edge of the seat, like two idiots. I still remember the kiss he gave me before he got up and raced off as if the Devil were after him. A kiss of liquid fire, the sort that leaves a scar. Shortly afterwards, when the train set off, I was leaning out of one of the windows in the corridor when I recognized the great wall on which the name of the city is painted in enormous letters; it was lit up by the sunset. On top of it stands the Mirador de Santa Elena. On an impulse I looked up. A man was standing there waving a handkerchief.

Yesterday, when I remembered that afternoon, I was the one who felt like crying as I leaned on the balustrade of the mirador, my eyes fixed on the intersecting lines. I went to the main post office to send Manolo a telegram. I know his New York address by heart, although I haven't often written to him. They live on the East Side. The clerk at the counter gave me a rather odd look after he'd read the text back to me: "We sing what we have lost," a line from Machado that he was very fond of. "No signature?" he asked. "No, there's no need." He shrugged: "It's up to you, it works out cheaper that way."

Then I felt like going on a spending spree, as always happens when I feel a depression looming. In a shop near the cathedral I bought a pair of jeans that I wore straight away and still haven't taken off. I think a size 44 would have fitted me better, though I don't know what Manolo would say. As I walked past shop windows, I looked at myself out of the corner of my eye, imagining the pressure of his hand on my waist, the rhythm of his steps next to mine, those sudden, intrepid words that would leap into my ear when I least expected them, slowly imprisoning me like a ring of fire, until night came. Had it really been worth giving up all that just to write an essay on eroticism?

I was hardly hungry at all and by mid-afternoon, feeling unusually bored with myself, I ended up at the bus station and travelled back to Puerto Real again. It was a strange afternoon, shot through with unreality, the sky full of churned-up, violet-coloured clouds. During the journey, the idea had begun to take shape in my mind, like a ghost ship ploughing through stormy waters, that I'm wasting my time here and that I must at all costs return to Madrid.

When I reached Calle de la Amargura and put the key in the door, that idea had almost become a definite decision. The tomb-like silence of the house closed round me. I stood in the corridor. "Come on, Mariana," I said to myself, "you can't go on like this, you'll go mad. Go upstairs right this minute, pack your suitcase, take a sleeping pill and tomorrow morning get the train back." My footsteps, however, would not obey my words. As I know all too well, such behaviour is very typical of stagnant situations like this: an inertia takes over that drives you to do exactly the opposite of what you should do.

As usual, for no reason, I went into the drawing room. It had just struck eight o'clock and was already getting dark, although I didn't put the light on. I went slowly over to the mirror with a feeling of apprehension. I guessed that what I most needed to consult the mirror about was not how my new jeans looked on me but my decision to leave. The mirror emitted a dull glow, like that of tarnished silver. The moment I stopped in front of it, I saw within it a shape that was in fact behind me, and I turned round with a start.

Mrs Dean was sitting in one of the armchairs on the other side of the room. She was sitting very stiffly, her eyes half-closed, reciting the rosary. She opened her eyes a little when she heard me walking over to her, but she didn't ask me if I wanted something; she didn't say anything. She went on praying regardless. I sat down in an armchair near hers and we kept silence for a while. If it hadn't been for the fact that her lips and her fingers were moving, albeit almost imperceptibly, she could have been a wax figure.

"I don't know what's going to become of us poor sinners," she mumbled at last, after uttering a long sigh.

It was one of those moments when the past gets jumbled up with the present, with your own and with other people's, when it's pointless trying to dam up your emotions, when you know only that you must seek refuge in another human being, as happens in response to a presentiment of disaster. I couldn't even swallow. I got up from my chair and sat down on the carpet at Brígida's feet; she was still whispering prayers, her eyes staring into space. At the other end of the room, you could just make out our two shapes inside the mirror crowned by that allegory of death. I noticed that Brígida had begun praying out loud, although still very quietly.

"The fifth sorrowful mystery. Jesus dies on the cross. Our Father who art in heaven ..."

Suddenly I surprised myself by giving the response to that Our Father, then to the Hail Marys that followed and lastly, responding with a resounding "Ora pro nobis" to the Latin litany that concludes the rosary, a bright string of extravagant epithets addressed to the Queen of Heaven, most prudent, most worshipful, most pure, most powerful. Brígida's voice grew more spirited, more lively, and she left pauses for me to give my response.

At last, she placed one hand on mine and looked at me. She said that this was the first time since Don Armando died that she had said the rosary in company with someone else. I felt overcome by shyness and didn't know what to say. Mrs Dean's hands felt rough. Neither of us moved.

"Forgive me for saying so, Señorita," she said suddenly, "but you're like lost sheep, all of you. And a flock without a shepherd is bound to go astray or come to some disastrous end. All this work, all this rushing around, taking on so many responsibilities, and what for, if there's no love? Can you explain it to me, you with all your studies?"

I lowered my head.

"No, Brígida," I said, "I can't."

That was when she began telling me how worried she was about Silvia and reproaching me for not having phoned her yet. She told me that Silvia had started drinking again and that it wasn't good for her to be there all alone, having to deal with sinking boats and disasters that even grown men would find hard to cope with.

"You could have such a good time here, the two of you together," she concluded, "going out, going to the cinema, talking and whatever."

My conscience began to prick me.

"Is she really that bad?" I asked. "Have you spoken to her?"

"Yes, two hours ago. She's got nothing to hold on to any more, she's going slightly mad, I think. I didn't tell her you were here, not that I didn't want to, of course ... but since you don't want her to know. That's the first thing you said to me the moment I opened the door the other day, when I heard you come in, almost before you said hello, do you remember? A fine way to behave when you go to someone's house."

93

She caught my eye and I simply gave a brief nod.

"I really don't understand," she went on. "It really bothers me that the Señorita doesn't know that you're here. It doesn't seem normal to me."

"The trouble is that I'm not very well either, Brígida. I just can't take any more problems. I've come here to rest."

"But you don't rest at all. Do you think I don't hear you pacing up and down in that wretched apartment and playing the radio at all hours of the night? Anyway, how can you possibly rest after what happened to Don Raimundo? Another poor, lost creature, may the Lord have mercy on him! And you just abandon him too when he most needs you …"

That was how I found out that Silvia and Raimundo had spoken on the phone and that he'd given her his version of events, about his suicide attempt and the fact that I'd disappeared from Madrid from one day to the next without saying where I was going.

"And all I can do is hold my tongue," Mrs Dean went on, "what else; it seems to be my fate."

She paused, crossed herself and added:

"Lord God, through the merits of Your most precious blood, forgive us the words we say when we should not and those which out of cowardice we swallow. You see what a cross I have to bear, knowing that you're here and that they're looking for you like some fugitive from justice. Who are you hiding from? From my poor Señorita? Our friends used to treat us more straightforwardly, more frankly, without all this confusion and secrecy. We may have had fewer friends then, I don't deny it, but they could at least be trusted."

"Has Silvia asked after me?"

"No. But not telling her is tantamount to lying, and it makes me feel that I'm involved in something I simply don't understand."

I promised Mrs Dean that I would phone Silvia at once. I gave her a kiss and went up to my room, leaving her feeling a little more consoled.

As I told you at the beginning, Silvia was pretty drunk, and one of the effects alcohol has on her is that it temporarily makes her lose her bearings. As soon as she heard my voice, without even asking me where I was and without any preamble, she started telling me some wild story about a workman called Fabián who was re-tiling the roof of the farm at Carmona and who had been making indecent proposals to her. She liked him, what did I think she should do? If she gave in to his demands, the gossip would spread like wildfire all round Carmona. And besides I already knew about her problematic relationship with sex. She couldn't understand how Fabián could fancy a woman so much older than himself, although, why deny it, it had boosted her morale no end. It all sounded like a bit of a shaggy dog story to me. It's not the first time that Silvia has built whole stories around one insignificant detail; she's occasionally told me as much herself. She says that, without these fantasies, life is very difficult to bear. Reluctantly, I decided to humour her, trying to find out the truth or otherwise of the story through the inflections of her voice. I felt increasingly uncomfortable, however, and in me that always manifests itself in a lack of attention. Silvia noticed.

"Listen, Mariana," she said suddenly, "would you mind telling me why the hell you've phoned? You don't fool me, you know. And don't tell me I'm getting aggressive. I've got my reasons. It's just one damned thing after another."

"I'm not telling you anything. I called to find out how you are, because I haven't heard from you in ages. What's so strange about that?"

"Liar!" she yelled. "You don't give a damn about me. You don't care about anyone. Not even Raimundo. You just clear off as soon as he becomes a nuisance. You've got him where you want him. That's the way you like it, isn't it? And anyway where the hell are you?"

"I'm in Puerto Real, at your house. But if you speak to Raimundo, don't tell him, please. I can't really explain, but I'm having a really hard time."

She burst out laughing and I felt as if she'd stripped me bare.

"Having a hard time, you! I'll make a note of that in my diary. What's up, have your defences failed you?"

Yes, my defences had failed me completely; all I wanted to do was cry.

"Please, Silvia, don't talk to me like that."

"I would never just leave Raimundo, never," she went on, getting more and more excited, "because I've always loved him, not like you. I'd give anything for him to look at me the way Fabián looks at me, even if it was only for ten minutes. You don't know how lucky you are. Everyone loves you, but you're incapable of loving anyone."

"If it's any consolation, Raimundo doesn't love me. He just makes me suffer all the time. If he tells you anything else, don't take any notice of him. Anyway, enough of that. I don't want to talk about Raimundo or see him ever again. That's over with, for good."

"Is that true?" asked Silvia, changing her tone.

"Absolutely."

"How can you say that without crying?"

There was a silence. The tears welling up in my eyes gave way to heartfelt sobs. Silvia softened.

"I'm sorry, Mariana, I've been drinking a lot. I just want to ask you one question, one that's really important to me. Do you think of me as a close friend? And don't tell me something you've worked out in your head; answer me from your heart, tell me what you feel."

I told her that I was feeling really bad and, besides, it really didn't seem like something we should discuss over the phone; that just enraged her and provoked the avalanche of "home truths" that resulted in last night's insomnia. At half past midnight I phoned her again, feeling absolutely awful. I needed to salve my conscience and to ask her forgiveness. I begged her please to come to Puerto Real, I needed to talk to her calmly. If she didn't, I'd come to Carmona. She took a while to respond. I realized that I'd woken her up.

"Thank you, Mariana," she said at last, in a very soft voice. "That's the first time you've ever asked me to do anything. I'll be there the day after tomorrow, as soon as I've sorted out a few things here; I'll be there in the afternoon."

She's coming tomorrow. But now the mere idea of confronting her weighs on me like a stone. I need to rest, I need to sleep. It's three o'clock in the morning. At least I'll go to bed today knowing that I've cleared up one thing.

At least now I understand why I've come to Puerto Real, Sofía: in order to write you this letter. I hope I haven't bored you.

96

Sleep well. I'll ask the moon to make sure you have a good night's sleep.

Lots of love,

Mariana.

PS Since there is simply no way I can get to sleep, I've got up and started going over my notes on eroticism. I've been doing it for a while now, but the cure is worse than the disease, because I don't like what I've written at all. And when I ask myself why I don't like it, what's wrong with this analysis that I undertook so arrogantly a few years ago, the wound of my most secret obsessions re-opens. Once when I was talking about this essay to Raimundo – with considerable enthusiasm because I thought I could see it all so clearly – he smiled and said that the weakness of my arguments lay precisely in that, that I saw it all too clearly, when eroticism is essentially dark and contradictory. According to him, I wouldn't deign to descend into these wells of darkness because I'm too afraid.

When I protested, he added: "I'm not saying that you haven't gone down there occasionally, but you've always done so like some cautious and sophisticated submariner, complete with breathing apparatus and safety devices that you've carefully checked beforehand to ensure that they don't fail you. That's what you teachers usually do. That's why your contributions to the clarification of complex problems are correct but inadequate. Eroticism is like a rising tide that breaks all the bounds of intelligibility, and you want to understand it without running the risk of letting yourself be overwhelmed by that tide."

"I don't like running risks that cancel out understanding."

"I know you don't, but you could use the experience of others who have run those risks. Why don't you re-read Bataille, for example?"

Ever since that conversation my work on eroticism began to smell slightly rancid; it acquired a whiff, which it's never quite lost, of something cooked up in the brain. Tonight, I'm more aware of that than ever before. My eyes have just alighted on a quote from Bataille that only increases my unease.

Human life — he says — has a tendency to prodigality. A feverish agitation latent in all of us begs death to carry out his work of destruction on us at our expense. Love and death are merely high points in a party to which nature invites the inexhaustible multitude of beings, for both love and death carry within them the limitless talent for waste for which nature has a propensity, despite the desire to endure experienced by all beings.

When I read this quote and copy it out again for you, I remember someone who would have agreed with it passionately, who lived life to the limit. You know who I mean. Weren't all his theories about desire in that same register? Although the fact is that they weren't even theories, they were simply waves that occasionally broke over you. Theories were what I deployed to oppose him, in a vain attempt to build a wall against the sea so that it wouldn't flood my house. I never dared adapt myself to his rhythm; I was never happy with him. It's time I told you that, Sofía. I had to imagine that he wasn't really like that in order to resist him and imagine that I controlled him. I submitted the sensual exaltation he aroused in me to a kind of alchemy that converted it into mere polemical excitement. I didn't enjoy him for what he was, I enjoyed the strategies I invented to put his love to the test, to explore it from the safety of my home territory and to channel its turbulence. It was through the Guillermo I invented and who did not exist — kneeling before me, dazzled, tamed by a calm, superior intelligence — that I merely loved myself more than ever. That was my first failure, although it took me a while to understand it, the first link in a chain of self-glorifying acts of which the only goal was to conceal my cowardice when confronted by tumultuous eroticism.

I'm sure you were better able than I was to follow his tendency to prodigality and waste, the sensual joy he found in living the present moment to the full, led only by his instincts. You were like that too, you too were drawn to the fire. It was written that you would meet and that you would love each other "despite the desire to endure experienced by all beings". Tonight, I envy you both retrospectively and I think that only my blindness and pride have occasionally made me imagine that you needed my absolution. How ridiculous! Not even Catherine or Heathcliff needed sensible Linton's forgiveness. The novel can't end in any other way, just as your story with Guillermo could never have had a happy ending either, because eroticism is a fire that consumes what it creates and inflames. That's all there is to it.

I suspect you knew this a long time ago.

It's nearly dawn now. Good morning, Sofía.

M.

VII

Conversation with Daría

I recognize now that I don't like reality, that I never have. I've done my duty by it as best I could when there was no way of getting round its laws, but I've never really been able to get the hang of the text of those laws, and there are so many of them. I keep the text in my head, held together with pins, but again and again I forget. I lurch from one shock to the next, untangling complicated knots that slow down the work, and I'm never quite sure whether I've undone them properly or not: I haven't a clue.

The same thing used to happen with maths exams. I never failed maths and I even got two B+s, one in the fifth year and one in the seventh. It seems incredible to me, but it's true. It's official. I saw it today, in writing and with an official blue stamp, in an old school book that turned up at the bottom of a large, untidy drawer I was rummaging through in search of a piece of paper that Eduardo had asked me to look out for some reason or another – I can't remember what it was now. I have a vague idea that it was yellow and rather crumpled. But even if I had found it, so what? I wouldn't learn anything new and I wouldn't have had any fun. It's just a second-rate hieroglyphic with no intrinsic interest whatsoever, one of many that throw us off the scent and conceal the genuine hieroglyphic. The genuine hieroglyphic. I repeated it to myself several times, syllable by syllable, distorting it by changing the stress, swinging back and forth on it. "Gen-u-ine-hie-ro-glyph-ic". I've always enjoyed playing with words, ever since I was a little girl. It's not without its risks, like grabbing hold of a ring which is, in fact, hanging in the void. That's also what makes it exciting.

I was sitting on the carpet in front of the open drawer where the bit of yellow paper might possibly be hidden and I was staring out of the window while I muttered the phrase to myself, taking it to pieces and then picking it up again by its tail. Evening was falling. A few pink clouds were passing, moving almost imperceptibly and almost imperceptibly changing shape, consistency and colour. Every shape they took on, each more suggestive than the last, was like brief slashes across the sky demanding to be deciphered, as they always have since the beginning of time: a variable and infinite text like that of our inner voyages. We travel along with clouds that disintegrate and darken, we change with them never realizing that we do, just as their fragile outline is condemned to fade and die before anyone has understood it. The genuine hieroglyphic lies in the clouds, never on bits of paper.

I continued looking for the bit of paper, though I did so unenthusiastically, against my will, not believing that I would find it. Anyway, when I opened the drawer, the handle came off (the screws were loose) and I was left holding it in my hand. That should have warned me that I shouldn't mess with things that are of no interest.

There are so many bits of paper though! The worst thing is that they proliferate of their own accord, tenacious as weeds, regardless of any interest they might arouse or not arouse. Each year, each month, each day brings another layer of papers implicating me, bearing my name and sometimes my signature, I certainly can't just forget about those. Have I lived so very long to have accumulated so much paper? Certificates, receipts, letters from the bank, notarized requests, statements of account, appeals, guarantees, newspaper cuttings, X-rays, birth certificates, old identity cards, deeds, life insurance policies, fines, leases, a book containing dates of family marriages and births. Whether I like it or not, these are things that have to do with me; one of these days someone is going to ask me to account for them, and on that day I will have to find the relevant piece of paper and recognize it by its physiognomy. They will demand this in peremptory fashion, not bothering to ask if I find the task repellent or not, the way they do when they ask you to identify a dead body and you have no option but to go over and lift up the sheet.

Yesterday, when Eduardo asked me to look out this obscure document and he saw the face I made, he was tactless enough to remind me that my dislike of administrative bumph has its roots in my pathology, in that obsessive shutting myself away in what the psychiatrist some years ago used to call "unreal experiences". Although he spoke of it in the past tense and acted as if it were of no importance, even managing to force a smile, there was the same impatient, authoritarian hardness I'd noticed in his voice when he said to me once (I can't remember when): "We're going to have to do something about you, Sofía. I hope you'll be co-operative."

Before I came across the school book, I was remembering how awful it was the first time Eduardo took me to see the psychiatrist, how I longed simply to disappear. The same symptoms resurfaced just remembering it. I stopped rummaging around in the drawer and, sitting there in the middle of the carpet, I twice asked myself: "What am I doing here? What does 'I' mean?" It did actually seem as if everything around me were spinning. I started to feel afraid, because that sense of strangeness increased at vertiginous speed: it began swelling inside my brain like a malignant tumour affecting my memory, my understanding and my will. I was surprised to find myself repeating, as if invoking the gods at a moment of terrible danger: "Memory, understanding, will," and I couldn't remember who I was or how long or for what reason I'd been sitting there on that carpet. Only by imagining it was Aladdin's carpet could I gain some respite from my anxiety, telling myself that I had to concentrate hard if I wanted it to fly. At that point, my willpower returned because that was what I really wanted, that was all I wanted: to fly out of the window across the May sky before the message from the clouds was erased.

Glued inside the school book with its hard blue covers is a small passport photo. At some point that girl with the blonde plaits and interrogative expression must have known how to solve mathematical problems; if not, she would never have passed the exams. But she didn't understand numbers. Numbers were simply unalterable ciphers and the names they bore never gave rise to fantasy. I went back to looking out of the window and my memory began to return. A little blonde girl in the mathematics class and the teacher saying to her: "You've got your he... in the clouds again, Señorita Montalvo."

She used to enjoy inventing words and taking to pieces words she'd heard for the first time, making different combinations with the dismantled pieces, breaking them up and putting together the pieces that occurred more than once. Long words were like dresses with a bodice, waistcoat and skirt and you could add the waistcoat of one to the skirt of another that had the same bodice or, the other way round, you could swap the skirt. Just by juggling suffixes or affixes around, for example, you could discover different aspects of peace, death, sanctity and testimony: pacify and pacific, mortify and mortality, sanctify and sanctimonious, testify and attest; it was quite a good game to play with a dictionary. Some bodices such as "philo", which meant love or friendship and "logo", which meant word, went with everything and allowed for fascinating variations. One day she put them together and created a really delightful character: the philologist, lover or friend of words. She drew him in her school book just as she imagined him, wearing mauve-framed glasses, a pointed hat and carrying a huge butterfly net full of spirals of words to which she added wings. Then she found out that the word "philologist" already existed, that she hadn't invented it after all.

"But it doesn't matter. What you did is understand it and apply it," Don Pedro Larroque, her teacher of literature, told her. "Never lay down your butterfly net. Catching words and playing with them is one of the healthiest occupations there is."

Giving them wings, in other words. And she gave wings to the words because she was their friend, and because being someone's friend means wanting them to be able to fly. She drew another, more detailed version of the philologist and this time he had blond plaits. Behind him stood an angel with thinning hair and an aquiline nose who was pinning a pair of silvery wings on his shoulders.

The mathematics teacher, on the other hand, didn't approve of these word games at all; they were proof that one was not paying attention to the really serious problems; they were a dangerous manipulation of two plus two is four, a waste of time. One fine day, he suddenly started talking about logarithms, and there was an unexpected and somewhat scandalous interruption. The girl with the butterfly net had stood up to ask if that word, which she'd heard for the first time, could possibly mean a mixture of word and rhythm. The other students looked at her open-mouthed and the teacher got angry.

"That's got nothing whatsoever to do with it, Señorita Montalvo. You've always got your head in the clouds," he said, looking at her severely. "You'd do far better if you paid more attention."

The blonde girl, who was beginning to come to terms with reality and to realize that what is important for some people is not important for others, sat down without saying another word and wrote in her notebook: "Logarithm: a word with no rhythm and no wings. Not important."

I look at her in the photo. There's a purple stamp whose smudged ink reads: "Instituto Beatriz Galindo"; it touches her shoulder and blurs the design on her jersey. She's quite pretty. What did she imagine logarithms were? How did she manage to struggle with them without knowing what they were? Not a trace remains. Now, if I say "logarithm", "digit", "square root" or "equation", I see a lot of little grey, articulated sticks creeping across the carpet like a procession of worms. You daren't even touch them. Units, tens, hundreds, millions, pi, three, fourteen, sixteen. They turn my stomach. They coil about each other, they seethe at my left side (overwhelmed, I've lain down on the carpet), and I look at them fearfully out of the corner of my eye, I see them march towards my feet, negotiate my waist, follow the curve of my legs. I can't move, I'm surrounded. I discover that there is another procession of equally fat worms moving swiftly down the right flank. These ones are green, and when they reach my feet, they turn the corner and merge their ranks with the greys. They mill around together, form groups, conspire, like the evil geniuses they are. They seem to weigh very little, as if they would disperse like a pile of feathers if I blew on them. An optical illusion. They weigh more than the carpet and between them they prevent it taking flight. They won't let me forget that they are there, just as the prisoner cannot forget the bars on his cell window.

These green worms are the dead hours, the rotting hours of my whole life, hours spent negotiating the reefs of reality in order to pass exams in subjects I remember nothing about, subjects I can't even remember being examined in, despite having struggled so hard with them. All I know about these subjects is that you have to face them each time as if it were the first time and that the fear of failure never goes away. It's very similar to the fear of losing the bits of paper that prove one has passed. You studied in order to get a good mark. They weren't optional. A pass in being a daughter. A pass in courtship. A pass in household management. A pass in conjugal relationships and doing one's duty by the in-laws. A pass in childbirth. A pass in smoothing over difficulties, in finding a place for everything and in putting a good face on things. A pass in active motherhood, although this subject, being the most difficult, is liable to continual revision. Such subjects, especially the last, can prove fascinating. It depends how you treat them. They do resemble logarithm problems in one respect, though, in that you never know how you're going to resolve them or why you have to. A breeding ground for the green worms and the grey worms of obscure, questionable, oppressive facts.

Daría came in without making a sound, as she usually does, startling me so much that it startled her in turn. Her arrival, however, provided contact with someone whose smell I recognize, like when you wake up from a nightmare and find friendly eyes gazing into your eyes. She knelt down and put her arm around my shoulders.

"What are you doing lying down on the carpet? Are you ill?" she asked. "I'm so sorry I frightened you. I came to ask if you wanted some tea. What's wrong? You're trembling."

I buried my face in her shoulder. We were sitting right next to each other because she'd helped me to sit up.

"I don't know what's wrong with me. I don't feel well, Daría. I just suddenly felt terribly dizzy."

"Have you been drinking or anything?"

She glanced round, but not surreptitiously enough for me not to understand what she was looking for, nor for her to understand that I understood. I followed the direction of her eyes. There were no bottles in sight. Daría blinked nervously. "Come on then, up you get. That's it. Breathe deeply. It's all right."

And it really was all right. I could walk perfectly well, I wasn't dizzy, just a little stiff, like when you've slept in an awkward position. I was breathing normally. And on the carpet, amongst the scattered papers, there wasn't a single worm, either green or grey, to be seen.

"Shall I pick up the papers on the floor? Good heavens, what a mess!"

"No, please, leave them for now, Daría."

But she'd already bent down to look at them and when she made as if to pick them up, all the certificates, receipts, bank statements, guarantees, X-rays, birth certificates, fines and old identity cards came back to life again. I broke down. I think I even covered my face with my hands.

"Leave it, I said. Leave it! I don't want to see it. Just leave it!"

I felt her hand on my shoulder, as if she were helping someone injured, and her tone of voice was like the one you use to console children.

"All right, all right, don't get upset. I was just trying to make sure no one would step on them. Shall I open the window? It stinks of cigarettes in here."

She opened it and I sat down in an armchair. The air coming in through the window wasn't cold. The sun had just gone down and the last remnants of the hieroglyph were fading in the pale sky.

Daría stood in front of me, waiting. Neither of us said anything. I saw that she was looking suspiciously at my mother's chest of drawers which, before, had stood against the other wall. But when? What do I mean "before"? I haven't written for days – how many days? – not bothering about the when and why of things, and I've lost the thread, that's what's wrong with me. I let my eyes wander from one wall to the other, as if lost. Then I looked up at Daría and saw that she was upset.

"It frightens me when you start moving the furniture about, it does really. Anyway, your mother's chest of drawers gets in the way there."

I didn't say anything. Shifting furniture from one place to another for no apparent reason was another of the things I used to do when I started going to the psychiatrist. That was doubtless what Daría was remembering when she looked at the chest of drawers. She has a surprising capacity for association of ideas. For the moment, to get back to the reason she came into the room in the first place, she asked me if I wanted a cup of tea. I felt that this was an attempt to re-establish normality.

"I'm going to bring you a bit of cake I've just made as well because, knowing you, you probably haven't eaten. I got here at four o'clock and, of course, there wasn't a scrap of food in the kitchen."

I looked at my watch for the first time. It was seven o'clock. I hadn't heard Daría come in. I said as much.

"Of course you didn't, you were asleep."

"Asleep? It's just that sometimes the days seem so long."

"They might to you," said Daría, "to me they just fly by."

"But I shouldn't sleep during the day, I shouldn't. How long was I asleep for anyway?"

Daría shrugged.

"Did the two of you have lunch out?" she asked, as if trying to help me tie up loose ends.

That plural evoked the image of Eduardo with his slicked-back hair, his Italian jackets, his look of being permanently stressed out, and I rejected it as a lie. He was a character who had appeared on the scene by mistake. Have lunch with him? Certainly not, how boring. Luckily, he hasn't asked me out to lunch for ages. Is it normal that I accept that so coolly? Since when? When did I start to care so little about his existence? I must go and see Mariana León. Not my old schoolfriend to ask if she's received my first batch of homework, but the psychiatrist who treats ladies in sequined jackets, executive wives with problem children, people whose head travels along one set of rails and their life along another. I need to see her because I can't remember where I had lunch today or what piece of paper I was looking for a moment ago, because I would be horrified if my husband rang me up and asked me out to the cinema, because I don't understand my behaviour and I can't control it. Because, in a word, I need a psychiatrist. I don't need Eduardo to tell me this time; he doesn't even have to know that I've found out for myself. I will deceive him, I will deceive them all. I've made my bed and now I must lie in it. Deceit is what appeals to me most at the moment, leading a double life. I will choose my own psychiatrist, because that's what I feel like doing. I've already chosen her. And no one knows it. It's a secret between Mariana and me, just like when we were small. How exciting!

"Don't just sit there staring like that. You look like you've had a shock." Daría was frightened by my silence.

"It's just that I can't remember if I had lunch or not, nor when I moved the chest of drawers; I can't remember anything, Daría, nothing! Do you think that's normal?"

Daría gave a resigned shrug.

"No, it isn't," I said emphatically. "I'm in a bad way, I am, I mean it. I'm going to have to do something."

"Now, don't start on that again. What you need is a nice cup of tea," she said, making as if to go out of the room. "I'm going to make it right now."

"OK, thanks. Put a bit of honey in it, will you? And would you mind closing the door?"

As soon as she'd gone, I looked for my address book which was in my handbag. Under L, next to Mariana's address, I'd noted down her telephone number the evening I met her at the exhibition. I resolutely dialled the seven numbers, turning the dial energetically, and my heart was beating hard. I didn't have to wait long. There were two rings interrupted by a light crackle.

"This is Dr León's answering machine. I'm going to be away for a few days. For any queries about appointments, please phone Dr Carreras on 5768527, that's 5768527. If you wish to leave a personal message, please speak after the tone. Thank you."

I mechanically wrote down Dr Carreras' phone number and then, when the tone sounded, I was about to hang up. Instead, I reacted angrily:

"Honestly, I'm surprised you've got any clients at all speaking in that frigid tone of voice. In fact, a patient of yours said as much the other day, she said you sounded as if you were speaking from the top of Mount Olympus. Your message is both uninviting and grammatically incorrect, because it sounds as if it's your answering machine that's gone away. Anyway, it's Sofía. I sent you some homework. Did you get it? And since then I've been writing things down in a notebook. It was working out really well, but I suddenly ran out of steam, I can't see the point in it any more. I need you to come back and tell me to write, because if you don't, it all seems like a hallucination I had; I feel that perhaps I didn't really meet you the other evening, when we had that conversation about the hare in the field. By the way, I can't remember how long ago that was, I've lost all track of time. I don't know if what I've got to say to you is personal or professional. Perhaps the answering machine sorts that out for you. I'd say it was more of a shaggy dog story myself. But, joking apart, I'm feeling pretty bad and I need to talk to you about various things. Call me when you get back from wherever it is you've gone. Lots of love and I'm so glad we met again. You didn't talk to me in that chilly tone of voice at the cocktail party. Goodbye."

I don't think my last words were recorded, I got cut off. But I suddenly felt calm again. Mariana León does exist. I didn't invent her. She's gone away, but she does exist.

When Daría returned with the tea, the room had recovered its usual physiognomy and brought back with it various facts about recent chronology. I'd moved the chest of drawers on Thursday, after Soledad had been to see me, because our conversation had stirred up a lot of things for me. It could become a chapter in the notebook. We were talking about her parents separating and that led on to other topics and set me talking. I was in a strangely excited mood, as if I were drunk. Soledad has always liked listening to me, ever since she was a child. Amelia had left the previous day. Old stories from the past surfaced, about Mariana and Guillermo, things I'd never told anyone. It was almost dark by the time we'd finished. Afterwards, I made some notes about the conversation and dated them. I think that's the last time I wrote anything, not in the notebook but on loose sheets of paper. Where could I have put them? It's fatal to write things on bits of paper. "I should write them out properly," I remember thinking, while I was moving the chest of drawers. "I just have to keep writing slowly, bit by bit."

Daría moved a low table over to the armchair and put down the tray with the tea and the cake on it. She cut me a slice.

"What are you thinking about?"

"About some papers I can't remember what I've done with. I haven't a clue where I put them and I need them."

"Just stop thinking about bits of papers for now. They'll be the death of you, those bits of paper. Have some tea. Then we'll look for them."

"All right, but sit down with me for a while. Are you in a hurry?"

"As you well know, being in a hurry all depends on how you look at it," she said, as she drew up a chair and sat down opposite me. "I've done all my jobs. But you can certainly tell I haven't been for a few days."

"You're right. By the way how's your lumbago? I forgot to ask."

"A lot better. Tomorrow I'm going to give the house a really good clean because Consuelo isn't a great one for hoovering or scrubbing. And since you never say anything to her ... She's a great one for avoiding her responsibilities. If she'd had the life I've had ... I'd like to see how she'd put up with a quarter of what I went through when my Elías was in prison. But it's pointless talking to young people about the civil war, what's it got to do with them, that's what they say, it's not their problem."

Daría's voice brought me back to a more comfortable world, connected, slow, full of common sense. I dunked my cake in the tea and it tasted really good.

"I don't know how you put up with her," she went on. "I always say to her: 'If you worked for anyone else ...' And the children are the same, they're just like you, the way they put up with everything. In fact, they're even more accommodating than you are. Even Consuelo says so, she says she just wishes that they'd ask her to do something, from which I gather that they don't ask her to do anything. And knowing her, if they don't ask her to do anything and she can do just as she likes, the famous refuge must be in a right state. Your mother must be turning in her grave!"

I was sipping my tea. Daría always provides the sort of information that brings you down to earth with a bump.

"I've told Consuelo already," Daría continued, "wild horses wouldn't drag me to that refuge. Once was enough. Why suffer unnecessarily? As for Encarna and Lorenzo, tidiness and obedience were never their strong points. And their friends are just the same. Don Eduardo doesn't like their friends, does he?"

"They don't like his for that matter."

"I know. They don't get on. Do you remember the rows when they were last living here, especially just before their grandmother died. Their father would say white and they would say black, and if you hadn't been there to intervene ... They made my summer hell. I can't bear to think of it."

"Which summer was that?"

"When you went to London to pick up Amelia and her friend. By the way, you should take more trips like that; you came back a new woman. It didn't last long, of course. What happened to that nice girl? Her name was Soledad, wasn't it?"

"Yes. She was here the other day. Her parents have split up."

"Well, better late than never. Perhaps the idea will catch on. I think it's a good thing. If you've got the money, why put up with something all your life if you don't like it? What's wrong? Are you feeling dizzy again?"

I shook my head and closed my eyes, but my head was spinning.

"You've closed your eyes again. If you like, I'll leave you on your own."

"No, don't. It's just that I want to remember things, when they happened, how they happened, how the things that happened before relate to what's happening now, and how other people's lives relate to mine, because everything is related, I'm sure of that. It's like trying to untangle the knots in a ball of wool that's all tangled up with other balls of wool, with thousands of balls of wool. It's driving me mad. I don't know where to begin, Daría, I can't concentrate."

"Why should you concentrate? It'll do your head in. Not even God can manage it, not the state the world's in nowadays, and he's so old now, the poor thing, he wouldn't even recognize the place. He'd say: So that's what happened to the little idea I had of making something 'in my own image'. A fine mess I made of that. And he'd do one of two things, either recognize that he'd made a mistake or lie down and have a nap. You like the cake then? It turned out really light, didn't it?"

"Yes, it's delicious."

"It'll be better still when it cools down."

"Daría, tell me something. When did they start treating me for my nerves? Was it the year I went to England?"

"There you go again! What does it matter? What's past is past."

"No, please, you must remember, because you remember everything. It was that year, wasn't it?"

"Yes, it was 1980. After the summer. Shortly after the children moved into the flat that their grandmother had left them. She died in September, rest her soul, and they moved in a few months after that. At Christmas, I think. I don't know if it was a good thing or not that they inherited from their grandmother when they were still so young."

"I don't know either, I don't know anything. And yet something hasn't worked out right, and it's my fault. I remember now that when I got back from London, that was when I saw things clearly."

"What things?"

"Well, that Encarna and Lorenzo don't accept reality as it is, that they don't want to be like their father in any way whatsoever. And I'm to blame for that. That's what I talked about to the psychiatrist. I understand them, I don't encourage them to feel that way, but I do understand them. I can't do anything about it."

"Well, I don't understand my daughter Consuelo and I don't encourage her either. And she's just as cheeky with her father as your children are. She even calls him an old fogey to his face. Terrible. If I'd ever talked to my father like that, I'd have got a good hiding. So don't blame yourself; with children these days, you just can't get it right. And what's happened with Lorenzo? Why doesn't he settle down and earn a living? With the contacts he's got now, Don Eduardo could easily help him."

"There's just no way, Daría. The more successful their father is in business and the more influential the people he meets, the more they despise money."

"That's because they've got some."

"They can't have much left of what they inherited from their grand-mother."

"Of course not, since they've done nothing but squander it from the start. It wasn't very considerate of them either to sell off all their grand-mother's good furniture for next to nothing. It was almost as if they couldn't bear to keep it in the house. Luckily, Santi took most of it. But he's so far away, in America … All that upset you quite a lot too."

"Not really. I couldn't bear to keep the furniture either, I'm not attached to old things. What upsets me, Daría, is having to make deci-sions. To take sides. To offer advice. To say some are right and others are wrong, to see myself implicated in the lives and destinies of other people, however close they are. That's what upsets me. They wanted to leave and they left, fine, but I couldn't be inside them and inside my brother and inside my husband, each fighting his or her own private battle."

"All right, don't get excited. Why the hell did I have to mention the refuge?"

"What did it have to do with me? And they were all waiting for me to decide, to say something, all arguing. I didn't give a damn either way, whether to sell it, buy it, share it out, mortgage it, I just didn't care. Do you know, even my mother's death left me cold. It would have sounded monstrous to say so at the time, so I didn't, but that's what I felt."

"She never loved you very much."

"No, she didn't. And she resented me. And I felt guilty."

"All this wretched guilt! As I said before, that's the fault of the person who created this world."

"It was marvellous that trip to England. When I came home, it was like landing back in hell. I haven't escaped from it since."

"Now then, don't exaggerate."

I sat looking out of the window. How long ago did I stop writing? And why? Writing rescued me from hell. I must find the notes I made after Soledad's visit. I'm sure there are some really key facts there. Daría had got up. I noticed that, while she was picking up the tea tray, she was looking at me again, as if she were spying on me.

nsuelo told me that you were fine a few days ago, that you
ng years younger, singing and making jokes all the time. She
aid, well you know what she's like, that she wondered if you had a
over somewhere or other and I said to her: 'If only she did!', and I meant
it. It's true, it would do you good. Isn't that what men do, look for
someone outside the home?"

"I'm not interested in things like that any more, Daría."

"Of course not, you've been without it for so long. I have the opposite
problem, I have to fight my husband off. Even these last few days, with
me crippled with lumbago, he didn't care. The bugger even said he liked
the smell of the spray the doctor had prescribed. Well, it's just as well we
can laugh about it! Honestly, I've never seen anyone whose expression
could change so much from one minute to the next. You don't even
realize it. You're a real case, you are."

"Yes, so Soledad tells me."

I stood up. I'd just remembered where I'd put the notes I wrote the day
that Soledad came to see me: inside a Patricia Highsmith novel I was
reading. With those notes, a few old letters and bits from the diary I
wrote during my trip to England, I could make a collage that might help
me to understand a little better what Guillermo meant to me. I put my
arm around Daría's shoulders.

"Everything comes and goes. I suddenly feel very well, cheerful. The
human soul is like the clouds: you never catch it in the same position
twice."

"I know that, so just let it be, and stop trying to invent traps to catch it
in. It's a bad habit of yours."

"It is, you're right. Perhaps I'll learn this time."

"No more hell and no more guilt. Women enjoy themselves most in bed
when they're about fifty; they're not afraid of anything then. My husband
may be stupid, and Elías certainly is, but at least he understands that. And
if yours doesn't, then you'll just have to look elsewhere and that's that."

I burst out laughing.

"It's not as easy as that, Daría. These days there aren't that many men
about, no decent men, I mean."

"You're right there. Anyway, I'd better go, if you don't want anything else that is, it's getting late."

I thanked her for her company and she said I shouldn't spend so many hours shut up alone at home, that I should go out more.

When she poked her head round the door to say goodbye shortly after that, her jacket already on, I'd just found *Deep Water*, the Patricia Highsmith novel. The papers were inside. "Write about Guillermo exactly the way I told Soledad about him this afternoon," I read. "Like a novel. As if everything that happened had happened to someone else. With the humour and disinterest he always advised me to cultivate in order to survive."

"Are those the papers you were looking for?" asked Daría.

"Yes. Thanks."

"You see how everything turns up in the end? And talking of papers, I forgot. There's a recorded delivery letter for you. A fat one."

I looked up from reading Guillermo's name.

"A letter? Where?" I asked, my heart racing.

"On the tray in the hall. It came earlier. Since you were asleep, I signed for it myself. Shall I bring it in to you?"

"No, it's all right, I'll go and get it."

I made an effort to speak normally.

"Right, I'll see you tomorrow then."

"Goodbye, Daría."

I waited until I heard the front door close and then I ran out into the hall to pick up what I already knew, even before I saw it, would be my first letter from Mariana León in years.

VIII

Solitary striptease

Dear Sofía,

This is the third letter I've written since I left Madrid, and I haven't give any indication of place or date to distinguish it from the other two which I wrote and intended to send to you, although subsequently I didn't, partly out of laziness and partly out of meanness. I've put them in a blue file I bought in Cádiz, along with my notes for my essay on eroticism. One of the letters, the one I wrote on the train, is even ready in a large envelope with your address on it, the other hasn't even got that far. The letters have a revitalizing effect on me. Re-reading them helps me pick up the thread of recent events and stimulates not only my recovering psyche but also my work which is gradually beginning to sort itself out. So I've decided not to send you the letter I'm writing now either. Your name and your memory serve as a mooring post for me but, on the other hand, I don't feel under any obligation to demonstrate that I'm necessarily concerned about you and your problems.

It's a very liberating decision. What a relief to confess to myself quite openly that this epistolary vice – taken up again thanks to your encouragement, of course – is, like most vices, a solitary one. What's more, I don't know if it's because the text of my unsent letters has caught a virus from the other meditations on love and sex which I keep in the same blue file, but it does all seems to me to belong to the same theme: the one which, arising out of the detour provoked by Raimundo, brought me to Calle de la Amargura and which, metaphorically speaking, has dragged me the length of that whole Street of Sorrows. I've been lurching down it for years now, drunk on unanswerable questions. They're questions I keep on asking out of professional habit but also because, deep down, I enjoy asking them. I've reached the point where I feel that the only meaning to life is trying to discover life's meaning, even though I know that nothing I do will clarify anything and that my researches will fail again and again. You see what a ridiculous pastime it is? It's like reading with unending enjoyment a detective novel in which the murderer never appears.

Anyway, as my father would say, at least it passes the time. He used to say that a lot. I always thought it was a banal thing to say, but once, when he was quite old, he explained that he was referring to the span of time allotted to each of us at birth.

"The unfortunate thing is that the amount of time you've been given isn't written on the tombola ticket they issue you with at birth. It's up to us whether we make it long or short; it's all a matter of learning to use it in accordance with the rhythms of our own body, like a sort of gymnastics. There's no point worrying about how long it's going to last. Such calculations are not for us to make."

Then, when he died, I often thought about what he'd said, because my father did always manage to get the most out of life and he hated unnecessary worries.

What matters is passing the time, as enjoyably as possible, of course, and taking pleasure in that inevitable passing. In this world, each person enrols for the sport that he or she most enjoys, and questioning everything is a sport like any other. I hold forth to the air for the pure pleasure of listening to the echo of my own voice bouncing back at me from the four corners of the room. So what? I should not therefore be surprised when Silvia accuses me of doing just that. It is, after all, what I enjoy doing: performing a solitary striptease. She herself helped me to understand and accept it. But I'll talk about Silvia later.

Think about it. When you look at life as it really is, that's all we have, the pleasure of breathing and using our own voice in its different modalities of sadness, indignation or enthusiasm: there is no other base element. I happen to be hooked on being in control of my own voice, turning up the volume to a shout or turning it down to a whisper, even if it's only to mention the lack of company. A purely rhetorical device, like the vocative phrases used by flamenco singers: "Ay, companion of my soul!", the only function of which is to render still more pathetic the absence of the person responsible for putting the singer through this hell, his beloved being completely indifferent to his complaints and having not the slightest desire to listen to them otherwise, what is the point of that solitary unburdening of the soul?

So in the end, Sofía, you who were once the companion of my soul, however we look at it, it's all a question of loneliness. Admitting that, breaking down the barriers that used to stop me saying so openly, allows me to advance more easily through a territory which I define and choose at the same time as I touch and explore it, which involves exploring myself, something I certainly need to do. For this territory is revealed and takes shape as I write. Or rather it is the writing itself as it is revealed and becomes more concrete, finding expression in the shapes that my eye discerns and transforms into words; with my writing I engender my own homeland, undisputed, albeit subject to change, my own rough, remote homeland that is always there waiting for me. Brooks rife with the red fish of the past imperfect, small serrated mountains of gerunds, steep slopes flanked by exclamation marks and suspension points, narrow canyons threaded by compound clauses, trees leafy with adjectives or bare of any, meadows glimpsed in dreams and which can only be reached by the fragile bridge of the conditional tense.

After putting a full stop after the word "tense", I looked up and took a deep, delicious breath of air, gazing across at the sea that stretches out, vast, before my eyes. And to put the finishing touch to what I've just written, I feel like giving an example of a conditional phrase which is, as it happens, particularly apposite: "If my friend Silvia had behaved differently, I would either still be at her house or I would have gone back to Madrid to resume my work."

Behind me, I hear an unmistakable voice, serene and implacable, the most familiar of all voices.

"And do you regret not doing so?" it asks.

"No," I reply quickly, "I prefer the present to the conditional."

"That depends on the consequences."

"Frankly, I don't care. I don't regret it at all."

"Only a short while ago, you were saying just the opposite, that you'd lost your balance and were like a boat adrift on the tides," insists Dr León.

"Forgive me for interrupting, but have you noticed those clouds? It's going to be a wonderful sunset this evening. Did I really say that about the boat?"

"Yes, you said Silvia had holed you below the water line. Do try not to lie to yourself."

"That's precisely what I am trying to do. But remember, there isn't just one truth, there are many. Every instant is full of atoms that refract it into a thousand possible sensations. And would you kindly keep your mouth shut and stop reminding me of what I said before and just let me enjoy what I'm seeing now."

I smile, absorbed, at the uncertain line of the horizon which the sun will soon stain fire-red when it plunges into the sea. "Let the air caress you, it's full of angels." That's one of your phrases, Sofía, one that you don't perhaps remember. Like the hare in the field, it belongs to your early attempts to conquer poetic territory. We were coming back from a school trip to Ávila, leaning out of the train window. I don't remember why, but I was in a bad mood. The wind was blowing our hair about. "I can't wait to grow up!" I said. You didn't say anything, you just pointed to a group of golden clouds hanging above the rocks. You said I should let the air caress me, that it was full of angels. All these years have passed and only now can I do as you told me to. Now that the phrase has suddenly resurfaced, fleeing from your homeland to mine, bursting through the barriers of time, I can savour the marvel without needing to understand; and the angels of the air really do fan me, they brush my lips with their wings, they tousle my hair. I resist asking what time it is and instead order another gin and tonic. The tide's coming in. Some waves have already reached the first steps that lead up to the bar here. The waiter, a very pleasant, dark young man, recognizes me I think. I came here several times with Manolo Reina, at the beginning of our idyll.

119

Tonight I'll play the tape that Manolo sent to me in Madrid after we stopped seeing each other. He's hardly written to me at all. Letters weren't really his thing, he disliked them, like the lover in the song:

> I don't know how to read,
> I don't know how to read,
> Send no more bits of paper
> That I don't know how to read.

I start singing the song under my breath, trying to copy the tone in which Manolo would have sung it.

> Through the post,
> Through the post,
> Just send me yourself,
> It's you I want most.

That voice of two summers ago is too much to bear. My breathing is growing faster and I don't want anyone to notice.

I half-close my eyes, and amongst the rainbow flecks, I think I can see a boat in the distance, barely visible. Perhaps it's adrift. Had Silvia not aimed a broadside at my boat, I don't think I would ever have reached the shelter of this port. On the other hand, it can't be denied that shots were fired and that the battle continues, the battle with myself stirred up from within by Dr León.

She won't ever quite let me forget about Silvia or prevent me uneasily reliving her presence from time to time, gushing through the valley of bitter mirrors, like pure quicksilver, invading the whole space, infecting everything. The worst thing is that I wasn't really in a position to complain. I was the one who had phoned her and asked her to come to Puerto Real. I told her: "I need to talk to you." I didn't need anyone to remind me of that.

She erupted into the house as night was falling and from the moment I heard her strident call from the foot of the stairs, my whole being was conscious of her there like a malaise. Firstly, because she was interrupting my work at a moment of genuine lucidity, just when I was managing to keep my personal sufferings from slipping into the framework of the text, and secondly, because she wasn't alone but with an American teacher she'd given a lift to on her way out of Seville and whom she'd invited to stay the night. They'd obviously stopped off at various bars on the way – I know what Silvia's like – and they were both pretty loaded, especially her. She was wearing a yellow dress and was talking so much that no one else could get a word in edgeways.

No sooner had the introductions been made than I realized that the presence of a stranger, far from inhibiting her urgent decision to discuss private matters, was in fact a stimulus. We were in the drawing room downstairs, I was feeling less and less in control and, incomprehensibly, the American teacher seemed to be enjoying himself. He was tall, blond and quite good-looking. He was smoking a pipe.

"Don't let Señorita Silvia drink so much," Brígida whispered in my ear the second time she came in with the drinks. "You know how sick she gets afterwards."

Those words increased my own unease. After all, I am her psychiatrist, the usual worries. Meanwhile, however, the thread of my mental discourse – which I had only with great difficulty resumed – snapped in various places and the beads scattered and rolled about the floor like futile tears. And you, Doctor, wouldn't let me cry out, you forced me to reply in measured tones to the intricate nonsense my patient was spouting, making me forget that I was the one to whom the word "patient" should have been applied, even if only in the sense that I needed all the patience I could muster to elicit a minimum of logic and moderation from that fevered voice. After an hour, Raimundo's name, mixed in with a few increasingly threadbare philosophical saws, had become part of a distorted story on the point of total disintegration, with all the hallmarks of a soap opera.

I felt a sudden need to free my mind from the whole tangled plot and try to work out for myself why I should agree to being implicated in that love story, why I should feel desperate, jealous, concerned about Raimundo's fate, filled with longing for his presence or something of the sort; and I have to confess that I couldn't. All I could think of was a phrase I'd left half-typed on my typewriter upstairs, something about solitary eroticism. I imagined remaining closeted with Raimundo in his house in Calle de Covarrubias, subject to his shifting moods, and looking back on the days that had passed since the afternoon I was sick in that bar in Malasaña, I suddenly saw them as a joyous voyage of liberation. I have avoided inflicting a terrible punishment on myself, I thought. I have escaped!

It was like a light bulb going on in my head, because the joy of understanding brought with it a decision to run away again. The bars on the windows of the house in Calle de la Amargura are, after all, easier to break. It was just a question of shaking off my two prison guards and calmly plotting my escape. I was extremely agitated and, if that wasn't enough, as I retreated further into silence, the American teacher, who was still drinking heavily, started asking me very direct questions, perhaps in the hope that by his intervention he might appease the aggressive, incoherent mood of his hostess. I simply smiled and he said that I reminded him of the Mona Lisa.

"No one ever knows what she's thinking," said Silvia. "It's one of her tricks."

"Perhaps she's thinking about that friend you both love," he said. "Only in Spain would you find such extremes of passion."

He was a Hispanist from Seattle and, as it emerged later on, a keen collector of Spanish idioms; I began to be afraid that he might even ask us for our opinion on Spain's entry into NATO or about Don Quixote's love for Dulcinea.

I wasn't the slightest bit interested in the Hispanist, or in Silvia for that matter, or in finding out whether or not it was true that Raimundo phoned her every day to tell her what agonies he was going through. I just wanted to go up to my apartment, without appearing too rude, because you, Doctor, won't allow me to be rude or to leave a patient in the lurch, however much I might like to. It is precisely that symbiosis with you which has been my downfall.

I tried to lead the conversation back to safer subjects and the topic that emerged, like a weak sun amongst clouds, was the irremediable loneliness of all human beings. It's too exhausting to spend one's whole life resisting loneliness. Wouldn't it be more sensible to come to terms with it? I spoke rather unenthusiastically on the topic, aware that I was merely performing a few preliminary, lacklustre passes. The man from Seattle, however, seemed to find my arguments enormously interesting.

"Everything she says is rubbish," Silvia riposted. "She's just trying to change the subject, in order to protect her secrets and stay safe inside her shell."

"Maybe I am," I replied coldly. "Why shouldn't I? Or do you really think that everything can be shared?"

She stood up and faced me, looking directly into my eyes, as if she were about to hurl herself upon me. My legs were trembling and my fingers were icy cold. I was afraid, afraid as I always am of losing control or becoming infected by someone else's lack of control. Silvia burst out laughing. When she gets like this, she sounds like one of those actresses who used to do the dubbing for old films.

"Certainly not! Share something with you? How could I, darling? The person hasn't been born yet who could share something with you. And do you know why? Because you wouldn't dare touch anything that might burn you. When have you ever ventured into the lion's den, eh, when? Never. No, your speciality is the solitary striptease."

She was clearly beside herself with rage and I felt responsible. Had I been feeling less fed up, I would have reacted correctly, outlining automatically and in rather pained tones my personal record as a seasoned traveller into the interior of the most diverse and darkest of lions' dens. That would have served as a balm to revive her faith and would have given me back control of the situation. In a word, Doctor, your good sense and your beliefs would have prevailed. Even in moments of deep despair, one must never confess to a patient one's own lack of vocation or of altruistic motives. Unfortunately, good sense did not prevail, although, given the rigid control you exercise over me, I still hesitated for a few moments before disobeying. In the end, though, to Silvia's utter incomprehension, I said:

"Yes, it is as it happens, so what?"

"What are you talking about?" she asked, disconcerted.

"The solitary striptease. I've developed a taste for it, I really have. And I'm glad. I don't know what you're looking so amazed about. Because I freely acknowledge the fact?"

Silvia was indeed staring at me, puzzled, helpless, as if struggling to understand.

"No," she said with a shaky voice. "It's just that I can't believe it, Mariana. It can't be true."

"What, that I acknowledge it?"

"No, that you like talking to yourself, thinking only of you, and that that's enough. That you don't struggle against loneliness."

The American teacher was looking at us as if he were contemplating an exotic landscape, his pale eyes swerving from one to the other.

"She didn't say that," he intervened, as if he were chairing a debate. "After struggling long and hard against loneliness, she has reached the conclusion that it's the wrong path to take, and I think she's right. Montaigne said ..."

Silvia grew indignant and began insulting us, saying we were both pedants, as if she suddenly saw us as allies lining up against her. She started taking old books off the shelves and hurling them on to the floor and against the walls. Then she fell back into an armchair and covered her face with her hands.

"Books, books, what a plague!"

I went over to her and sat down on the arm of her chair, cursing my profession. I put a hand on her shoulder.

"Come on, Silvia, don't drink any more. What have the books got to do with it anyway?"

"They have a lot to do with it, they have a lot to do with everything. Leave me alone," she said, sounding like a sulky child. "Don't you quote books at me, you can save that for Raimundo, that's how you turn men's heads, by quoting from books."

"I haven't heard her quoting from any book," said the American.

"And who asked you to stick your oar in?" yelled Silvia.

"I think that as long as I remain in the room, I should be allowed to offer an opinion," he replied calmly and a touch ironically.

Silvia told him rudely to go to bed, but he simply started filling his pipe again and took no notice of her. I was exhausted and reluctant to make much of an effort for anyone. I'd got to the point where I couldn't stand this stupid contest and had reached the conclusion that by arguing with Silvia I was merely fighting a losing battle. But I had a vague intuition that she had fired a shot below the water line of my boat or, rather, of Dr León's splendid liner. I got up.

"Let's just leave it, Silvia. I'm going to bed. We're all tired."

"Don't use the plural. You might be. You, you, you, that's all I ever hear!"

"Well, I *am* tired. To be more precise, I'm fed up to the back teeth, because it's impossible to talk to you, it's like talking to a brick wall. It's one thing to lose the thread and quite another to have no thread at all and yet still persist in trying to sew."

"Are you serious? What thread?" she asked in a voice that had grown suddenly weary. "I'm sorry, we'll talk properly now. I'm listening."

The American professor was listening intently to our exchange. He took out a small pad, carefully noted down a couple of idiomatic expressions that had caught his fancy and poured himself another drink, seeing that Silvia was doing so too. It must be said that the situation was one that demanded a stiff drink or two.

"I'm sorry, Silvia, but it just bores me. This whole business is an unholy mess."

The professor laughed out loud with enthusiasm, still scribbling, and interrupted us to check whether one of the expressions he had noted down was possibly rather dated. "Didn't Valle-Inclán use it in one of his plays?"

"Oh, shut up, Norman, don't be such a bore!" Silvia said angrily. "Come on, Mariana, please, give me an example. I really want to know, please."

"An example of what?"

"I don't know, of me losing the thread."

I mustered all my patience and set about picking up books from the floor.

"For example, you said earlier that my speciality was the solitary striptease. You were the one who said that, weren't you?"

"I don't remember. But so what?"

"Because then, when I agreed with you, you leapt down my throat and called me a liar."

"You mean we're in agreement then?" she asked uncertainly, her eyes dim. "Is that what you mean?"

I agreed reluctantly and at that point I noticed that Norman was looking at me rather insistently. From the street came the sounds of conversation and muffled laughter. A little boy fired a cracker and peered in, scrambling up the bars at the window, before leaping back down again. I envied him the way the prisoner envies the bird that visits his cell but can come and go as it pleases. We heard laughter and the scamper of feet running away. Silvia's voice had grown sad. She sank back into her chair.

"You and me in agreement, just like that. You're saying that to shut me up, as if I were a mad person to be placated. She knows a lot about mad people, Norman, it's her job."

When she addressed the American teacher, she noticed that he was staring at me. Since I didn't know how things stood between them nor what her intentions were, I was afraid she was going to kick up a row about my possible resolve to make a conquest of him. I went over to the door, prepared to take drastic action.

"Let's just leave it, please; besides, what does it matter? I'm sure your friend here isn't interested in all this."

"On the contrary, I find it fascinating," he assured me, entirely unmoved.

"He's not my friend," Silvia said abruptly, "I just said that if he wanted to sleep here tonight he could, that's all. I've got so much room here, I can invite anyone I want. A friend! That's all I need. On the way here, he kept saying how tired he was. He seems to have woken up."

She came over to me in a confidential manner and put her arms around me as I stood by the door, trying to stop me leaving. She was already extremely drunk, but it was ridiculous to hope that she would recognize it. She muttered something to me about how, if I liked Norman, we could come to some arrangement. I pretended to ignore the suggestion.

"Look, I really am beginning to feel tired," I said in a conciliatory tone. "Tomorrow's another day. I'm going upstairs. Goodnight."

"But tomorrow you won't want to see me. You've just said that what you like best is being alone. Or did I say that? Please, don't go, Mariana."

We looked at each other and her face seemed suddenly utterly grim. When I think about it now, my face must have expressed only rejection.

"We don't need you anyway!" she shouted, "Why don't you just leave! I don't want to see you!"

She stumbled back into the room, almost falling into the arms of Norman who was sitting on the sofa at that point and had moved over to make room for her.

"She doesn't want you," Silvia was saying in a thick voice. "She doesn't want anyone. But I do. You know, you're terribly handsome, darling. Kiss me."

I stood there looking at the room full of tapestries and old paintings and I suddenly felt terribly sad. It seemed to me that the people occupying it were just three anachronistic ghosts who'd wandered into the wrong theatre. I accepted my liking for the solitary striptease and I understood that my only refuge lay in writing. Silvia knows better than anyone that we are all always alone and the proof of that were my failed attempts to explain. Besides, those attempted explanations had long ceased beating their wings, like the fat moths that had flown in through the window while we were talking and now fluttered round the lamp, some falling to the floor as if struck down by some fatal fit. That fleeting but intense vision is the one that remains burned on to my retina as a symbol of the second prison I have rejected in the space of only a few days.

I slipped upstairs, packed my things and waited for dawn, listening until the noises in the house had died down. At one point, I heard Brígida's voice and I seemed to hear her steps coming up the stairs and pausing outside the door of my apartment. The light was out, though, and if it was her – I can't be sure – she didn't have the courage to come in.

Rarely have I waited for the dawn with such longing. I left a short note on the table as well as a poem by Pessoa, a poem which you, Sofía, used to like a lot.

> This morning I left the house early
> having woken up even earlier
> not in a mood to do anything much.
> I couldn't decide which way to go,
> but the wind was blowing hard,
> pushing at my back,
> and so that was the direction I took.

I liked that touch: it affirmed me in my decision, anticipated the pleasure of my escape and, more than that, represented a homage to your passion for Portuguese literature. It was like sidestepping the apparent addressee and replacing her with another less hostile one.

I placed the keys on top of the note together with a sprig of jasmine. I knew that Silvia would be more irritated by the fact that I had returned her keys than by the message. Nevertheless, I had decided to break off relations with her and I needed that symbolic act.

I gingerly opened the door and tiptoed down the stairs, until I got to the massive street door that always creaked a little. When I left, with my suitcase in my hand, I didn't dare look back. The fear of being followed made me breathe faster for a while and only gradually did my breathing grow quiet again. It was still dark and, hearing my footsteps echo down the deserted street on my way to the station, I remembered a painting by Remedios Varo entitled *Breaking the Vicious Circle* which depicts a woman who bears inside her breast a forest encircled by barbed wire. Nothing consoles me quite so much at this moment, Sofía, as the thought that you might know that painting.

All that happened two days ago, I think. Or possibly three. Later, if I consider it worth while, I'll work out the dates and tell you all about this beach hotel plagued with German and Danish tourists, the hotel where I'm holed up in order to continue with my solitary striptease.

And yet, now that the sun has just set, leaving a sort of bloody trail across the sea, and I set off once more on the thorny journey down the alleyway of night where every bend could conceal some unexpected beast lying in wait for us, I watch with envy the silhouette of two young people holding hands, walking barefoot along the beach. To them, time is an enchanted, infinite garden. Every now and then they stop, bend down and pick something up from the sand, running up the beach when the waves threaten to catch them, laughing, hugging each other. Then they move on, their arms about each other's waists. They walk slowly along at a light, rhythmic pace. Unmistakable. They will not leave each other's side tonight.

The light in the lighthouse on the promontory to my right has just been lit. I finish my gin and tonic and ask the waiter for the bill. He looks at me. He smiles. This time I'm sure he's recognized me.

"What's happened to Señor Manolo? He hasn't been here for a long time."

I try to imagine that Manolo's just got up to go to the bar and greet a friend and will be back in a moment. Here he is. I wait for his touch on my shoulder. "Right then, my love, shall we go?" He had such a wonderful voice! And that way he had of placing his fingers lightly on the whole world contained in the present moment, and of looking at things obliquely, as if he wasn't looking at all.

"I haven't heard from him in ages. He lives in America now."

The waiter bursts out laughing as he gives me my change.

"What's he doing so far away? He won't last long in America, you'll see. I know him. He's a Cádiz man born and bred. If you write to him, send him regards from Rafa."

"I'm afraid I hardly ever write."

"Well you should; if you don't, someone else will get their hooks in him. He's a really nice bloke. You look good together."

I liked the fact that he used the present tense. I smile, thank him and get up to go. Then suddenly I feel a stab in my side, the poisoned arrow of my old anxiety which, despite all my efforts to deactivate it, will, I know, preside over my insomnia tonight. I'll try to ease it by listening to the tape recorder. I've brought the tape that Manolo recorded for me shortly after we said goodbye and which he sent to me in Madrid. I remember that I had a lot of work at the time and it was a few days before I listened to it. It didn't have the same impact then as it does now. Like good wine, it improves with age. Even so, however tightly I shut my eyes, when I'm actually listening to it, I rarely manage to experience that voice as recent and addressed directly to me. It lacks his breath, his face, his eyes.

My notes on eroticism would really come in useful here: they're impatient to be brought into the foreground, anxious to burst through dams and swell the waters of this letter, if you can use that term of a discourse which, though originally intended simply to flow into the blue file, is now more like a tributary of it.

Basically, no one loves or talks or writes in order to convince anyone of anything, but rather to convince themselves that they're still in good shape and can still perform the acrobatics that test both mind and body and, in particular, the measured relationship between them: a miraculous balancing act, as easy as breathing, or so you'd think.

A couple of weeks ago when Raimundo was on a respirator in the intensive care unit, I thought a lot about how little importance we give to the unnoticed, tenacious, precise activity performed each day by the lungs in order to keep us supplied with air. Everything – the rhythm of the body, our eyes, our ideas, our gestures and our words – depends on that supply of oxygen, but even at that moment, when I was in a state of great anxiety, I was thinking it from the privileged position of one who was able to breathe. And it's always like that. The fact that Raimundo, Silvia, Manolo or you continue breathing at this moment is like an abstract certainty, which I can neither enjoy nor believe in, because it doesn't concern me. If I said otherwise, I would be lying.

I'm back in my hotel room, which has a small balcony. I had a simple supper consisting of a sandwich and a glass of milk, and there are loads of stars. I'm still besieged by memories of Manolo Reina who, even if I decide to send you this frankest of letters, will be nothing but a name to you. At our age, Sofía, there are few things, either pleasant or alarming,

130

which can truly be shared. And love, of course, least of all. That's why it spawns so much literature.

I said to you before that writing is my homeland. One day I'll invite you to visit it, like when we were children and we used to read each other's diaries. However, the pleasure of inventing it and the difficulties of cultivating it are mine alone, just as the necessary determination and boldness to create an imaginary landscape, one that will make an apple tree suddenly spring up in your bathroom so that you can rest in its shade from the plumbing problems created for you by your downstairs neighbour on the seventh floor, are yours alone; a fleeting, spacious shadow that will refresh only you when you succeed in invoking it, even though the surrealism of the scene amuses me. I cannot be part of it.

Yes, we'll visit each other one day. You'll come to my homeland and I'll go to yours and each will view the homeland of the other through the eyes of a foreigner, always aware that what they reflect will be avidly picked up by the other's watchful eyes. What do you think? Well, this, that and the other. A long discussion might ensue and then we'll say goodbye. That will be it. I don't mean that it will be unpleasant visiting each other, far from it. We've already tried it and certainly yours (your first batch of homework which I often re-read) has proved a revitalizing tonic to my dried-up, neglected garden because, ever since, I've been pruning, raking and pulling up weeds.

I did thank you, although I can't remember in what terms. It's a mile-stone that's lacking in my blue file and I miss it now, I mean my first letter, the only one I posted to you. I suppose that by now you'll have received it and it pleases me to think that it will have given rise to further despatches.

If you want me to be honest, though, at the moment my interest in your new batch of homework isn't born of altruism. I'm simply dying to know your response to what I said to you, so that I can get it back again because I've completely wiped it from my memory, although I do remember uncorking a bottle of champagne and feeling very happy. Much happier than I would have felt if you had been by my side because I was free to imagine you as I wanted to imagine you. I mean that I need you to return to me, reflected in your remarks, the sample of earth that I sent to you. I await it as if it were the result of a biopsy, because it's quite possible that you may have discovered, hidden in some fold of the earth – for you don't miss a thing – the evil weed of mendacity.

I'll find out when I get back to Madrid, although I don't know when that will be; it all depends on what changes take place in the humours in the crucible of my soul, not to mention the deterioration in my relationship with Dr León.

IX

Coming to terms with time

Dear Mariana,

Just above the words "Keep writing, Señorita Montalvo, always be a writer" – the words of Don Pedro Larroque whom you bring back to life by quoting them – just above the word "always", in fact, a tear has fallen and then another, and I've had to push to one side the letter I'd so longed for and which has more than fulfilled my expectations in order not to drench it. I also laughed a little, and when I laughed, I missed you even more than I had when I cried because, you must admit, it's funny that his name should resurface the moment I write "Dear Mariana", just as if time hadn't passed and he were someone we would see in class shortly, explaining Jorge Manrique's *Coplas* which he always read with a tremor in his voice, however hard he tried to disguise it.

> For if we see the present
> how it is gone and over
> in an instant,
> then, if we are wise,
> we will count the years not yet lived
> as already past.

I copy out this verse in my best handwriting, just as I did in the middle of the first page of my literature notebook in the third year – do you remember it? – with a flower drawn on the left and a few dried leaves on the right, because it was thanks to that decorated page, and to the fact that it caught your eye, that we became friends in a new way. I said to you – I think it was that same day – that when he read Jorge Manrique, Don Pedro's voice could as easily have been that of a lover as of an old man.

You thought that was extremely funny. Now I know that only someone who has known a great love and lost it could evoke that frieze of perfumed ladies in silk dresses, those gentlemen and minstrels of the court of King Juan, could transport them from yesteryear to today and have them parade through an inhospitable classroom, making of the teacher's platform the site of a tournament which, though spectacular, is condemned to die, as transient as vegetables in a vegetable patch.

> What has become of all the ladies,
> their headdresses, their robes,
> their perfumes?
> What has become of all the flames
> that burned in the fires lit
> by lovers?
> What has become of all that poetry,
> of the harmonious songs
> they played?
> What has become of all the dancers
> and the gilded dresses
> they wore?

Listening to that calm, vulnerable voice, I had my first experience of being pierced by the enigma of time, as if by a treacherous dart, capable of provoking the most unexpected mutations. It excited and troubled me to peer into that abyss, indulging in a kind of anticipatory nostalgia. "What will we be like when we're twenty years old, Mariana? Will we remember this sunny afternoon?" And you, always so sensible and Cartesian, said: "What does it matter? You're talking in abstractions. We won't be twenty for ages. We're only in the third year." Then, we still measured time by school years, and now it's nearly three whole schooltimes ago since all that happened.

Don Pedro Larroque must already have known quite a lot about the ravages of time; that's why his eyes would mist up behind his glasses when he recited, as he gazed out of the window, "Let no one deceive himself/thinking that what awaits him/will last any longer than what he

134

has already seen." His voice made me tremble inside. Sometimes he would pensively stroke his thinning hair, threaded with white. And we were unable to decide whether he was handsome or ugly, old or young. Until one day we found out, because he told us himself in class, that he was the same age as Jorge Manrique when he was pierced by an arrow during the assault on the fort at Garci-Muñoz: thirty-nine years old. "So old and still single," I said to you sorrowfully. If he's still alive today, he must be about eighty. If we ever chanced to meet him, he might not even remember us. And yet he still speaks to me through your mouth, just as Jorge Manrique spoke to us through his. You see, I'm still grappling with the same problem, the problem of time.

The most remarkable thing, Mariana, is that I've lived all these years without giving a thought to Don Pedro Larroque, but, you won't believe this, I was in fact thinking about him shortly before I got your letter, or, rather, he just stepped quite nonchalantly on to the stage to complete my evocation of him with yours. He too encouraged me to write, using a phrase I'm not even sure he ever said, I may have just invented it, because I've gone over and over these memories on my own and sometimes – maybe the same thing happens to you – I rather unconvincingly and unnecessarily elaborate on them, like those women who continually and rather pointlessly keep changing their hairstyle when they sense that their husbands no longer find them attractive. "Never lay down your butterfly net, Señorita Montalvo," that's what Don Pedro or his ghost said to me a while ago. I remained unmoved, however, and could find no use for a phrase which, besides, was addressed to a remote little girl, a spent force, who has nothing whatsoever to do with me, condemned for all eternity to hunt wax butterflies studded with diphthongs. A pretty image, I suppose, almost surreal, but it's a scene preserved in amber where the air doesn't move and never will move until my faith in that child and my relationship with her are revived by means other than artificial respiration.

However, getting a letter from you in your handwriting – still instantly recognizable even after all these years – in which you say: "Keep writing, Señorita Montalvo, always be a writer": that's different.

The word "always" recovers its talismanic powers, lifts the lid on a coffin in which lay Sleeping Beauty, Señorita Montalvo and me, now known as Señora de Luque, and simultaneously restores the colour to our cheeks.

Do you know, even if our old teacher were dead, as he might well be, his words, simply because you revive them in my memory, cut a path through the weeds hiding Sleeping Beauty's castle from the eyes of the profane and have the same direct effect on my heart and senses as our recent conversation which, by the way, was languishing and becoming increasingly vague and questionable without any further response from you. In other words, the hare in the field was beginning to look in need of a respirator, along with our years at school, Guillermo and the clock that stood at the end of the corridor in your parents' apartment in Calle de Serrano. In fact, for several days I kept asking myself: "Did I really see Mariana? Did she see me? And, if we did see each other, what did she see when she looked at me? Did she really tell me to write?" Now, on the other hand, I know for sure that I didn't invent it because you've sent me a plan of the room you were sitting in when you wrote, and acknowledged receipt of my homework, and you ask me to carry on writing because you remembered what I said to you at the cocktail party and because you even remember the colour of the dress I was wearing at my house that June afternoon when Guillermo was already beginning to cause me grief, before you went to Barcelona and I stopped seeing you altogether; it was a red dress with a square neckline that my godmother sent me from Paris. Just like in a fairy tale, don't you think? I'll tell you the story of that red dress later if it seems appropriate, although suddenly there are so many stories jostling to be allowed into the light that I don't know where to begin. For the moment, I'll simply enjoy your letter and luxuriate in your "Do you remembers", like lying back and letting the sun touch my skin after a long winter.

We don't realize, Mariana, how wonderful it is to be able to ask someone: "Do you remember?" and see that they do, they do remember. Memories cultivated alone form a tangled skein inside us, they snag on thorns; you get to the point where you can't differentiate between what actually happened to you and other incomplete scraps of scenes you saw in the street or at the cinema; but the worst thing is that, by constant rummaging around in that jumble, yesterday turns vampire on you, it thins the air and clouds the light of the moment you're actually living. It's difficult to escape from the tumour of the past without harming the fabric of the present, delicate and fragile as a petal.

Something similar happens with delayed letters, especially when you re-read them hoping that the text will provoke in you the same surprise, the same excitement as the first time. A vain hope, of course. Surprise is a hare, as you very well know, and if you go out hunting for it, you'll never find it sleeping in a field. My daughter Encarna says that old letters should have a "use by" date written at the bottom of the page, like medicines, and should be thrown out after, at most, a year, instead of being allowed to accumulate in a cupboard.

I've just looked at the date on yours. You finished it a week ago, although you probably posted it much later. It hasn't yet had time to lose its curative powers. Your "Never stop writing, Señorita Montalvo" is freshly cut, full of vitamins; it's still having a salutary affect on me, which is why I started crying. It was just what I needed to hear. It was an enormous relief!

I sat for a while with my elbows on the table, my chin resting on my hands, enjoying the tears running down my face, like when you go to the cinema to see a love story, realizing how good it feels to cry like that, not out of sorrow or despair. I recognize the feeling, I mean it can't be the first time I've cried in this gentle way that exorcises evil spells and unties black knots, but I can't calculate the time that separates me from that other time, assuming it ever existed. You see, Mariana, and I want to tell you this straight away so that you can see that, at least in this respect, life has not changed me, I've never been able to work out dates and times and I've never felt interested enough to bother. I hope only that time will welcome me, that I may enter its sacred space without fear, instead of pestering it from outside, defending myself against it, measuring it. That's what happiness consists of, in saying, as Guillermo used to say: "Now is always" and believing it and being able to transmit it to other people. And even as I remember this and remember Guillermo's eyes fixed on the stars when he said it to me the night I met him, the word "always" here at my side, written in your handwriting, winks at me like a lighthouse through the fog, slightly blurred by my two recent tears, which means that you too still use a fountain pen, another coincidence.

Anyway, that's enough of preambles and meanderings. My anxiety has melted with my tears and we've reached a clearing in the wood. We'll pause here, if you don't mind.

I feel, with little room for doubt, that now is the time for Guillermo's story, even if it does emerge all mixed up with other stories it might bring with it, and there will be a lot, I warn you, because I'm not going to be the one to take a scalpel to them. I don't know how you feel about it, but I'm ready to have a go. At this moment, in this "now" encamped between two opposing poles of "always", I feel I've reached a strategic place on which to set up my telescope and scan the distance, not forgetting the focal length I've adopted nor, of course, that it might be necessary to correct it. And although this place may seem metaphorical to you, it exists, and I'm treading solid ground. Believe me, please. Besides there are no minor characters around today to interrupt us. Would you like to come with me into the story-telling area, Mariana?

I should just warn you that I'm going to change my style, since you've given me carte blanche to choose. I'm going to keep the epistolary style in reserve, because you never know when you might need it as a flourish, but for the moment it's of no use to me. There's one very practical reason for that: I'm not going to be able to send you the letter.

Since I need to imagine your cardinal points, however approximately, while I sort out the odds and ends I need for this elusive story that concerns us both in equal measure, I decided to phone Dr Josefina Carreras to find out where you are and how your friend Raimundo is. She sounds like one of those actresses who used to do the dubbing for old films. She says she can't help me and that she's not allowed to give your address to anyone. Suddenly it was as if a bridge had been blown up in front of me, but I didn't hang up.

"But I imagine she phones you to find out about her clients."

138

"Of course, sometimes."

"Fine, so how is she? Is she well?"

"Why wouldn't she be well?"

"Because, my dear, people often aren't. Do you never feel unwell? Or do psychiatrists have some sort of papal dispensation?"

She gave an embarrassed little giggle, perhaps because the dilemma that provoked her first direct question was beginning to feed into her mental computer: she wants to know if I'm a friend of yours or a patient. You're all absolutely obsessed with that. But suddenly I feel in an extremely good mood and, as always happens when I feel lighthearted, I feel like having a bit of fun, like doing a bit of play-acting. I put on an extravagant tone of voice. Dr Carreras must imagine me with a cigarette holder in my mouth.

"A friend of hers?" I ask in a languid voice. "Do you believe I'm a friend of hers, lovey? Eh? I'll give you a minute. Kindly put your brain into gear."

There's a silence.

"I don't have to believe anything," she says at last.

"Really? You don't believe in anything? Not even in Freud?"

Her voice sounds suddenly irritated.

"I'm sorry, but are you being treated by Dr León? That's all I wanted to know."

"Well, let's see, at the moment only by letter. A kind of long-distance treatment."

"Long-distance? How odd. I don't understand."

I try to give my reply a tone that is both confiding and mysterious.

"I'm not surprised. It's a delicate matter. There was a misunderstanding between us, a suspected robbery; I hope that you, with your professional discretion, will know how to keep a secret; it's a case that's been filed away for a long time and has only been looked into recently. Any evidence, however insignificant, could prove decisive."

"I still don't understand."

"It doesn't matter. By the way, do you happen to know if a friend of Dr León's who tried to commit suicide is now out of danger? Or perhaps he's gone away with her. His name's Raimundo, half-patient, half-friend according to my information. I tell you that for your records. Do you know him?"

"Well, I only know him because he's been calling a lot lately," she says, sounding slightly agitated.

I notice that she immediately regrets having told me this. I take advantage of the opportunity to continue the game.

"I see," I say, exaggerating my impersonation of a detective. "Therefore they have not gone away together and you know where he is. Am I correct?"

"I don't know anything. I didn't say that."

"All right. You're beginning to bore me, but don't worry, I won't compromise you further. Many thanks for your collaboration and try going out to the cinema a little more often."

I don't know if by now Dr Carreras will have come to any conclusions about the mental illness I'm suffering from. For my part, I've come to the conclusion that writing to your address here, without knowing when you'll be back, is a complete waste of time.

This, then, has ceased being a letter and will simply be another addition to my homework exercise book. As you will see for yourself, one day, it's really just a collection of fragments of mirrors. It's an ill wind, etc. Guillermo's story can't possibly be reflected in one single, full-length version, like a perfectly intelligible and utterly innocuous romantic novel. It deserves a different treatment, which I will invent as I go along, because I don't just want to tell the story, I want to investigate it, to throw some light on the perplexity provoked in me by its fissures, its cracks, its *trompe l'oeil* effects. I'm going to use a collage technique and will be fairly free with chronology. Apart from the version given in your letter – which is fragmentary and partial – I have on hand other elements that might help me refresh my memory: various love letters and letters of farewell whose use-by date has long since passed, pages from a diary that I began after my mother's death and something much more recent and more useful in literary terms: a few notes, which I'm going to write out neatly, notes made a few days ago after my conversation with Soledad. (She's my youngest daughter Amelia's best friend, and there are various mentions of her in earlier pages in this notebook, so I won't repeat myself. You can tie up any loose ends yourself.)

The investigation begins. Now would you mind just moving out of the way and listening, because I'm talking about you to someone else. We'll see what happens.

"How long was it from the time Mariana first mentioned Guillermo until I met him? I don't know, about six months. To be honest, it seems distinctly odd to try and work it out ..."

"What's odd about my wanting you to tell me the truth?" asks Soledad.

And in the silence that follows I sense an atmosphere very similar to what a suspect must feel when he suddenly finds a detective hard on his heels. I've been reading a lot of detective novels lately.

"Well, since you ask," I say, suddenly thoughtful, "it's because, during a period when apparently nothing much was happening, a lot of things happened without my realizing it. It was obvious or, rather, it gradually became obvious that Mariana no longer enjoyed my company; it reached its peak that Christmas. To me it felt like a mutilation, a void."

"But how long did it last?" insists Soledad. "Honestly, sometimes you remind me of my mother."

"Let's see. The second half of September, October, November, December, January and February. Yes, what I told you originally, five and a bit months."

It's beginning to get dark in the room. We've been talking for a long time. She's watched me count on my fingers and is now waiting, deep in thought, as if grateful to me for that pause. I'm grateful to her too. It seems amazing that the most significant episodes in a person's story are the most carefully stored away in hidden folds in the memory. I suddenly feel like cutting myself off from everyone, the way I did during those months when it seemed to me that nothing was happening, and to curl up inside them and relive them in silence. For that is what those months were, I can see it now, the curling up of a caterpillar preparing, all unknowing, to become a chrysalis. By understanding that, I recover them.

"I'm sorry, go on," said Soledad. "Do you mind if I switch on the light?"

I shake my head and the red glow of the table lamp makes Amelia's room shift momentarily back to the time when she and Soledad were just beginning to be friends and to tell each other all those things which, at that age, you can't tell your mother. I came into the room one afternoon and I found her there, in the same place she's sitting now. I'd never seen her before. A nine-year-old girl in a sky-blue dress looking me straight in the eye. I'd heard their laughter from the corridor when I came home. They fell silent, but I could still see the fun glinting in their eyes. I noticed Amelia hiding some bits of paper, but pretended I hadn't. "This is Soledad, a friend of mine from the French lycée," she said. "She's staying for tea, if that's all right." I went over and gave her a kiss. I was carrying various parcels. Later on, Amelia told me that her friend thought I was very pretty. "Why should I mind? I've bought some croissants. I'll call you in a minute." I'd also bought a packet of Tampax for Encarna who had just started her periods. I remember that while I was preparing tea for them in the kitchen, listening to Daría's chatter, the fleeting vision of those papers being hurriedly squirreled away safe from my presumed vigilance was like a knot in the pit of my stomach, a warning that Amelia too was beginning her escape from childhood, was beginning to have secrets from me.

Soledad looks slowly round the room, then she pours herself a little more tea. Perhaps, like me, she too is remembering the first time she had tea in my house. A layer of time added to all those other layers, like stirred embers, that have lit our whole conversation this afternoon, one moment a soothing glow, the next a pitiless blaze. In the red light, she looks tired. A little while ago she was crying. "Phone Soledad. She's very sad about what's happened to her parents," Amelia said to me before she left the day before yesterday. "I think it would do her good to come and talk to you." Was it the day before yesterday? Soledad puts her teacup down on the table and looks at me.

"It's an occupational hazard this preoccupation with dates; if I can't place myself in time, I can't get a fix on anything," she says, by way of an excuse, when she sees that I haven't gone on with my story about Guillermo. "It's not that surprising really, what with the thesis and Richard ..."

She's based in Paris now, writing a doctoral thesis on the relations between Spain and France in the years prior to the Spanish civil war. While researching in the Archive d'Affaires Étrangers, she's recently met an older man, a teacher who she's mad about: he's so interesting, so mysterious, so old school. She hasn't gone to bed with him of course; she doesn't even know where he lives, only that his name is Richard and that his father was a Republican and was shot. Richard was born two months later in a small village in the south of France. "You see," she says with a satisfied smile, "he could be my father." Her questions about my memories of the post-civil war years and about things I might have heard tell regarding the Republican Government are interspersed with other more urgent questions (not really addressed to me) about the event that has interrupted her *amitié amoureuse* and her work: her parents' sudden divorce, which has also become material for research. She's desperate because they won't help her. She's hardly seen her father, her mother won't say a word and she needs to discover the key to this whole unexpected process; she refuses to accept what she can't understand.

"You were always the same," I say, smiling. "Don't blame the thesis or Richard. Ever since you were a little girl you've always wanted to understand everything instantly. 'And when did that happen?' Imposing an order on life. And it's not always possible."

"That's true. Fancy you remembering! I was always asking questions. I must have been unbearable. In the cinema the people behind me always had to tell me to shut up."

"You're still the same now. The other day, at that Mastroianni film, Amelia kept telling you to let her watch the film in peace."

(They came to pick me up at the Ateneo. In the notebook I bought at Muñagorri's, I was describing Gregorio Termes' party. I've begun another one now. What's happened in between? Time is so confusing. I meditate fleetingly on the comfortable ambiguity of the expression "the other day".)

"Well," says Soledad, "it's just that they'd added things to the film that don't appear in the Chekhov story at all. You must admit that the opening scene with the waiter is pretty far-fetched."

I don't say anything because I don't feel like analyzing the film with her right now, especially given the tide of thoughts it brings with it. It made me think a lot about the relationship between love and lies, about the treacherous nature of words, about our need to have someone to listen to us and the difficulty we have in confronting our own past without embellishing it, in other words, reality versus illusion, the usual thing. And I think it was because I got involved in such reflections that it suddenly struck me as absurd to go on writing in that "me me me" style (Encarna's term for narcissism) in a notebook which, in all probability, is going to be read who knows when by a friend who is no longer my schoolfriend but nothing more than a fashionable psychiatrist. Then I felt depressed. I've often begun diaries with varying degrees of enthusiasm and the bubble has always burst for very similar reasons. When you're a young girl, fine, but there comes a time when you think: who is going to read this? Anyway, I don't want to go into all that now. Soledad won't accept any unjustifiable diversions and we've gone off at quite enough tangents in our conversation already.

I pour myself another cup of tea and simply say that Mastroianni is one of my favourite actors. She smiles. It seems that her Richard has a touch of the Mastroianni about him, but he's more like Mastroianni in his earlier films, when he was younger, without the spare tyre and the bags under his eyes.

"Well," I say, "what with that and his air of mystery, he must be really something."

She says that he is, or did I think I had exclusive rights on that. We both laugh. And I think how, at least in that respect, girls today and girls in my day are just the same, though that, perhaps, is all they have in common. If you mention a film star, the description of a new lover is bound to follow. Earlier I'd received a belated reward in this respect. The first time Mariana told me about Guillermo, she said he had a face like a wolf, but she didn't compare him to James Dean, because James Dean's films didn't even exist then, he would still have been just a snotty-nosed kid with a sulky face ignored by everyone. A short time ago, however, when I was talking about Guillermo to Soledad, I was able to say that he looked like James Dean and it was a relief to have her agree with me when I showed her a photo of him, three-quarter face, wearing a polo neck sweater. She's picked it up again now and is looking at it.

"I haven't got a photo of Richard," she says. "There's one on the jacket of a book he's written about Marat, but it's not very good of him. Besides I left the book in Paris. You can imagine how it was. I left, as they say, with nothing but the clothes I was wearing and as soon as I see that my Mum is a bit better, I'll go back. But I don't know, she's so passive about it all, it drives me mad."

Soledad has shadows under her eyes and when she gets heated, her long, expressive hands wave about to emphasize what she's saying, trying to clarify her meaning. They push back her hair from her face, feel for a cigarette, stroke my hands. She asks me to forgive her continual interruptions and I tell her that everything in life is an interruption and that she shouldn't struggle so hard to separate one thing from another because they're all seething away together simultaneously however hard we try to avoid it, the banal mixed up with the serious, the present with the past, the necessary with the dangerous, and if you really want to understand something, then that's the only way you can do it, by accepting that confusion as a valid way forward. That's why it's so difficult to write a novel.

"Are you writing a novel?" she asks with genuine curiosity. "Amelia thinks you are."

"Well, I've tried to do so several times. I've got loads of files hidden away somewhere containing the beginnings of novels. But then it all gets so complicated."

"That's why you need dates, don't you see?" says Soledad, impatiently. "Things get confused because there are no dates."

"And for other reasons too. There are a lot of characters in a novel and it's a matter of harmonizing the version given by one character with all the other characters' versions. And, of course, they tend not to dovetail, because not everyone experiences events in the same way. Not all the characters tell the truth or rather what they say depends on the circumstances. Memory is very fickle. And then they change, we all change without quite knowing how. Unless you take into account lies and incomprehensible transformations, dates are no use at all."

It suddenly occurs to me that the beginning of this novel should coincide with an analysis of those five and a bit months during which the person who is now Dr León became a stranger to me. And since Soledad demands dates, I could choose an afternoon in the second half of December when I'd had an argument with my mother and had decided to go over to Mariana's on the off-chance, at the risk of not finding her in. It was snowing. It must have been about the 20th or something like that. I found her in the middle of packing her suitcase because she was going to spend Christmas in Barcelona at her grandparents' house. I noticed at once that my visit was inconvenient. I noticed something more serious than that too: I realized that we were no longer friends. A key date for that period: the last time I cried in front of her.

(By the way, Mariana, I need to make a parenthesis here and return momentarily to the epistolary style, the only one suitable for reproaches. My conversation with Soledad, which I'm now salvaging with its corresponding literary adornments, took place before I got your letter. I've just re-read it in search of similarities and, frankly, I have to say that you've been most unfair. There's not one mention of those five and a bit months. They simply don't exist for you. It's as if the breakdown of our relationship dates exclusively from the day when your friend told you that she'd seen me with Guillermo in the woods. But what about before? Who first began to grow away from whom? Soledad

146

is right, you have to put dates on events; you can't just tell things the w...
you wish they had been, because it just won't wash. The question "How...
is the gold become dim?" which, according to you, tormented you
during that whole spring, was the very question, if you think back carefully, that I asked you in your house while the snow was falling outside in
the street, on precisely that afternoon when I turned up without warning
just before Christmas. Don't you remember how you behaved towards
me or the tone of voice you used telling me not to be so childish when I
burst out crying? Well, seeing that you can't answer me, I'll leave this
parenthesis in order not to suffocate inside it as if I were stuck inside a
tunnel. I'll describe the scene to you from the outside, just as it came into
my mind, like a flashback, before I got your letter, just as I was telling it
to Soledad. This all arises because of a gesture she made, an impatient
lift of the eyebrows, exactly like a gesture you made that afternoon. The
usual association of ideas.)

"There's no reason why change should be incomprehensible," says
Soledad, irritated, frowning. "You're just like my Mum, it's as if you
want to hide behind the idea that everything's a mess, and that there's no
answer or explanation for anything, in order to escape from reality,
rather than confront it. Well, that's what she does anyway, I don't know
about you. She's afraid of reality, she always has been. She's afraid of
growing up."

I close my eyes in order to remember.

"I hope you grow out of this Peter Pan phase," says Mariana, irritated,
frowning. "It's lasted much too long, it's quite worrying really. What
about all those people who are starving or in prison and have really
important reasons to cry? Have you ever thought about that?"

Her face was all blurred through my tears and, perhaps because of
that, her gestures, as she stuffed things into my suitcase, seemed to me
unharmonious and unconnected with their objective. She was wearing a
pair of black cords. It was the first time she'd spoken to me like that, at
least face to face. On the phone, I'd already noticed that she was sometimes abrupt and impatient, or else she wasn't home or had a lot to do. I'd
gone to see her precisely because I hadn't heard from her in such a long

time – apart from brief, reluctant telephone messages – to find out what was going on between us. Something was going on, she couldn't deny that. And my tears had started flowing beneath the snowflakes of her monosyllables, colder than those falling from the sky and dancing in the light of the streetlamps; come on, please, don't be so childish, she said, and stayed where she was. I couldn't accept that it was so difficult to ask her questions; I couldn't identify that fear of being indiscreet with a loss of confidence and love. I didn't think – and I told her so, even though it required an effort – that having a boyfriend was any reason to distance oneself like that from a friend, on the contrary. If I ever fell in love, I was sure that I would love the rest of the world much more, that I would be better, more generous, happier, have three times my usual energy. Or was it that she'd had an argument with Guillermo and didn't want to talk to me about it? I pronounced his name cautiously, as if it were the name of a troubling ghost. Without replying to my question, Mariana said that my idea of love between a man and a woman was pure Walt Disney and she'd had her fill of literature. All that was just personal stuff, bourgeois complacency. We were grown-ups now, weren't we, and really serious things were happening in the world, in our own country, for example. But she didn't look at me when she said that. I dried my eyes and leaned against the wall.

"How is the gold become dim?" I said as if to myself. "How is the most fine gold changed?"

And for the first time I understood that questions like that never have an answer. I understood too that I was confronting myself for the first time and that my sole comfort was an acceptance of my own vulnerability. I knew that I had to write, that writing was my one refuge.

"Why have you got your eyes closed?" asks Soledad. "Aren't you feeling well? I'm sorry, I'm being selfish, I'm making you ill with all my problems."

She has come over and knelt down next to me; she rests her head on my lap. There's a silence. I start to stroke her hair very slowly, as if she were a child, a child – I recognize with silent amazement – wise enough to help me reconstruct the blurred areas of a story which I had begun telling her reluctantly in order to distract her from her own ~~her~~ her fears.

"I'm sorry, Sofía," she says. "It's just that I have to talk to someo~~n~~ The last few days have been unbearable. I'm just so tired of playing mother to my own mother."

I go on stroking her hair and I tell her not to take it so much to heart, but I don't lard my advice with long explanations. I just say in English: "Take it easy", and I know that I've hit the mark because, years ago, when she and Amelia were beginning to make some progress in their English, we used to love saying that phrase together, like a spell, in fact just repeating it very slowly but loudly (take-it-easy-take-it-easy-take-it-easy) used to make us laugh so much that, however bad a mood we were in, we could always laugh ourselves out of it; it would undemonize us, to use Amelia's expression. "Do you remember?" I ask, and of course, Soledad does, how could she not? The verbal jokes of early youth are the last thing to be wiped from the memory, even when all the other texts have become confused and tangled. And she laughs, which is what I wanted, to see her undemonized.

"But that wasn't the word Amelia used," she points out, "it was an even stranger word: 'unbewitched'. She still uses it. She said it to me when we said goodbye; she told me that what I needed was to get myself unbewitched."

She's been talking in a low voice, without raising her head from my lap, as if asking me to go on scratching her head and talking to her about whatever; she makes herself more comfortable and indicates her forehead, and I tell her that she's got lovely hair, that she shouldn't ever think of cutting it or perming it, and she wags a finger to indicate that she won't and lets out a slight purr of pleasure, and I realize how important physical contact is between two people who love each other. I don't mean sexual contact, what a bore; anyone would think it was the only kind of physical contact that existed. Whenever these viatica, these moments of communion, occur along the way, time becomes eternity; you may not know where you're going, but you feel that you're in good company and on the right road; your contact with the other person calms you and

.issipates the mists shrouding your existence. I'm so glad that Soledad came and that she allows herself to be stroked like a kitten.

"Sometimes, when you're alone, you just lose your sense of direction," I say.

"Instead of being bewitched, you just feel bewildered" she says, laughing. "They couldn't be more different, could they? And yet they sound similar."

And I say yes, that at bottom everything's a question of words, of combining them, of playing with them, that's the good thing about literature, which people say is dying out because of videos; but that won't wash, it's nonsense, people still love inventing stories that will move other people or convince them of something, even if it's a lie, well, what do you expect, it depends on how they say the words to you and how you listen. Isn't love itself mainly a question of words? At least, the sort of love that appears in novels and makes you cry, it obviously has something, and she nods, at the same time lifting her hair to reveal the back of her neck. Once, many years ago, a teacher of literature at school advised me never to put down the butterfly net I used to catch words in; he said this because of a collage I'd made which I entitled "The Philologist"; the teacher's name was Don Pedro Larroque, and it's thanks to his advice that I'm still here, because literature has saved me from many a black hole.

"Do you remember that dictionary game?" says Soledad. "Who was it who invented it?"

And yes, I do suddenly remember; I invented it to entertain the children. It consisted in each person looking up an unusual word in the dictionary and then writing down the true definition along with two or three invented ones as different as possible one from the other, "tropical fruit", "resentful attitude" and "inhabitant of a mountainous region", for example, and the other players had to guess which was the real meaning. Sometimes people came up with such convincing definitions that they suited the word better than the real one did, as happens sometimes with first names that seem to have been given to the wrong people.

"You were brilliant at the dictionary game," I say to Soledad, while I begin massaging the back of her neck. "We always lost when it was your turn to invent definitions."

"Oh yes, just there, on my neck, that's wonderful!" she replies.

She undoes a couple of buttons on her blouse, makes herself more comfortable, and I notice the beneficent energy flowing out of my fingertips.

I go on talking and thinking at the same time, as if I were travelling along two parallel roads, a feat of acrobatics, by the way, that certainly stimulates the imagination. I imagine that I'm a witch doctor whose magic potions cure him as effectively as they do the sick person he's treating. It's quite a frequent daydream of mine, with slight variations as to my age and the clothes I'm wearing and the landscape and the identity of the people who come to me complaining of being ill, but what remains constant is the sense that the witch doctor's spells are a direct verbal application and will only work if he pronounces them. Generally, the words leave his mouth the way they do in comics, but the bubble disappears like smoke; indeed, it is essentially transient; then it is erased and cannot be repeated. It's something very special, you have to pay close attention in order to catch the words in the air. Besides, that is precisely what cures the witch doctor and allows him to go on practising his profession, otherwise he would turn into a simple beggar.

"That's great, you've got really positive energy in your fingers today," says Soledad.

"So has your neck, it's a reciprocal drug."

Thinking about the virtues of reciprocal drugs, I remember a very long, monotonous song that I learned from my grandmother and that I used to sing to my children to send them to sleep. It began:

Holy St Anthony
pleaded with the Almighty
that by his divine grace
he enlighten his understanding
so that his tongue
might tell of the miracle
that thou didst work one day in the garden
at the tender age of eight ...

It's very odd, that "thou", because it suddenly breaks the third person style and seems to be establishing a dialogue with the Creator himself or with St Anthony as an old man. It's not very clear; but my grandmother said that was what it was, that the song had always been sung like that, and who was I to give her lessons, that I was a clever clogs, an expression she used meaning that I was a know-all or something like that. And the miracle consisted in this: one Sunday, when he went off to Mass, his father asked his young son Anthony to keep an eye on the various birds that used to forage for food around there and stop them coming into the vegetable garden and pecking up the seeds because then everything would be wasted; and the little boy stayed behind to look after the vegetable garden. However, realizing that his efforts to frighten away the large and various flocks of birds were all in vain, he chose instead to address them with great sweetness and persuasion, so much so that hundreds of these pecking birds, and every one of the species is mentioned in the song, had flown down to sit near him and listen and obey him; when the father came back from church, he was amazed to find his eight-year-old son telling stories to the birds in order to try and make them see reason. It was a very long song, though, and therefore an excellent lullaby because, in the end, informed of the miracle, the bishop himself arrived, having said that he would only believe it if he saw it with his own eyes. And by the time the bishop arrived, both the sleepless child and the mother rocking the cradle would have fallen victim to the same quieting effect of that naive, interminable song. What I used to notice too was that I felt in less of a hurry for the child to go to sleep and the annoyance I'd felt when I began the song ("As if the general irritations of the day weren't enough, she now wants me to sing 'Holy St Anthony' to her.") would have disappeared; I would concentrate on singing each verse properly without leaving out a single one and I didn't need to check the results of the remedy by glancing at the bed because I felt them in myself, in my calmed nerves, and the child would go to sleep because of that, because I had calmed down. I've forgotten some of the verses now and that worries me, not only because it shows me how much time has passed since I last sang it all the way through, when Amelia was a baby,

but because I remember that, at the time when I had my last chil[...]
needed the relaxing effects of that nocturnal drug more than ever. By
then, it had become obvious that Eduardo and I had nothing in common,
neither in the realm of dreams nor in the real world.

That memory automatically makes me tense up. I fall silent and the
silence becomes awkward. The fluid magic that had connected me to
Soledad is dispelled, and she notices. She sits up, thanks me and smooths
her hair.

"You get better and better at massage and you sing too. Anyone would
think you were a professional!"

"Well, it's certainly not because I get a lot of practice."

"If you'd gone on much longer, I would have fallen asleep."

There is a silence. Soledad has buttoned up her blouse and is looking
at me, as if disoriented.

"What were we talking about before?"

"Before what? I suppose we were talking about time; I don't know if
you've noticed, but we haven't talked about anything else all afternoon. I
think we were trying to account for five and a bit months of my life."

"That's it. But something's wrong, you seem sad."

"No, I'm not, don't be silly. It all came up because of that business
with dates. And I think we were saying … oh, I don't know. Time, after
all, is an unreliable refuge and not to be trusted. If, for example, I say: 'the
afternoon went on for an eternity', what do you understand by that?"

"That you were bored."

"You see, I understand something entirely different by it. For me the
eternal is the one thing that doesn't weigh on you: it's when time passes
without you noticing because you're so happy. For that very reason,
though, since each person experiences time in his or her own way, there
have to be rules, of course, otherwise it would be a mess. So it's no bad
thing to settle accounts with time. Dates are important, you're quite
right. Five months are five months, after all. By the way, what time is it?
Haven't you arranged to meet your mother?"

"Yes," she says, glancing reluctantly at her watch. "But I've still got a
bit of time."

She's gone very thoughtful. She doesn't like being reminded of her mother. I can tell by the excited tone she uses to lead the conversation back to her obsessive theme.

"Yes, the importance of dates. I'm fed up with telling her that. She could at least differentiate between what came before and what came afterwards, don't you think? Any process, whether it be judicial, psychological or historical or whatever, needs to be put in order, it's elementary, my dear Watson. But she won't, she can't, she lives in a state of perpetual chaos."

Her eyes fix on mine as if imploring advice from a sensible person. I refuse to talk to her about my own chaos and instead put on a sensible face. This story of a failed marriage is already beginning to bore me a bit, though, and I set to thinking again about those five and a bit months before I discovered love – and that relaxes me. If I start rummaging around in those months, a lot of things are bound to emerge. What I remember most is that I wrote endlessly. Poems, the beginnings of novels, a diary. I've lost some of those notebooks, others I burned. Some I still have. At the time, I was consolidating my love affair with literature, although it never became a commitment. And if my love still endures it's because it was always fluctuating, contradictory and dangerous, just like the love I felt later for Guillermo. That's why I still remember him. There are love affairs that belong in novels and love affairs that end in marriage.

"It's impossible to clarify anything with my Mum," says Soledad. "She just blocks things off all the time. I mean, at some point she must have noticed that things were starting to go wrong with my father. Nothing happens just like that, from one moment to the next. Don't you agree? What are you thinking about, Sofía?"

"Well," I say, "don't be so sure. There are some changes that tiptoe in and others that suddenly emerge like an eruption. Or a miracle. I don't know. It depends."

"Do you mean love?"

"Yes, but irritation too and all the other moods that we experience during the day, so that one moment you want to die and the next you find life intoxicating. Your mother's having a rough time, so don't keep on at her. She's probably trying to understand it all herself. Sometimes the skein can only be untangled by the person who got it tangled up in the first place."

Soledad sighs and changes the subject.

"She hasn't got many friends. Why don't you phone her some time?"

"She'd find that a bit odd; I hardly know her. I only saw her that day at the airport when you and Amelia were off to Brighton. She seemed to me to form an indissoluble unit with your father. That was ten years ago, wasn't it, you who like dates so much?"

Soledad nods. Her face has darkened while she's been shuffling through a pile of old photos I got out to show her. Her face has an obsessive look about it, concentrated, absent, a bit like the boy in the polo neck sweater. Although he might have a thousand faces. He would have done well in films.

"I'd like to know if she'd had a Guillermo in her life. Why can you tell me about that, but she can't?"

"Very easy. Because I'm not your mother. I don't burden you with the responsibility of my stories and yours aren't a burden to me, however much we love each other."

She looks thoughtful.

"That's true. That's what Amelia says too."

Her words create something like a whiplash inside me. I feel suddenly cast out from the refuge, exposed once more to the blizzards of reality.

"What does Amelia say? She was very odd with me when she was home this time."

"She's worried about her brother and sister."

"Right, well so am I. But what does she say about me? Come on, if it's not a secret that is."

"No, of course it isn't. All right, she says that between you and her there's always an area of half-truths and that however much you try to treat her like a friend, you're still her mother, and there's nothing anyone can do about that. Besides … oh, nothing."

"No, please, tell me, whatever it is. Besides what?"

"I don't know, she thinks that you tend to stick your head in the sand about certain things. She means it in the nicest possible way, it's not a criticism. She loves you a lot and she worries about you more than you can imagine. But she's been over your situation again and again, so it doesn't come as a surprise to her. Well, it doesn't to me either, but since I've been living abroad for a long time ..."

"What doesn't come as a surprise?" I ask.

And I realize that I'm diving into a pool of icy water.

Soledad looks at me awkwardly, as if she regretted saying what she'd said. Then she looks away.

"That Eduardo doesn't love you."

I look down uneasily. This is an area I don't like rummaging around in. Encarna, the most direct of my children, knows that all too well. Do I love him? Have I ever loved him? I need to go to the refuge and talk to Encarna about this and other things and to Lorenzo too, even though he drives me mad. His father can't go on thinking that he's finished his degree and has found a job. And I can't go on sticking my head in the sand. It isn't just Eduardo's fault if he and I hardly ever speak to each other. I don't know why I say that he's disappointed me if I never wanted to find out what he was really like anyway. I just took it for granted that I knew what he was like and left it at that; you only fall in love with what intrigues you; I wasn't in love with Eduardo when I married him and that's where the problem began. It isn't his faults that are the problem; you don't stop loving someone because of their faults, but rather because you're no longer interested in interpreting those faults or understanding them. He doesn't even get on my nerves. I can't complain; he's not to blame.

But that's enough of that, I don't want to get bogged down in guilt, because it doesn't agree with me at all. Encarna's always telling me that no one is to blame for anything, that it's just the remnants of a Judaeo-Christian education, and Lorenzo's the same, only he's more categorical: "Oh, cut the crap, Mama, things happen and that's all there is to it, so don't go on about it", and there's nothing more to be said. Is it really true that they live so untouched by any feelings of guilt or sin? Our conversations always end the same: "Don't worry, forget all that stuff and just switch off," and for a moment I feel fine, as if I were floating, but then I see that with them nothing ever gets resolved, everything is left pending. You can choose not to talk about things and it might even seem that you've stopped thinking about them too, but you haven't; you still think about them, perhaps even more; they scrabble about inside you, digging ruts and, who knows, they might hurt your spleen or your pancreas – that's where I sense the erosion is taking place. Eduardo bores me, bores me to death. I can't be sure that I know everything about him but what I do know, I don't give a damn about. Why don't I just tell him? Of course, he must realize, but telling him would be a very beneficial unburdening, what they call a catharsis, and the only possible way of ending it – with a lot of shouting and slamming of doors. But no, please, not that.

I look at Soledad, looking for something to hold on to, just as she looked at me a moment ago. She must notice the anxiety in my face. I can't even breathe, I feel that steel blade sticking in my ribs again. It makes me feel even worse to know that I'm burdening her with my anguish. I look down.

"I'm sorry," I say in a feeble voice.

I know that tears have begun to fall on to my hands. It makes me furious. Soledad holds out a Kleenex to me.

"Here you are, don't be silly. You cry all you want to."

Her voice is very soft now. Is that the same voice she uses when she consoles her mother? Or does her mother upset her more than I do?

"Was your mother in love with your father when she married him?" I ask.

"She says she was, madly in love."

"So you see, it's all the same. It all ends the same," I say so quietly that I think she might not have heard me.

At least, if she has heard me, she keeps silent. She can't be enjoying the turn the conversation is taking one bit. She said before that nothing about our situation surprises Amelia. And yet, I can't remember ever having said to my children that I wasn't in love with their father when I married him. I did say it to him. I cheated of course, using those famous half-truths, only mentioning Guillermo in passing, as an unimportant love affair. And Eduardo was practical, sure of himself. He believed in the politics of the *fait accompli*. He wouldn't give up until he'd got me to say yes and having first made me pregnant. "You'll come to love me eventually," he said, "it's always best for the man to love the woman more than she loves him. Besides, I love you enough for both of us." And I liked hearing that. I wanted to leave home as soon as possible. And have children. It wasn't Guillermo's fault either. There are men you marry and others you remember for ever like lovers in a novel. I knew from the beginning that Guillermo belonged in the second category.

I told him as much many years later when I met him again in London. Funnily enough, it was he who suggested that I divorce Eduardo so that he and I could get married, or else just go off together; everything would sort itself out. But I didn't want the novel to finish like *Anna Karenina*. "No, Guillermo, I don't want to end up like Anna Karenina," I said to him with sudden lucidity the night we said goodbye. We were in the blue-wallpapered room of the London bed and breakfast he was staying at and I was looking out of the corner of my eye at our entwined bodies reflected in the mirror on the wardrobe which, as it happened, wouldn't close properly. It was a rather shabby room, but welcoming, like the landlady, a Mrs Morrison, who treated him like one of the family. He'd lived there ever since he separated from his wife or, rather, since she left him. He didn't tell me much about it, only that it was a brief marriage and that they'd had no children.

"The only thing I don't understand, and nor does Amelia for that matter, is why you and Eduardo don't separate," says Soledad.

I shrug my shoulders.

"I don't know, out of cowardice, I suppose. I'm terrified of violent situations, anything aggressive. I've never even been capable of slamming a door. Maybe it's because my mother was always slamming doors."

"You don't have to slam the door. You simply talk to him. Eduardo's a reasonable person, he's not a savage."

"No, but even the idea of talking to him frightens me."

"I don't see why."

"Well, you may not, but that's the way it is. You've no idea how far back I'd have to go to pick up the thread. Threads! There are loose ends everywhere, it makes me dizzy."

"Come on, don't get all worked up about it. I just meant that you should talk to him about your relationship, calmly, about what's happening now; I don't mean that you should haul out any dirty linen."

"I find it harder and harder to talk to him, not only about that, but about anything. It just wouldn't be right."

"Oh, I don't know, leave him a letter like they do in novels."

"That's easy enough to say. And where would I go?"

"To the refuge. You throw everyone else out and move in. Just like that. That's what Amelia says you should do."

I'm gradually calming down. I can no longer feel the knife in my ribs now when I breathe.

"Tell me the truth, when did Amelia tell you about all this? About Eduardo and me, I mean."

"Now let's see, what date would it have been? When we were together in Brighton. Or perhaps before that. But especially then."

"In Brighton?"

"Yes. Well, we spent all day together, slept in the same room and everything; we didn't have any secrets, you know how it is. And naturally we talked about our parents. Well, less about mine. I didn't think mine had a problem."

"But Amelia thought we did?"

"Yes, of course, huge problems. She was very upset about you, she felt bad that she was having such a good time. She'd cry sometimes when she read your letters. That's why she encouraged you to come and fetch us."

My letters? It's incredible how many things we forget. I must have written so many letters in my lifetime, letters I've now completely forgotten about. I feel a sort of blind, retrospective remorse, the worst kind. It's like a slug, leaving the dirty, sticky trail of all the unintentional pain we caused on the neatly folded memories stored away in crates alongside the apples and the thyme.

"Poor Amelia. Did she really cry? I don't remember having written to her complaining about anything."

"You didn't really complain. But you did write to her a lot, really lovely letters. Sometimes she'd read out whole paragraphs to me. I don't remember quite what you said. Nothing concrete, all very poetic, but you were definitely depressed. I seem to remember you saying something about 'coming to terms with time'."

"My usual theme. That's hardly a clue. And was she the one who encouraged me to come and pick you up? Yes, you're right, I'd forgotten. I suppose she didn't really mean it."

I have a sudden longing to be alone; everything that interrupts the evocation of my arrival in London feels like an obstacle. I had written to tell them not to come and meet me, that they shouldn't worry about me. I took a taxi from the airport. "Victoria station, please." I kept checking that I had all my luggage, and I liked travelling alone after all that time. I felt as if I'd sprouted wings. Free and alone, with a thirst for adventure. The first chapter should be: "Reunion with Guillermo at Victoria Station", that's where the novel should start. Me, weighed down with luggage, asking about the times of trains to Brighton, and then colliding with and nearly falling into the arms of a tall stranger. Just like in the films. Sorry, I said. But he wasn't a stranger. It was the blond wolf, with a few grey hairs.

"Well," Soledad is saying, "you do always tend to enjoy yourself most just when things are coming to an end, and we'd settled in by then, we both had a boyfriend of sorts, and the truth is that when you did finally decide to come and fetch us, we weren't really looking forward to it that much. Amelia thought that we'd have to act as chaperones while you went into ecstasies over the Palace Pier and the grey pebble beach you see in all the films. Anyway, we were in seventh heaven when you called from London saying that you'd happened to bump into some friends and that you were going to spend a week at their house, that

London was, after all, more interesting than Brighton. It was as if we'd come up on the lottery, I can't deny it, especially since, according to Amelia, you sounded really happy."

Yes, I was happy. He was with me in the phone booth. Before that he'd swept me up in his arms, right there on the platform surrounded by my suitcases. It was like a dream. He took me off to the bed and breakfast where he was staying, just as if it were the only logical continuation of that encounter, the only possible one. And I found it natural too, I didn't put up the least resistance, I didn't ask any questions. I was in a complete daze. What a time we had, especially the first few days. Then things changed a bit, although the initial enthusiasm was still there. The mirage began to fade. I'd been fascinated by the image of a Guillermo who had remained true to his rebellious dreams of youth, refusing to adapt to a society that was hostile to him, refusing to compromise himself for money. Gradually, though, it seemed to me that he made rather too much of this, that my eagerness to listen to his words was like petrol poured on the flames of a story that no one else was interested in any more. (That was precisely what the Mastroianni film was about.) I began to suspect that he saw me only as a kind of life-line and then he begged me to leave my husband and go and live with him, completely destroying any credibility that all his hymns to freedom might have had. That was later, though, because I saw him again after that. Well, the truth is, I can't really remember how the time passed.

"Then, do you remember, when you finally arrived that Saturday, laden down with presents, Amelia said to me: 'You see how different she is when she's on her own? Doesn't she look lovely? She comes to life without Dad around, she enjoys everything. Don't you think so? She's a new woman.' And she was right, I noticed it too. You did seem like a new woman, although," she adds after a silence, "you do tend to change a lot anyway."

"Everyone changes," I say distractedly.

"But you change from one moment to the next."

If I weren't feeling so churned up, I would confess to Soledad the reason why the woman who got off the train that brought her from London to Brighton seemed, indeed was, a new woman. But that's another story; if I put it in now, it will conflict with Soledad's chronological criteria. She prefers things to be told in the order that they happened, quite apart from the fact that I'd have to tell it to her slowly and with plenty of time to spare. It's better to write it down. I think it would be best told in the third person.

Soledad is still looking at me, disconcerted. She must notice that I'm not the same woman who, only a few moments ago, was massaging her neck.

"Yes, it's true, I do change a lot," I say with a smile intended to cover up my sudden boredom. "But doesn't this all remind you of one of those never-ending stories from childhood?"

"It's my fault," says Soledad. "Where were we?"

"What do you mean?"

"Where did we get to in the story about you and your friend."

"Ah, yes. Do you know, I can't really remember."

Tiredness is contagious, I've often noticed that. There's no need for physical symptoms like yawns, for example, to know that both the person who's speaking and the person listening are running out of energy. That's how you can spot the boring bits in a novel; they become leaden precisely where they became leaden for the author. You know it for sure, although there's no way of proving it and no one has yet invented an apparatus with which to synchronize one person's boredom with another's.

Soledad is going through the photos that lie in a pile on the table, as if trying, without much conviction, to rekindle the embers of this straggling tale. She's picked up one showing Mariana leaning against the trunk of a tree. It was a photo I took of her in Aranjuez. She's wearing a V-necked blouse.

"Your friend's really lovely," says Soledad.

"Yes, she still is. As I told you, I saw her a short while ago at a cocktail party. Maybe she's had a facelift. She seems so sure of herself. She's a bit frightening in a way."

"Keep to the subject. We'd got to the point where she told you that she had a boyfriend and then five and a bit months went by before you met him. And during those months, what happened? Something must have happened."

"Nothing much that I can remember. I hardly saw her at all and, when I did, she seemed distracted, distant. The few times she spoke about Guillermo it was just to make a casual comment, although I did get the impression that it was a rather difficult relationship. 'You must introduce us some time?' I said. But then she'd change the subject and so I stopped saying it. Something had broken between us, I don't know what."

"Following different courses at university can drive a wedge between people," says Soledad. "I was talking about that with Amelia just the other day. That's what happened to us."

"Yes, that can have some influence. Oh, and Mariana had got into politics, I didn't tell you that. Well, nearly everyone was at the time, even Eduardo; Eduardo was a member of FUS, can you imagine, but then you probably don't even know what FUS was; the Federation of University Students, or something. It doesn't matter, I didn't know at the time either."

"Weren't you interested in politics?"

"Not much. It was just sort of background music to me. Now I know more about what was going on in the world then than I did at the time. I almost feel I could write a doctoral thesis like yours, it all seems so far away …"

"And was Guillermo a member of FUS too?"

"No, he had no time for politics either. He was a free agent. But I didn't know that until later. Since Mariana didn't tell me anything about him, I just assumed he must be an activist too."

"And why do you think she didn't want to talk to you about him?"

"I couldn't understand it at the time."

"And now?"

I was beginning to find this interrogation horribly tiring and it must have shown in my face.

"Well, when you explain things with hindsight, you squeeze out all kinds of reasons from them, but then you only drink the juice of the ones that taste least bitter."

"You're deliberately going off the subject because you don't want to tell me about Guillermo."

"Maybe. It's just that I'm a bit tired."

"Just tell me one more thing. Did you fall in love with him the moment Mariana introduced you?"

I sat staring out of the window, as if trying to establish the cardinal points. No, not that direction. It was north-east, and there was a full moon. It was 27th February, I'll never forget that date. I knew that something would happen that night. I needed to get drunk, to forget about Mariana, to open myself to life.

"She didn't introduce us," I say. "I met him at someone's house, near Pozuelo, where we both happened to end up. Neither of us were great friends of the people there. It was a birthday party. They were all very trendy types, the sort who'd taken down the Virgin of Lourdes and replaced her with Che Guevara. I'm sure you know who Che Guevara was."

Soledad smiles.

"Yes, I know Che Guevara, I've got that far. On the other hand, you didn't know who James Dean was."

"Exactly; anyway, his appearance there caught me completely off guard, because it really was like an apparition. To cut a long story short, when I found out later that this James Dean *avant la lettre* was Mariana's Guillermo, it was too late, though I know that sounds like some sloppy torch song. I'm sure you know what happens the first time a man awakens feelings of love in you. It's useless trying to struggle against the tide."

"Yes," says Soledad, "useless."

"Well, you've understood the most important part then. The rest of the story will have to wait until another day, because it's very late."

"Okay, Scheherazade."

She looks at her watch, stands up and says that it is indeed late.

I accompany her to the door and we give each other a kiss. We're both very sad.

164

"Thanks for the massage," she says.

"Thank *you*. That was the best bit of the afternoon."

"No, it wasn't. It was all good."

When she leaves, I feel very upset. I promise myself that I'll go on writing, which means, as always, beginning to write differently. Instead, all I do is move the furniture around and smoke one cigarette after another.

X

The shadowy key

I've slept in many hotel rooms in my life, Sofía, and what I remember most about them all is that feeling of confusion when you wake up, those few painful seconds accompanied by the question "Where am I?", while your still drowsy eyes blindly seek some reference point that might give a clue to the identity of that unfamiliar space and remind you why it was you had ended up sleeping there.

In this room, opposite my bed, hangs a large etching – the first thing I see when I open my eyes. It depicts an old ship, its sails unfurled as it negotiates a narrow channel between two icebergs. Slightly out of keeping, don't you think, considering this is the south. I suppose one day I'll come across the image of that sailing ship again and associate it with my inability to note down details of some recently evaporated dream, although I may well confuse the hotel with another hotel in another country and may not remember if it was winter or summer nor, of course, what the dream was about, since I haven't as yet managed to write down the plot of any of my dreams. I'm dreaming an awful lot these days. I know the symptoms. Does your head feel heavy when you wake up, as if you had a weight between your eyes? Yes, Doctor, that's exactly how I feel. And then you spend a while feeling somehow absent from everything you look at? Yes, yes, sometimes it lasts the whole morning. Oh well, don't worry, keep trying to remember your dreams, even if only fragments, it's important. And write it down so that you don't forget it. You need to free yourself from your dreams.

Underneath the picture, there's a kind of long desk with a mirror and drawers, which is useless as a writing desk because there's hardly room

to put your legs. Besides, it's almost entirely taken up by little card
pyramids informing the client of the dialling codes for Spain and abroad,
dates and times of excursions, prices in the coffee shop and for the sauna,
ironing and other sundry services. The management of this kind of hotel
never seem to consider that a guest might occasionally want to make the
room a home from home. There are no cosy little corners.

I asked for an extra table and have placed it next to the French
windows which take up the whole of the wall opposite the door. It was
the only place it would fit. I had to push the desk with the cardboard
cones a little further up because otherwise, since it's quite large, there
wouldn't be enough room for me to squeeze past so that I could still reach
the handle that operates the blinds.

The first thing I do when I wake up is raise the blind and open the
French windows which lead on to a small balcony with wickerwork
furniture; I do this almost mechanically, the way an alcoholic reaches for
the bottle. The salt-sea light bursts in like a burglar and strips the
icebergs of their spurious power, relegating them to the realms of
fantasy, along with all the detritus of my night-time images, although
even such a clear-cut delineation of territory does little to lessen my
bewildered state. On the contrary, it merely increases it. It's spring and
this is a village on the south coast of Spain; the sailing ship and the ice are
a complete irrelevance, really; just forget about it, a whim of the owner
of the hotel you happen to be sleeping in. Okay, but why am I sleeping
here? What am I looking for, what am I escaping from? Something
happened in today's dream which might give a clue, a disguised clue, but
I can't remember now. What was it? Someone was saying "Don't give
her anything to eat", yes, that was it, someone in the same room as me,
although we couldn't see each other, and the person or ghost in question
could not have known that I was listening. Besides it was a coded
message; that was the most important thing in the dream itself. Wait a
moment. This is data for research. What were you reading last night
before you went to sleep?

I look at the new table, so crammed with books and papers that it
looks as if the table and I had been here for a year already, a disquieting

thought that vanishes along with the feeling that I've woken up surrounded by ice. I don't really like the way the table is positioned, at an angle like that; it doesn't look particularly welcoming and I keep bumping into it. A detective novel – that was what I was reading, *Talking to Strange Men* by Ruth Rendell, about a young Londoner obsessed with coded languages. Ah yes, and a few paragraphs from Katherine Mansfield's journal. On the cover there's a photo of the writer taken in 1920, her eyes dreamy, anguished, and her very black hair cut in a Japanese-style fringe. She died childless. I wonder where the original of this photo is now, the photo from which she looks out at me as if at a complicit doctor, "I hardly need you to tell me what the problem is, do I?" She didn't have long to live, she died when she was thirty-four; TB was difficult to cure then and she knew it, she says so in her journal.

When I began studying medicine, Koch's bacillus was no ghost from the past. What I didn't know, and you may not know this either, is that it was named after the wise German man who discovered the bacillus; we're rarely aware of all the people concealed in our conversations and our thoughts, like a sturdy framework for the cloth on which we embroider our own lives. I can see the oval portrait of Robert Koch now, a Sagittarius born midway through the nineteenth century, neat and tidy and sporting a bow tie, a little white beard and round glasses, just as he appeared in my encyclopedias. It's over a century now since he announced in Berlin, after long experimentation, that he believed he had isolated and discovered the bacteria responsible for tuberculosis. He died in 1910 in Baden-Baden, ten years before Katherine Mansfield posed for the photo I have before me now and which, unintentionally, superimposes itself on that of the wise and kindly old German, because everything superimposes itself on everything else. Anyway, as I was saying, when I began my studies, Koch's bacillus still enjoyed some of its former glory and was still carrying people off, a powerful monarch in decline from whom other hordes have now stolen the sceptre, with no bespectacled superman to do battle with them – there will always be some kind of plague. The victims of Koch's bacillus were defenceless, rebellious, pale young people, the high-risk victims of a shipwreck, brothers and sisters of the moon, gazing with their Katherine Mansfield eyes into the seeming void. They would die dreaming of other mountain slopes and a more enduring love, struggling in vain between that longing for the infinite and the bonds of a body which they perceived as a prison. The whole of Katherine's journal is like that, an arduous journey where her confessions of impotence alternate with her efforts to combat it and leave some testimony of it, as the allotted time separating her from death dwindled away. Who would have thought, Sofía, that when we were reading *The Garden Party*, a collection of rather precious stories when you think about it, its author was suffering like a dog and was writing everything down in this sombre, heartbreaking journal, strong stuff, you've no idea. Or rather I hadn't: maybe you already know it.

I buy these books when I go for strolls in the village, in a rather odd shop I've discovered where they sell a little of everything. I feel as if I were setting up home – stupid, eh? – and I always come back to the hotel with a bag full of various useless bits and pieces. A bad symptom or, at the least, disquieting. So I'm reading a bit as well now, just whatever takes my fancy, picking up things without rhyme or reason, it never goes much beyond a pinprick. That doesn't only happen with books, Sofía, it happens with everything, because I'm restless, rootless. I change position all the time, change my posture, my focus, I try out different styles of writing and feel at home in none of them, always searching for some reference point in literature, in my dreams, in conversations with forgotten patients and even in the faces of the people wandering about the hotel; I'd like to know how they run their lives, these other people, how they organize their time. Because, as my father said, what matters is how you pass the time, pass it as painlessly as possible, so that the broken glass of that all-devouring time does not remain impaled in your flesh.

Pride is the only thing that keeps me from phoning you, Sofía, from crying out to you: "Please, come!", and it's also what stops me sending you this letter; I don't want to burden anyone with my boring disquisitions. And yet, as soon as I listen to my feelings, it's always your name I hear. Or rather, my name, because when I try to remember the tone of your voice, that voice says "Mariana", that's what it always says, with a slight stress on the "i"; I say it too, I imitate you, you see, as if anyone could. I can find neither my voice nor my place in the world – that just about sums up what's going on for me – and I have to steal it from someone else, anyone, I have to resort to supplanting my neighbour, dead or alive, real or fictitious, and plunder their respective territories. I don't think you do such things, you're not like that; however embattled you feel by domestic life, you know how to create a place for yourself, even at a cocktail party; you know how to surround yourself with invisible walls that protect you. That's what I most envy about you, your ability to isolate yourself; it's what I most envied about Guillermo too.

And I suddenly think: could the fact that Katherine Mansfield appears in my dreams, assuming she did, also be a tendency in my subconscious to identify myself with you? I say that because of your first batch of homework; it's on my table and I've read it so many times now that everything I've written since seems to contain the detailed descriptions that are so characteristic of your writing. It's odd, you didn't need me or anyone to tell you: "Write down your dreams." The night before we met at Gregorio's exhibition – which already seems centuries ago – we had been together on the moors at Gimmerton, that is, Emily Brontë was warning us that in a few hours we would see each other again for real – not that you bother with interpretations. It seems that you were as real to me there on that spring hillside as you were when you stopped studying the fried-egg picture and turned round so that we stood face to face, looking at each other in the midst of that crowd; what I notice most about you is how little you change. You just tell things the way they are, you don't complicate matters; it's as if everything belonged to the same world: day-to-day life and miracles, Señora Acosta and the Brontë sisters, the unreal and the tangible. You were always like that, and it used to infuriate me. "You're mad, Sofía, you talk about Yolanda, the daughter of the Black Corsair, as if you'd just seen her and been talking to her."

And you would look at me with your bemused, transparent eyes and say: "Of course I do, because I have seen her and met her, haven't you?" That was precisely what I envied about you – although I don't think you ever knew it – the fact that you didn't see any boundaries between life and literature, that you always had your head in the clouds. I envied you deeply and wanted to be like you. It never worked, and that, of course, made me angry. It was as if you could fly and I couldn't, and what made matters worse was that you didn't even realize you were flying and that other people couldn't see the same landscapes you saw. I sometimes used to pretend I could see them and would deceive you just by observing you and stealing your light, your words. That's what I used to do: I would use any scraps of material that you inadvertently dropped and out of them I would make dresses which you thought were original, but which I knew were not. I eventually began to feel awkward about this, and that soured the unstinting approval and enthusiasm with which you greeted those imitation Montalvo dresses, caricatures of the ones you made. And so, after a certain age – this confession is long overdue – I decided to reject that symbiosis with you, a symbiosis I had struggled so hard to conceal from myself. I went to the opposite extreme, by exaggerating our differences. It often happens.

Put like that it sounds so cheap, so elementary, my dear Watson: the doctor in me always resurfaces. On the other hand, the thread of my dream has been broken for ever and the face of the person who said "Don't give her anything to eat" is fading; it was very hard to make out, but I think it was Katherine Mansfield's pale face, with the dark, fixed eyes of the dying; I turn the book over; I don't want to see her face any more. I've got a splitting headache! It's time I ordered breakfast.

I usually have breakfast on the terrace ("Coffee, toast and orange juice for room 203"), because the buffet downstairs offers too many tempting proteins and I already have difficulty doing up the jeans that I bought in Cádiz. Before they bring my breakfast, I look at the time, turn on the radio and take a shower. That's when the day lays itself before me like a blank cheque, white and inert, with no surprises and no provocations.

...lize again that life lies in those rubbish tips of detritus and confu-
...ion which I've explored so many times without ever once getting my
hands dirty, prodding them from above with a walking stick in order to
analyze the etiology of the various bits of detritus and attempt a
classification. Not an easy task, because they form an amalgam with the
organic matter and from the resulting mixture there arises a strong smell
which, though occasionally stimulating, is more often than not merely
nauseating. I've persevered, with varying degrees of conviction, in my
task of rummaging around in other people's rubbish with my right hand
and holding my nose with the other, often thinking that I'm deceiving
those I try to help and submitting them to a painful, pointless experiment,
wasting their time and their money, because the only way you can catalogue life is by falsifying it; life bespatters us, attacks from more than one
direction at a time and grabs us round the neck like an octopus; you
simply have to get through it as best you can, each person risking his own
skin. Sometimes it works out well and sometimes it doesn't; there are no
rules. Knowing that only increases my unease.

Write down your dreams.

"That's easy enough to say," a middle-aged widow said to me once, a
woman tormented by the urgency and frequency of her sexual desires
and by her need to suppress them. "They're either dreams and you take
them as such, or you write them down and then they stop being dreams.
Besides, I've got quite enough to do being a widow by day instead of
singing at the top of my voice whenever I feel like it and, by night,
feeling that I can't go out into the streets to look for a man, because I
wasn't brought up to do that kind of thing, and then there's the fear of
actually grabbing what you need, and fear of what the children will say,
because whether you like it or not, they're bound to find out. In my
dreams, though, that's precisely what emerges; what do you expect? I
never dream about white weddings and shopping and visiting, making
meals and packing suitcases and always going to the cinema with the
same man, I never dream about that because it's boring, and no one in
their right mind would want another twenty-odd years of having to grin
and bear it, but I wouldn't say no to a bit of fun. But you can't talk about

172

such things and that's why you end up with your nerves shot, becaus
only at night, in bed, that I miss Luis. I love everything to do with beu.

Her name was Almudena and her husband came from a higher social
class than her. I've got it all on a tape which I typed out while I was in
Puerto Real. I'd been meaning to do it for ages and yesterday I was re-
reading her file – how work piles up, and what's it all for in the end?
Almudena Sánchez, widow, from Portillo. She often came to see me and
her conversation was liberating, unadulterated and exuberant, she left
me speechless and, of course, demolished all my arguments.

One day she said: "I'm telling you all this so that you can write it
down; that way it doesn't go to waste and it helps me to get it off my
chest, that's why I talk to you, because you're not shocked by anything,
as is only right, and that suits me. But I don't come here so that you can
cure me; that doesn't even enter my head, because there is no cure for
life, Doctor."

No, there isn't. That was exactly what I was thinking last night when I
was listening to the tape that Manolo Reina recorded for me, listening to
his voice, a voice that still makes the hair stand up on the back of my
neck, and I remembered Almudena who, by the way, hasn't been back for
a while, and who used to say that the most difficult thing for certain
women was to resist dressing up a passion rather than simply suffering it
or enjoying it, that it was best to eat it raw, just as it came.

She said: "I think it must be because, as young girls, we're all given
recipe books full of stews, and then we read all those magazines about
how to doll ourselves up; it seems that we also need stews and dolling up
to justify that 'until death do us part' business, which is a complete lie,
because when death does part you, it's just as if there was never anything
there. Well, you can see the effect it's had on me."

She was so funny, Almudena, she was like an Italian film actress, and
bright as a button, the sort of person who seems to be able to read your
mind. And last night, when I was out on the balcony listening to
Manolo's voice and looking up at the stars, for some reason, I suddenly
remembered her face; I seemed to see that mocking look of hers:

"What is it with you? Are you made of stone? People in your line of business never give anything away. Why don't you tell me something too?"

That was when I suddenly started talking to her. At first, I was talking to Manolo. I'd pressed the stop button on my cassette player to interrupt his talk at a crucial moment: he'd begun imitating the purring of a cat, something he does very well, especially right in your ear, and then I heard the sea, "Special effects, Mariana", and then, changing his tone of voice, he kept repeating my name again and again, very slowly, as if he were just breathing in and out, and after a pause, against a background of waves crashing, I heard his voice again: "I need you right now, do you understand? Now, now, now, I can't stop thinking about you. Can you hear the sea?" And I put in a blank tape in order to reply to that message of nearly three years ago, because his voice is really something. Even bottled it can make you drunk, make you lose yourself, and that was what happened: I felt as if I were lost in a labyrinth that abolished time and blurred perspective; the noise of the waves down below must have had some influence, so unchanging, so eternal. My hands were shaking as I slotted in the blank tape, in my haste to take advantage of that coincidence of rhythms, to fit my vertigo to his. "Yes, I can hear the sea, I can hear it, you have such an amazing voice, please, talk to me some more, but listen too, now, now, now, I need you now as well; do you enjoy hearing me say that?" And suddenly, without transition, I stopped whispering and I thought, but he's got another girlfriend now, another life and we're separated by thousands of miles, what am I talking about and to whom? It's just a trick of the senses, there is no coincidence of rhythms, we're not even in the same time zone, it will be mid-afternoon in New York and he wouldn't even be looking at the same stars I'm looking at, and tears started to trickle down my face. Perhaps he's gone to the cinema with his girlfriend, a thirty-year-old yuppie; what's she like I wonder, he never sent me any photos, but I bet that Sheila woman is domineering, she probably doesn't even give him room to breathe; it'll be five o'clock in the afternoon in Manhattan, they live on the East Side, maybe he's lying down in his apartment waiting for her to come back from the art gallery, or perhaps they've got a dog and he's taken it out for a walk, or else he's buying a tin of something at the supermarket. What does it matter anyway, why imagine him as the recipient of this ill-timed message? It wouldn't make any sense to him at all.

And that's when I remembered Almudena, who had so often complained that psychiatrists never tell you anything, and I simply changed conversational partner, just like that. Now I was telling Almudena all that stuff about the dog and the supermarket and the overpowering New York girlfriend, seized as I was by a ridiculous fit of jealousy, so intense that I couldn't stop crying and had to use a Kleenex. "Just to show you that we psychiatrists aren't made of stone," I concluded. Even I find it odd, this obsession with Manolo Reina that has gripped me these last few days, much more so than when he was here with me and spoke with great conviction about a future in which we would share dreams, books and journeys – a prospect I actually found rather hard to stomach – and I used to quote that line to him about: "We sing what we have lost." Deep down, though, his plans for the future gave me a future too, which is why I could allow myself the luxury of rejecting them, because they made me someone with solid foundations and a life to look forward to. That summer, when I visited the house in Calle de la Amargura for the first time, life was a long road full of crossroads well provided with different inns where I could spend the night; I could even spend the night out in the open, like the hare in the field; I could escape if I wanted to and transform myself into a solitary, unsociable hare; I could be mistress of my own fate. What I can't bear is feeling that I've been ordered to leave. That's what it comes down to, love for me is just a pretext: it gives me the opportunity to play at all or nothing, to run the risk of losing without ever actually giving up control, to leave the table when I want, not when I'm told to. For me, Almudena, men have always been a pretext. You see me crying now? Well, two weeks ago I was crying just as bitterly for another man, and I thought it was the end of the world, but the reason my world fell apart was more because I felt I'd been told to leave; what right had he to tell me that I needed a psychiatrist?

And out came the tale of Raimundo and, of course, Silvia. I even told her about Guillermo, although, to be honest, I haven't thought about

Guillermo in years. By the time I went off to university in Barcelona, I could think of his face without the slightest tremor, and I confessed to Almudena that what had impelled me recently to romanticize this former love was your reappearance, Sofía, which has stirred up so much muddy water and set me off on this crazy, solitary striptease, so much so, that I ended up talking not only about you and the letters I write to you and don't send, but also speaking directly to you as well when necessary, and to Raimundo and Silvia and Manolo, so that the terrace gradually filled up with all these ghostly presences and my monologue became increasingly fevered; perhaps I should apply for a theatre grant from some progressive drama company, although doubtless someone has already come up with the idea of the multiple interlocutor.

My creative impulse ran out of steam, however, and by the end of my peroration I had returned to the theoretical rails, as if it were an impeccably prepared lecture in which the proper names were mere footnotes. I used them in order to guide my discourse towards an unhappy ending. Like a naughty child who delights in dismembering all her toys, I continued my autopsy on sexual passion, becoming more and more Dr León before a distant Almudena, showing off my lucidity but all the time knowing that I was obeying a defensive reflex action, knowing that all my theories about love are merely an experimental vaccine against the poison incubating in the black hole being relentlessly dug by loneliness.

What did I have to tell her, anyway? What had I learned from my erotic experiences? Well, to sum up: that we cannot get inside anyone else's skin, however fondly we may imagine we have achieved this through a momentary illusion of oneness. That's what I thought I saw so clearly as I sat crouched on the terrace in my silk pyjamas, mumbling into the tape recorder, my voice sounding oddly opaque, quite different from the voice with which I'd responded to my illusion of oneness with Manolo. I saw that love is pure adventure with no real point to it, at least according to the agnostics – a chilly belief, bright and tinged with the same bluish light as the moon on the dying waves. Don't you believe it, Almudena, there is no oneness: every being is radically different from every other being, although sometimes we happen to break on the shore

176

at the same moment, like the waves that chase each other and coincide for an instant on their foamy peaks – yes, exactly like the waves, I repeated sadly, rocked by their dull, uniform murmur down below on the beach – enjoy, dissolve, allow those who follow behind us to pass over; and so it goes, on and on. We are discontinuous beings and there's nothing we can do about it. It's hard to bear, though. That's why we cling so hard to the amorous encounter as if it were our last hope, out of a nostalgia for a lost continuity, Bataille said as much: we resist having to die shut up inside our own decrepit individuality. Sexual excess is a substitute that tries to remedy the isolation of the self, but succeeds only in projecting that isolation on to someone else. If you're lucky, your projection may coincide with the other person's, but even then all you have are two individuals who, if they share anything, share only a state of crisis. It may be the most intense crisis imaginable, but it's also the most insignificant. It's just like the waves, chasing each other, enjoying themselves and then dissolving separately.

At one point, I was so blatantly summarizing recent readings and making use of bits of an article that won't come out right, that I came to an abrupt halt. I think it was then that I pressed the stop button, because I remembered how difficult it was to fool Almudena Sánchez and I imagined her mocking look as she half-closed her rather myopic eyes surrounded by laughter lines and said: "Come on, Doctor, you're going all round the houses and missing out the really important thing: how was it with that young man with the nice voice? Wouldn't you like it if he suddenly phoned you from reception and said could he come up to this moonlit room; however shortlived the illusion of oneness, it needn't be so very brief, it depends on the man." I don't know if I actually said something like that out loud to myself, possibly copying Almudena's voice, I'll find out when I replay the tape, if I can ever bring myself to listen to it, I've left it on the table. At the moment, even the thought of it makes me feel sick – all those incomplete statements lying in their little glass coffins!

I was wide awake and filled by a growing sense of disquiet; and, once I was in bed, that led me to pick up the detective novel and Katherine

Mansfield's journal. I need more than ever to write, Sofía, but I'm bored with the essay: none of my attempts at starting it are any good, and I keep looking for other literary models in order to find a way out of all this unfinished business. I'd like to talk to you about these problems. We could rummage around together in the pile of stories, both mine and other people's that I keep without knowing why I keep them, although what I do begin to understand is that the friction of all these things rubbing against each other creates a kind of phosphorescence that disturbs but also guides me; it's the same phosphorescence that appears in my dreams.

I was silent for a while, my head resting against the balcony wall, and almost holding my breath ("That's enough, don't think about anything, be still") as if I wanted to purge myself of all those words and simply allow myself to be filled by the smell of the sea and the cool night breeze; we don't even know how to enjoy that any more ("You do make things complicated, Mariana, you'll drive yourself crazy; go on, have a good cry"), and to the bluish light of the moon sweetening my tears were added the endless beams of light from the lighthouse that you can see to the right of the beach, high up on a promontory.

To the left of that lighthouse is the little bar Manolo took me to several times that summer. He really liked it there. "Shall we go to Rafa's bar?" In fact, he was the one who told me that if I ever fancied escaping from my mad clients and having a good think about them, there was an excellent hotel nearby, and he pointed it out to me when we went to get his car to drive back to Cádiz, a blue Fiat Uno with three dents in it. That was the first time I saw this place, glinting in the sun of a slow, fiery sunset that we stopped to savour with the wind in our faces until the last glimmers died away. "It looks as if there'll be an east wind tomorrow," he said. We'd spent all day in the open air, stopping and swimming at different beaches along the coast. It was like having serum injected into your veins, one of those rare days when everything feels new and every moment revitalizes you. And that red sun, as it sank into the sea, seemed to be ridding me of fear for ever, impregnating every subsequent moment with freedom. "The hotel's fantastic, I mean it. They have really good bands on at night. By the way, do you like to dance?" I said that I did, and we agreed to go dancing there one night, but the occasion never arose. That was at the beginning of our brief affair. We stood there together halfway up the hill, holding hands, until the last red sliver of that great globe of fire carried the day off with it, a day whose promises of continuity I've so often unsuccessfully tried to retrieve. Now that I think about it, that's what I was trying to do last night when I was talking into the tape recorder: to relive those beginnings, to eternalize the very essence of transience. It was what Katherine Mansfield was trying to do, poor woman. One thing is clear, though, there's nothing like taking a shower to help you understand things.

Fully awake now under the shower, the provisional words in Mansfield's journal, as stripped of rhetoric as the moans of the dying, bring back to me her longing for the infinite, her vain, inexpressible feeling of revolt. Everything you postpone goes bad – she knows that – and it fills her with despair, not having enough time to leave some mark on the world; and in last night's dream, what she did was to pass on to me the torch of that burning disquiet. "Don't give her anything to eat"; of course, now I remember, she splits off to become another person who orders her to write and pay no attention to the excuses of inertia. "One of the KMs is sad," she writes. "Well, leave her alone. Don't give her anything to eat." That was the key: don't feed your despair.

There you have it, Sofia, the shadowy key, hidden beneath the intermittent throng of images that Dr León advises me to control, images that gallop along vaulted corridors the moment we close our eyes, that remove the dam built by our will and the clock in order to suppress the natural desire of those images to break free. For they were born to break free and then die. The stirring speeches we address to the ghosts of our little private theatre – and the order in which we address them – are all outmoded too: shifting, ambiguous characters who, in this kaleidoscopic outpouring, change face, name and status, disguising themselves in the garments left discarded on the floor by their antecedents.

Even in dreams, I find the metaphor of the theatre a valid one. Abandoning oneself to dreams or to daydreaming is like entering the theatre and only half-remembering what went on when you leave, knowing that it will all be lost if we don't get a chance to talk to someone about it. And then, of course, it is lost anyway.

All this wealth of imagery spirals and whirls away down invisible drains, exorcised by the light that puts flight to the bats, dissolved into the shower water that slips over my skin.

Once I'm showered and dressed, I open the door to the chambermaid who brings me my breakfast and the local paper, and I think again: the day is a blank cheque.

"Do you want breakfast on the balcony as usual?"

And I say "yes" and that expression "as usual" troubles me, because I wonder how long I've been here. I notice that, as she advances into the room, the chambermaid casts an incredulous look at the table piled ever higher with papers.

"You were right when you said you needed another table and I said why couldn't you make do with the wicker one; you couldn't fit another thing on there."

And I again think of Katherine Mansfield and I notice in the reluctance with which I prowl around this area, like someone queuing up at a social security office and not even knowing the colour of the form he has to fill in, that I have rarely felt less clear about the kind of work I've come here to do, even though, on the other hand, the urgent need to do some proper work injects me with a forgotten sense of faith about this whole project with its perilous reefs and changeable nature. Everything still remains to be resolved, I think to myself, and what I should do is ...

I step aside to let the chambermaid pass, because I don't in fact know what I should do, apart from wake up a bit. I follow her out on to the terrace and, as I pass the table, I glimpse various bits of paper that I scribbled last night by way of memoranda containing advice and warnings to make better use of my time today, as if I had guessed I would need to counteract the opium of the string of thoughts provoked by these fragmentary nocturnal images.

The one thing I am clear about, however, is that these hybrid images are life itself which I vainly struggle to dam up in my organized, sensible, daytime writings. In these images beats the pulse of time passing me by, in them you can glimpse time's true face. Perhaps I should take a chance and write a poetic text, a novel perhaps, where I could give free rein to all these contradictions and abandon all this psychoanalysis. I experience that temptation like a sharp pang. Perhaps I should begin by describing the sunset that evening when Manolo Reina pointed this hotel out to me for the first time. That's certainly what you would do, Sofía.

The chambermaid has left my breakfast on the table out on the balcony and is looking at me perplexed because I'm blocking her way out.

"Is there anything else?"

"No, thanks."

"Well then, I'll see you later. Enjoy your breakfast. They asked in the sauna if you would be down before eleven o'clock."

"I'm not sure. I'll give them a ring in a moment."

From the balcony you can see the luxurious swimming pool and get a glimpse of the interiors of other rooms which, like mine, face on to it. On nearly all the balconies, towels and swimming costumes are hanging out to dry. I'll tell you about my neighbours in room 204 another time. They merit a whole letter to themselves. It's a glorious day and a hotel employee in orange overalls is cleaning the bottom of the still empty pool.

What shall I do after breakfast? Despite Katherine Mansfield's advice, my will, as if cut off from its body, will remain at the mercy of errant instincts that will take me out of the room and end up carrying me off somewhere, not that my wandering footsteps give me any special pleasure, obsessed as I am by the relationship between the different bits of paper on the table in my room, by the questions that they pose. And I'm suddenly filled, like a lightning flash, by the certainty that as soon as I get back to Madrid and walk into my office, this feeling of uncertainty will vanish. Seen from the tightrope I'm walking along, my office looks like a bolthole. However, I know that I have to confront this vertigo of indecision out of which something worthwhile might just emerge, a new direction.

You get to the beach by some rather steep steps leading down from the swimming pool. The beach is made of very hard sand, and when the tide is out, as it is today, you can walk along it to the village. It's about five kilometres, although I usually take the other road that goes inland.

I cross my legs and calmly spread butter on my toast. Having breakfast in a luxury hotel when we're grown-ups ... How I wish you were here, Sofía!

XI

From one room to another

Thinking is like jumping from one apparently unconnected room to another, rooms that belong to the present and the past, some still accessible, others closed for ever or in ruins, ours or other people's, one moment a settled dwelling place, the next a temporary refuge of which all that remains is a smell or a shifting shadow projected on to the ceiling – what city was it in? – where it took me a while to go to sleep and I could hear noises in the corridor, a hotel, the house of some acquaintances – how did I get there? – rooms that move, split in two, swap size and decor when they appear in dreams at the service of a plot cobbled together from films and novels, and you walk through them in disguise, not quite daring to recognize them, struggling to understand what dark force has brought us back to stand on these particular thresholds, and struggling to remember where that long corridor led to that we can see beyond.

Memories are scattered throughout rooms that one's thoughts visit when the mood takes them in an unpredictable rhythm outside our control. Thinking is like jumping from one room to another and, should you find yourselves embarked on this adventure, don't expect it to make any chronological sense. Each room contains four or five more inside, like Chinese boxes, except that every now and then someone behind you muddles them up, transforms them. All you know is that the one outside is the one whose walls you can see and touch just at the point when your mind takes off and starts to drift.

"It's nice that stuff about the rooms, very poetic, what else? Keep writing, don't stop!" I mutter to myself. Sometimes this is said in hushed, serious tones if the message my lips pick up emanates from a classroom, now perhaps renovated or long since disappeared, in the Instituto Beatriz

Galindo; and at other times in a warmer voice, near at hand ("Go on, Sofía, wherever it leads you and whatever the subject") when it emanates from a certain consulting room that I've never entered, but which contains a couch as well as a familiar clock and lamp.

I'm so pleased that in her letter Mariana understood how important it was to describe the room in which she works, pleased that she felt the need to draw the curtain in order to go on talking to me differently, because the sight of that couch was distorting her words. How well I understand that. I've got a small notebook crammed with thoughts on the significance of moving furniture or changing rooms. In that same auxiliary notebook, I've written a poem, "The House with the Balcony", inspired by our childish interpretations of the changing shapes of clouds. The house that the child Mariana used to see reflected in them gradually changes its shape inside the poem until it becomes the one she describes to me as an adult, a house incorporated for ever into mine, even though I've never entered it, just as what I write connects with what she writes, although we each of us go our own way, and neither she nor I know if we'll ever meet again, or when.

"The dreams that we had then were divergent dreams, just like the divergent lives we both now lead." Go on, Sofía, even if it's in hendecasyllables. Go on, wherever it leads you and whatever the subject. That's what Mariana tells me to do, and her letter, so often read and re-read, is a constant source of daydreams.

Since I got her letter, I've been sleeping on the divan in Amelia's room because I sit up until late into the night writing and looking through old bits of paper, threading together and trying to understand forgotten stories that summon up insomnia, night butterflies that will only allow themselves to be pursued without witnesses and on tiptoe. "Never lay down your butterfly net, Señorita Montalvo." No, I've got a firm grip on it now. It was in fact lost, stored away, without my realizing it, in some cranny of this room which has also undergone changes over the years; it's the last room I decorated when I was excitedly expecting my last child.

It wasn't even really my decision to stay in this room while Amelia's off travelling through the clouds. It just happened, like anything that's really worthwhile, like any change which is revolutionary by virtue of its sheer simplicity: inconceivable until it happens. So, I've abandoned the matrimonial bed, just like that. I think it was something of a relief for Eduardo. The first night he acted surprised and felt obliged to ask me what I was doing.

It was late and he must have seen the light under the door because I heard his footsteps stop outside, as if he were wondering whether to come in or not. Finally he did come in and stood there rather awkwardly, staring at the lamp and the papers scattered about the table. He didn't look well and he wore that expression of perpetual inner tension which is reflected in his inability to hold my gaze.

"You're up late."

"As you see."

"What are you doing?"

"Writing. Personal stuff."

He wasn't in the least bit curious. Everything about him now exudes a mixture of suppressed impatience and indifference.

"Oh well, that's no bad thing."

"No, not as far as I know; I'm doing it on doctor's orders."

He seemed slightly troubled and asked if I'd gone back to the psychiatrist. I looked down at the table and, like the light from a lighthouse, my handwriting winked amiably up at me from my notebook and from the loose sheets of paper. I smiled. I felt completely in charge of the situation.

"No, of course not. Don't worry. It's just that I have this alter ego who keeps telling me to write. A kind of controlled schizophrenia, if you like. You get another person to tell you what's going on in your life and that other person, who is also you, looks at it all from the outside. Then, when you want to remember it, that other person has separated off from you and ends up actually existing. That's what happened with Álvaro de Campos and Alberto Caeiro."

He was looking at me more and more uneasily.

"Who?"

185

wo of Pessoa's heteronyms. And there's another one too … now what was his name?"

"I don't know. You're in a funny mood!"

I rested my chin on my hands and sat staring into space. I've been reading Pessoa's work recently and I felt like using it to explore the stagnant waters of Eduardo's soul, as if I were throwing in a baited fishing line.

"My character is such that I detest the beginnings and endings of things," I recited, "because both are definite points. My spirit is entirely constituted of perplexity and doubt. Just as the pantheist feels himself to be a tree or even a flower, I feel myself to be several beings …"

"Please, Sofia," he interrupted me impatiently, "don't go all sublime on me. I don't know what you're on about."

"Okay, okay. It doesn't matter, don't strain yourself."

He tried to soften his reply.

"It's just that I'm dead on my feet, you don't mind, do you?"

"Not in the least. Sleep is free. 'Between the world and myself there is a mist that prevents me seeing things as they truly are, as they are for others. I do not ponder, I dream. I am not inspired, I rave …' Ricardo Reis, that's the name of the third heteronym. I just remembered."

"Great, I'm so glad it won't keep you awake at night. Aren't you tired?"

"Tired? Please! Do you know what I'm going to do? I'm going to sleep here tonight so that I don't bother you later."

There was a brief pause.

"Okay, if that's what you want," he said. He told me again how exhausted he was and that he was going to have a bath. We said goodnight and I heard his footsteps headed towards the Escorial. And that was that.

Then he was away for two days travelling and he hasn't mentioned my moving into Amelia's room since he got back; it's as if he accepted this provisional truce. His sister Desi phones him a lot. I've noticed that he's in a very odd mood lately and I know a storm's brewing. For the moment, though, he leaves me in peace.

Since I can't get up the strength or the will – if I ever do – to hold a proper conversation with him, one that will breach, or at least try to breach, the wall that separates us, I find it frankly uncomfortable lying beside a gentleman who arrives in the early hours of the morning and doesn't even tell you where he's been, and who must find my efforts to disguise my insomniac fidgeting and my attempts at regular breathing as distressing as I find his efforts to muffle the buzz of his secret obsessions and to give a tinge of normality to the few words he addresses to me before or after getting into bed.

The bed consists of two beds with sturdy legs and solid sides joined by a common headboard. During the day, they're covered by the same bedspread, a present from my sister-in-law Desi. According to her, it's made to a very exclusive design; the word "exclusive" melts in her mouth like sugar icing. It has a pattern of pink and grey diamonds on it. It's a bit stiff and difficult to fold. The beds are awkward to make, being so close together, pretending to be one, and because they're quite heavy and it's hard work manoeuvring them about, it's best done with two people.

"Maybe it's the heavy mattress," Daría says, "but they're harder to shove together than a husband and wife who don't get on."

I know what she's getting at, of course. The absurdest thing from her point of view is having to smooth the bedspread out so that it looks like it's one bed, something which she sees as a real cheat.

"Why not just accept that there are two of them. That way you can each keep to your own side and turn over whenever you want to without bothering your neighbour. You could put up a screen between them too – you've got the money – one of those Chinese ones with birds embroidered in silk; they look lovely. Now that would be real luxury. It's not so long ago that you gave me that double bed when you moved out of the other apartment."

We had a double bed in our apartment in Calle de Donoso Cortés, where we lived when the children were born. It was made out of old wood inlaid with metal and, like Eduardo's family, it originally came from Teruel.

It was there before we got married, when he lived alone in the apartment. It was flanked by a hideous great desk (I have no idea where it came from or where it went to afterwards) and by shelves supported on bricks and books in piles on the floor.

I remember the first time Eduardo took me there. It was at the beginning of autumn; I'd just finished with Guillermo and I was feeling very sad. A gentle light filtered in through the green shutters and a cool breeze drifted up from the street.

"It's like a scene from an Italian neorealist film," I said, as I stood at the door of the bedroom.

"And you look just like a girl out of an Italian film, with that slightly hobo look of yours," he said. "You go with the decor."

That was the first time he'd called me a hobo.

"It must be because I feel sad. Besides I rather like ramshackle things."

I didn't say why I was sad and he didn't ask me.

We'd had lunch in a bar nearby, and it had never occurred to me that he wanted to go to bed with me. Some things just happen like that, arbitrarily, without you realizing it or being alerted to the possibility. It was in that house that I fell pregnant with Encarna, which was why we got married. It was a rented flat with a fixed rent; it had a very strange layout, with various tiny little rooms that you couldn't imagine any use for, and a kitchen with an ancient stove. The only rooms that were well decorated were the ones at the back where Eduardo had set up a lawyer's practice with two friends, friends of my brother Santi as well.

Later, when we got married, the owner let us make alterations because he was a relative of Eduardo's and because we were considering buying it from him. I couldn't really be bothered, but Eduardo was keen. For some reason, tearing down walls has always given him a thrill. Out of those three rooms, like recesses in the large intestine of the corridor, emerged one room which, though rather irregular in shape, was nice. We made that our bedroom and put the big bed in it. Since it was high up, it looked out over a fairly bright courtyard. I got married when I was three months pregnant and the work went on for some time. I suffered badly with morning sickness. I had stopped writing completely.

Sometimes, when I emerge from the pretentious Escorial-type bathroom and I look at this present bedroom with its diamond-patterned bedspread, I have to make a real effort to reconstruct how our life was at the beginning in Calle de Donoso Cortés, what we used to talk about at night. The fact is that Eduardo's feverish desire to earn more money, whatever the cost, surfaced early on in our marriage and invaded the territory of his political ideals with suspicious speed, so fast indeed that by the time I finally realized what had happened, his new obsession had displaced his ideals completely. His sister Desi had married an extremely wealthy businessman, quite a bit older than her, who started off as a petrol-pump attendant. Eduardo saw him, and still sees him, as a role model. He was the one who got him into the import/export business which, according to Eduardo, had a big future. For me the word "future" sounded even worse in the context of business and money than it had when used to adorn political speeches. Needless to say, I was not over-fond of that goddess of the future, hauling behind her everything but the kitchen sink. Eduardo soon began to complain that I didn't support his plans or spur him on in his ambitions.

So at night, apart from mingling bodies with varying degrees of enthusiasm in the great Teruel bed, we mostly talked about money. Or rather he did. I remember a sensation of dampness and sadness, of disappointment.

"You never seem to be listening when I talk to you," he used to say.

And it was true. His words were born as if ready anaesthetized for memory. I thought very slowly at the time, as if my ideas had to make their painful way down muddy tracks. I used to stare up at the ceiling and listen to him, with no idea what to say, nor even if I was expected to say anything. Apparently it happens to certain women while they're pregnant and after they've given birth. I don't know if that's true, but that was certainly the case with me.

To be fair, though, even before I knew Eduardo, several people had already complained that I seemed distracted when they gave me messages or talked to me about practical things. Oddly enough, conversations about politics, so popular amongst people when I joined university, also failed to hold my attention; they produced in me, instead, a kind of strange distrust. God had died and so you had to find replacement idols. I, who hate any kind of preaching, was not at all amused by the verbal aggression of those clandestine dissidents. I certainly wasn't going to dethrone Christ and put Che Guevara in his place. As I think I've said already, that was one of the things that had distanced me from Mariana ever since our last year at school. That impatient eagerness to unearth every act of injustice and to declare one's solidarity with all the disinherited of the earth seemed to me particularly insincere in certain people of humble origin who, by dint of perseverance and pride, had managed to shine in their studies.

Such was the case with the young man from Aragón with thin lips and a permanent frown who occasionally attended the meetings organized at home by my older brother Santi, although it took me some time to notice him. I used to call them the conspirators. Memory is a fickle thing, and we can't know for sure by what criterion it decides that certain settings will be remembered for all time, whilst others that witnessed far more significant scenes in their day, are relegated to the realm of shadows. I say this because the room in my parents' house, where Santi used to meet with the conspirators (and which is now incorporated into the apartment next door, inhabited by other people), tends to burst into my meditations at the most inopportune moments and appears in my dreams with such persistence that I've begun to consider it part of my anatomy, like a sort of benign tumour growing in a fold of the brain, something upon which no surgeon would be able to opine if an autopsy were ever performed. I don't recall anything particularly noteworthy happening to me in that room, although my fate was in fact being decided inside it.

It was the biggest room in the house; it had a corner balcony and was always full of cigarette smoke. I slept in the room next to it and, at night, the conspiratorial murmurings kept me company and provided a kind of background music to my solitary daydreams that struggled to find some echo in my writing. Apart from my brother's, though, I didn't pick out any other voice.

"Have you met my sister?" he would sometimes ask them when we happened to bump into each other in the corridor. It seems that I used to stand there looking as if my mind were on other things, doubtless the same head-in-the-clouds expression with which my maths teacher had reproached me years before when he was discussing logarithms. Some would say that, yes, they did know me, that we'd already met, and they even greeted me by name. I became quite familiar with their names too, but I couldn't always fit faces to names. I could never remember the country boy from Aragón, Eduardo Luque, who had graduated with a law degree at the age of twenty-one and was responsible for making a certain scruffiness fashionable amongst members of the group. He himself later told me that Santi had introduced him to me five times in five different places and I never once recognized him, and that, it seems, was what most aroused his interest.

To get back to the room with the balcony: the strangest thing is that my unconscious, as far as dreams or daydreams are concerned, associates it with Guillermo who never set foot in it or in any other room of the house for that matter. Now is the time to admit it: Guillermo only touched my daily life very tangentially, and our brief relationship developed in a kind of no man's land where there was no room for either past or future. That's why, however hard I try, I find it so difficult to describe our relationship, just as I do to map the extent of its influence. Perhaps my memory – which might not be as capricious as it seems – has chosen the conspirators' room in order to hide Guillermo amongst the curls of cigarette smoke because, in the months prior to our first meeting, that conspirators' den, separated from mine by a thin partition wall, was often my only bridge to the outside world, a frontier between history and fantasy, a sort of handhold when the tide of unreality threatened to overwhelm me. Those periodic high tides also beat against a fragile little boat that bore the words Mariana-Guillermo written on its side. The hyphen that separates those two names symbolized for me the pain of absence and the fear of the unknown.

The winter, which that year had begun its rigours in early October, seemed endless. I have before me two letters from my godmother, which I won't copy out for fear that this story will end up lasting as long as that winter. Reading them, however, is helping me to reconstruct the feeling of anxiety and rootlessness that accompanied my unconscious wait for love while, in the room next door, a chorus of male voices was busy forecasting the political future of Spain.

Sofía Montalvo, my godmother and namesake, lived in Paris; she was my father's cousin, and my fantasies about a possible youthful romance between the two of them date from early childhood. The radiant figure of the fairy godmother often appeared in the stories I invented for Mariana when we were small, but I didn't tell her about my own godmother for a long time. When, one afternoon, I told her that my godmother had the same name as me and lived in Paris, she grew very thoughtful, as if trying to find some *raison d'être* for that unexpected information. She always wore the same expression when she was plunged in deep thought like that: she would stare into space and place one index finger, slightly crooked, across her lips, as if requesting silence. I had christened this look "her detective face".

I remember that we were in a café in Calle de Hermosilla, where we'd gone to have tea when we came out of school. I always associate the smell of cream cakes with the décor of that café and the mixture of excitement and pleasure you feel when you're fourteen years old and go into a public place with a friend and exchange confidences with her in a hushed voice, a feeling of self-importance and of faith in life that will never be repeated. I looked at Mariana, perplexed by her sudden silence, and saw the expression on her face. My godmother's name still floated above the cream cakes and above our heads, mingling with the coils of smoke from Mariana's cigarette. I didn't smoke at the time.

"That must mean something," she said at last in a very serious voice.

"What? The business about my godmother? It means what it says; there's no need to put your detective face on just because I've got a godmother in Paris."

"But you never told me about her before."

"So what? You haven't told me about yours. I imagine you've got a godmother too, haven't you?"

"Yes, but that's different. Mine's a great aunt and extremely boring."

Mariana's family seemed far more attractive than mine and I felt flattered that she should envy me my godmother who, from that moment, rose considerably in my estimation. I had to confess, however, that I had had very little to do with her and she might well turn out to be boring too.

"No, she can't be," said Mariana. "Besides, you idealize her. If not, why are there always so many godmothers in your stories, tell me that? It must mean something."

I think that the tendency to complicate things so typical of psychiatrists was evident in Mariana ever since she was a child. Of course, her ability to impose her personal interpretation of the facts on others was as striking as its influence was difficult to escape. She considered the subject of my godmother for some time, convinced that it could serve to explain certain aspects of my personality and my rather cool relationship with my mother. My mother obviously couldn't stand "SM II" as Mariana dubbed my father's cousin, and she'd tried to make me dislike her too.

Anyway, the fact is that I had a godmother in Paris. I say "had" because she's since died. We'd met only rarely, but she wrote to me sporadically and the two letters that made me mention her now were written in reply to one I wrote to her in which, it seems, I told her that I'd lost my best friend for no apparent reason and asked her not only for consolation, but also for advice on how to win back her affection. She was of the opinion that certain adolescent friendships are simply a stage we go through, like a bar rest in music, before more important loves come on the scene. My godmother's handwriting is a little like mine, only spikier. I don't know if Mariana would also find that significant. It had never occurred to me before today, confronted by her unfolded letters. She wrote on very thin bluish-coloured paper.

"Be quiet, be quiet, princess, says the fairy godmother ..."

I don't much like Rubén Darío's poetry. Too many swans and water lilies and wingèd horses riding forth to meet us. And yet, when I see those lines from his famous poem "Sonatina" copied out in Sofía Montalvo's handwriting, I have to admit that she was something of a sibyl. Viewed in retrospect, it's obvious that what I needed to do that winter was to fall in love. What other explanation could there be for that continual weakness of the joints and my detachment from any incentive the world might offer me? Ah yes, "the sighs that escape her strawberry mouth which has lost its laughter, lost its hue"; there was no jester on earth could have made me laugh with his pirouettes. Mariana's disappearance had done no more than prepare the ground for my transformation into womanhood and predispose me to receive the flame of love as soon as it appeared. But its fiery rays did not emerge from the conspirators' room, although one of them had already noticed me – or so he says – with voluptous intent. I, of course, had not.

It wasn't that I didn't know that men liked me – of course I did – but it was information gathered on different occasions and kept in reserve, something about which I had not yet formed an opinion, because it neither altered my plans nor changed the rhythm of my breathing.

Consequently, I didn't usually realize when a boy liked me; it was nearly always Mariana who put me wise and even then I didn't accept it with the readiness that real beliefs provoke in one's heart. Nor did it trouble me to imagine beforehand the possible upsets love might bring in its train.

"The strange thing is," said Mariana perplexed, "that you're capable, on the other hand, of inventing the most delightful love stories and are reduced to tears by the sonnets of Garcilaso and Petrarch."

"I know, I don't understand it either."

She liked it when men liked her; she said that just noticing that someone was attracted to her gave her a sense of power. She had an innate ability to influence people, which she presumably still has, although she's of the opinion that she lets everyone else do exactly as they please. I'm not sure; I think she may be deceiving herself. Anyway, I don't want to go into that just now. I'll leave it until I tell Guillermo's story, if I ever do, because this narrative, or whatever it is, is turning out to be a very rough and rugged path.

Returning to my godmother's prophecies: the fact is that the symptoms of languor, diagnosed by Rubén Darío as the heralds of an awakening of the senses, more or less fitted what I felt that winter, although the would-be prince didn't live in Golconda or in China but in Calle de Sagasta. I've never been in that house, by the way, although I've looked at it from the outside and still do when I'm passing. It has pot-bellied balconies decorated with rather ancient wrought-iron work. I think Guillermo's grandmother still lives there (or at least that's what he said in London ten years ago, so that "lives" is more than a little improbable). It's one of the houses that appears most frequently in my dreams: it has a lot of circular, slightly sloping corridors; all the rooms are on two levels, connected by a staircase, and I'm always standing on the upper level looking down. I recognize the house out of pure intuition, just as you might say that a study in someone's house reminds you of Madame Bovary's, although, of course, none of the readers of that novel has ever set foot there.

I think I've already mentioned that it was very cold that winter. In the course of it, apart from the incomprehensible distance between Mariana and myself, I'd realized something else: that my parents' relationship with each other was steadily deteriorating.

(At this point, I feel a sudden need to revise what I wrote the other day about my conversation with Soledad. At first, I looked for it in this same notebook, but the bit that interests me now is in the previous one. I must just say here what joy it gives me to have one full notebook and another one half full. I've found it now. Soledad told me that when she and Amelia were sixteen years old they spoke quite naturally about their parents' relationship. That didn't happen in my time. I never said anything to anyone about my parents not getting on with each other, not even to my brother, although I was sure he must have noticed it too. Now, I think that the silent, solitary suffering which that discovery produced in me may have influenced me in my desire to hide from my own children the deterioration in my relationship with Eduardo. Not that it did any good.)

Two particularly chilling dates stand out in that period of wintry isolation, associated in my memory with the murmurings of the conspirators: one was my visit to Mariana (which I've written about in the previous notebook) and the other was the last day of December. In the morning, my mother asked me if I had any plans for the night and that, if I hadn't, I could go with them to the house of some friends of theirs, the sort of lifelong friends you get in all families. I didn't fancy that at all, so I said that I'd arranged to go out with a group of university friends.

"Who?" my mother asked me. "You said you didn't have any friends at university."

"They're not close friends, but you don't have to be on intimate terms with someone just to see in the New Year."

"Well, I'm glad you've got up the courage to go out," said my mother. "You could have invited them here. You know I always like to meet your friends."

I shrugged and didn't reply. My mother couldn't resist trying to keep a check on my movements, a cover for certain matchmaking tendencies.

"By the way," she said, "there's a postcard for you from Mariana in Barcelona. Have you two fallen out?"

I was furious. Her question clearly revealed that my mother had read the postcard.

"Why are you always poking your nose into my things? Give me that postcard."

"That's precisely what I was going to do," she said, taking it out of her apron pocket. "You get more peculiar every day, my dear."

I grabbed it and flounced out of the kitchen, giving the swing door a kick. It still is a swing door. The kitchen is one of the few things that hasn't changed in the refuge. The changes in physiognomy that house has undergone from the time my parents got married up until the present day would require a whole notebook to itself. (Before I forget, I must go to the refuge.)

I went into my bedroom with Mariana's postcard. It depicted a snowy landscape with Christmas trees and a Santa Claus all dressed in red and laden with presents. The snow on the mountains and Santa Claus' beard were covered in bits of silver, rough to the touch. I looked at it for a while before turning it over. The words were as cold as the landscape it depicted and referred to our last encounter at her house. Cold upon cold. "Happy New Year, Sofía. When are you going to grow up?" With even more certainty than on the afternoon when we said goodbye, I thought:

"She's not in love, she can't be. A person in love would give off a different glow, would be capable of warming others with her own fire." I tore up the postcard and threw it in the bin, while I asked myself again if that ghostly figure, Guillermo, with his wolf-like face, really existed, if he was with her in Barcelona and if he too would denounce the bourgeois complacency and concern for the individual that Mariana had accused me of. Looking at the scraps of Santa Claus and snowy mountains glittering in the bin, my eyes filled with tears when I thought of Mariana and Guillermo and I silently wished them all the best.

I didn't feel that I'd reached the end of any particular stage in my life, but I made a decision to grow up in my own way. I didn't go to a party; I wanted to see the New Year in on my own, and that night I sat down to write. It was the first time I'd done that, writing not to give pleasure to Mariana or to my literature teacher, but out of imperious need, because there was no other road I could take. It was a question of life or death. I knew it was a very steep road, but I enjoyed the fact that I was capable of climbing it and that I would do so alone. When I heard the noises in the house of people coming back from their respective parties, I turned out the light and got into bed with my clothes on. I hadn't had any supper, I hadn't noticed the passing from one year to the next, and it seemed to me impossible that so many hours had gone by.

In the months that followed, I stopped inventing sentimental stories with more or less happy endings and, instead, noted down my feelings in starker, more urgent form. I wrote aphorisms and poems dedicated to myself. I used red ink for the poems born out of moments of euphoria and black ink for those in which I bemoaned my own impotence to give expression to what was oppressing me. I would return to the ones written in red ink when I was feeling low and they served as some consolation. I learned how to feel my way forwards, how to wait without hope, how to expect no answers from anyone, how to feed myself only on my own hunger to live, however moribund that felt. That has been my guiding principle throughout my life, not to become an embittered woman, and to cling on to whatever is available in order to achieve that. Of course, there's no better salvation than the pen. Thank you, Mariana, for reminding me of that. I've nearly filled half of the second notebook now, although this one is slimmer than the others.

When I used to shut myself up with my books at home or in a corner of the Ateneo library, the need to explore the void into which I'd been plunged by Mariana's absence swept away all my intentions to study and overflowed into poetic babblings which seemed to me to put me in touch with the very heart of the world. Urgent interrogations hurled into the void were scattered like electrical charges throughout the pages of all my class notebooks, amongst dates of battles, inventions, cultural revolutions, deaths of kings, births of saints and poets, commemorations, plagues and shipwrecks. I tossed my poems into that stormy sea like the flowers of a belated offering. And sometimes I dated them too.

There's one dated 27th February entitled "Thaw". I wrote it in the morning. That evening I met Guillermo.

XII

One day and two doors

I noticed her immediately and paid her particular attention because she aroused very contradictory emotions in me.

I think it was the way she had of taking the cigarette packet the receptionist was holding out to her, a gesture that seemed to be the end result, after much rehearsal, of successive shots selected for a glamorous advert with a slogan like: "Marlboro, the natural elegance of the artificial", or something of the sort. My hands are not what they were, Sofía, and precisely because I try to ignore the fact or to present it to myself as a phenomenon of no significance, when I suddenly see them as someone else might see them, for example, alongside other, younger hands, hands in which the blue veins are not yet prominent and the knuckles still wrinkle-free, the evidence of my own decline leaps out at me and the dread settling of scores I've tried so hard to avoid overcomes all my evasive strategies. The odd thing is that this woman, who immediately became a suitable subject of research, didn't seem that much younger than me, an impression that was confirmed when I saw her closer to.

We'd first met at the reception desk, just when I'd arrived with my luggage after a sleepless night, undecided as to where I should stay, still unshowered and with my soul in torment; one of those occasions when your eyes feel puffy and swollen. It was midday. She was just coming in from the swimming pool to buy some cigarettes. She was wearing a short bathrobe open over a spotted bikini that revealed a large expanse of firm, brown stomach. She was barefoot.

We looked at each other. Her face had acquired the peculiar inexpressiveness which is the fruit of much leisure and constant efforts to keep at bay any emotion that might cause unwanted wrinkles. She'd obviously been under the plastic surgeon's knife more than once as well, but she had the hands and feet of a geisha girl.

Shortly afterwards, when the bellboy had taken my luggage up to room 203, explained how the television worked and finally left, wishing me a pleasant stay, and the sounds of music from outside were drifting in and wrapping themselves around me, I suddenly realized with absolute clarity, as I stood there paralyzed, looking about me, that I was quite incapable of deciding how long I would stay here. I'd prescribed this holiday to myself as a kind of urgent sleep cure intended, in principle, as a simple halt on the road before going back to Madrid, but I now began to perceive my stay as an unknown quantity, a stay whose duration I would only discover with the passing of time.

"You don't have to decide now. At the moment, we have a room free for a week," the receptionist had said in a conciliatory tone, like someone trying to smooth away the difficulties of an awkward situation.

It *was* an awkward situation. The moment I saw those velvety hands pick up the packet, take out a cigarette and light it, I had experienced a sort of withdrawal, what Dr León calls "flashes of absence", and I saw in the receptionist's obsequious but disconcerted smile the awkwardness caused by the absorbed expression and deafening silence with which I greeted his question about how long I was thinking of staying.

"All right. Thanks. It's just that I don't know yet. It all depends on some news I'm waiting to receive," I replied distractedly, whilst I watched the woman move off again, her bare feet like flowers.

I thought about her for ages and her figure became an obstacle in my longed-for conquest of sleep. Beneath her statuesque gaze, an old, barely repressed dispute had surfaced in me, one in which envy and disdain for the woman-as-sex-object alternately brandished their weapons, with neither side achieving more than passing victories. Now it was envy's turn to take up a strategic position.

As I contemplated with glazed eyes the engraving of the iceberg which I had just discovered, I told myself it must be depression brought on by a sleepless night, by the hard time Silvia gave me. I dismissed any plans for the future and promised myself a deep, uninterrupted sleep. "When I wake up, my brain will function better."

I was, in fact, utterly exhausted and drained, so much so that I didn't even have the energy to take a shower. I hung the "Do not disturb" notice outside on the door handle, took my pyjamas out of my suitcase and, before pulling back the sheets on the bed, I went out on to the balcony, with its wicker furniture, intending to lower the awning.

The swimming pool, which is surrounded by a low stone wall that faces on to the sea and is scattered with brightly coloured sunbeds, low tables and striped sunshades, brutally invaded my senses, filling me with a desire to stay for ever in this leisurely, pleasurable world, to submerge myself in it, safe from all responsibility, detached from any problems or regrets, camouflaged in the tropical garden of its conventions. I leaned out a little further.

Beneath my terrace I saw the oval counter of a Cubist-style bar with black and pink stools; that was where the music was coming from; together with the smell of the sea, it sapped my will still further and sharpened my already alerted senses. They were playing a Beatles song:

> I'd like to be
> under the sea
> in an octopus's garden
> in the shade ...

I first heard it in Barcelona in the house of a Catalan boy I was going out with at the time, Sergi Casal. I remember it because it provoked one of our more or less political arguments, the last I think. He wasn't a steady boyfriend. I've never had a steady boyfriend. He lived with his parents, rich but rather cultivated people, in a spacious house in which he enjoyed an unusual degree of independence and all the privileges of an exceptionally gifted only child who was clearly a born leader. He's now a well-known paediatrician. I've met him occasionally at conferences. He loved the Beatles.

"How stupid!" I said. "Don't you realize how stupid the words are? 'I'd like to be under the sea in an octopus's garden in the shade?' But then their lyrics are all pretty stupid. In an octopus's garden, what an idea!"

"Only poets would come up with something like that," said Sergi. "If you're expecting poetry to be logical, then your intelligence must be getting rusty. You'd better watch it, Mariana, my love."

I got very agitated. The message that the Beatles were sending to everyone, gilding the pill with a sprinkling of poetry, was worse than stupid or absurd. It was an escapist slogan, like "Let it be", "Here comes the Sun" or "Yellow Submarine", foolish longings to immerse oneself in unreality, which, in the long run, would do a lot of damage to people, it would depoliticize them and make them more indolent, more sensual, it would lower their defences and undermine their critical faculties: What does it matter, forget about it, here comes the sun, everything's fine as it is, just let it be, and on with the party. It was, I realize, a fairly visceral speech.

"What difference is there," I concluded, "between them and that much-anthologized reactionary Manuel Machado, he of the spikenard soul of the Spanish Moor? 'My will died one moonlit night/when it was beautiful neither to think nor to desire ...', there you have it; we don't need four twits from Liverpool to tell us that."

Sergi was standing by the cocktail bar pouring himself a drink; he put the record back on, having momentarily taken it off, as if he wanted to make it clear that it was my words that had interrupted the Beatles and not the other way round. For a moment I didn't even realize. I'd got myself very worked up and I was quite breathless. Sergi came and sat down next to me on the sofa and took my hand. He was smiling, half-ironic, half-seductive. The song that advised us to seek refuge in the shade of an underwater octopus garden again began to climb the green-wallpapered walls of the room that were just beginning to be plunged into a pleasant penumbra, "I want to be under the sea" spun and bounced against the walls, threatening to distort reality. I wanted to say something, but Sergi placed a forefinger across my lips.

"You're so wild sometimes, Ninotschka!" he said, almost whispering in my ear. "If you weren't so gorgeous ... Come on, please, be quiet, 'let it be'. Would you like something to drink?"

I got up without saying a word and left the house, slamming the door. I realized at once that I'd over-reacted and I stopped by the lift. I was sure that he'd come out and call me, like in the films, but he didn't.

It was growing dark. I remember walking down Calle Aribau, crying with rage, staring up at the balconies and remembering Andrea, the heroine of Carmen Laforet's novel, *Nada*, who lived there; I was enjoying imagining that I might meet her and take her by the arm like an old friend. Perhaps she was about to go back to that dark house where she lived with her relatives – you once said that the oppressive atmosphere of that book reminded you of *Wuthering Heights*, Sofía – she would arrive having wandered aimlessly about the city in her faded dress and would stand indecisively outside the door of the house, in no mood to go back upstairs and shut herself in; I'd call to her: "Andrea!" and we would recognize each other instantly. I began walking more slowly, as if surprised at myself. It was a long time since I'd suffered such hallucinations, which before had almost always been kindled by yours, Sofía, and usually at night, for it was that forgotten goblin Noc, father of all stories, who set the world upside down. My heart turned over to see him pirouette back into life, hanging from the bars of an old balcony in Calle Aribau, by the light of the streetlamps. Andrea-Noc, one of those associations of ideas so intense and arbitrary that in one's memory they displace the reasoning that motivated them, though the latter might still be pure poetry. "You'd better watch it, Mariana, my love. If you're expecting poetry to be logical, then your intelligence must be getting rusty." Sergi was right. Why was I always on the defensive?

I realized, however subterraneanly, that my tears had ceased being a tantrum provoked by wounded pride. They were now purely poetic and illogical because they were provoked by my nostalgia for a character in a novel with whom I had never before identified. The reason I remembered her then wasn't so much because I felt alone and misunderstood in the streets of Barcelona, as Andrea had in the 1940s, but because *Nada* was one of the first novels that you passionately recommended to me, Sofía, although your mother wouldn't let us read it. At that moment, newly expelled by my own pride from the octopus garden that Sergi was offering me, I sought refuge in the memory of our first clandestine readings together, of the time when you led me by the hand into all the story gardens, when surprise was a white hare only ever to be found by those who didn't go out hunting for it. In other words, it was you I missed as I walked down Calle Aribau, for I needed to tell you all my woes, dating from way back, from the moment I stopped telling you about them. I needed to hear your opinion about almost everything. The memory of our two heads together under the lamp in my room with Carmen Laforet's novel on the table before us, that was what brought back to me the longing to hear your night-time footsteps accompanying mine. That's why Noc had come back to life as well, only to be immediately eclipsed, of course, because without you, he grows bored. It was you that Noc and I needed to find, not Andrea. I found that association of ideas extraordinary. My vocation as a psychiatrist seemed ever clearer. Ah, yes, to investigate the tortuous paths of the inner world! By then, in my final year of medicine, I'd almost made up my mind.

Now that I think about it, though, perhaps there was another element in my unease on that night walk through the streets of Barcelona, perhaps that secret controversy about the woman-as-sex-object had begun to insinuate itself into my thoughts, a controversy in which my position has not always been clearly defined – odd in a person like me, so fond of defining everything. I was insulted that Sergi had called me "gorgeous" in order to conclude an argument which I had thought was a serious one, and yet, on the other hand, I've never been able to survive without men letting me know, in one way or another, that they find me attractive, although I prefer them to keep their distance, not to get too close. I've always been like that, ever since I was eleven years old, as you well know, Sofía.

"But how can that possibly be enough?" you used to ask me sometimes, mystified.

"Well, I don't know if it's enough exactly, but knowing that I please men feeds me, perks me up. But I don't want to get involved."

"What do you mean 'involved'?"

"I mean involved, tied up – that's what the word means really – dependent on someone else."

"Does that frighten you?"

And I used to say that it didn't, that it wasn't fear exactly, but it was.

One night, at a birthday party at Sergi's house, shortly before the octopus garden argument, I got drunk for the first time in my life, me who had always claimed to be able to hold my drink and know how to control it. There were a lot of our friends there, mostly men, all of whom I had doubtless been flirting with. I can't remember a thing, but it seems (or so I found out later from one of their girlfriends) that I burst out crying and kept repeating that I was a fraud and that I would give up all my studies and my concern for the future of the working classes if I could only lose my fear of pleasure, the good life and men. That was where I got the nickname Ninotschka.

Anyway, a lot of time has passed since that evening when I first heard "Octopus's Garden" and I put up much less resistance now to those words imperceptibly infiltrating my blood; what a shame you can't go back to being twenty-something again, when crying in the street actually improved your looks, you didn't even have to glance at yourself in a shop window to check, you just took it for granted, everything seemed designed to beautify you, nothing left a mark. That was what I was thinking the other day, shortly after arriving here, when I looked out from the balcony of room 203 and that Beatles song was playing, spreading in gentle waves over the pool area until it slipped through the stone balustrade, rolled across the sands and plunged into the sea. "I'd like to be under the sea in an octopus's garden in the shade," I certainly would, what fun! "In our hideaway beneath the waves," yes, and never have to raise my head again, never, just turn my back on everything, hidden away in a secret garden.

At that moment, a waiter went over with his tray to one of the tables under the sunshades, and when he'd set down the Martini and the dish of olives he was carrying, I noticed the hand with its perfect nails emerge from the depths of the sun bed to sign the chit that the waiter held out to her. It was her, the woman I'd met in reception.

She sat up to sip a little of the red liquid through a straw and then elegantly spear an olive. She oozed boredom. "I've spent so much time poking around, looking for the causes of that boredom," I thought, "as if I were a supernumerary at the parties where it mainly occurs, picking up the pieces left behind in its trail of destruction." I couldn't take my eyes off her though. She'd got up and was making her way towards the diving board; after a brief shower, she climbed the steps. Naturally, she wasn't wearing a swimming hat. She wore her hair short. It was dyed, I think, doubtless using only the finest products.

Once she was up on the diving board, silhouetted against the sea, she looked up at my room which is immediately opposite. She smiled and waved before performing an impeccable dive into the turquoise water. I stepped back as if I'd been caught out. That was when I realized that someone, on the balcony next to me, had noticed my presence, perhaps the same person for whom the wave from the diving board had been intended. He was a thin man, but I could only glimpse his blurred silhouette through the frosted glass screen that separates each balcony from its neighbour. He quickly looked down. I guessed that he was reading a newspaper.

I came back into my room, hurriedly lowered the blinds and lay down thinking that I really should take more care of myself, perhaps get my hair cut and, of course, lose at least eight or nine pounds. I imagined how exciting it would be to go waterskiing, to be able to do the crawl properly, to go sailing, or to plan a holiday with someone capable of solving all your problems. I rejected that last idea as utterly false. In the lift, by the mirror, I'd seen a notice listing various facilities: sauna, toning tables, massage, hairdressing salon, swimming lessons. I decided that I wanted to go back to Madrid a new woman, someone Raimundo wouldn't even recognize. Then I rejected the idea of Raimundo as false too.

It was very relaxing lying between those well-ironed sheets in the half-darkness that was threaded with the noises coming from outside, and yet I kept tossing and turning, unable to get to sleep. My ambition to become the body beautiful was accompanied by my disdainful rejection of the person who had provoked it. Opposed to my troubling desire to be like her was a haughty belief in my own superiority and the parallel temptation to find some occasion on which to reprimand her for the vacuity of a life whose sole stimuli lay in consumption. I amused myself imagining the various circumstances in which that conversation might take place and ended up convincing myself that she must, in any case, be extremely boring and utterly without interest, a production-line model.

The suspicion that I already knew her, that I'd seen her somewhere else before, alternated with the feeling that I was remembering someone over whom I'd exercised some influence, possibly a patient of mine. With the couch in between us, I would never have envied her. I was sure of that. I knew too, however, that I myself had no desire to go back to the room with the couch, a room I identified more and more closely with the lion's den. No, not that; just thinking about it made me break out in an anxious sweat which, by contrast, made an imaginary dive from the diving board seem even more delicious. She was down there, sliding like a mermaid through the turquoise waters, while I pinched at fat on my stomach, absorbed in sordid soliloquies. With the couch in between us, I would never have envied her. Of course not. However, she hadn't come to my consulting room. We'd met on her turf; it was my turn to play on enemy territory. And I could do one of two things: I could throw in the towel or accept that I was at a disadvantage and be aware that in this territory, the kingdom *par excellence* of the woman-as-sex-object, she, at least in principle, looked like winning.

Or so I thought before I got up to get a sleeping tablet, swallow it down with a little bottle of Vichy water that I got out of the fridge, and slipped back into bed where I abandoned myself at last to sleep.

I woke up at about six o'clock. I half unpacked my suitcase, showered and made my first walk to the village by the path that takes you away from the beach, not knowing if it would be a long or a short walk, not even wondering why I was going there, just letting my legs carry me along.

That first afternoon I discovered the shop I've been back to many times since and to which I was attracted by its hybrid appearance: part-clearance sale, part-haberdashery and part-secondhand bookshop. I bought a toothpick holder made in China in the shape of a little dog, a ruled notebook and Katherine Mansfield's *Journal*. The stop for the buses that run regularly between Cádiz and other villages along the coast is in the same street. I asked for the timetables.

I walked aimlessly about, immersed in a pleasant sense of unreality which, by contrast, intensified the reality of my own body, lending my gaze a mixture of tension and ease – a very rare combination in me, Sofía – a perception that comes from simply concentrating on taking in the concrete world and considering its boundaries, colours and reflections. On my way there, past various houses, I'd noticed several paths going off to the right down to the sea. I didn't follow any of them but I'd paused on top of a small hill in order to orient myself. The tide was out and I saw that, if I wanted, I could walk back along the beach to the hotel from the village. There were no rocks or buildings to block my path. Although I didn't make a decision there and then, the possibility of that night-time return by the seashore kept me company on my wanderings round the village as I strolled about and noticed that evening was falling and it was growing colder.

I'd forgotten my wristwatch, I'd probably left it on the shelf in the bathroom, and I felt that was a good omen. "I won't put it on again until I'm back in Madrid," I promised myself and, for the first time, the idea of returning to my work schedule presented itself to me as something imminent; I found the thought unbearable. Besides, with every day that passes, I'm getting deeper and deeper into trouble with Josefina Carreras, the doctor who's been standing in for me ever since the Raimundo affair and who must, by now, be extremely worried. I've only phoned her once from Puerto Real. "I must phone her tomorrow," I said to myself, knowing that I wouldn't.

I suddenly felt very hungry and decided to have supper in a rather ramshackle, high-beamed restaurant in the village, apparently attended by only one waiter, a man of uncertain age and with a rather ghostly air about him, who smiled subtly, as if everything he said carried a double meaning.

"Shall I remove the other place setting or are you waiting for someone?" he asked, while he noted down my choice from amongst the list of dishes he'd recited from memory, never once taking his eyes off me.

"No, I'm not expecting anyone. You can take it away if you like, and could you bring me a chilled dry sherry?"

He made a gesture with his lips as if blowing me a kiss and remarked that we Spaniards don't much like being alone. I smiled reluctantly.

"There's more room in the back, if you want to think," he added.

"Think? No, no, I'm fine here."

"I mean at the back, beyond the bar. By the back door."

"No, really. Thank you."

He made that same gesture with his lips again and I realized it was a nervous tic. Then he went back to the bar carrying his tin tray and disappeared through a small door.

The dimly lit restaurant was a kind of vast, windowless bodega with a rather Buñuelesque look. There appeared to be too much wall and the large still-life paintings in oils seemed to have been placed here and there to cover up some imperfection or a camouflaged window. It was, I imagined, still early to have supper. There was only one other table occupied, by a young man and a not so young woman. I could have chosen any other place to sit, since the restaurant was empty, but I couldn't resist sitting next to them. They had attracted me the moment I saw them. They were an intense couple with a story to tell.

Although I only caught fragments of their conversation, by the time the waiter had taken away the hors d'oeuvres, I'd already ascertained that this was a reunion and that she had found the time between meetings much longer than he had. It would have been much easier to clarify the story if I'd been able to see their respective expressions, especially during the lulls in conversation, of which there were a large number. My best bet, though, was to disguise my growing curiosity which even I found excessive. I was incapable of saying: "This is not my business." I took out the Katherine Mansfield book and started leafing through it with feigned interest. If they noticed me, they might take me for a foreign teacher on holiday. We were separated by an ancient sideboard on whose upper shelf, underneath a still life of melons, stood a desiccated, one-eyed seagull, one of its glass eyes having fallen out.

Whilst I enjoyed the meal and pretended to be holding a silent dialogue first with Mansfield and then with the desiccated seagull, I realized that they, on the other hand, had little appetite and that the woman was drinking more heavily than her companion. Her voice oozed repressed passion and, the more she drank, the more the resolutely cheerful tone she'd initially adopted to ask him about his job, places they remembered or mutual friends, gradually gave way to another more inquisitorial one; the questions came faster and ended on a shrill rising note that overstepped the bounds of good manners. I've always been able to detect a disparity in affections by the unequal distribution of questions and answers exchanged by lovers. In the case of these two, who had clearly once been lovers, the woman asked the questions and the young man put up with them. He answered briefly, grudgingly, or else did his best to change the subject. His voice grew livelier then and he'd head off down some impossible tangent which she would impatiently cut short – "That isn't what we were talking about" – and which he would finish with a "Sorry", a forced laugh and silence, his silences becoming more and more frequent, though I could only allow myself sideways glances to investigate further. He didn't ask any questions at all. There wasn't a tremor, a trace of emotion in his voice, apart from an occasional note of slight irritation.

I thought to myself, he doubtless feels uncomfortable in a situation not of his choosing, but which he feels obliged to control, since he has no option but to grin and bear it. The important thing is to watch your reflexes, not to lose face in front of your opponent, not to give anything away, but to wear her down; in short, a defensive strategy. His unease derived from the encounter itself, it didn't go beyond that. For him it was all a matter of keeping control of the situation to which I was a witness, a spectator, and emerging from it gracefully, with everything neatly resolved. I opened my handbag and took out the notebook I'd just bought. I wrote: "Like an actor or a bullfighter. Problems of skill and invention brought to bear on each segment of the fight or text. A surrender to the present moment."

Her unease, on the other hand, like that of most of my female patients, like mine when I get out of my depth, was of quite a different order. To one's present unease are added distorting echoes that make it hard to find the resources needed to confront this conflict and to analyze its particular characteristics. It's known as "secondary disturbance" in my professional jargon. The problem is that one doesn't know how to set boundaries to that attack from the past nor how to immunize oneself against its contagion. The present situation is contaminated by the muddying presence of other situations which are withered and deformed by memory. I spent the whole of my supper thinking about this.

When I'd had my coffee and asked for the bill, they had spent some time in silence and still no one else had come into the restaurant. I suddenly felt terribly anxious and I was gripped by a strange suspicion: I felt that the couple, with their tense silence, were transferring their problem to me, somehow implicating me in their quarrel. I needed to flee from that evil spell, to deactivate it with words, the way characters do in fairy tales or the way you cry out in a nightmare just before you wake up. I realized that I had to say something to them, however banal, simply in order to prove to myself that nothing of what was happening to them was happening to me, that I did not in fact know them, and so untangle myself from their plot.

With an effort, I managed to wrest my gaze from the one-eyed seagull and to look straight at the neighbouring table, full of uneaten food, and at the faces of the people occupying it. She had put on a pair of tinted glasses, resting her cheek on one hand whilst, with the other, she was engaged in making little trails of sugar and breadcrumbs across the table cloth. I decided to speak to him – he'd just lit a cigarette – and he immediately responded to my look with an almost knowing smile.

"Would you mind telling me what the time is?" I asked.

He pushed up the sleeve of his jacket to reveal on his wrist a large, old-fashioned watch which he immediately covered up again.

"Half past. Half past ten."

"Thanks."

At that moment she grabbed his arm, furtively slipped her hand inside the sleeve and felt the young man's forearm. She seemed beside herself.

"Stop it, Eloísa, please! What are you doing?" he said, pulling away, deeply embarrassed.

"What do you mean, what am I doing? What's this? You said you never wore a watch, don't you remember? Time is measured in other ways, you used to say ..."

"Well, so what, it's no big deal. I'm fed up with all your 'don't you remembers?' I've changed my mind, that's all."

"No, that isn't all. You should have told me. Don't I deserve notification of such an important change? It's as if I didn't really know you. Say something. Why are you wearing that horrible watch? It's horrible."

His voice sounded dry and cutting as he removed himself from the hand that gripped him. Covering the watch protectively, he said:

"It isn't horrible, Eloísa. If you must know, it's a present from a person I love very much."

"You see, you see? How long have you been wearing it? What person?"

I went over to the bar to pay my bill, pursued by Eloísa's sobbing. I didn't even listen to what the waiter was saying to me. I didn't even wait for my change. My feeling of claustrophobia was so intense that I'd almost broken into a run by the time I crossed the threshold of the back door that opened on to an alleyway. It was completely dark by then; I felt cold and put on a pullover I had in my bag. I didn't feel safe until I'd wandered down various streets and lanes that led me farther and farther away from that place. Even though I was feeling calmer, I continued to walk briskly, not looking back, until, at last, I worked out where I was.

I left the village and walked on to the beach; when I reached the shoreline, I took off my shoes and started walking back to the hotel whose lights I could see in the distance in front of the lighthouse sending out its broad silver beam across the quiet surface of the sea. For a good while, the final question asked by the woman in the tinted glasses – "What person, tell me, what person?" – intercut with sobs and getting no reply, echoed relentlessly inside me, intensifying my sense of flight and the vague feeling of having left unresolved something that wasn't entirely alien to me, something irreparable. A very distant image surfaced in my memory of the scene in Raimundo's house which had only just avoided an equally catastrophic denouement. Never again, never again would I fall down such precipices.

The tide was a long way out and it was nice walking along with the waves washing over my feet. I rolled up my jeans above my ankles. As I walked along, I was idealizing my return to the hotel, my need to furnish my room according to my taste alone, to make myself a little home, a refuge where the phone would never ring and I would never have to ask anyone when I woke up from a nap: "Do you fancy going for a walk?" or "You've gone very quiet, what's wrong?" I suddenly realized that thanks to that contretemps with Raimundo – so absurd, so far away – I was enjoying the air of an Andalusian night redolent with salt sea and the freedom you get from the knowledge that no one is going to demand to know why you're late, that no one even knows where you are.

It had been a long time since I'd gone for a walk on my own at night, still less in such a deserted place. All I could hear was the dull murmur of the waves that came to die at my feet. From time to time I would stop, turn my back on the beach, wade a little further out into the sea and wait to be pierced by the magic arrow of the stars which, according to you, only strikes people who are calm and unworried, the same people in whose hearts Noc's stories take root and find shelter. As you see, Sofía, evoking your memory is my one true anchor, or rather, as you *will* see, because one day I hope to share my impressions of this journey with you. You're the one encouraging me to write them down, the person structuring and holding them together, like an invisible skeleton that will endure when everything else has disappeared.

I was just coming up to the rear of the hotel, which was crowned by a red neon sign displaying the hotel name in reverse since most customers, of course, arrive by the front drive and park their cars there. From the beach you get to the swimming pool by some rather steep steps cut into the rock which I'd noticed when I leaned out of my window that morning. I stopped on the first landing to look at the balconies outside the rooms, trying to locate mine and failing to do so with any exactitude. Some were lit up, on others I could see people sitting or moving about. It must have been quite late. From inside the hotel I could hear blues music playing and as I went on up, with my eyes fixed on that façade, a feeling of strangeness rose in me like a fever. You know the feeling well, Sofía, that sudden sense of being uprooted that makes us cut our links with all our usual reference points, blurs the outlines of the world and carries us off along the coasts of literature. How much time had passed? Did one of those little unlit balconies really belong to my room? I couldn't even remember the number or how the furniture was arranged. Why did I call it mine then? I have to conquer it first with my eyes, I said to myself, and then inhabit it. I'll call Josefina Carreras to tell her that I'm staying on. Brief visits are like footprints in water.

I'd just got to the top of the steps and had sat down to brush the sand off my feet, roll down the bottoms of my jeans and put my shoes on. I could hear a piano playing; it was closer now. There was a brief pause, and then I heard the first chords of "Strangers in the Night". It was at that moment, just as I stood up and started walking back towards the hotel foyer, drawn by that melody, that I was gripped by a strong temptation to write a novel, a temptation I surrendered to. Why not? Only days before, I'd been filled by hundreds of ideas and possible beginnings, but my previous commitment to the essay I was writing had placed a barrier before them. It's an old project gone into hibernation; it revived, spread its wings and gleefully took charge of my will. I seemed to see you smiling a satisfied smile: "Of course, enough of theories. Write a book with a cover like a romantic novel. The essay on eroticism bores you, admit it, it's gone stale on you." You're right. Anyway, I could use some of its more inspired bits, without bothering with quotes or conclusions, simply as an adornment to the central argument: mature woman escapes. I remembered all the unsent letters I'd written to you since I took the train south and my enthusiasm redoubled. "For Sofía and for Noc, from afar." I searched in the sky for the Great Bear, I felt your hand in mine and my eyes were filled with the tears of childhood. The stars despise our mean little tales, our chronological order. It could be a sort of disorderly diary with no very precise before or after, written out of those feelings of strangeness, playing with the contrast of unexpected emotions, with the alternating current of disparate moods that imperceptibly transform a person.

For example, as I was thinking this and walking nimbly and cheerfully across the pool area – completely empty at that hour, with all the sun beds taken in – I looked at the diving board reflected in the still water and I had to ask myself if I was the same person who, some hours before, had given rein to those tortuous meditations on woman-as-sex-object that had scattered now like a flock of black birds. The piano music was coming from the foyer which is separated from the swimming pool by columns forming an archway. I went over there, humming the words that Frank Sinatra has forever dedicated to all strangers passing in the night.

What fun, Sofía, entering a hotel by the back door! A great improvement, don't you think? I didn't like the woman who arrived this morning by the front door and I'm sure you wouldn't have either if you'd seen her. Let's hope she doesn't come back. Listen, I could use that two-doors idea in the novel, don't you think? One day and two doors. I arrived like someone washed up from a shipwreck and I return like a detective. Yet another coincidence: at the restaurant with the seagull I came in one door and went out the other. Is that significant? It would be such a laugh if you were here! You'd say: "Come on, don't put your detective face on now, we're just about to tiptoe into this luxurious foyer. Have you noticed how sweet the music sounds and how shiny the floor is? And you like an urchin, with the bottoms of your trousers wet. Let's play at being Heathcliff and Cathy when they went into the garden at Thrushcross Grange at night and climbed up on to a window ledge to peer into the Lintons' living room. Don't make a sound, Mariana, or they'll set the dogs on us."

The pianist was black and only a few people were listening to him, scattered amongst three or four tables placed round a small dance floor. I leaned, half-hidden, against one of the columns leading into the foyer while I waited for him to finish "Strangers in the Night", then I emerged from my hiding place and went straight over to one of the empty tables, the one nearest the piano. There was a little light applause to which I added my own, loud and long. The pianist repaid me with a smile and I responded with another.

"Excuse me, do you know 'Treachery'?" I asked when I'd sat down.

"Sure I do. I'll play it for you with pleasure."

"It's for a friend of mine actually," I murmured. "It's one of her favourites."

The waiter came over and asked if I was staying at the hotel. I said that I was but couldn't remember my room number and I indolently held out a business card so that he could confirm my name at reception. I found all this immensely amusing and, needless to say, it was all done for your benefit, like my request for the pianist to play 'Treachery'. I ordered an iced coffee. Then I closed my eyes to enjoy to the full the melody he was beginning to play for you, the young Sofia, because time doesn't exist.

> Who knows where you are,
> or what adventures you're having -
> now that you're far away from me!

I hoped that you would be about to embark on a lovely adventure, something that would get you out of your matrimonial rut and away from your plumbing problems.

When the waiter brought me the iced coffee, I languidly opened my eyes and that was when I saw him. He was on his own, sitting directly opposite me, with his long legs crossed and holding a half-empty glass of whisky in his hand. He was wearing a suede jacket and he couldn't take his eyes off me. Can you believe it? A nice-looking executive, a bit like Gregorio Termes, intrigued by the lady with the windswept hair and no make-up, wearing her detective face. I held his gaze for a moment. He's not a very interesting type, but better than nothing, and he could prove useful to the novel. He was obviously bored.

When the pianist had finished playing "Treachery", I took out the notebook I'd begun at the table in the restaurant of the one-eyed seagull and started writing furiously, notes for what I'm writing now, several days later. I felt flushed, beautiful, happy. Every time I chanced to look up, I'd find the eyes of the man in the suede jacket gazing into mine. He's been looking at me ever since.

What I didn't know – and I'm sure you'll find this very amusing – is that he's with the woman-as-sex-object. They're my neighbours in room 204.

XIII

The red dress

I was wearing a very special dress, a red dress. Everything happened because of that red dress or, rather, because of the feelings it released in me when I wore it that first time. I've often gone over the early stages of that night and, even allowing for the continual retouching that memory performs on favourite scenes from the past, I think I can say with some confidence that the red dress was the main focus. As soon as I close my eyes to relive certain details – certain angles or forgotten figures – the first thing that explodes in the middle of everything else is the colour red and my body coming to life again inside that fiery sheath whilst my eyes follow a silhouette, also surrounded by a red glow, which is kneeling before a fireplace, trying to rekindle the flames with a bellows. I'm sitting on a sofa behind him. He's a man whose face I have yet to see.

The university friend who took me there was called María Teresa, I can't remember her surname; she wore glasses, talked about female emancipation, chewed her nails and swore, a custom still unusual amongst women of the time. She moved in the same circles as my brother Santi; they were all members of the same student movement, although, as far as I know, she never set foot in the conspirators' room. Very few girls went there, apart from the occasional girlfriend who came to pick one of them up, something which my mother, by the way, did not at all approve of. Since María Teresa preferred to engage in political plotting in the bar to attending classes, our relationship consisted mainly of an exchange of lecture notes – with me in the role of lender – which, to judge by the insistent, agitated way she always asked for them, seemed to be a matter of vital importance to her. Her tense face reflected either her eagerness to move me to pity or her anticipated indignation at any possible refusal, and she had a hesitant, breathless way of formulating her request.

These symptoms were not unfamiliar to me. When we were doing our baccalaureate, Mariana and I were always playing around with ideas and one of the things we invented was an era of rudimentary culture which we christened "copiomanuensis inferior" whose individual members were obsessed with obtaining, as their prime source of nourishment, other people's lecture notes. We even got as far as drawing comic strips depicting the copiomanuenses, little creatures with insect heads and sucker-like lips. They wore leather loincloths and carried a quiver full of arrows over their shoulder. While the lecture notes were sleeping, they would tiptoe up to them, kneel down and suck their vitals from them, although often they would risk going out to hunt them down in order to carry them back to their caves and offer them up as trophies to their wives. Mariana and I wrote the text of those adventures together, over my original drawings. Only a short time ago, I found one of the strips inside a book and I gave it to Encarna because she liked it so much. She says she wants to put me in touch with a friend of hers who writes comics. However much we love each other, though, Encarna can never share the pleasure Mariana and I got from inventing the nomenclature – the 'notadocus' and the 'notasaurus' – and the laughter when we passed the latest of the comic strips from desk to desk in class: no one else in the world can share that, apart from Mariana. I wouldn't enjoy talking about it in such detail now if I hadn't seen her recently at Gregorio Termes' exhibition and we hadn't laughed together about the hare in the field, the password by which we recognized each other amongst all those strange people and which first gave her the idea of setting me homework to do. Keep writing, Señorita Montalvo, wherever it leads you.

As you see, today it's the turn of the copiomanuenses, who were definitely not on the agenda, all because tonight I sat down to write with the firm intention of clarifying the Guillermo affair. It's pointless having firm intentions. Perhaps all these tangents I allow myself spring from a strange certainty that the name Guillermo does not mean the same to her as it does to me, and that the stories it evokes in each of us will not necessarily unite us; they might quite possibly have the reverse effect, as Mariana hints in the one letter she's written to me. Yet I'm sure that those childish cartoons of antediluvian hunters are still hidden in some fold of her memory, as clear in her mind as they are in mine, and that they will unite us, as long as we have breath in our bodies, because they belong to the realm of certainty. The landscape was very rugged and planted with some sort of cork trees; the lecture notes used to fly above the rocks and the shrubs in the guise of enormous, flattened birds. At other times, they took the form of kangaroos or giant lizards with strange geometrical profiles; they escaped by taking sideways leaps into the undergrowth, and, with their bulging polyhedral eyes, they would watch the advance of the enemy. Regardless of whether they ran or flew, however, their skin was covered in lines of dense calligraphy, giving them the veined appearance that marked them out as targets, even at a distance – the prey most coveted by the arrows of that tribe of huntsmen.

Anyway, María Teresa belonged to that species of copiomanuenses which I had believed to be extinct, and, without the support of Mariana and her comments, I found it extremely tedious having to deal with that surviving example of the species. So surprised was I to find that the species was still in existence that, at first, I thought she must be some kind of optical illusion; after all, the subjects you study at degree level are hardly elementary. I just couldn't conceive how anyone could possibly gain any advantage from the hunting and capture of other people's lecture notes which were difficult to interpret even for the person who'd written them, or, indeed, for the teacher who'd dictated them, because lecturers tend to summarize what they've read in various books and then add a few points of their own. It also depends on the mood they're in when they give the lecture and on their capacity for concentration and on how well they've slept. At first, I tried to discuss these matters with María Teresa and to impress on her the futility of her labours as a copiomanuensis in comparison with the advantages afforded by getting the bibliography at first hand. Unfortunately, she never showed herself to be in the least receptive to my advice, which she thought was just meanness on my part, nor to the matter under discussion, despite the fact that by going deeply into it you would get to the very heart of textual analysis which, after all, is what the study of literature is all about. It was like talking to a brick wall. Bearing in mind, moreover, that María Teresa was not famous for her sense of humour, I soon realized that our talks on the subject had no future, so I accepted her limitations and stopped asking for the impossible.

We'd never really spoken to each other for more than half an hour at a stretch, except on that evening when I wore the red dress for the first time. I seem to remember that she was wearing a three-quarter-length corduroy jacket in black or grey, though I'm not sure. She has been saved for ever from the fires of oblivion not because our conversation that evening revealed unexpected affinities between us that had remained hidden until then, but because what happened that evening performed the miracle of converting that late example of "copiomanuensis inferior" into "the girl who took me to the party", a transformation which has elevated her to a higher plane in my memory.

As I said before, I've done little lately but think about Mariana, writing all this down for her in the hope that one day she'll read it. That's the only justification I can give for having gone on at such length and in a rather flippant tone about such a colourless figure as María Teresa; I remember how much Mariana always liked subplots and minor characters. Now, unfortunately, I feel unable to leave anything out because it seems wrong to put in lots of details about one thing but not about another, so if I continue in this vein, who knows how many pages I'll have filled by the time we finally get into that house with the fireplace. I'll probably fill this entire notebook. Still, I'm enjoying myself and there's no one here to call me to account. So there it is. I can't see any harm in it.

The first thing I have to explain is the red dress.

My godmother had just sent it to me via some Paris friends of hers, Monsieur and Madame Richard, who were visiting and had come to see us at home the previous evening. My parents had been arguing on the phone about the visit a short time before; he was calling from his office to say that he might be fifteen minutes late and my mother reacted sharply and angrily: there was no way she was going to receive them if he wasn't there. I don't know how it all ended. I went out and when I came back they had already arrived.

I can see myself now standing in the inhospitable living room we called the "screen room" with the parcel from my godmother clutched to my chest, sensing through the paper the soft texture of what I was convinced was some really chic dress, whilst I reluctantly listened to my parents' conversation with that slightly older couple. I think the husband was someone important, someone on whom my father, for whatever reason, wanted to make a good impression. My mother was wearing make-up and high heels. They were planning a trip to Toledo the next day, a city that the Richards had never visited. I'd only been called in to receive the present they'd brought for me and I realized all too clearly that if I gave in to the temptation to sit down, I would end up being dragged along on that tedious excursion. The atmosphere at home had been very strained ever since Christmas and I'd often had to do what I could to mitigate it and to ease tensions, forgetting my own griefs for once. After all, I was the daughter, a daughter who could be very nice when she wanted to be and who spoke French well, a skill which, in that particular case, was rather to my disadvantage. Suddenly, though, all I wanted to do was to open the present; I found everything else unbearable. That desire became as powerful as my desire to escape from the living room and from the cranes and butterflies embroidered in grey silk on the screen from which, oddly enough, I found it hard to look away, as if my eyes felt safe there.

Mme Richard was an elegant woman with a small, expressive face, and my mother was struggling to keep up a conversation with her without betraying her total lack of interest; unfortunately, the rictus of boredom on her face let her down. My father was talking about the destruction of the Alcázar in Toledo and about the *Burial of Count Orgaz*. M. Richard was very keen on El Greco, and Papa said nothing to contradict him, although within the family he'd always described El Greco as a specialist in portraits of TB patients. I dragged my gaze away from the cranes on the screen and looked at Papa. His alarm at this uncomfortable situation was revealed in a nervous tic barely noticeable to anyone who didn't know him and which consisted in an intermittent clenching and unclenching of his jaw. It was his silent way of asking for help. He looked at me and realized that I'd noticed.

"What's wrong, Sofía?" he asked rather harshly. "Why don't you sit down?"

"I'm sorry, Papa, but I was just about to go out and, besides, I want to open my godmother's present, you don't mind, do you?"

Ever since I was a child, I'd always known how to speak to my father in exactly the tone of voice he liked, a mixture of gentleness and firmness. It came to me naturally and had an immediate effect.

"You could just as easily open the parcel here," said my mother.

"I know I could if I wanted to, but ..."

"But what?"

There was a silence.

"But, as is only to be expected, she would prefer not to."

It was the French woman who had spoken. She smiled kindly. My mother didn't respond, but I could see that the threatened storm, darkening her brow, was growing imminent.

"Sofía might well have sent her a note inside the parcel – you know what a one she is for writing people little notes," continued Mme Richard, "and letters from godmothers are secret aren't they, *chérie?*"

I stooped to give her a kiss.

"Yes, Madame. Thank you for being so understanding."

"You always manage to get your own way in the end, don't you" said my father who had clearly been won over.

"That shows she has a strong personality," remarked M. Richard.

Mama didn't say anything. I said goodbye politely and almost flew out of the room.

The red dress was indeed accompanied by a note. I read it before trying on the dress.

"I don't know if this will fit you," the note said, "but fire knows no sizes. May all your ghosts be burned up in this bonfire and your body come to life again."

It was exactly my size and fitted me like a glove. As for the resurrection and the burning of ghosts, which were very much auguries in keeping with those formulated in fairy tales, I have to confess that I stood for a long time looking at myself in the mirror, waiting for some marvel to occur. The girl in red split off from me, as if she were a stranger; she smiled a sensual smile with which, as it grew wider, she seemed to be inviting me to participate in some dangerous exchange of confidences. She withdrew then advanced towards me with languid steps, holding her arms above her head and then slowly lowering them again. The dress had a square neckline, quite low-cut, with two clips at the corners. Of course, neither the dress nor that way of moving were really my style, but I thought I looked lovely. When I think about it now, the greatest transformation consisted precisely in my pleasure at discovering that different look and liking what I saw. I don't think I'd ever before gazed at myself in a mirror for such a long time, it was like a form of hypnosis.

I abruptly awoke from the trance when the door opened and my mother appeared to tell me that there was a phone call for me. Her surprise, initially motivated by the fact that I hadn't heard the phone – which was in the corridor immediately outside my bedroom – only increased when she saw me converted into a kind of Marilyn Monroe figure rehearsing for a role. The oddest thing of all was that I didn't even feel embarrassed. On the contrary, I exaggerated my theatrical pose and made a brief curtsy.

"Whatever's wrong with you? What are you doing?"

"Nothing. I'm just trying on the dress that Sofía sent me."

"And why all those strange gestures?"

"Please, Mama, can't I have a bit of fun? Surely, we don't always have to treat life as if it were a third-rate funeral."

She stepped aside to let me pass.

"Really!" she said. "It looks outrageous on you. It makes you look like a tart."

I sighed as I watched her walk away down the corridor. Then I leaned against the wall and picked up the telephone.

It was María Teresa and I must admit to being disappointed, not because I was expecting anyone else to phone me that evening, or rather precisely because of that: since I wasn't expecting anything, there was room for the unexpected. And while I listened to the usual request for lecture notes, formulated this time in a tone of panic, I bent one knee to rest my foot against the wall and stroked the skirt, soft as suede, clinging to my thighs.

"Are you still there, Sofía?"

"Yes."

"I thought we'd been cut off. It's just that I've got really, really behind with my notes. I haven't got any notes for the History of Grammar since before Christmas, can you imagine? Are you listening?"

"Of course."

"So when can we meet?"

Tomorrow was Sunday and I'd decided to spend the whole day in the Ateneo to avoid family entanglements. I arranged to meet her at seven o'clock in the bar there.

So Sunday was the day I first wore the red dress. With an overcoat on top, of course, because I left the house early and it was cold. I wore my coat unbuttoned, though, in a slightly provocative fashion.

I've never paid much attention to the division – much more rigid then than now – between everyday clothes and evening wear; besides, I think it's bad luck to delay wearing a new dress for the first time. Anyway, as I was walking along and looking at myself out of the corner of my eye in shop windows, even I had to admit that it wasn't really a suitable dress to wear to study at the Ateneo. I felt rather uneasy when I realized that my choice had been influenced less by caprice and more by my mother's dismissive comments and my eagerness to go against her wishes. I had already begun to glimpse something which would become ever clearer as time passed: to free yourself from the influence of the other lives that touch your own, it's not enough to slam the door and flounce off down the street.

I didn't get much work done that Sunday and I didn't write anything much either, apart from a short poem entitled "Thaw" which actually isn't that bad. It speaks of the longing with which a numb soul awaits the arrival of spring, like the advance of an army brandishing burning torches. I wrote it at one sitting. The rest of the time, however, I spent making several false starts to a letter addressed to Mariana, tearing up each successive draft and throwing it in the wastepaper basket. I couldn't find the right tone and that was because, instead of thinking about what I wanted to say, I kept trying to second-guess how she might be feeling about me, and the crossings-out were a reflection of my all-consuming insecurity. Finally, I opted for a jolly tone, but that didn't work either. In the last version that I tore up, I'd included a new comic strip of the copiomanuenses and a little drawing of the red dress with tabs on the shoulders like those cut-out clothes for paper dolls. It was no good. Mariana wouldn't be amused by those drawings, she wouldn't think them a stroke of genius, or at least I couldn't be sure that she would. So I gave up, as hopeless, a venture which I am perhaps resuming today. You can only feel free to decorate letters with drawings when you are certain, rightly or wrongly, that the addressee is going to enjoy the contents immensely and find the letter all too brief, "Keep writing, Señorita Montalvo"; then it doesn't matter what you put, even if it's silly, because anything that you write about with real feeling automatically ceases to be silly. That's what it's all about.

At a certain point in the afternoon, I began to feel very uncomfortable and to wonder if it wouldn't have been a better idea to have joined my parents and M. and Mme Richard on the trip to Toledo because at least there I would have felt useful and in my place. They were thinking of staying the night. It worried me imagining them walking down those narrow streets, wrestling with their inner tensions, trying hard to make it a memorable day. Their pointless wanderings weighed on me from afar, and I reproached myself for being selfish, a selfishness which, in the end, had destroyed my own illusions of fulfilment.

Sitting at the desk opposite was a balding young man with the look of someone cramming for an exam; he was compulsively underlining strings of sentences in different coloured inks. Every now and then, he would sigh deeply, scratch his head and stare at my neckline, at first surreptitiously and then more and more boldly. This contributed to my growing sense of unease and my inability to concentrate. The afternoon had taken a strangely boring turn. From my satisfaction at seeing the image reflected back at me in the mirror, an image that presaged disquieting transformations, I was now sliding down the slippery slope of distrust and self-consciousness about my own mistakes towards a blind desire to throw stones at mirrors and to smash every one of them.

Finally, I collected up my books and went down to the bar half an hour before I'd arranged to be there. The afternoon seemed endless.

When María Teresa arrived, we had a coffee and I handed her my notes on the History of Grammar which she immediately weighed in her hands and, overwhelmed, leafed through them – a task she undertook by wetting one fingertip – more in order to count the stapled sheets of paper than to get even the slightest idea of the contents; it seemed to plunge her into a terrible depression.

"Forty pages! Did he really give you all these notes! It's an awful lot, isn't it?"

There was a shadow of reproach in her voice.

"Well, they're the notes from January and part of February, you've got the dates there. Look, you hardly ever come to class, what do you expect?"

"There are more important things than going to classes," she said rather bitterly.

"That's your business, I'm not going to argue with you, but don't come complaining to me afterwards. You might as well just stop studying."

She was still looking at the notes.

"Do you know all this already?" she asked.

"No, I don't. I'll look it over when it's time for the exam. And can you copy them out more quickly this time; you kept the last lot for ages."

"I'll try," she said. "There are an awful lot of them."

Sighing, she put them in a grubby blue file, paid for the coffees and we left together.

"Have you finished studying for the day?"

"Yes, it's been fairly fruitless anyway. Some days are like that."

227

We started walking in silence towards the Plaza de Santa Ana. It was one of those windy, clear-skied evenings that you get at the end of February, and, in the trees at the end of Calle del Prado, you could glimpse glimmers of spring. I stopped to look in the window of a secondhand bookshop that's still there today. Every time I pass it I remember. There was a large print in sepia and red depicting a nineteenth-century lady reclining voluptuously on a sofa. In her right hand, which was resting on her lap, she was holding a letter that she had presumably just finished reading. Her eyes, staring out of some invisible window, still glowed with the fire provoked by the words of that absent lover, words that completely impregnated the whole scene. At one time, that discovery would have given rise to one of the many novels I used to invent for Mariana when we were small, novels filled with dreams of romantic love. From how many poems and songs had we imbibed the inflamed air of a lover's absence? For absence is the air that extinguishes the small fire and kindles the large. Suddenly, when I saw myself reflected in the window, with my red dress on beneath my unbuttoned overcoat, staring at that paper lover, I realized that I wanted to discover for myself, just as Mariana had, the difference between the real and the painted. I realized that it was no longer enough to invent stories or to have them told to me; what I really wanted was to fall in love. Well, I may not have put it in quite those terms, but that's how I always remember it when I pass that bookshop now. I was utterly absorbed, though; my heart was beating fast and the dress worn by the woman in the picture was red like mine.

"What are you looking at?" asked María Teresa.

"That engraving. I really like it."

"The one of the woman reading the letter? Well, I don't. It's really kitsch."

We walked on. There were a few jumbled, steely clouds in the sky. It was just the sort of night I would have stayed over at Mariana's house, since my parents wouldn't be back until the following day. I felt a thrilling mixture of nostalgia and rebellion. I missed my friend intensely, but I needed to burn all my ghosts, to break the tyranny of the vicious circle. There must be some route along which I could escape towards the unknown.

"Where are you going?" asked María Teresa when we reached the Plaza de Santa Ana.

"I don't know. I might go for a walk. Is that your Isetta?"

"Yes. I can drop you somewhere if you like."

María Teresa had stopped next to a two-seater car, round and transparent, one of those so-called "bubble cars". It was designed a bit like a helicopter cabin and the door opened at the front. It was a fairly cheap Italian model, and in pre-consumerist Spain they were, briefly, all the rage. I looked enviously at María Teresa while she lifted the oval door of her Isetta and revealed the two passenger seats. I'd never been in a car like that and I suddenly had an intense desire to do so. It looked a bit like one of the little cars on a children's roundabout.

"Where are you off to?" I asked.

"I'm going to the house of some friends of mine; they live in a commune near Pozuelo. It's someone's birthday. They said I could bring anyone I liked. Your brother will probably be there. Do you want to come?"

With sudden enthusiasm, I said "Yes", and that was how I came to ride in that rather surrealist glass contraption towards the house with the fireplace. My brother wasn't at the party. There was no one there I even dimly remembered, no one who would notice my presence. My fairy godmother had prepared the scene well.

The people who had started setting up communes around that time prided themselves on flouting bourgeois convention and always paraded a mild degree of untidiness and disorder as evidence of their spontaneity and lack of inhibition. They gave any mention of people like Marx and Simone de Beauvoir a modern, efficient slant by skilfully intermingling such remarks with statistics on the number of people in exile, the birthrate and unemployment, a few records by Raimon or Brassens and the joys of free love. When they held a political meeting or a party at one of these communes, usually houses on the outskirts of the city rented by

229

a group of people, no one visiting the house for the first time – having been brought there by a friend – could expect to be introduced to anyone else or to be told which of the people present were permanent residents or the identity of the parents of the children rushing around.

What's happening to me as I write this is very strange, a kind of free association of ideas. I seem suddenly to have discovered the underlying pattern – taking into account all the apparent differences that might disguise the similarities – that forms the basis of "elite" gatherings like the one the other day at Gregorio Termes' house, gatherings where, because everyone considers themselves to be one of the elect, a fellow conspirator, the motto is: take no notice of anyone else. I bet Gregorio was one of those 1960s trendies who didn't wash very often, lived in a commune and launched furious attacks on the bourgeoisie. He might even have been at that house in Pozuelo when María Teresa and I arrived in her Isetta.

There were two large, rather shabby rooms in the shape of an L, which were separated by a sliding door that was open at the time. The door that gave on to the garden wasn't shut either and María Teresa simply pushed it open without bothering to ring a doorbell. The walls were lined with cork and there was a staircase up to the top floors where, to judge by the intermittent sounds of voices, laughter and music drifting down, most of the party guests were gathered. There were very few adults in the downstairs part, but there were a lot of children lying about on the floor reading comics or playing with wooden building blocks. Others came and went from the rather unkempt garden where I could see a swimming pool with chipped tiles and some greenish water at the bottom. There was a dog too.

I think María Teresa almost immediately disappeared upstairs. She may have said hello to someone first. She may have asked if I wanted to go upstairs with her. I don't know. I don't remember anything about that. From the moment I went into that L-shaped room full of shelves supported on bricks, posters pinned to the cork walls, half-empty bottles, toys, pillows, ashtrays and books scattered about the floor, I had eyes only for a blond boy in corduroy trousers and a check shirt who was crouched by a fireplace and a dying fire in the right-hand corner of the room, carefully stirring the embers with a poker. Oblivious to anything outside himself, his look of absorption gave the impression of someone engaged in a task of fundamental importance: reviving a fire. I've no idea how long I stood there looking at him before walking slowly but inevitably over in that direction.

On the way, I spotted a tray of drinks on a small octagonal table and paused to pour myself a glass of wine. It was cheap red wine and the cups were made of paper. There was no cut-glass goblet, no amber-coloured liquid, nothing that suggested the love potions that transformed the Infanta Flérida or subverted the will of Iseult; there was no apparent reason to be on guard. I took the first sip nonchalantly, as if I were merely making a pause on my journey. It did me good and I gave a deep sigh, a feeling of shrugging off the past, of weightlessness. I was staring, enthralled, at the embers of that fire and at the figure kneeling before it trying to rekindle it. I may have been going to his aid, but I was still in no hurry to arrive; I knew where I wanted to go and that was enough. I scrutinized the possible access routes to the area (bounded by a sofa and two armchairs) where the blond boy had taken refuge. I was just like the lost boy in fairy tales who, glimpsing a tiny light, in a distant house, shining amidst the darkness of the forest, stops to savour that moment of sudden hope and amazement. If only I could go back to that moment when time stopped! I often do go back, albeit along paths that do not take that octagonal table as their starting point, but different places that superimpose themselves, parts of the woods I inhabit now. The scene, however, is always the same.

It's a still photo like the ones at the beginning of certain films that freeze the image of the actors while, to the right, their real name appears alongside that of the character they've been chosen to play. The girl in red: Sofía Montalvo. We still don't know what's going to happen to them. It's a familiar picture postcard that creeps into my dreams, which, when I least expect it, interrupts some task I'm doing, an errand or a tedious discussion, and sweeps me out of the shadows and into the light. You've got your head in the clouds, Señorita Montalvo. What are you thinking about, Sofía? I'm in another time, another place, inside the bubble, unable to understand how I came to re-enter it, afraid that it will burst in the heat. No, that's not true, there's no fear. The girl in red wasn't afraid, and you are the girl in red. You're standing in the middle of a strange room, about fifteen paces from the fireplace and you've just raised the paper cup to your lips. Keep still! Concentrate. You mustn't take your eyes off the shoulders of the blond boy who, as yet, doesn't even know of your existence, just as you don't know that the force calling you springs from the curve of those shoulders; you don't know that you've just taken a sip of a love filtre because no one would suspect a paper cup. You're smiling, you've drunk a toast to the fire, and your coat weighs heavy on you. Concentrate on your body, you can move a little now, as if you were looking at yourself in the mirror. Action!

I refilled my glass and drank it down in one. Then I went over to the fireplace following an oblique route, stepping around the various bits and pieces scattered on the floor, intent on every step I was taking. The armchairs were large and placed very close to the sofa. I didn't want to push them aside in order to open a narrow point of access nor to go through the two gaps left in front of them, nearer the fire, because either of those options would betray my presence. Instead, I took off my overcoat in order to feel freer in my movements and hung it over the back of the sofa; then, sitting on the left arm, I let myself slide slowly down on to the seat swinging my legs in an arc through the air. At that moment, he'd just turned over the one large log that was still burning. It didn't look as if it was going to take. I stayed completely still for a moment. I didn't even pull down my skirt which had ridden up some inches above my knees – it was quite close-fitting. My heart was beating very hard like when you ring the doorbell of a strange house and you can hear the footsteps of someone coming to open it and you know there's no turning back.

Then something very odd happened: I realized that the blond boy had noticed my presence, although I hadn't moved and he hadn't turned round. However, when he reached over to the right to pick up the bellows, and when he applied them to the heart of the embers, he did so in the knowledge that someone had invaded his territory. I curled up in one corner of the sofa expecting him to turn round either out of irritation or, at the least, curiosity. He didn't. He had very nice hands and the gestures he made seemed increasingly delicate. He was making every move for my benefit; he liked the fact that I was watching him. I don't know that it's possible to understand these things, they seem so devastating at the time; I only know that when it happens, there's no point asking for guarantees or demanding a re-run. It's simply a question of faith. That was how it was. Those gestures were dedicated to me; perhaps he'd glimpsed me out of the corner of his eye, the way a bull glimpses the swirling cape, who knows? He was no longer concentrating on the fire, although he continued to tend it in a more and more desultory fashion, with no success whatsoever. It had become instead a theatrical fire, a pretext for showing off to me his hands and the back of his neck. Besides, there was no way that bit of wood was going to take, it was far too big; what he needed was some kindling.

I half-closed my eyes and rested my head on the back of the sofa, ready to improvise my role as soon as I was given my cue. He had to give it to me, since no one else had appeared. It was bound to be a question, that's how dialogues between people who don't know each other usually start. It wasn't up to me to speak first, I preferred to reject that possibility. But why waste time on conjectures? The important thing was to muster all my serenity and to savour the intense excitement I felt at the idea of saying "Yes" to whatever invitation or challenge might be put to me. A most unusual game was about to start, a very ancient game, the great, exciting game of which everyone has some experience but which, until then, I had only participated in through films or books. Mariana was convinced that I was poisoning myself with all those literary love stories and that the false trails laid by novels and films would confuse me when I tried to apply them to my own story.

"I won't have to ask anyone for help, don't you worry," I protested. "I'll know exactly what to do when the time comes."

"And how will you know when the time has come?" insisted Mariana.

"Because I'll be in a mood to please. My body will tell me, and my

233

imagination and my intelligence will increase in obedience to signals from my body; they too will want to rise to the occasion."

Everything was happening just as I'd predicted, with the added help of an auspicious gift. My imagination had a lot of catching up to do if it was to be on a par with a body that had been in the mood to please for the last twenty-four hours and which, unexpectedly reviving under the spell of a fairy godmother, had dressed as if for a gala and had rehearsed in front of a mirror for an unrepeatable party, a body which was also longing for its turn to become a mirror too. It was the same body that had just silently slipped off its shoes and put its feet up on the sofa with theatrical nonchalance, a gesture, by the way, that seemed to find a response in the other actor and to provoke a half-turn of his head, so tenuous and brief, however, that the girl in red didn't have time to do anything more than glimpse from beneath her eyelashes the contour of a memorable throat. Luckily he didn't actually say anything, though the danger had been there.

My hands were trembling a little. I knew that I had to remain alert, without appearing to be so, ready for whatever words the young man, as worthy of being loved as Calisto or Romeo, might blurt out, possibly while still with his back turned to me, a treacherous blow that would make any reply much riskier.

Anyway, the important thing was to lose my fear and to feed my imagination. I couldn't disappoint my godmother. She had dressed me in red in order to see if someone would want to play with me, in a game whose rules I would have to pick up as I went along. Things weren't going badly. It was clear that the other player had appeared, even if, for the moment, he remained an enigma. As the incarnation of that enigma, however, I could not have asked for a more evocative figure. Besides, not everything depended on him, much depended too on my own ability to decipher the enigma.

Thus I brazenly adopted a horizontal position and, since night was falling, decided to invoke an old friend who had always stood as godfather to my stories and daydreams: the goblin Noc. I folded my hands in my lap and, with my eyes shut, I asked him for the necessary wisdom to solve the enigma and for enough courage to assume his powers of fascination. I asked him to spark in the blond boy's mind the necessary curiosity and desire to listen to my solitary fantasies – all the crazy stories that were dying for lack of an audience – as well as for the wit to sew those tattered stories back together again and for the wisdom to understand that he was the reason I was telling them and for the patience to wait for the right signal, O Noc. I asked him to inflame me with all his inspiration so that I could dress my words in gold and see them reflected back at me in the eager eyes that had as yet not even looked at me; untie my tongue, O Noc, I asked him, but at the same time curb it, as you did with Scheherezade, help me to time my pauses so that there is always something left to tell, something more to listen to; I'll continue tomorrow, I'll be back tomorrow, amen, O Noc, amen.

"I'm going into this completely blind," I thought suddenly, in a moment of lucidity that dispelled my feeling of intoxication, "because he still hasn't even looked at me or spoken to me. It may be that his face won't be the right face and his voice won't be the sort that demands a response or invites a reaction. If that's the case, then it's best that he takes his time before looking at me, don't you agree, Noc? It would be better if he never looked at me and never moved. Tell me if he moves, I've no intention of opening my eyes."

And Noc, the little god with the pointed ears, who always presided over the night-time tales I invented for Mariana, smiled mockingly as he hovered above me. Not that I was thinking about Mariana at the time, she didn't enter my thoughts for a moment.

From upstairs came the sounds of "Je ne regrette rien" sung by Edith Piaf. French music, naturally. My godmother wouldn't overlook a detail like that. The perfect soundtrack for a film. It was, in fact, very much like a scene from a film, the way the girl in red smiled rather dreamily, her eyes tight shut, while she listened to the lyrics as if to the words of a prayer. "Je m'en fous du passé", yesterday doesn't exist, I've left it all behind, no, I regret nothing, neither the wrongs people have done me, nor the good, what does it matter, I've lit a bonfire with my memories, with my sorrows and my joys.

And then, of course, I did think about Mariana, but as you might think about something to which one has bade a final farewell. Perhaps that's what she felt when she fell in love, and at that moment, it seemed logical to me that she hadn't wanted or had been unable to share her love with me. I understood it from afar, without pain, with that strange vagueness mingled with certainty with which one sometimes understands things in dreams or the way you see a city lying beneath you as the plane begins to climb carrying you away from that city, possibly for ever, and you say "There's so-and-so square, so-and-so building, such-and-such park" and press your nose against the window. You can recognize those places laid out as neatly as the paths of a cemetery, goodbye, *Je ne regrette rien*, I'm off to other lands. The truth was, I was saying farewell to my childhood, and on her behalf, to Mariana's childhood too; she'd never much liked solemn ceremonies.

The best way to keep control of a situation is to rise above it. I closed my eyes, stopped thinking about the blond boy's fire and lit my own instead, my own Piaf bonfire, in which the voices of childhood and all the stories I'd read and invented in order to keep myself amused while I waited for love burned and crackled like dry leaves. I lost all notion of time.

"Don't cry," I heard someone say in the gentlest of voices. "Don't you feel well?"

I opened my eyes. The blond boy had sat down on the floor next to the sofa and was looking at me. My silence and possibly my look of terror at seeing him so close, so unexpected, encouraged him to put one hand on my knees and unselfconsciously to stroke them. That caress lasted only moments, but it proved decisive, it determined my whole future.

"Don't cry, please," he was saying. "You're trembling."

I was drowning in emotion. I think I've said elsewhere in these notebooks who the blond boy looked like, so there's probably no need to say anything further, but in a way, never having seen a James Dean film, he made an even greater impression on me. I hadn't noticed him sit down beside me and I couldn't remember why I'd started to cry. There were just too many surprises all at once, and then the *coup de grâce*, that subversive caress that cut the ground from beneath me; it meant that, after all my agonizing, the plot was now demanding its freedom, was now completely out of my control. I swung my legs round so that my feet were on the ground again, and smoothed my skirt. Nothing was going as I'd planned.

"I didn't mean to cry, I mean, I wasn't intending to," I said like an idiot, whilst I raised my hand to my cheek as if to feel the tears for myself.

"Really?" he asked, suddenly amused. "What exactly were you intending to do?"

I looked away because I couldn't hold his gaze. The fire had gone out completely by then.

"Well, I intended to tell you, amongst other things, that you haven't a clue when it comes to lighting fires, that you can't do it without kindling or paper faggots. Plus a bit of faith, of course. What are you laughing at? There's another thing I could ask you: why are you laughing?"

"At that expression 'paper faggots'. I thought only my grandmother used it. Look, gorgeous, I didn't ask you why you were crying, I only asked you not to do it. That's a bit different, wouldn't you agree?"

He'd called me "gorgeous", but only jokingly, not the way I would have liked him to say it, the way I would have said it to him if I'd dared, and then an alarm bell rang: Be careful! He must be sick to death of people telling him he's gorgeous, he's probably unbearably vain; O Noc, please protect me, I'm beginning to get out of my depth.

"Yes, it is slightly different," I said, "I'm sorry. Do you always get your own way?"

I felt a bit awkward. It was more or less what my father had said to me before I'd gone off to my room to try on the red dress. I was saying things I didn't intend to say, the words were coming out all wrong. I decided to put things right.

The blond boy had grown serious, staring into the fireplace. Suddenly, he didn't seem so young. "He's one of those people who changes with the light," I thought and felt pleased.

"Well," he said, "not when it comes to stoking fires. I don't seem to have got my own way there."

"You probably didn't have enough faith."

"Probably not. Are you going to cry any more?"

"No."

"Right then, you'd better dry the tears that are left."

He held out a spotless handkerchief which he produced from his pocket, but there was nothing of the Don Juan about the way he did it. Everything he did was right. I carefully wiped away my tears and we looked at each other smiling, with a degree of mutual curiosity too. A tentative look.

Pointing to the fireplace, I said: "Do you want me to have a go? There are still a few embers burning. I didn't like to suggest it before. Do you know where I could find some kindling or some old newspapers?"

"I've no idea. I've only been here once before. Thanks, anyway, but your faith is of no use to me, I'm afraid. You see, it was a sort of wager I made with myself, and I lost. That's all."

"I'm sorry," I said.

"I'm not. *Je ne regrette rien.* It was a fire that was doomed to go out from the start."

He knelt down on the sofa, facing the back, and looked out through the window at the dark garden. In profile, he was even better looking.

"Do you like Rabindranath Tagore?" he asked after a rather long silence.

"Yes I do, but he's not exactly fashionable. I'm surprised you like him."

"I have no pretence to being fashionable and, anyway, I didn't say I liked him."

"What then?"

I knelt down too and put my arms over the back of the sofa. It seemed to me that a tale was about to unfold.

"You see," he began, "when I was a child, I liked him a lot. Or rather my grandmother liked him a lot."

"The same grandmother you mentioned before?"

"The same. And I read so much of him that I got hooked on his poetic language; it became as familiar to me as the language of the street.

Absurd, don't you think? I knew whole passages by heart. I was a big fan of Tagore for a large part of my childhood. Then, because all my friends thought he was kitsch, the sort of writer prim young girls read, I became ashamed of what I'd once enjoyed immensely. Maybe I'd had enough of him too. Anyway, I disowned that particular passion."

He was speaking very slowly, as if to himself, and now he'd fallen silent.

"That often happens," I said. "The same thing happened to me with Hermann Hesse."

"But something that had such a profound effect on you always leaves traces. For example, I've often wondered …"

He broke off suddenly and shrugged, still looking out of the window.

"What?"

"Well, it's silly really. I've often wondered what someone smiling behind a mask of utter absence would look like; it's a phrase of Tagore's, I don't know if you remember it. For years, I dreamed of finding a girl with that expression on her face. I knew I'd recognize it, although it wasn't what you'd call a very precise description. The girl never appeared of course and I'd almost forgotten the phrase. Years have gone by without my once remembering it, that's what's so odd."

There was a silence that seemed final. The noise upstairs was growing louder. They were playing jazz now.

"Why are you telling me this?" I asked at last in a faint voice, thinking that Noc had obviously gone over to the other side.

"Because before, when the fire went out and I turned round and you were lying there with your eyes closed and wearing that red dress, crying and smiling at the same time, I suddenly remembered Tagore's words, with absolute freshness, as if I'd read them for the first time or was inventing them myself, 'How you smile behind your mask of utter absence!'; you seemed so far away and yet so near. Your face tends to change a lot anyway."

"So does yours."

He wasn't looking at me, but it was marvellous to hear him talk.

"There's something slightly out of synch about this whole meeting, don't you think?" he added, in another tone now. "It's obvious that Tagore's 'mask of utter absence' has simply stumbled on to the wrong stage set."

"Do you think so?"

"I'm positive. If you mentioned Tagore's name in this house, they'd immediately label you a petit bourgeois. Anyway, what are you doing here wearing a dress like that. It just doesn't fit."

Now he was looking me straight in the eye. Only it wasn't just my eyes he was looking at.

"What doesn't fit, the dress or me being here?"

"You being here. The dress, well, the dress is amazing. The people upstairs are all in jeans and baggy T-shirts."

I suddenly felt delighted with the red dress, with my own body and with my desire for adventure. Now it was my turn. I decided to dive in with a response straight out of a black-and-white movie. I made use of my gift for mimicry.

"Seems to me, stranger, that you're in an awful hurry to light one bonfire with another," I said in a phoney Hollywood voice.

I hit the mark; he burst out laughing. What a relief! Suddenly it was as if we'd been friends all our lives. Who knows what happened to achieve that change of tempo in such a short space of time?

"And you're pretty quick on the draw with the kindling too, kid. You're not from these parts, are you?"

"Guess. I'm sure you don't want me to give you a summary of my life, after all that pretty talk about masks of utter absence."

"Good God, no. That would be dreadfully common," he said. "I don't expect anyone to sum their lives up for my benefit or to expect me to do the same, and I hate being told to get a move on, or people who say things like: 'where do you stand on this?' or 'we must act responsibly' or 'there's strength in unity'. And I don't like being with crowds of people either. The ideal number is two. Can you accept that?"

"I'll try, boss."

He sat up and bent over to put my shoes on. Then he took my hand.

"In that case, I don't know what we're doing here. Let's go. I don't imagine there's anyone you have to say goodbye to."

I let him pull me towards the door.

"Not really. Do you?"

"No."

When we went out into the garden, I looked up at the sky. The first stars had come out and the moon was huge. I suddenly remembered that I could get home at whatever time I liked; I took a deep breath and felt happier than I've ever felt again in my life.

"Do you know where we're going?" I asked.

"No idea. I shouldn't think you do either."

"No. I don't know this area and I haven't got a car."

"Glad to hear it."

We set off past the houses, along unfamiliar streets. Holding his hand, I thought what a miracle it was that his blood was flowing through his veins at the same time as mine was flowing through my veins, and that he should have discovered in my face the mask of utter absence, and that the moon looking down on us was also shining on wild seas, solitary mountains, remote roads, noisy cities, rooftops, valleys and night birds and would continue to do so into the future; and the words in my throat, O Noc, were like waves waiting to drown everything.

We stopped beneath a streetlamp and before he kissed me, he said: "Doesn't it feel to you like now is always?" And that was when I knew that this was a love affair that would slowly murder me, because it was not a love that would last.

That's all one can recount of a love story really, the preliminaries, the moment when it first burst into flame.

If one day you read this notebook, Mariana, which, after all, is my reason for writing it, I want you to know that your name wasn't mentioned once that night, nor for some time afterwards. He simply said in passing that he'd broken off with a girlfriend who had proved too rational and domineering for a reader of Rabindranath Tagore. He said that he'd vaguely expected her to turn up at that party, but she hadn't.

"You mean at the party with the fire that refused to light?"

"Exactly."

I didn't ask him anything else because the night was full of riddles and symbols and brilliant replies. No probing questions allowed.

And although hours later, in a place in the old part of Madrid where we danced boleros, my heart gave a strange lurch when I discovered that his name was Guillermo, I calmed myself by thinking that it isn't, after all, such a very unusual name.

"Is something wrong?" he asked me. "You've gone very quiet. Why are you looking at me like that?"

"I don't know. How am I looking at you?"

"Oddly."

"It's just that you look so different in profile."

When you looked at him properly and, given that one couldn't as yet compare him to James Dean, Guillermo could be said to have something of the wolf about him. That had been the only distinguishing feature you'd given me the first time you talked to me about your boyfriend, but it had never occurred to me that a wolf might be blond.

XIV

Literary echoes

Dear Sofía,

Yesterday morning, when I went to leave the key to room 203 at reception, the receptionist asked if I'd finally decided how much longer I would be staying. He smiled when he said the word "finally". He has very regular, white teeth and takes every opportunity to flash them at people, even if a smile isn't always appropriate, like those television presenters who gabble the script, giving scant attention to the natural pauses in the text, as if they considered pauses a kind of nervous tic added for the benefit of the studio lights rather than the laws of prosody. They probably hired him because of his teeth. They're worthy of a toothpaste ad. I call him Mr Colgate.

Anyway, whether deliberate or not, that "finally" stood out in his sentence as if he wanted to draw my attention to the fact that it was an adverb of time and to alert me to the need to come to terms with dates, a subject, by the way, which I usually give considerable thought to the moment I open my eyes. Or rather, it's the noise of it buzzing around me like a bluebottle that wakes me up, and my early morning endeavours to muster some willpower are inevitably directed towards inventing ways of shooing it away. His question, therefore, troubled me greatly. It was like a headache suddenly getting worse again just as it had started to disperse. Besides, in a strictly literal sense, it was not, I think, the first occasion that the young man with the impeccable smile had suggested that I should come to terms with time and dates.

I'd gone down to the sauna for a while to see if I could get rid of the hangover brought on by a night rich in nightmares. Silvia and Josefina Carreras were travelling in some sort of wagon and were looking for me

243

in a wood. The driver, dressed in heavy winter clothes and sitting as still as a statue, turned out to be Raimundo. It was pitch black. They passed very close by me and I hid behind some trees because I was afraid. I coincided in the sauna with the woman-as-sex-object. Afterwards, back in my room, which was newly cleaned and smelling of air freshener, I experimented with make-up and various outfits that I threw down on the bed as I discarded them in my search for the one that could best withstand my critical gaze. The clothes neurosis. I have sheaves of notes on the subject in my files. There are days when the neurotic relationship between a woman and her clothes intensifies, especially when it comes to her most recent acquisitions which lose their significance within the space of a few days. A sort of lucidity mingled with impotence makes us hate them and consider them to be somehow a trick, a palliative. The one item of clothing that never disappoints me, which is why I always end up wearing it in situations like this, is my tailored gaberdine suit – which is getting on a bit and makes no attempts to disguise it – without a blouse underneath but with a flowered scarf tucked in the neck. Apart from being an old friend I can trust, it makes me look much slimmer. I don't know if you noticed, but I was wearing it when I met you at Gregorio Termes' exhibition. As for my hair, recently I've decided that it looks best up. Or at least that's what Raimundo says. I still have the rubber band I used that last night I spent at his flat. How many things connect and are summoned up, Sofía, when you stand in front of a mirror in search of the most suitable and solid figure to present on the balcony of the new day, for we never know what the day will bring us.

This kind of game, whose initial intention is to make peace with one's body in order to make one's soul feel at ease inside it, soon bursts the bounds of that preliminary stage and seizes control of any subsequent decisions, taking over the helm. A kind of usurpation of your own will takes place and the will finally bows before the argument that you have to get some reward for all that time spent on meticulous rehearsal. We end up accepting the servitude of going out and soliciting someone else's appraising glance in order to judge whether or not the results are good, because our own mirror has grown too tarnished. After spending nearly an hour pondering whether to clear my table, sit down and write or to spend a day lounging by the swimming pool or to catch a bus in the village and go off somewhere in search of improbable adventures, I opted for the latter.

The guest in room 204, who was leafing through a newspaper in the foyer, got up when he saw me come out of the lift and went over to the reception desk to ask if he had any mail. His question interrupted the one the receptionist had just asked me and that helped me to gain time. We almost touched; he smelled of expensive cologne and the question about his mail was just one of many excuses he invents to get close to me or to follow me from afar with his eyes. The suspicion that on some nights he might even eavesdrop from his terrace on the conversations I hold with my tape recorder feeds conflicting feelings of repugnance and curiosity that charge our subsequent encounters with an electric tension. Of course, I might well be imagining all this; ever since I've been staying here, my imagination has produced mostly nonsense with a marked tendency to erotic fantasy. I've only seen him at the swimming pool once. His legs are rather too thin for my taste, but straight and strong. I've come to the conclusion that his relationship with the woman-as-sex-object lacks stimulus, indeed the same may apply to his whole life. She's probably one of those women who says: "Not now, dear, you'll mess up my hair." When he's with her, he avoids looking at me and I've even managed to persuade myself on occasions that we really do have something to hide.

I stood there, deep in thought, staring into space and chewing my thumbnail, a gesture you're familiar with, Sofía, and which you once christened my 'the lady's off to Cairo look', after that romantic song that my mother knew and the tune of which I now forget, though I'm sure you'll remember it. Thank God you exist.

"You see," I said, thoughtfully, "it doesn't depend on my will alone."

"I'm sorry, Señora, what did you say?" asked the receptionist, although I was not, of course, addressing him.

"My decision to leave, I mean. It doesn't depend on me, do you see? Or at least not exclusively on me. I'm sure you understand."

There was a pause. My neighbour in room 204 reached out a hand to take the letter the receptionist was holding out to him; his hand brushed my arm and we exchanged a fleeting look.

"Sorry," he said in such a low voice that I only felt obliged to reply with a kind of sigh.

"You do understand, don't you?" I insisted.

"Of course, Señora, perhaps tomorrow you'll be able to tell me something."

I fixed my eyes on the pigeonhole. My breathing always gets faster when I do so. It was empty, naturally, but knowing that doesn't calm my nerves at all. The receptionist, who caught the disquiet in my eyes, gave the impression that he was striving hard not to be apologetic.

"There's nothing for you, I'm afraid," he said, his smile broadening.

"And there haven't been any messages either?"

He dutifully plunged his fingers into the pigeonhole. We were both acting with a fairly acceptable degree of complicity, acceptable even to more reluctant spectators.

"No, Señora, I'm terribly sorry."

"How strange!"

My neighbour's envelope was typewritten and was stamped with the name of some boring bank or company, I couldn't quite see what, but I saw his name: Daniel Rueda. I knew he was Spanish because I'd sometimes heard him arguing with the woman-as-sex-object. They mostly argue about money, because she spends a lot. The only other conversations I've overheard – although in fact they're rarely seen together – have been about crosswords, a pastime in which she eagerly immerses herself although apparently without the necessary general knowledge to know the name of the philosophical doctrine according to which everything is determined by the ineluctable decisions of destiny, eight letters, or the name, five letters, of the Australian relative of the dog. But then again, they are Spaniards.

He withdrew to the armchair from which he'd come and disappeared from my field of vision, although doubtless I did not disappear from his.

I stood there thinking how dull it must be to open an envelope like that mid-morning and I wondered how long it had been since he last received a letter that made his heart beat faster, assuming he ever had. He looks about forty-five. When he was young, people still used to write love letters. Dear Daniel. Daniel, my love. For the love of God, Daniel, tell me that you still think about me, tell me anything. Why don't you write to me, Daniel? It's a good name. Temptation surfaced in me like a fleeting desire to create mischief but was immediately transformed into a literary idea. It could make a good beginning for the novel I'm thinking of writing and which has already undergone so many false starts. Opening with a minor character is always a good idea, isn't it, Sofía? In fact, the thing I like most about your homework is the almost immediate appearance of Señora Acosta. They're fascinating, these minor characters, if you know how to use them. Anyway, Daniel Rueda could be the catalyst for my story. One day, a letter written on creamy beige paper and addressed to Daniel Rueda appears in the pigeonhole for room 204. The woman-as-sex-object picks it up. A violent scene ensues, in the dining room, for example, or on their balcony – I'll work that out later – but in a place where I could overhear fragments of the subsequent altercation. Daniel swears that he knows nothing about the woman, but in the days that follow, his glances in my direction become more and more inquisitive because he's beginning to nurture the strong suspicion that the letter might have been sent by me, a suspicion I pick up on and which troubles me, although I try not to show it. And yet, how can I put it, I don't mind if I show it a little bit; you know me, I'm not averse to provoking extreme situations. There's an intensification of that atmosphere of desire between us – all of which is based entirely on that toing and froing of glances – even more so when he realizes that I'm beginning to lose control and feel unsure of myself. It intrigues him to detect symptoms of insecurity in a person with such a haughty demeanour and such resolute step and he sets out to study the symptoms; he becomes, in a way, a detective of my behaviour. What do you think? It could be a good starting point for the central plot: the progressive psychological disintegration of Mariana León who is suffering from persecution mania. Who is she running away from? Why is she running away? Although initially attracted by the glow of the inaccessible, when he applies his magnifying glass, Daniel becomes a witness to the transformations of the suffering soul reflected in it, to her changes of attitude and mood. Difficult to carry off, of course, but interesting as an idea, don't you think? The whole thing will depend on the text of the letter, the letter has to be really convincing; it depends too on how I pace his growing suspicions. As an adornment to the plot, I could use the receptionist whose intervention to confirm that my handwriting is indeed the same as that of the unknown lover could add a touch of the thriller to his researches, although that might be a bit forced.

I'd been leaning on the reception desk for a while, saying nothing. Mr Colgate's eyes, completely divorced from his smile, betrayed a certain unease.

"Would you mind if I had a look at my form?" I asked, scarcely realizing what I was saying and immediately regretting this unexpected and inappropriate request.

"What form?"

"The one I filled in when I got here. I imagine I did fill in a form."

"Yes, of course," said the receptionist, confused. "Do you want to know what day you arrived?"

(You should shorten this scene which will just pad out the text and which leads nowhere. It's a mistake. You have to break the vicious circle as soon as possible. Leave the hotel.)

"It's just that I'm rather forgetful lately," I replied lightly. "I don't even know why I'm asking you to look for the form, so how am I supposed to remember how long I've been here? It doesn't matter. Don't worry. Anyway, until I hear further news, it's probably best to forget what day it is and just enjoy my holiday to the full, don't you think?"

The receptionist had started rummaging around in the filing cabinet and looked up, startled. "... staring up into the seeming void", I recited mentally, dedicating the phrase to you. This time his smile was a little late in appearing. He froze. I think he was moving from confusion to surprise.

"As you wish, Señora," he said. "However …"

He stood there looking at me as if trying to calculate my capacity for understanding before he continued speaking. Yes, I really must include the receptionist, though he should have a more sinister air, perhaps dressed unseasonably all in black. That would give a Kafkaesque touch to the story. You used to say that minor characters are always rather Kafkaesque, although it might also be said that all the people in Kafka's books are minor characters. They either have no name at all or, at most, an initial. They make our existence seem merely relative, make it more ambiguous, more tenuous. For them, arriving does not necessarily mean arriving anywhere in particular.

It was late evening when K. arrived. The village lay in deep snow. The hill on which the castle stood was hidden, surrounded by mist and darkness, without even a glimmer of light to show that the castle was there. For a long time, K. stood on the wooden bridge that led from the main road into the village, staring up into the seeming void.

We used to know the opening paragraph of *The Castle* by heart and we'd incorporated it into our secret jargon. Sometimes, seeing that you were distracted, I would ask you what you were thinking about, and if you just shrugged your shoulders and continued gazing up at the ceiling or the sky, I'd say to you: "Come on, that's quite enough staring up into the seeming void." It was like throwing you a lifeline to haul you back up to the surface again, the lifeline of literature. Laughter would immediately burst forth again, the knowing laughter that always reunited us, until I started taking life too seriously. "Okay," you'd reply, "I'll just cross the wooden bridge and I'll be right with you." The Spanish translation was published by Emecé Editores, Buenos Aires, do you remember? The logo of the publishing house was an open book with a capital E on either page. How evocative initials can be. It occurs to me in passing that the name and surname of the unknown lover could have my initials, Magdalena Lastra, for example, or perhaps Marta Lucena. That would be fun.

With evident effort, the receptionist completed his interrupted sentence.

"However," he went on, "if you do plan to stay longer, we may have to change your room to another one on the first floor. That's what I meant to tell you before, Señora. Do you understand? Another room which would have to be a single room. You wouldn't mind moving to a single room would you, unless you're expecting a visit from someone, that is?"

He articulated the words very slowly, as if he were speaking to a foreigner or a mental defective.

I wanted to move on to another scene. I said no, I wouldn't mind at all and I wasn't expecting any visitors, just a message. I asked him to tell me as soon as he received any letter, package or telegram addressed to me. That was what really mattered, that was the only thing that was important.

"Whatever time it arrives, do you understand?"

And my voice sounded so genuinely pleading and concerned, I alarmed myself. Watch out, ML is bordering on dementia.

"Don't worry, Señora, I'll keep you informed, but, as you know, the post always arrives at the same time."

I walked across the foyer towards the main door. A sideways glance was enough to tell me that Daniel Rueda, or DR, was still watching my every move; I wasn't thinking about the letter I was going to write to him, though, I was thinking about the letter I still had not received. I am seized at the most inopportune moments by the certainty that, when I least expect it, a letter addressed to me will appear in my pigeonhole; it's like the unexpected smile on the monster's face in horror films. I must be prepared. No one must notice any hint of emotion when I pick it up. It will mean, though, that they have found me out. It would be best not even to open it, just take it as an alarm signal and make a more thorough escape this time, leaving no loose ends. For example, I should never have been so chatty with the taxi driver who drove me from Puerto Real (because, in the end, I decided to take a taxi).

It was a lovely, cool, sunny morning, with a sky covered now and then by clusters of fast-moving, capricious clouds, clouds going nowhere, being frayed and buffeted by the same breeze that rules and mitigates our passions, our highs and lows. I took a deep breath and consoled myself with the thought that, for the moment, nothing has happened that forces me to make a decision. I was wearing very comfortable shoes and, as I walked up the rather steep hill away from the hotel, my breathing became as light as my steps, feeding on the open air, like a butterfly fluttering its wings having barely escaped drowning in the whirlpools of a river.

Get your bearings, Mariana, keep your feet on the ground and just enjoy what's around you; above all, enjoy the fact that you're alive and can see all this. Your fantasies are getting out of hand, inhabiting some almost airless place, where you lose all sense of distance. Don't let them muddy the present, whose enjoyment consists, as you well know, in making small adjustments to your mind and checking how the machinery's working before plunging it into a sea of dreams. If the Universe is not to swallow up their ship, fantasy and logic need to go hand-in-hand like two sisters, always together, always hand-in-hand; you've often given others the same advice. Perhaps now it no longer works for you precisely because you've said it so often. Try to hear it as if for the first time, as if someone you love very much were saying it to you, inject it directly into your veins. Now tell me, who is going to write you a letter, if no one knows where you are?

And yet I still expect a letter to come. It might come at any moment. I know they're looking for me, Sofía. I know that for sure. Even in the most perfect crime, the criminal always leaves some compromising clue as he makes his escape. At night, I devour detective novels and, sooner or later, the face of the detective always ends up taking on the angular features of Josefina Carreras.

The last time I phoned her was from Calle de la Amargura. There doesn't at the moment seem to be any very pressing work problem requiring my return to Madrid, but I noticed little tremors of alarm in Josefina's voice. What had happened to me? It was like a complete personality change, she couldn't understand my running away like that, that sudden, unexpected disappearance, my giving her no warning,

her only a brief note on her office desk: "I hope you won't mind
n for me for a few days. My friend is out of danger now. I have to
go away for a while. I'll call you."

"Thank heavens, you've phoned," she said to me. "I was worried sick,
Mariana, surely you can understand that. It's not like you. You didn't
even leave me a telephone number, an address, anything."

I can't bear being checked up on, that was why I was a bit abrupt.

"Don't worry, I'll give you the phone number now. But don't give it
to anyone else, all right? I'll be back soon. Has anything urgent come
up?"

She said that wasn't the point, she just wanted to know how I was. As
far as she was concerned, the only urgent matter was finding out how I
was or what had happened to me.

"Something must have happened," she said, when I remained silent.
"Are you with your friend?"

I gave her an incomplete and unwilling summary of the situation. She
only knew about Raimundo by indirect references I'd made about him,
but she doesn't like him. She says he's ruining my life. I tried to exclude
Raimundo as the catalyst for my trip, motivated in part, I said, because I
fancied a change of air after all those days spent at the hospital, but above
all by professional reasons. I felt responsible for a former patient of mine
who really needed my help and in whose house I was staying. Since Silvia
had just notified me of her imminent arrival from Carmona, I considered
this only a white lie. Besides, I always lie a little to Josefina because she's
such a pain and tends to take my affairs too much to heart, to live them as
if they were her own.

"You're incorrigible, Mariana," she said. "You're too generous with
your time. I don't know how you keep it up, especially considering how
people repay you."

I felt embarrassed by the warmth of that compliment. It provided too
stark a contrast with the pitiless image of myself that Silvia had given me
over the phone. Yet I almost prefer Silvia's insults to Josefina's dog-like
devotion, although what I prefer most of all, naturally enough, is to be
left in peace.

"Don't be so silly," I said impatiently. "Sometimes you sound like my maiden aunt. I don't feel I'm the victim of anything or anyone, I've told you so hundreds of times. And if I get into a mess, I'm to blame and no one else."

Then I regretted having spoken to her in that tone and I apologized. It's just that sometimes she drives me mad with her totalitarian judgements and her complete and utter lack of humour. You may ask how I manage to get along with her at all, and I really couldn't say. She was a student of mine, she had a very unhappy childhood, and we've been together for eight years now; it's one of those collaborative efforts about which one can change nothing. I recognize her qualities of loyalty, honesty and competence, but, Sofía, if I tell you that she's rather like a member of the copiomanuensis species, you'll know what I mean. I'm sure you haven't forgotten the copiomanuenses. Like almost all of them, she's very uptight, doesn't drink, wears glasses and is of medium height.

I gave her Silvia's telephone number in absolute confidence and we left it that if I wasn't going to be in Madrid by the beginning of the following week, I'd tell her. I don't even want to start thinking about where this week has gone. She said again that I sounded strange and that she was worried. She must be even more worried now, since I haven't given any further signs of life and since Silvia, with whom she will doubtless have made contact, has no more clues to my whereabouts than those enshrined in a poem by Pessoa. Up until now, Josefina and Silvia knew nothing about each other, but it's not hard to imagine the sparks that will be flying from their recently formed alliance nor the alarmist mess they will have created between them and Raimundo, because Raimundo will be involved too, that's for sure. The three of them are making their investigations. The three of them have started looking for me, sniffing around the neighbourhood. "She can't have gone far," they murmur. They'll end up finding me.

I was so deep in thought that I jumped when a car drew up beside me. DR was at the wheel. I'd stepped back towards the ditch. He wound his window down and a face appeared that suddenly struck me as being utterly vulgar and inexpressive.

"I'm sorry," he said. "Did I frighten you?"

"Well, yes you did a bit, to be honest," I admitted, while I looked at him hard to make sure that I wasn't just imagining him as I had my persecutors.

For a few moments, the fear of being discovered by them was diverted into another. Now I would have to explain to DR about the letter. Why else would he be talking to me? Then I remembered that I hadn't actually written it yet.

"I'm sorry," he said, "I just wanted to ask you if you'd like me to give you a lift somewhere. I'd be pleased to. I'm heading in the direction of Cádiz."

He spoke quickly, in a flat, nasal voice. I decided I didn't want to string him along.

"Thanks, but I'm not going anywhere in particular. And besides I like walking."

"You didn't mind my asking, did you?"

"No, not at all."

"Well, goodbye then. And enjoy your walk."

"And you enjoy your drive. Goodbye."

The car drew away and I stood there for a few moments, watching him move off. I smiled. At least I'd got the approving look I wanted. All I needed now was for something to happen that would be rather more exciting than being picked up by a fussy little individual like him. It was best to relegate him to the workshop where I store up scraps of literary material. I only had to hear him speak to dismiss him as a suitable protagonist in a love affair. Nevertheless, it's a scene I could use in a novel if I changed the dialogue and, of course, the tone of voice and the intention behind his look. In the novel, DR has already received a letter from Marta Lucena.

Before setting off again, I made sure that I had my notebook in my pocket. No, it would be better to find a stationer's where I could buy some good writing paper and matching envelopes. A light bulb had just lit up in my head. Suddenly, what I wanted more than anything else was to sit down in a café in the old part of Cádiz, write a letter to DR and send it to him for real. I remembered a big café with mirrors on the walls in Callejón del Tinte where I sometimes used to meet Manolo. It would be empty at this hour. I could spend a really nice morning there. As far as literature was concerned, adventure was assured. It was better than nothing. I quickened my pace, humming to myself.

When I reached the village, the bus for Cádiz was just about to leave. I managed to get on it, but just before I did, I bought a newspaper to read on the journey. When we reached San Fernando, a news item in the local paper leapt out at me, left me breathless. Manolo Reina is showing some of his paintings in a gallery in Cádiz. Surprise is a hare, Sofía, if you go out hunting for it, you won't find it sleeping in a field. The return of that phrase seems even more appropriate now, given the number of coincidences with the first occasion I said it to you after all these years. The hare obviously likes to turn up at art exhibitions after I've suffered an attack of clothes neurosis which always ends up in my choosing to wear the tailored gaberdine suit and the printed scarf around my neck. There was a photo of the artist leaning against the wall between two of his paintings. What can I tell you about the artist? He's wearing a white open-necked shirt and a leather bomber jacket, his hair is a bit untidy and he's smiling nonchalantly. The painting, on the other hand, looks totally phoney to me. Of course, you can't really judge in black and white and still less printed on bad paper. Nevertheless, I can see that he's changed his style and that he now goes in for the smudge and blot technique. He used to paint very poetic watercolours, seascapes full of light. The remarks he makes in an interview given to the newspaper don't correspond to the way he used to talk either. He speaks of the telluric nature of his work, about essential environments, about decontextualization. And to think he used to laugh at all that jargon!

Anyway, he's in Cádiz and, to judge by the dates of the exhibition, he was there when I sent that unsigned telegram to his address in New York and I was pursuing his memory down streets and in places where I might quite easily have bumped into him. I'd rather not arrive unannounced, though, because this meeting might have its difficulties. There's every chance he's with the American gallery owner, and that she probably bought him the trendy jacket he's wearing in the photo, and that he smiled smugly when he tried it on. I can see them reflected in a mirror in their New York apartment, she's standing behind him, her arms around his waist, her eyes full of love. He turns round to kiss her: "Thank you, honey." They're bound to speak English together and she … Well, best not to think about her. She has no part in your happiness this morning and she has no right to spoil it. Just forget about the gallery owner, pretend she doesn't exist. Eliminate her. Manolo can't have forgotten you. You have to plan things properly. You must try to see him alone.

When I got off the bus, I felt reborn, magnetized. Suddenly, a brilliant light tore through the fog of fantasy, drained the substance from the cerebral soup I'd been cooking up. The images of Josefina, Silvia and the man in room 204 retreated like wounded dragons. At last, something real was going to happen to me, my heart was really beating, I could really see the boats anchored in the bay, my eyes calculated the distance, my body revived, what joy to be alive! I couldn't predict how things would turn out, but I felt very pretty in my tailored gaberdine suit and I fancied nothing more than plunging into the adventure of seeing in the flesh the man who spoke to me from the tape recorder at night and said: "Come, I need you."

When I read the interview in the newspaper more calmly and with more attention in the first bar I went into in order to think things through and to have a drink (which turned out to be several drinks), my enthusiasm cooled considerably. It was clear that she was with him. He referred to her as "my manager", but, a few lines on, it became clear that his manager was a woman: HER. She'd encouraged him to change his style, she'd given him a new rigour and consistency, she'd had faith in his talent and introduced him to the New York market where his name was beginning to be known. The success of a recent exhibition in a gallery in Lexington Avenue confirmed that. While he was showing the interviewer a few cuttings of reviews, he remarked: "You see, Jesús, no one is a prophet in his own land. You have to go abroad to get any recognition."

"And come back so changed we don't even recognize you," I said, sharply, not realizing I'd spoken out loud until I saw a solitary man, sitting at the next table to mine, giving me an amused, knowing look.

"I'm sorry, I didn't mean you," I said.

"I thought not," he said smiling. "Don't worry, there are more of us every day, people who talk to themselves, I mean. There are hordes of them in Cádiz alone. You're not from here, are you?"

"No, I'm not."

"It doesn't matter. It's the times we live in. The way I look at it is that psychiatrists would be out of a job if it wasn't for people like us talking to ourselves."

"How right you are," I muttered, before turning my back on him and immersing myself in the task of reading between the lines of what Manolo had said.

Had that experience made him feel more a "citizen of the world" than just a boy from Cádiz? Well, no, the proof was that, on his return to Spain, he'd decided to hold his first exhibition in Cádiz, as a homage to his home town. Later, in a month or so, the same exhibition would travel to Madrid and Barcelona. "Unless I sell all the paintings here, of course," he concluded. "You're certainly on the up, Manolo," commented the interviewer, "and that goes for your morale as well as your prices. You're a changed man!" "I've always been an artist at heart," he replied, "but I must admit that launching yourself on the big wide world does change you. You learn a lot of things, you know?" "For example?" "Well, that you have to blow your own trumpet, because, if you don't, no one else will."

By just after two o'clock, after ever briefer intervals of optimism, my morale had hit rock bottom and my wandering about the city had become a kind of painful flight with no goal. I scanned the horizon cautiously and suspiciously every time I turned down a new street or went into a book-shop or a café. Needless to say, my clothes neurosis had resurfaced and I bought two or three entirely unnecessary items of clothing. I didn't dare go anywhere near Puerta de Tierra where the exhibition was being held and, though I dialled Manolo's old number again and again, first from a shop and later from a phone box, no one answered. My desire to see him on his own increased in inverse proportion to my confidence and ability to invent a stimulating, witty pretext to do so. It became an increasingly frenetic desire that clouded my mind and weakened my will to control it. "I can't, I can't," I said to myself, "I don't know what to do, but I must do something."

My arrival at the café in Callejón del Tinte, which I'd imagined as the refuge where I would write my letter to Daniel Rueda, eased my tension slightly. Firstly, because at that hour – lunchtime – it was completely empty and, secondly, because its welcoming gloom was not only conducive to reflection, it also brought back to me, like so many precious stones, moments from that distant summer which I'd tried in vain to recapture on other occasions.

I went straight over to a table in the back, the same table where Manolo had sat opposite me in silence, never taking his eyes off me while I continued to pontificate and where, for the first time, he'd put his hand on my hand as it rested on the table.

"Don't you think so?" I asked.

"What? Do you want another sherry? I do."

I nodded. He got up and went to order another two glasses at the bar where he stayed for a while chatting to some friends. Night was falling. I'd just met him at an exhibition of his water colours. I thought I'd dazzled him with my verbal brilliance, but when he came back, the only thing on my mind was whether he would put his hand on mine again. He did. I couldn't bring myself to look at him.

"You talk a lot, don't you? And you just confuse everything with words, they stop you enjoying things," he said.

"How do you know?"

"I always notice what is unnecessary. I'm a specialist in the field. There may not be a lot of money in it, but nevertheless I know my subject. You liked my paintings of sailing boats, didn't you? Fine. I knew that. Words often serve only to make you distrust what you're saying, to get lost in them."

"Do you think so?"

"I think you should look at me a bit more and not think so much. I like it when you look at me."

I did so and he squeezed my fingers harder.

"Thanks," he said. "Shall we try not saying anything for a while, just to see what happens?"

And suddenly, life formed a quiet pool in that brief space between his eyes and mine; it had begun to flow gently and transparently like the waters of a river into which you can fearlessly plunge.

I tried to remember. That afternoon, Manolo had said that he only painted when he felt like it, that he considered life and art to be an adventure and that his one ambition was to be happy. My pompous speech, which he cut short with that unforgettable period spent gazing into each other's eyes, had been all about the joys of hard work and the possibility of making the demands of work an adventure too, of creating a harmony between belief and feeling and purifying the mixture in the still of technique.

"Good grief!" he'd said, smiling.

Why did it trouble me, then, the fact that he'd succeeded as a painter and was pleased with himself? I couldn't put it down to his change of style, especially since I couldn't give an opinion on paintings I hadn't even seen and about which, I had to admit, I didn't feel the least bit curious. The root of my unease lay in my refusal to accept that the New York gallery owner, who until then I had stubbornly thought of as a minor character, could have had so much influence on him.

Anyway, I couldn't testify to those changes until I saw him face to face. I needed to see him more than anything else in the world, to read in his eyes whether or not he'd forgotten me. No, he couldn't have. He said that he liked me because I was free, because he never knew what I might say next. I had to play that card, to find out, whatever the price, if he still considered me an antidote against monotony. I sensed that at that very moment he was feeling my absence, as I was his. It's true that I'd hardly eaten and, on the other hand, had drunk quite a lot, but that sudden, inner presentiment revived me. No reproaches, simply take up where we'd left off, with a sporty, nonchalant air: "As we were saying yesterday ..." Just the way he liked it.

I took out the writing paper and matching envelopes that I'd bought in a bookshop. It didn't have the Statue of Liberty on the front like the paper on which I wrote to you, Sofía, that one letter I sent to you at the beginning of this turbulent month of May. Instead it had a sailing boat, which isn't bad either. I placed a sheet on the marble tabletop and started writing:

Dear Manolo,

I'm in the café in Callejón del Tinte where you first told me to stop speechifying. I don't want to go and see your exhibition because it seems to me that your paintings are getting dangerously close to being daubs and because in Yankeeland you seem to have picked up a very pedantic way of speaking. I want to know if you only use it in interviews or if you need taking down a peg or two, as you did with me. In other words, I want to see you, I need to. No speeches, I promise. Just so that we can look into each other's eyes for a while and see what happens. An hour would do. What do you think?

Consult your diary. I'll give you a deadline. I'll wait for you the day after tomorrow in the little bar on that long beach where we watched the sun go down one endless day. I'll be there from 6 p.m. onwards. Rafa, the waiter, sends his regards to you and was of the opinion that you wouldn't stop long in America. He thinks we're still going out together. I'm staying in the four-star hotel that you can see from there and which you recommended to me; at night, they have a pianist playing. By the way, you still owe me a dance. I could dance with a man by the name of Daniel Rueda, but I don't fancy it. He has the marks of an executive. I hope you haven't become an executive too. You look very handsome in the photo in the newspaper. I need to hear you and see you.

I'll wait for you the day after tomorrow at the bar. As you would say, that's an order.

Lots of love,
Mariana

I put the letter in an envelope and sealed it without re-reading it. Perhaps I should have left out the allusions to New York; it might sound like a reproach. Despite the fact that I'd partially recovered my euphoric state, I was afraid to go over it again. I remembered your golden rule: "Never ever cross anything out." This was no time for doubts.

I got up and went over to the phone and realized that I felt so dizzy I had to grab hold of one of the chairs. My gestures weren't very assured and harmonious either while I looked in my address book for the telephone number of Manolo's parents, which I found neither under M nor under R and which in the end I found under P, where I'd also noted down the telephone numbers of other friends' and clients' parents. I dialled the number and a woman with a very soft voice answered. I asked her for the exact address of the house and if I could leave a letter there for Manolo.

"Well, they're staying at the Hotel Atlántico," she said.

"Won't you be seeing him?"

"Of course I will! He's supposed to be coming over this evening."

"Well, I'm going to leave the letter in your letter box, if you don't mind, because it's nearer for me. You will give it to him, won't you?"

"Of course I will, dear. It's Rosalía, isn't it?"

"No, no, I'm a friend of his from Madrid."

When I reached the front door of that house, my legs were trembling. I looked around. There was no one in the street. I hesitated for a few moments wondering whether I should tear up the envelope, which I was clutching in my hand inside my pocket, or put it in the box. The latter option prevailed and I slipped it in quickly, as nervously as someone depositing a letter bomb. I ran off, as if fleeing from myself. I went to the nearest taxi rank where I caught a taxi to bring me back here. I spent most of the journey with my head thrown back and my eyes closed, like on that day, suddenly so far away, when I drove with Raimundo from the hospital to his flat in Calle de Covarrubias. Only now there was no one by my side to stroke my hair.

All this happened yesterday, Sofía. I've spent today in the hotel, writing to you and feeling very excited. I'd give anything to have seen his face when he read the letter and to know if she was by his side when he picked it up. I feel afraid again, the wake of disquiet that's always left by decisions taken under the influence of alcohol. On the one hand, I can't wait for the time to pass, on the other, I'm happy here, cocooned in the unease of the unresolved, of events refracted into a thousand possible endings because, as yet, there hasn't been one, feeling safe and at the same time trapped in a web of unfinished business.

Writing to you, though, is calming my anxieties a little. The most meaningless things seem to acquire meaning when you go over them often enough. Ultimately, that's what's so important about stories, regardless of how they're going to end: I mean, recording how they began, don't you think? That's what you did in your first batch of homework, going over in minute detail all the things that happened before our meeting. (By the way, I hope you've kept your homework up.) I'm merely brazenly copying the system you use.

I'll continue, Sofía, even though I don't quite know where it's leading. Lots of love,
Mariana

PS The people in room 204 left today. However, as minor characters they still seem highly significant to me.

XV

Encarna's junk room

There's a room in the house which has never been renovated in any way, although it's changed its shape and its name according to circumstances that have imperceptibly changed us as well. At present, it's called "Encarna's junk room".

When she and Lorenzo moved to the refuge, she left some of her things in the room because that's where she always slept, and every now and then she renews her promise to come and spend an afternoon or two throwing out what she doesn't need and removing anything that's in the way. Of course, given her natural dislike of purges or for definitively giving up on anything, this is a promise she's never kept. Since she made the promise in good faith and, after hints dropped by Daría, has given us permission, for the time being (one of her favourite expressions) to use the boxes and shelves that remain empty, the fact is that everything we don't need or don't know where to put ends up there. Stick it with Encarna's junk for the time being, we'll decide what to do with it later. A gradual, complex coexistence has grown up between the things that were there already and the things that continue to arrive, and the room – which opens on to the central courtyard and has been called by turns "the small blue room" and "the goat" – has taken on, in its current incarnation as junk shop, the peculiar mixture of openness, obscurity and disorder that characterizes its former inhabitant; indeed this is even more marked than when Encarna actually lived there. The whole room is like a provisional warren presided over by that phrase "for the time being", and it has the wholeheartedness characteristic of generous souls prepared to give shelter to emergency cases, problems, secrets and pilgrims from any race or country. It's as difficult to define as a smell, but equally unmistakable.

When something has been given up as lost for ever, sooner or later, even though no one can remember having taken it there, it's almost certain to turn up in Encarna's junk room, although, as a general rule, it's never there when you look for it, at least not on that particular day. On the other hand, you do usually find something else that you were looking for obsessively and fruitlessly on another similar occasion, as if time, through these small acts of wickedness, these tricks and consolation prizes, wanted to demonstrate that it is governed solely by the laws of its sovereign caprice and gives rewards only when it feels like it, in short, that it is the master. For some reason this continues to surprise us, as if it were something that had happened for the first time and for which one must find a logical explanation. "Look, would you believe it, I've finally found the big scissors and I went through this whole box when I was looking for them before! Who could have put them there? It was about time they turned up …"

Time has the upper hand, as regards its decisions and its gifts, if we're capable of receiving those gifts with gratitude and grace. The hours are almost never empty if you crack them open, and rare indeed are the hours that do not carry in their breast something we find indecipherable or unworthy of consideration, for we stubbornly care only whether or not it coincides with what we had asked for. Of course it doesn't. It almost never coincides and you'd better get used to the idea. The hours of our lives are like a Father Christmas of the "take it or leave it" variety: they don't like entreaties and they don't like demands. Our flatly rejecting the pact they propose and the fruit that they offer is tantamount to laying down the early foundations for hardening of the arteries. If you do accept the terms, it's best to do so gladly and with an alert mind because that's when you get unexpected extras. As we know, surprise is a hare and if you go out hunting for it, you'll never find it sleeping in a field. But we always forget that just when we most need to remember it. Even I do, and I repeat it to myself often enough.

By the way, I've been studying the collage of the white hare emerging in the middle of a cocktail party where only two young girls notice its appearance, a surrealist herald who presides, amongst fragments of mirror, over my first notebook. I began a third notebook in order to tell the story of the red dress after a lapse of nineteen days it seems. How odd "writing time" is! It really does control things: it imposes itself as absolute master, especially when we've assumed it has fallen silent for good, then it erupts again after a long absence, ready to sweep us up in its drunken swell and overturn any appearance of simultaneity, a tyrannical whirlwind that bowls us over and whirls us around to carry us off wherever it fancies. Abandon yourself to it, Sofía, don't be afraid, that only makes matters worse. It defies vertigo. It doesn't allow you to protest at the bends in the road, it won't let you shut your eyes or suggest another route. You think it's time to enter Encarna's junk room? Right, let's go. Afterwards, you'll understand why you had to go in there.

I felt very restless last night and I gave in to the temptation of looking for photos of the children when they were little. I don't like sticking them in an album because I always feel as if I were dissecting butterflies instead of merely hunting them in order to admire them close to for a moment before letting them fly away again; as a consequence, they're always all over the place, mixed up with letters and papers or inside books. Anyway, I couldn't find the batch I was anxiously looking for: two rolls in black-and-white that my sister-in-law Desi took on the beach that summer we spent with them in Suances, the summer after I'd had my last child.

Higinio, her husband, had bought an old two-storey house there which used to belong to a famous family who had come down in the world and were torn apart by multiple squabbles. For some years it had remained empty and, according to them, it was in a pretty terrible state. Higinio had spared no expense in modernizing the interior, nor stinted on any detail that might contribute to their comfort. He had left the façade and the garden as they were, though, limiting himself to correcting a few imperfections.

"I owe a lot to this garden," he used to say. "Sitting there on that bench, I became the man I am now."

His father had worked for many years as a gardener in that house, and sometimes, if Higinio had behaved himself during the week, his father would let him go with him, on the clear understanding that he didn't make any trouble, that he sat quietly and didn't speak to anyone except to say hello or if spoken to.

"I did as I was told," he remarked. "Nobody encouraged me to do otherwise. Things were different then, of course, and when I look back on it now, I can't really see much wrong with it. The rich man in his castle etc. If we're not equal, then we're not, why go fooling ourselves? And if you want to get yourself a better position, then you earn it with the sweat of your brow, that's all there is to it."

Sitting on that bench in the garden, beneath the old magnolia tree, while he watched the shifting movements of the fleeting, white shadows that appeared on the upper gallery or strolled along the box-edged paths or, with extraordinary nonchalance, climbed the stairs to that unknown paradise, Higinio had nursed his first desires for social revenge, his ambitious dreams for the future had sprung into being and he had promised himself that he would not cease in his endeavours until he had as much money as the ladies and gentlemen of that house.

Now, according to Eduardo, he's got more than they ever had. He's a rather watered-down version of Heathcliff, though, since I doubt that any of those vague female shadows he spied on from the garden ever died of love for him, or even uttered a sigh. He lacks any kind of devilish charm; he's jovial, enterprising and fanatically clean and tidy. He's also a bit on the ugly side. He must be about seventy-something now, but he takes care of himself and he doesn't look his age. He married Desi when he was in his fifties and they haven't had any children. Although they often talk of adopting one, they've never actually taken any steps to do so and now, whenever that possibility resurfaces, it has clearly been relegated to the attic where we store all the regrets and failures which, as we grow older, we try to present to others in a sugar-coated version.

They had arranged the right wing of the ground floor for guests — three bedrooms, a study and a bathroom — all very cute and modern, apart from some of the rather valuable heavy furniture and paintings that the previous family had left in the house in order to push up the price a bit. Although it was very cleverly done, that contrast provoked a certain feeling of unease in me, as if, amongst the shifting sands of my personal life, it picked up the echoes of a silent battle between the authentic and the false, and the weight of that discord between two alien strata of time added to my own inability to adapt to the present and be reconciled to the past. Besides, although the rooms in which we were to be the first guests were furnished and decorated in almost excessively good taste, they were cold and dark because they faced north and the outer wall was covered by ivy so thick that it obscured part of the windows, thus cutting out some of the light. Higinio refused to prune it because that was how his father had liked it and the former owners had always respected his wishes.

From the moment we arrived, all this only increased my already considerable reluctance to participate in other people's joys or to follow the thread of stories I felt had nothing to do with me and was made worse by my habitual unease about moving (only exacerbated when plans for the summer holidays are afoot), plus the tiredness brought on by the journey and my concern because Amelia, who was teething, had diarrhoea. The tour of every room in the house, to which Desi and her husband submitted us as soon as we arrived, proved utterly exhausting and I couldn't bear to listen to the detailed explanations they went into about the renovations; how much better the whole thing was when compared with its former, highly irrational layout, the story behind each and every object. It was like being dogged by an implacable guide, only worse, because in this case there were two of them and they continually interrupted each other, a habit they cultivate even when they're not showing people over the house and which they find hilarious, considering it proof of their loving symbiosis. I've always found Desi's relentless optimism and energy rather inhibiting. She's not exactly someone I'd go to when I felt like crying, and that night I really did. I found it almost hard to breathe. It had been unbearably hot all day and a storm was threatening.

I remember that I left the table when supper was over and put Lorenzo and Encarna to bed in their respective rooms. Once I was back in our own bedroom, while Amelia was eating her supper, I took advantage of the fact that Eduardo had stayed behind for dessert and sat down for a

lf-suppressed weep, what I call an emergency weep, indispens-
relieving distress, although it doesn't give me any real respite or
time to fantasize. By the time Eduardo came into the room, I'd just
finished changing Amelia's nappy, put her in the cradle and was gazing
wearily at our half-unpacked luggage. My eyes were dry though. There
was a rumble of thunder, and I got up to close the window that was
banging against the wall. It was raining. Just as well. I breathed in the
delicious smell of wet earth for a few moments before returning to my
precarious inner world whose futility contrasted with the wild forces of
Nature. I could hear fat drops of rain bouncing off the gravel in the
garden and the loud whistling of a sudden wind shaking the branches of
the trees. Eduardo had remained standing with his hands behind his back
and when I turned round our eyes met. He looked very severe. He
immediately began reproaching me for my negative attitude, for the
discontent apparent on my face and my obvious indifference when other
people spoke to me. I didn't seem to realize how insolent the expression
on my face was sometimes.

"What expression?" I asked, frowning again after that brief moment
of peace.

He shoved me towards the big mirror on the dressing table and
switched on the three-branched wall light overhead. He was gripping me
by the shoulders as if afraid I might run away.

"That expression! Do you see?"

Yes, I saw. I shook him off and turned out the light which was falling
directly on Amelia's cradle. I remember that scene with absolute clarity
because, years later, when I went to the psychiatrist and he asked me
when I first had the feeling that I was living with a stranger, that was the
image that first came to mind: the two of us reflected in the mirror, while
the rain was beating down outside. What I saw in my expression was
something resembling hatred.

"I just don't like being treated badly or perhaps you don't know that,"
I said. "I doubt that you do, frankly, since you know almost nothing
about me."

He was so taken aback that, at first, he didn't react. Normally, I didn't

268

say anything – a bad habit of mine. You keep choking things back and then, suddenly, you explode at a moment which seems entirely incomprehensible to the person on the receiving end of that ill-defined outpouring of malaise whose causes cannot really be justified. I realized too that, according to the matrimonial rulebook, I had used the wrong expression when I said I felt I'd been treated badly, because although Eduardo had occasionally slammed the odd door, he had never raised his hand to me. He seized on that at once.

"What do you mean by 'being treated badly'?" he asked.

I shrugged and felt suddenly weak, and I noticed that tears, that most cunning of female weapons against clear thinking, were again clouding my ability to explain in logical terms any of the confusion which I myself had helped to create. I withdrew, like a snail inside its shell, at the least threat that my behaviour might be questioned. I thought of Mariana, as I often did in moments of weakness. She hadn't mistreated me physically either; she'd simply refused to understand my need to explain myself. But had I really fought to make her understand that need, appealing to a logic from which stammered words and tears were excluded? The truth is that I hadn't, and I felt a terrible nostalgia for that golden age of our friendship when we had no need for long explanations to understand each other, when even a hint of sorrow in the expression of the other was soon dispelled by a touch or a joke. "Come on, Sofía, that's quite enough staring up into the seeming void." And the void would become precisely that, only a seeming void to be filled instead with hope. The golden summers passed and nothing ever happened, but the unexpected was always just about to happen. "Quoth the raven, 'Never more!'"

Eduardo took courage from my silence.

"I really don't understand you, Sofía, I really don't," he said. "Are you referring to something that happened today?"

I stared at him abstractedly. Through my tears he looked blurred. Today? Where did that "today" date from?

"What do you mean what am I referring to?"

"What's wrong with you? Honestly! I'm referring to what you said about being treated badly. Don't make me lose my patience, please. Explain yourself. What were you referring to exactly?"

"I don't know. Nothing in particular. They're just things that you feel but can't explain."

"Especially if you don't even try!" he shouted.

I realized that he was quite right, but I didn't know how to placate him. At that moment, that was all I wanted to do, to sweep the whole affair under the carpet, along with all its awkward ramifications. I just wanted him to stop shouting in case he woke the baby.

"Look, just forget it. I'm sorry. You're right. Just leave it, I'm probably just tired."

He looked at me, beside himself with rage, and I realized, as I had before, that you can't pacify someone else's anger if, at the bottom of your heart, you feel no tenderness for the angry party. On the other hand, I was the one who was crying, and as long as my crying meant that I put my need for unconditional acceptance above other people's demands to be understood, the dispute would remain unresolved. There's nothing in the world more absurd or more boring than a matrimonial squabble.

"It's all very well you saying leave it, but you're crying," he exploded, "and people don't cry just because they're tired. What do you want, tell me? What is it that you haven't got? People treat you badly you say … honestly! You waltz through life as if the world owed you a living and wasn't giving it to you. At least stop crying! I've had enough! I really don't know any more what it would take to make you happy, I'm serious."

The word "serious" has remained fixed in my memory as the adjective to describe that moment because, suddenly, alerted by an almost imperceptible noise, I dried my eyes and looked over at the door. It had slowly swung open and Encarna was standing barefoot on the threshold in her nightshirt, looking at us wide-eyed, not moving. That summer she was wearing plaits.

"Why are you crying, Mama?" she asked without a shred of shyness, in an almost critical tone of voice.

Her father, who had his back to the door, turned round, looking very embarrassed, while I tried to erase from my face the bitter look that had started the argument.

"I'm not crying, love. I'm just a bit upset."

"You are crying, he makes you cry," she insisted.

"Don't say such things. Papa's very kind."

Eduardo lost his temper.

"This is a great start to the summer!" he said. "Do you mind going back to bed and leaving us in peace?"

We'd both gone over to the door by then. I crouched down and gave her a hug.

"Off you go, sweetheart, it's late, why aren't you in bed? I thought you'd already gone to sleep."

"I can't. I'm afraid. There are people walking about in the garden."

"Don't be silly, it's the rain."

"No. Something else is happening. Do you know what's happening?"

She put her arms around my neck and tried to whisper in my ear, but her father unceremoniously parted us. Ever since Amelia was born, it had been clear that Encarna was jealous and she started demanding the total attention that no one had ever deprived her of until then. Her brother had never overshadowed her or provoked any jealousy; on the contrary, she seemed to feel maternally protective towards him. Doubtless this was because when she learned to speak, "Zenzo", as she called him, already formed part of the elements with which she began to enrich her vocabulary or else because, despite being a boy, he always submitted to her wheedling – a submissiveness which, according to Amelia, has still not entirely disappeared. One thing is certain: ever since she was a little girl, she's always been remarkable for her self-confidence, initiative and clear thinking. That was why it was so strange that, especially in her relationship to me, she should suddenly have become so babyish, given she could already speak English, read fluently and was a leading light at her school. Eduardo maintained, possibly quite rightly, that I collaborated in that regression, that I spoiled her too much.

"Come on," I said to her, "I'll take you back to your bedroom and you can tell me what it's all about."

"She doesn't have anything to tell you that I can't hear too," Eduardo said irritably. "That's quite enough of all these silly whims. You're eight years old now."

"So what?" she said. "Adults have secrets too."

I noticed that she was finding it as difficult as I was to hold back the tears. Her father took her hand.

"That's enough," he said, in authoritarian mode. "Either I take you back to your bedroom or you can go alone. As you wish."

She let go of her father's hand and lowered her eyes.

"I'd rather go alone," she said. "Goodnight."

And she left, a resentful look on her face.

When we were alone again, the noise of the rain falling on the trees in the garden had intensified. My throat felt tight and I kept listening carefully in case the sound of Encarna crying in the room next door should give me an excuse to go and see her. I heard nothing, only the rain and the wind tearing at the branches of the trees. Perhaps she'd put her head under the sheets to cry, just as I used to do when I was little. And again the past, like a stab of pain, clouded my ability to surrender myself to the present and to understand it. No, she wouldn't be crying as I used to do, it was different. I hardly ever felt supported by my mother, but then I thought: was I so sure that it was different? Did I know for certain what Encarna needed from me at that moment? Of course I did: she needed my unconditional love. But there were the others too; I couldn't avoid the responsibilities incurred by my multiple maternity, nor by Eduardo, nor by the criteria he imposed, still less by my secret desires for solitude. It was a question of maintaining a harmonious balance between opposing forces, that was the crux of the matter. In a sudden moment of lucidity, I realized that talking to Eduardo about this matter — or matters — whose importance seemed self-evident to me, would be a step towards my own maturity and that I should not wait a moment longer for the right time or the right tone of voice in order to begin that analysis of these unresolved problems. This particular moment would do, why wait for another?

Suddenly, it seemed to me utterly irrelevant for him to break the silence in order to resume the conversation we were having before Encarna had appeared in the doorway, as if his words had been carried away by the hurricane winds of the night, leaving no trace.

"Who has treated you badly, tell me? You've been made welcome in this house, haven't you?"

I said we should just forget it, it didn't matter any more; but it did matter to him, it was his one obsession. I sat down on the bed, my eyes fixed on the floor, plunged once again into apathy. He kept on and on about it and finally told me what had hurt him most: the way I had snubbed his sister. According to him, I hadn't been sufficiently enthusiastic in my expressions of pleasure and gratitude, in marvelling at the beauty of the house and praising Desi's incomparable talent for interior decoration.

Throughout that summer, the alliance between Eduardo and his sister grew stronger; he has always felt unbounded admiration for her and he never tires of praising her organizational abilities and her domesticity, her energy, her wonderful cooking, how well she understands her husband, her social graces, her altruism. Whenever I came across them talking together, they would immediately fall silent; not that I cared, I wasn't even curious. Besides, I felt equally excluded from the conversations they held in my presence and in which I didn't always attempt to participate. The topics would be plans for excursions in the area, gastronomy, types of car and, above all, what a bargain they'd got when they bought that house, profiting from the economic difficulties of a now ruined family.

"Well, you know what they say," Desi would say, "peasant begets gentleman begets pauper."

Higinio would light a Havana cigar and savour her words with evident satisfaction.

"Who'd have thought it! If only my father, may he rest in peace, could see us now!" he would say, looking out from the terrace, where a maid would serve us coffee, at the dark fronds of the garden.

I thought it was a very gloomy garden, overshadowed less by the thick, sturdy trees than by the impalpable presence of the people who had lived in it before us and who, it seemed, had left little joy behind them in the air.

Encarna didn't think the garden was a very happy place either and she didn't enjoy playing in it, but she told me that all the endless stories she invented before going to sleep came in from the garden through the window and would all crowd into her head together. She liked that, but it frightened her too, because she wasn't inventing them herself and sometimes she didn't understand them.

"It's like reading," she said, "I get the story from what's down in the book."

"Yes, yes, but with these stories from the garden, who's making them up?"

She adopted a confidential tone, looking around her first, even though we were alone sitting in the garden, underneath the magnolia tree in fact. Lorenzo had gone off to play football with some friends. Amelia was asleep in her cradle and the others had gone off on one of those long car trips planned in detail the night before and in which I did not always participate. It was a very cool afternoon and the birds were singing. She tugged at my sleeve to draw me closer.

"There are some little men who sit on the tops of the trees," she said, giving a fearful glance upwards. "You're the only person I've told. It's a secret. You won't tell anyone else, will you?"

"No, don't worry, I won't."

"It's nice having secrets, isn't it?"

"Yes, very nice. But tell me, have you seen them yourself?"

"Nobody sees them, because they only come when the sun's gone down and it's beginning to get dark, and even then not always. Some nights they don't come at all, they only come when they want to. And they're not the same ones every night, it depends on the weather."

She looked at me. I didn't say anything. I made a gesture encouraging her to go on. Children know when someone believes them. My childhood wasn't so very far away that I'd forgotten that.

"They're the ones who tell me the stories," she continued, "and they blow them into my room and up into my head through my ear.

But because it's very narrow, the stories bump against each other and they arrive in my head in bits because they talk a lot and interrupt each other, like Aunt Desi and Uncle Higinio, especially on cloudy days. And then, of course, I'm the one who has to sort out what they've put in my head. The same thing happens when I read a book with lots of different characters in it, I have to make room for what they say, do you know what I mean? Just so that I can understand them, because not all the stories will fit in my head at once, there are too many, you pick up one and they all fall to pieces. Does that happen to you too?"

I said that, yes, exactly the same thing happened to me, exactly, although I hadn't heard the men in the garden, and that when I couldn't understand things in the order they came in, a sort of cloud would appear in front of my eyes that covered the sun; I'd always been like that, ever since I was little. In order to see the light again I had to invent a story that would explain the others.

"But," I said, "if you don't tell that story to someone else or write it down, that gets forgotten too and you find that when you want to remember it, it's all in bits. I mean everything tends to get broken and you have to stick it back together again; that's how it is, a bit from here and a bit from there, everything's in bits."

Encarna burst out laughing. She bent over to tear out a page from a newspaper that had fallen on the floor and started ripping it up and throwing the fragments into the air, while she sang:

"It's all in bits and pieces, everything's in bits!"

I laughed to see her. Then she came back and sat on the bench by my side, kissed me and said:

"You understand everything so well. I'm so glad that you can't fit everything in your head at the same time either. I mean there just isn't room, is there?"

"Of course not. Far from it."

Then she explained to me that she noticed it most when she saw maps of countries with all those rivers and mountains and frontiers. If you started thinking that all those things actually existed at the same time

275

with people moving about and animals and fields of corn, you'd get dizzy. The same thing happened when you stared at the stars for a long time. That was even worse, because they looked so small and yet they must be enormous, even the ones that looked like specks of dust. And there were hundreds and millions of them and something was happening on every single one of them and we knew nothing about it. She felt small as a grain of sand or an ant, and then she'd be afraid and when she slept she would dream of universes.

My heart turned over and we looked at each other in silence, as if testing the possibility that we were sharing a rare and precious emotion. She looked at me questioningly with shining eyes, almost on the verge of tears.

"Don't ask me to explain it any better," she said. "It's very difficult to explain, but it's very frightening."

"Let's see if I've got this right. You dream that you're falling from a great height and you fall and fall and you keep bumping into planets and you can't see the ground or where you're going to land, is that it?"

"Yes, that's it, but the most frightening thing is that you can see yourself falling, the way you watch a star falling. I watch myself falling from down below, it's horrible."

"Well, all nightmares are a bit horrible and they're always about the same thing, about falling."

"I'd love to be able to fly, like Peter Pan, even if it was only in dreams. When you were little, what did you imagine Peter Pan looked like?"

We were so busy talking about Peter Pan, Scheherezade and many other mutual friends, that we didn't even notice that we'd missed tea. It was as if that day, the storytellers in the trees had got up early and come swinging down from the branches to sit around us as we named them: Hans Christian Andersen, Lewis Carroll, Robert Louis Stevenson, Collodi, Elena Fortún, Daniel Defoe, Perrault, Jules Verne, Salgari. We came to the conclusion that even in that garden it was sometimes possible to have a nice time and have good chats.

"Yes," agreed Encarna, "just as long as there are no adults about."

That afternoon marked the beginning of our intense summer friendship, comparable only to the friendship, also sparked off by literature, that had existed between Mariana and myself years ago when Don Pedro Larroque used to read the poetry of Jorge Manrique to us in class. When I relived my early fear of the precipice of time that Manrique had first made me peer over, an unexpected reward emerged from that same abyss. The enigmatic and mutable deity of Time suddenly stopped the vertiginous spinning of her wheel. What she was offering me with that truce was not, as on other occasions, the embalmed remains of a lost childhood, but a new childhood: the one my daughter was inviting me to share.

In the days that followed, I talked to her about Mariana. And about Noc. That summer Noc came to life again. We decided that he was, without a doubt, the chief of that band of little men who perched at night in the garden and adorned the trees with streamers of stories that changed colour according to the atmospheric conditions. We also understood – each in our own way – that the alliance Noc was forging between us was threatened by a set of circumstances that meant it would not only be shortlived but that it must also be secret.

That summer, Lorenzo ignored his sister almost completely and, encouraged by Higinio and Eduardo, who both clearly favoured him and were of the opinion that he should liberate himself from female company, he fell in with a group of rather simple-minded, sporty lads who were a bit older than him and whose friendship was a source of great pride. Encarna, on the other hand, didn't hit it off with anyone and preferred to read everything she could lay her hands on and then wait until she could talk to me about it when we had time to spare and no one would interrupt us. Those moments weren't always easy to find, especially for me, although the incentive to find them provided a salve for my anxieties and depressions. In fact, I became more friendly towards the others and sometimes, when we were together in a group and some of the phrases they said touched on our code of shared words, the smile and knowing look my daughter and I would exchange repaid me for my other woes. I considered myself privileged compared with those not fortunate enough to enjoy such a talisman and that made me more inclined to pity them and, as a consequence, to treat them more kindly. That talisman, however, was a coin which, like all coins, had two faces and sometimes it came up tails.

Encarna and I had come to a tacit agreement that we should not make a display of our closeness but rather hide it and that was exactly what gave it the emotional edge that characterizes the relationships of those crossed in love. In our case, however, there was an added inconvenience that detracted from the truth and joy of my rejuvenation. The recovery of my childhood became merely a mirage when I had to combine it with the trials and tribulations caused entirely by my unavoidable commitment to the world of adults in which Encarna could have no part. For example, during our talks alone, when she referred to "the grown-ups", excluding me from that group, my smile was clouded by a fatal awareness of my own duplicity. The same thing happened when she asked me what I was thinking about and it was something that I couldn't tell her, almost always something to do with her father. Sometimes I thought I could see in her eyes the same aversion towards him that was gathering strength in me. If that was a feeling we shared – something I never dared to ask – the suspicion that I was right, far from binding us together, cast a dense shadow over all our games and jokes, a shadow that separated us.

I remember one particular morning on the beach, shortly before our return to Madrid. Eduardo and I were still dragging around with us the remains of a rather bitter but nonetheless subdued nocturnal squabble; during our stay at Suances we had made considerable progress in our ability to keep down the volume, even though what we were saying was pure dynamite. I've more or less forgotten what sparked the argument, although I remember some complaint about how rude and rebellious Encarna was becoming, I, of course, being the only person responsible for her existence and upbringing. (In fact, neither then nor more recently has he ever deigned to discuss Lorenzo's upbringing with me, as if he considered that he had exclusive rights over Lorenzo's successes as well as his failures. I think that, deep down, Lorenzo is the only one of our children in whom he feels disappointed.) As usual in that kind of battle, fed by a clash of moods in the two warring parties rather than by the

278

apparent subject of the argument, we reached neither con̶
agreement. It's a well-known fact that our mood, being a g̶
element, is subject to unforeseeable fluctuations and is as capricious
the clouds. Just as not even the most expert painter will ever be able to
capture the changing shapes of the clouds, we can never foresee when
our soul will swell to such a size that it invades the space reserved for
another, still less remember afterwards the fortuitous cause of that colli-
sion, the shape it took or the bubbles into which it melted. What does
happen, when you love someone very much, is that you can sense when
their storm clouds are building and sometimes manage to withdraw your
own so that they don't conflict. I've never known very much about
Eduardo's clouds; I've simply never felt interested enough to think about
them. He must have them though. I only remember that on the night in
question, the clouds dispersed before the storm broke. He wearied of it
before I did and I took advantage of that to pretend to be asleep. As I've
learned to my cost throughout the time we've lived together, that
pretence can be a double-edged sword, because, fearful that the other
person is also only pretending to be asleep, you dare not move or put the
light on in case you stir up the embers of their grievances again.

Anyway, by the time day was dawning in the garden, coinciding with
the first gurgles and slaps from the cradle announcing that Amelia was
awake, I still hadn't slept a wink, going over and over certain painful
obsessions, the sort that only emphasize the diffuse sense of guilt that so
often clouds my happiness, stops me dreaming and makes everything
about me seem opaque; it's like a dull, persistent ache I can't quite locate.
I got up feeling very low and in no fit state to discuss *Twenty Thousand
Leagues Under the Sea* with Encarna, as I'd promised I would. All I
wanted was to sleep for hours on end, to stow away on Jules Verne's
submarine and to wake up amongst complete strangers.

Desi, on the other hand, whom I happened to meet in the kitchen, was
in an excellent mood that morning, enthusiastically preparing croquettes,
sandwiches and piles of other delicious picnic food. I remembered that
we'd arranged to spend all day on the beach with another couple who
also had children, one of whom, I seem to remember, was in Lorenzo's

gang and quite a good friend of his. As soon as I'd fed Amelia and changed her, I felt obliged to help Desi and to pay her a little attention, an extra effort that completely drained my reserves of energy, so much so that at one point I felt faint and had to sit down. She herself said I looked ill and asked if I was pregnant again.

During breakfast, she remarked on how lucky we were that it was a fine day and that we would have one last chance to savour the delights of the beach, something the rain had prevented us from doing for several days. She also decided who should travel in which car, gave various orders to the maids and was obviously thrilled at the idea of capturing us all in the lens of her new Leika, photography being one of her many hobbies.

"At last," she announced, "we're going to be able to take some photos that will be a proper souvenir of the summer. What with one thing and another, this is the first time I've been able to get you all together."

Encarna, who was sitting opposite me, kept trying to catch my eye while I was studiously trying to avoid hers. She didn't say a word all through breakfast. The previous evening, at the end of a conversation about submarines that Desi had interrupted, her look of irritation was as exaggerated as the promises she was always trying to extract from me whenever I left her to go and deal with the many other things I had to do. I realized, with a sorrow that lasted all night and further poisoned my insomnia, that I had to put a limit on the demands of that affection, simply because I couldn't respond to it with the same degree of exclusivity, even though it was my greatest source of light and energy. As she herself had sensed intuitively when she spoke of "dreaming about universes", you would have to have a thousand lives and a thousand hearts and a thousand heads if you wanted to give full and proper attention to all the shipwrecked images and feelings simultaneously clamouring for asylum.

"What's wrong, Mama?" she asked me afterwards when we were going out to the cars.

I said that nothing was wrong and that she should try and be nicer to her Aunt Desi, that sometimes, to judge by her expression, you'd think she was being tortured. I spoke to her in an impatient, rather cutting tone.

"I could say the same to you," she said, "except that when you ask me what's wrong I always tell you, even though you don't always tell me what's wrong with you."

"Tell me what's wrong with you, then?"

"I don't want her to take photos of us all together and to tell us to smile. I don't feel like smiling like an idiot just because she tells me to."

The photo session that day proved to be utterly exhausting, mainly because Desi didn't want to take the photos all at once, but only when the light and the composition seemed right. She'd recently finished a short correspondence course in photography and she was like an omnipresent being spying on our comings and goings, smiling the instant smile of someone hoping to spring a surprise, but at the same time demanding the victim's collaboration, neglecting to find out whether or not the surprise is to the liking of the person on the receiving end.

At the most unexpected moment she would say: "Don't move, please, stay exactly as you were. What a photo! Lorenzo, don't put your racquet down, that's it, but be careful not to block your sister. No, Sofía, you go a bit to the right, just the way you were before."

"But I don't know how I was before."

I was in such a state that any "before" involved a search that caught me up in a dangerous spiral, drawing me even further away from participating in the present moment. I remember with gratitude the company of those people – their faces now nothing but a blur – who came with us on the picnic, because they talked a lot and not only exempted me from taking part but helped to ease the tensions that might otherwise have arisen between Eduardo and myself. They were particularly concerned about the housing problem – I think he'd invested money in the construction industry – and Eduardo said that he'd decided to buy a bigger apartment because when Amelia grew up, there wouldn't be room for us in the apartment in Calle de Donoso Cortés. Although he barely looked at me when he said this, various remarks made by Higinio and Desi made it clear that he had often discussed this with them, and that they just assumed I knew about it. I simply said that I hated building work and hated moving.

"We all know that. I hoped you might come out with something a bit more original," said Eduardo.

I didn't say anything else.

Shortly before they called the children for lunch, I escaped and went for a walk along the seashore as far as the rocks. I sat down on one that was hollowed out like a cave and stayed there absolutely still and lost in thought watching the tide rise. I found the idea of returning to Madrid even more oppressive with the extra burden of Eduardo's plans which he'd never before spoken about in such a peremptory manner. My eyes filled with tears to imagine the children growing up and our settling into that new home (then just a nebulous idea with no precise location and now as clear and inescapable as it is laden with memories). Encarna, who had followed me, came slowly up behind me and put her hands over my eyes just when a wave exploded at our feet and splashed our faces.

"It's Sinbad the sailor!" she said.

"You startled me, sweetheart! We'll have to go back, the tide's coming in. Come on."

She looked at me.

"Are you crying or is that just where the sea splashed you?" she asked me.

"It's where the sea splashed me."

She put her arms around my neck.

"Do you know why I want to grow up?" she said in my ear.

"I don't know. You're always saying that you don't want to grow up."

"So that I can have a house of my own and you can come and live with me. A little house with balconies, overlooking the sea. And you wouldn't have to do anything, just tell stories. We'd let Noc come and visit at night."

"And what would we live on?"

"On the money we earned from telling stories. In lots of places they pay people to tell stories, you said so yourself."

I burst out laughing and gave her a kiss. For a few moments she had managed to turn the apartment in Calle Donoso Cortés and the one

282

where I'm now sitting and remembering that forgotten dream into a small house with balconies that opened on to the sea.

"You love me very much, don't you?" she asked.

"Very much, of course I do, you know I do."

"And we'll be together for ever and ever, won't we, whatever happens; the others don't matter."

"Look, the tide's coming in really fast now."

"Don't be frightened, I'll go ahead and you can hold my hand. Don't slip. I'll be your captain."

Desi suddenly appeared and took the last photo of the reel when we were beginning the descent, hands held and with our backs to the sea which had grown wilder and had just splashed us with another of its waves. We didn't notice her until she said:

"I came to call you for lunch. That will make a lovely photo, you'll see!"

And she was absolutely right. That's the photo I was looking for last night.

All the dormant feelings of that summer, so vague it might never have existed, slowly awoke from their anaesthetized sleep whilst I searched, ever more eagerly, for the two yellow envelopes where I last saw those photographs; what stands out in them, with the unmistakeable glow of a treasure, is the protective smile of Encarna as a little girl when she'd just invented, as a refuge for our future, a fairy-tale house that was later swept away by the sea, as implacably as it sweeps away the names in a heart pierced by an arrow that lovers trace in the sand.

I promised myself that if I found it, I'd get an enlargement made and buy a silver frame for it. That promise shattered, however, when I suddenly remembered the present-day Encarna's sarcastic smile when she's ridiculing certain houses belonging to the *haute bourgeoisie* whose coffee tables are so cluttered with family photos framed in silver and tortoiseshell that they're reduced to the status of a mere ornament, "with no room to put a book, a glass, an ashtray, or even lean one wretched elbow".

memory of that expression of Encarna's brought with it the
memory of the party at Gregorio Termes' house and the silent return
home in the car with Eduardo; not only has he not been out with me
since, but our subsequent conversations wouldn't fill three pages of this
notebook. This stark realization brought me abruptly back down to
earth. The imaginary and the everyday are like two enemy planes; one is
always shooting down the other. The effects of the fall take the form of
that coming to terms with time I've referred to again and again ever since
I started writing this. I began my first notebook, the one that begins with
the collage of the hare set amongst fragments of mirror, on the first day
of May, that is, the day after the party at Gregorio's. Earlier on, I wrote:
"Nineteen days, how odd 'writing time' is!" But what I rarely consider is
that, running on parallel lines to this project which has plunged me into
fictitious time, there is also real time which I've mentioned only very
tangentially, if at all: the "unreal experiences" that the psychiatrist
mentioned years ago. I obviously find it less painful to rummage around
in the events of the past than to ponder what's happening around me now
as I submerge myself in the task of filling up pages and re-reading them.

For example, earlier in these notebooks I mentioned that Eduardo and
I no longer sleep in the same room and that it's up to me to take the initia-
tive — since he won't — of starting a conversation that might open a
breach in the wall that separates us. What I didn't say is that we both
know the real cause of the silence that began when we drove back from
Gregorio Termes' party, and since then the silence has only thickened.
When I went out to the swimming pool that night to greet the month of
May on my own and I stood there looking up at the moon, I heard the
noise of someone scurrying away into the bushes, though not so fast that
I couldn't recognize Eduardo's walk and his broad shoulders vainly
trying to hide the reddish glow of his companion's hair. I've deliberately
tried to forget this scene, I've tried to erase it, and when it resurfaces I
have to acknowledge that the tears that made it seem blurred and uncertain were not tears of jealousy but of longing for my lost·youth. In fact,
the following day, I woke up singing "Yellow Submarine" and decided to
embark seriously on the literary salvage of a part of that lost youth. In

short, I'm still a victim of that stubborn tendency with which Encarna so often reproaches me: trying to seek refuge in the past. Of all my three children, she knows me best, even though she no longer dreams of building a little house with balconies overlooking the sea so that we could live there together.

"I must talk to Encarna," I thought, while I continued looking for the photo taken on the beach, "with the present-day Encarna."

When I thought that, I looked around me, because my search for the photo had inevitably brought me back to her old bedroom, now converted into a junk room, and even the smell of the place evoked her fugitive, indecipherable presence. I felt in corners and recesses, along shelves, like someone playing at blind man's buff, but I was pretty sure that it would not be that longed-for childhood I found.

"I must speak to her, tell her to give me a good talking-to, to tell me what a coward I am, to be my captain again. I must put out into that sea of changes, set sail 'stripped of any luggage' and head off to unknown ports."

Completely forgetting why I had gone to the junk room in the first place, I continued going over what has been happening outside myself during these last nineteen days while I've been busy filling notebooks. I haven't seen Lorenzo or Encarna; they've rung me up occasionally or Consuelo has mentioned that she's seen them and that they're fine. But I need to see them in person, in their own surroundings, to step down from my fantasies and present myself at the refuge.

And what about this Mariana I talk so much about in my notebooks? Where is the real-life Mariana, what can have happened to her? That night on the borders of April and May, while I was listening to the rambling confidences of a patient of hers, she — although I didn't know this at the time — was writing me a very long letter in which she encouraged me to go on with my homework before she set off on a voyage, destination unknown. But where is she now, what air is she breathing, apart from the air I breathe into her when I evoke her? I phoned her again three days ago, and the doctor standing in for her, Josefina Carreras, answered at once. She said that she's very worried because Mariana has given no sign of life and nobody knows where she is. She was so upset, she didn't seem like the same woman who spoke to me the first time; it would seem that psychiatrists are human too. She said that if I was a friend of hers and received any news from her that I should, please, get in touch with her immediately. She kept asking about the nature of our friendship and I didn't like that at all. I said that we were very close friends, but I didn't want to tell her my name or how long we'd been friends, although she asked me this in an avid tone that seemed both rude and rather disagreeable. "That's irrelevant," I said and hung up. Suddenly, I don't know why, I feel closer to Mariana than to anyone else and as if I were the guardian of some secret of hers. For some days now, I've been watching the mailbox with particular excitement, but without anxiety. I'm sure of two things: that Mariana is fine and that she'll write to me or phone me from wherever she is before she contacts anyone else. Dr Carreras doesn't know why she left Madrid, but I do. She was escaping from the problems of that friend of hers who tried to commit suicide. She says so at the end of the one letter from her that I've received: "One of these days, I'll phone you up and we'll arrange to meet, but not just now. I need to feel stronger. I really don't know how I've managed to keep going these last few days. I may leave Madrid for a week or so." Of course more than a week has passed now.

Anyway, what does it matter how much time has passed! I've filled two and a half notebooks, haven't I? That's enough. I wonder if this paper plane that lifts me above reality and allows me a better view of it will ever take flight again. As soon as I start taking account of hard facts and try to fit them in with imaginary ones, nothing coincides and I feel lost. She seemed lost too when she left. Hers is not a very pleasurable profession, poor thing. What slavery, listening to all those mad people. I can't stop writing, it's the only thing that will cure me, and besides, one day, I'll have to show her the notebooks. I'm writing them for her because I want to and because they may help her to understand things that affect us both. And, if I don't go mad in the process, I'll be able to listen to her problems with a clearer mind and to those of the children and to Eduardo. Yes, Eduardo too, why not? I'll ask him to tell me about the redhead if that will help him get it off his chest. Everyone gets tired of everyone else: it happens in novels and even in the best families – the worst thing you can do is lie to yourself. I'll explain that it isn't jealousy that stops me having this conversation, just laziness and fear of change, for our separation would involve having to think about moving, about building work, invoices, a whole new batch of papers to deal with. That's the plain, unvarnished truth. I'm not going to play Lady Bountiful or the grand romantic at this stage. Although it might offend him to hear me talk this way. He might prefer to believe that he's hurting me.

I was so absorbed in these thoughts that I was startled to see him standing silhouetted in the door of Encarna's junk room.

"What time is it?" I asked.

"I don't know, midnight I think."

"So late."

"Yes, I'm shattered. What are you doing?"

"I was looking for some papers that Encarna needs," I lied.

And that pointless lie made me realize fleetingly that it's much more difficult than it seems to be honest and that some things are not so easily resolved.

"What's happened to those two?" he asked distractedly, as if out of duty. "They seem to have disappeared from the face of the earth."

"They're fine. Lorenzo's still working in that architect's office and Encarna is writing, as you know."

I had lied again, because Lorenzo hasn't worked in that architect's office for ages and hasn't even finished his degree, something I can't bring myself to confess to his father.

"Actually, I don't see them much either," I said, adding: "If you want some supper, there are things in the fridge."

"No, I've just been out for a business supper. I'm almost dead on my feet."

"You'd better go to bed then. Oh, Desi called."

"What did she want?"

"I don't know, she didn't tell me."

"I'll phone her tomorrow. Goodnight."

He was about to leave when he turned round. He spoke now in an irritated tone.

"You need a brighter light in here. You look like a ghost crouched beneath that bare bulb hanging from the ceiling. I've told you before, this room gives me the creeps."

The aggression in his voice when he spoke of Encarna's junk room, evidence of all the things that separate us, seemed to crash blindly against Encarna herself, against all her tenderness, her idealism and her insatiable quest for honesty.

"Oh well," I said sharply, "we can always call in Gregorio Termes and he can turn it into a sauna."

He frowned and disappeared without saying anything more. The pending conversation was deferred yet again, but it didn't feel like a lead weight now and I couldn't rouse any sense of regret at all.

As expected, I didn't find the photos from the summer in Suances, but what did turn up was a ruled notebook with oilcloth covers that attracted my attention. The words "Sombre Tales" were written on the first page. Only a few of the pages had been written on, in Encarna's handwriting; she's always beginning notebooks and then not finishing them. Judging by the date given underneath the title (written in block capitals and underlined), I reckoned she must have begun it in her first year at university when she was about the age I was when I met Guillermo. While she herself has given me more than enough opportunity to contrast our respective childhoods and even to fish for them with the same net, I have very little material by which to compare her adolescence with mine, apart from data provided by my own interpretation of reality which is unreliable and hardly rigorous.

I'm not usually one for rummaging around in other people's papers, but the recent evocation of that summer in Suances had left me with such a thirst to discover what transformations had taken place since then in Encarna's soul that I absolved my curiosity of all guilt, arguing that it was, after all, a literary text, not a diary. I picked up the notebook, switched off the light in the junk room, tiptoed across the corridor to Amelia's room, closed the door quietly behind me and lay down fully clothed on the divan, ready to devour that sombre tale. For it turned out to be only one tale and, although it was only fifteen pages long, one was quite enough.

I don't just mean because of its remarkably high literary quality, but because of the shudder that ran through me when I compared the poems I was writing at that age, full of longings for an ideal love, with the frank, sinister tone of "Exile with no Return", the one sombre tale, possibly incomplete, that appears in the notebook hurriedly written and with few corrections. Eloy, a boy of fourteen, is travelling with his parents through a barren, uninhabited landscape in a sleek car driven by his father; the car is adorned with wreaths of chrysanthemums as if it were a hearse. In the back seat, where he's lying down pretending to be asleep, the adolescent, who is described as being like Icarus with broken wings, imagines a fatal accident from which he emerges unscathed. The detailed description of the fictitious accident, accompanied by the evidence which the judge requires from the sole survivor once the corpses have been removed, alternates with the real-life dialogue between the father and mother in the front seat. By the fifth page, I felt such a weight on my chest that I had to take off my glasses and rest for a while. Following the thread of that matrimonial conversation, as dull, futile and cruel as all the conversations I have with Eduardo, Encarna — alias Icarus without his wings — reflects upon the antagonistic tendencies that cohabit in her brain: on the one hand a desire to examine and under-stand everything and, on the other, an adherence to moribund beliefs whose abandonment would mean abandoning paradise. She confesses her early indignation at the cowardice and duplicity of her parents, her inability to continue to idealize them and her disgust at having been born into a world whose laws were written without her acquiescence. If he falls back into the temptation of an idyll with his mother, Eloy will have nothing left of his own to tell, apart from the exploration of his soul through the twisted, falsified data that she herself shows him. Although he knows that freeing himself from the family bonds will mean embarking on an exile without return, he decides to renounce the lie. Suddenly a blinding flash forces him to open his eyes. When he sits up, the hearse is surrounded by the flames of a devastating fire. He only just has time to crawl to safety.

When I finished reading "Exile with no Return", I felt like someone waking from a nightmare and although, when I looked about me, I could see no fire, my soul was in flames.

The need to see Encarna coincided with a fiery, urgent desire to escape from the apartment, to rebel against the lie, to cast off my moorings. "I must talk to Encarna and tell her everything that's happening to me and what I'm feeling now, I can't delay for even a minute longer; of all the people close to me, she's the only one who understands me." The refuge suddenly appeared before me like that little house with balconies overlooking the sea which her childish imagination had built to offer me asylum. "You wouldn't have to do anything," she'd said to me, "just tell stories." And that is precisely what I needed to do. She herself had just shown me that stories can be sombre, that they don't always need a happy ending, indeed, that such stories must be told in a detailed, skilful way even if they don't have a happy ending; perhaps, when you think about it, they require even more skill. Of course, it's very difficult to know how and when to end them, to hit upon the right unhappy ending. That's exactly what has been happening to me ever since I started these notebooks. I write nothing but unfinished stories, fragments, and I bind them together as best I can but they're still nothing but odd fragments, alive and kicking, trying to elbow their way into the plot. There's nothing there, just a whole life into which they've flowed and into which many more continue to flow, each one singing its own song, all those intermingled waters, all that mud; and without leaving the house, every box I open, every cloud I see passing by my window, every word I hear and every book I start to read, breaks into a thousand pieces, each reflecting new fragments of life: shattered stories. The only almost-happy ending these incomplete stories can have will be that of being handed over to someone who will smile tearfully when they receive them.

I looked at the clock. It was half past midnight. I replaced the notebook in a box, put on my jacket, picked up my money and my keys and then, just as I was about to leave the house, I retraced my steps and went back into the kitchen. It would be more sensible to call the refuge first before going just to see if Encarna was there or had gone out. I was in no mood for futile journeys.

As soon as I picked up the phone, I realized that I'd interrupted a conversation; Eduardo was talking to someone on the bedroom extension.

"Please, Magdalena, don't make things any more difficult for me than they already are. I'm just asking you to be patient for a little while longer. I'm having a bad time of it too, you know," I heard him say in a tense, nervous voice.

I put the phone down carefully on the small table in the pantry, like someone cautiously removing an insect that might prove dangerous. I moved away a few steps, not knowing what to do. If I hung up, then Eduardo would hear me and might suspect that I was checking up on his private conversations. Leaving it off the hook created two problems that arose from the same unknown factor: how long that conversation would last. I didn't have the courage to stand there until it ended, and, being skilful enough to make my click coincide exactly with that in the bedroom would mean having to listen to all the ins and outs of their colloquium. Leaving the telephone in the pantry off the hook and forgetting about it, which in the end was the solution I chose as the least bad option, meant that if, as was quite likely, Eduardo wanted to make another phone call, he would realize anyway, when he couldn't get a line, that I'd listened in on the conversation.

"At least," I thought with relief, "I won't be here for him to demand explanations of me or to feel obliged to explain things to me." There was another advantage too – my sudden flight at that hour of the night would no longer be judged an incomprehensible, capricious act; it might even appear logical. That subplot, which had appeared like a hare in a field, not only made my desire to leave the house more urgent and overwhelming but it also gave my actions a most opportune justification.

I tore a sheet off the message pad and wrote: "I'm going to sleep at a friend's house. You don't know her and she hasn't got a phone. But don't worry, I'm not going crazy and I won't throw myself off the viaduct.

Tomorrow or the day after I'll call you at the office and we'll talk. I don't feel like it now. And I have no intention of doing anything I don't feel like doing ever again. Goodnight, S."

During all my pondering, and especially when I was writing the note and placing it carefully underneath the earpiece so that Eduardo would be sure to find it, I could do nothing to prevent a whole series of fragments of that crazy story from pouring into my ears, increasing the already abundant flow of all the other unfinished stories and unsettled accounts. Magdalena, whom I identified – possibly mistakenly – with the redhead in the garden, was complaining and making demands and he was trying to placate her, assuring her that everything would work out and sprinkling his promises with affectionate epithets like "Darling" or "Sweetheart". What really stunned me was a sentence I heard quite clearly because it was said just at the moment I was lifting the earpiece to place the note underneath.

"Patience?" she was saying in an angry voice intercut with sobs. "Do you think I haven't been patient enough? Well, if you must know, Desi says that she doesn't know how I put up with it, you just ask her."

I left the kitchen, walked down the corridor and out into the street.

XVI

A cry for help

I just phoned you at home and you weren't there. In fact, no one knows where you are. A woman with a young-sounding voice answered. I asked if she was your daughter, but she said no, she wasn't, she was just the help. Her answer left me speechless, unable to react, because it echoed the stark words I was bursting to say even while I was dialling your number, a sort of SOS: "I need help." The words were surfacing as unstoppably as a round of machine-gun fire and I wasn't even sure I'd be able to finish sending my SOS without bursting into tears.

The young woman, Consuelo she said her name was, speaks extremely fast and muddles everything up, constantly alluding to people and situations she imagines I know about. She seemed very anxious to find out whether I was calling from my own telephone or from a public phone box. It seems your husband has been trying to get out of her the name of some friend of yours who isn't on the phone, in order to find out where you spent the night. This struck her as very strange, she says, because you don't have that many friends and certainly none without a phone, "Who do you know who isn't on the phone these days?"; she thinks you probably just said it to put him off the track.

I listened to her impatiently at first, then with a bewilderment that gradually became curiosity and then a kind of subterranean energy that decanted all my troubles from my soul to yours. What started as a cry for help from me was transformed into a desire to help you instead and into the conviction that I could. I don't know if you've ever had a similar experience; you get to the house of some friends feeling really bad and fully intending to say: "Look, I'm feeling like death, just bury me quietly," only to find that they are in the grip of some problem that may or may not be more serious than your own; that doesn't matter, what's important is that you have a better understanding of it than they do because you can see it from the outside, and that clears your mind, distracts you from your own problems and gives you back the will to get your own atrophied brain working again, in short, to live, because our need to live always revives a little when we feel useful and able to help.

I found it hard to concentrate, though, because I'd been awake until dawn prowling various blind alleys, not knowing whether I should stay here, keep running or go back to Madrid; all three options seem equally wrongheaded because, when you're in that kind of mood, feeling that you don't belong anywhere, and that the only person who'll be missing you is someone who bores you rigid anyway, you just lose the will to go on. Some of the time I spent writing and the rest I spent exhuming dead letters from that cemetery of the woes of love, my own and other people's, whose feet are littered with the withered flowers left by those who swore never to forget that special moment when they uttered the fateful words "for ever", with the addition of a précis of my notes on eroticism, so aseptic and obedient to their epigraph and which, up until now, have never exuded any poison or evil smell nor have they ever overflowed from their little box. Hidden words, lies disguised as truth, mingling and embracing and turning wild somersaults, crossing the streets of my brain, riding roughshod over it, as if at a Carnival dance where the main fun consists in not asking anyone's name, where they live nor what ails them, and of which all that will remain afterwards are scraps of torn clothing, amnesia and broken glass. It made no difference if I switched off the light or covered my head with a pillow: the table – a lacerating reminder of the desk that awaits me in my consulting room in Madrid, full of delayed correspondence and matters pending – continued to emit from its provisional corner that strange phosphorescence peculiar to corpses and ghosts. I knew that there, in that pile of papers, lies the focus of the conflict, as well, of course, as its possible clarification.

It may have been that second suspicion that resisted last night's destructive impulses and stayed my hand each time I was gripped by a desire to tear up bits of paper indiscriminately. In the end, they were all reprieved. Three times I stuffed them in the bottom of my suitcase and another three times I dug them out again from amongst the layers of crumpled clothes I'd thrown on top to cover them up, the third time when day was already dawning, a dawn which, paradoxically enough, also blinds me. "I never thought that out of light would come the dark," to quote the words of an old Alberto Pérez song.

Still singing that song, exhausted by all those useless thoughts going round and round in my head, I slumped into an armchair and let sleep overwhelm me. I dreamt that I was walking along the beach towards the village in order to pick up some papers I'd left behind in the restaurant of the one-eyed seagull, papers that were essential for an understanding of Manolo Reina's feelings towards me and which could also prove compromising to him. The waiter with the nervous tic had kept them for me, but it proved too dangerous actually to go there and retrieve them because this was just one episode in a long, confused spy story in which you, Sofía, were also implicated. Day was breaking. I was feeling afraid and kept looking cautiously all around me as I walked along the seashore, my arms hanging like lead by my side. Suddenly I spotted a figure coming towards me from the opposite end of the beach, a figure that became progressively clearer as it approached. Then I saw that it was a woman: you. You were waving some papers at me, I recognized your smile and then we ran towards each other and embraced, weeping for joy, not saying a word, right there in the middle of the deserted beach.

I woke when the sun was already quite high above the sea. I got up from the armchair and immediately went to find your phone number which I had looked up when I was in Madrid and had written down in my diary under E for Emergencies, although this was the first time I'd ever used it. It had come to me, like a bolt from the blue, that I can't wait any longer to hear your voice, not one minute longer, that it's ridiculous to keep suppressing that irrefutable, spontaneous desire for the sake of some idiotic sense of *amour propre*. It's not just that I don't mind you seeing me looking a complete wreck, I actually need you to see me like this, I need to cry and be consoled by you, I need to tell you how badly everything's turned out, how stupid I've been.

That's why having to make an instant adaptation to the sharp tones of that still unfamiliar voice, emerging moreover from a place I can't even imagine, required an extra effort of tact and caution as if I were finding my way in the darkness of a strange room. The only advantage is that Consuelo doesn't appear to require any immediate reply to anything that she says, she prefers the scattergun appproach, you know what I mean; and although it was a bit of an effort to follow what she was saying, it also gave me a breathing space to swallow my tears. On the other hand, although I didn't have the consolation of hearing your voice, I did at least have the consolation of getting recent news of you, news from last night; it wasn't only in my dream that we embraced. I now know that while I was ruminating on my sorrows, my eyes wide open as an owl's, you were awake too, no doubt desperate for a friendly word, for it's never lethargy that prompts us to leave home at unseemly hours and seek refuge in another bed, by the seashore or between the four walls of a bar, it's the need to talk. It does seem odd in your case, since, according to Consuelo, you hardly ever go out.

What she found even odder than you spending the night away from home, however, was that your husband should be so concerned. What did it matter to him if you slept somewhere else or in Amelia's room, for all the notice he takes of you? "Because," she added, "even if you're not that close a friend of hers, she's probably told you already that they don't sleep together any more." She added that she thought you'd be a fool to come back and that all men were the same; they only want you when you're not there for them any more. She thinks you're at the refuge, but she hasn't told your husband and has no intention of doing so, because if you've lied to him it's because you don't want him to catch up with you; everyone lies for the same reason. And she's not going to tell on you because she certainly doesn't want him to find you. She'd do the same for anybody on the run from whatever or for whatever reason; after all, everyone has their reasons for wanting to escape, so you should always be on the side of the fugitive, it's only natural. The proof is that when children play cops and robbers, no one ever wants to play the cop, apart from the odd creep, of course, you always get one. It's the same in the films; you nearly always feel sorry when the thief gets caught. These are all stupid comparisons – she continued – because, as I doubtless know, the only thing you're guilty of is being fed up with being ignored. Anyway, if I was the close friend she mentioned and I did know where you'd gone, the best thing I could do was to keep quiet about it. She's very pleased to know that you've got friends, but I can rest assured, she won't breathe a word, she'll be as silent as the grave.

That was when she asked my name, if I didn't mind her asking. I said it was Mariana and that I was sure nothing bad had happened to you. I said it partly to calm her down, but also because in a way it was true that I had given you refuge in my room last night simply by repeatedly asking you for refuge for myself, by addressing you out loud: "What shall I do, Sofía? Tell me what you do when you lose the will to live. All the solutions I dish out to other people are useless, just as it's useless my having analyzed the phenomenon of jealousy a hundred times before and always reached the conclusion that it's irrational and counter-productive. Listen to me, I need help, I'm up a blind alley," just as if you were lying in the bed next to mine and really could hear me.

Consuelo said that she's not worried about you either and that all she wants is for you to have a good time and get the most out of life, for you've always treated her better than her own mother and that's why she loves you, quite apart from the fact that you're a real scream. She said that on the days when you wake up in a good mood, no one can touch you when it comes to inventing words for songs, they simply pour out of you, and if you dedicated yourself to that alone, you could earn even more money than your husband without having to get involved with lawyers and all that rubbish, there's a huge demand for good lyrics these days, even singers like Ramoncín run out because they can't find people to write good songs for them. She says that you've probably gone to the refuge, although she has no intention of trying to find out whether you're there or with me, she'll leave that for the cops.

I didn't ask her what refuge she was talking about because, by that point in the deluge of chaotic information, the whole story seemed to me about as unreal as my letter to the hotel guest in room 204. Indeed, precisely because of that, because it sounded a bit like the stories I invent when I start daydreaming, I started putting it in order and correcting it in my own style on the basis of the information provided by that crazy script. I not only managed to escape for a moment from my own troubles, I also managed to share the excitement and risks of your night escape and to relate them to the confusing spy story that had slipped into my dream. I could see the two of us running hand-in-hand down narrow back streets, searching for that shadowy refuge that may have provided us both with a hiding place last night. I felt relieved to be able to calm your fears in the arms of my fears, to know that I'm not the only one they're after and that if we add your capacity for invention to my talent for disguise, we can throw any detective off the track, however troubling his appearance, however acute his sense of smell.

What I told Consuelo, when she let me get a word in, was that I'm not in Madrid and I haven't seen you recently, which makes it even more likely that you are at the refuge, but I asked her, please, could she tell you to call me urgently the moment you turned up. I gave her the number of the hotel and she assured me that she'd written it down correctly, as well as the code for Cádiz and my room number. I also asked her to tell you personally and no one else. She repeated that she would be as silent as the grave and we said goodbye.

As a result of that conversation, I've unpacked my suitcase again because now I have a reason to stay, to await your call. I've proved to myself once again that dealing with someone else's problems is the best remedy for paralysis of the will. I've spent several hours writing a kind of composition, just as I advised you to do, and, as a consequence, I've tidied up the papers on the desk, torn up many that were unnecessary and found others which I thought were lost. They're much less troublesome than they were last night.

That's because you exist, Sofía, hidden away, looking for a space in a refuge from which I want to rescue you; that's why everything I write is like a tunnel dug completely blind and I'm like a mole advancing along this subterranean gallery of words, my only guide being my desire to find you in order to ask you for help and to offer help in return. Sometimes I stop scrabbling at the earth because I have to come up to the surface again, even though it may prove risky, and then I shin up trees and my words help me to leap from branch to branch, to scale walls or swim the murky green waters of moats, always furtively, always led by a faith that only grows stronger in the face of obstacles, like in those films about captives in mortal danger, when their liberator, who always arrives at the last possible moment, will also be liberated from some dark threat as soon as he releases the prisoner, which is why he summons up all his genius and skill; and so my need for you to hear my message and for me to wait for yours ceases being a source of anxiety and becomes instead an incentive that motivates and colours not only these words opening up a path towards your possible refuge, but also the thread of words that they carry with them, all the words I've been writing to you from the moment I caught the train to Puerto Real, scattered to the winds like wild oats, and which now, restored to life on the paper where they lay, come to the aid of the others, in hot pursuit, like the rearguard of an army leaping on to their horses at the sound of the bugle.

I'm writing nonsense, I know; any old twigs or dead leaves will do to withstand the cold of waiting, to rekindle the fire of the story I want to tell you before returning to the dungeon of common sense, before my tears cool and the guard whispers: "There's really no need to go on about it so, you've had your fling, you're quite safe, it's time you came to your senses." No, I don't want to drink that potion just yet, I won't place myself in the hands of Dr Jekyll León, for her to return me to a world of genuine miseries for which I am responsible; I reject even the thought of being treated and pacified by Dr Jekyll León, of being transmuted into her, I want to escape, Sofía, distorted in grotesque mirrors, it's me, Mariana, calling to you, I want to feel able to weep freely with you over a possibly irrelevant but painful love affair that brings with it many previous sorrows, stillborn tears and sighs stored up since our years at university, when I decided that I would have to choose between attending to other people's feelings and paying attention to my own and I knew that if I wasn't capable of sorting mine out for myself without asking for help, I would be of little use to anyone else; it seemed a painless decision to make at the time, it may even have made me seem more attractive, with my distant Ninotchska smile, the Lauren Bacall look, be sure to repress your instincts. But Manolo said that was a lie, he said I had fire in my veins, and that it was fortunate that I wouldn't die in ignorance of the fact; that was three years ago, better late than never; his name is Manolo Reina, as I think I told you in one of the other letters, but he doesn't love me any more. My fault entirely, I lost him out of sheer wilfulness because I wanted to return to the prison of common sense that I've spent years longing vainly to escape from, just as I've spent years, many more years, knowing that you, my soulmate, are the person I want to call in order to find consolation, that you're the only one capable of consoling me, though I've refused to acknowledge it; I need to cry, to pour out my heart to you, I won't let Dr León submit me to treatment, "she can't tell me what I need to hear." I just hope that these mad, jagged words reach you and scratch at the windows of that strange refuge where you're huddled and that you recognize my tears in the raindrops beating at the window, because here at least it's begun to rain. I wish I had that passage from *Wuthering Heights* that you liked so much: it's near the beginning, one stormy night, when the face of Catherine the child peers in at the attic room that was once hers and where Lockwood is now sleeping; through the shattered window he grips her ghostly fingers and reaches the awful realization that he's been touched by a story, albeit in dreams, from which he will never be able to free himself, a story he subsequently learns about through Mrs Dean and then recounts to us, and to you in particular. Copying out fragments of a novel that still illuminates your dreams, Sofía, incorporating it into the general hieroglyphic of our lives past and present, would be another channel open between you and me as we are today, an aerial bridge linking our memories, fears and disappointments, a spell to invoke the reply I await so eagerly: "Did you call me, Mariana? What did you want?"

If I didn't believe, with all the vehemence of certainty, that soon (tomorrow at the latest) your voice would come flying over rivers and mountains to say those words to me, to find out what's happening, what's wrong with me, why I'm holed up in this hotel on the Costa de la Luz, alone, paralyzed, your voice saying that you're in no hurry, please, don't cry, I would put a match to all these attempts of mine at a solitary striptease, haunted by the tentative, empty spirals of a love story with no happy ending – a story that could never have ended happily – and I'm going to tell you something that can be stated very simply, something that only hurts when it stops, that I'm in love with someone who no longer loves me, and I'm going to tell you all about him, what he's like and what an extraordinary voice he has, because his voice doesn't change, Sofía, it's terrible, his voice is exactly the same, his hands too, he makes the same gestures, you can't imagine what it's like hearing that voice say: "So how are you? You're looking really good, Marianilla," using a diminutive as a distancing device, in a way he never did before, and me saying: "Fine. As you see, something still draws me to the south. I'm working on an essay at the moment and I'm a bit tired," all the time staring at those hands as if hypnotized, just as if I were seeing them inside a frame, those hands producing a lighter, lighting it and casually holding out the flame to me, without a tremor; as I tell you what they meant to me, that voice and those hands, which some incomprehensible evil spell changes before my eyes into the same hands as before, I don't know whether to believe it or not, whether or not to investigate further, to abandon myself to the hallucination or to flee the danger, telling it all to you, Sofía, higgledy-piggledy, just as it occurs to me, the way my patients talk incoherently to me about illusions lost for ever, out of the shock, inevitable when you rekindle spent fires and seek amongst the shadows what could only exist in full sunlight, when your understanding, blinded and dazzled by the light of a fleeting summer that defies questions, simply opened out to receive a gift with no tomorrows, something pleasurable, natural; to ask you, Sofía, where am I going to put all these crazy, fragmentary but still vibrant images of this man who no longer reacts, is no longer surprised to see me, where am I going to put them all, tell me, what am I going to do with them? It's like finding some valuable object broken into a thousand pieces and you don't know whether to keep the pieces or to throw them away and the main cause of your perplexity lies in the discovery that until that moment you hadn't realized how valuable it was; if I wasn't sure, I mean, that you were going to listen to me, however garbled the story, however I distort the facts of a tale that only your attention can redeem from triviality, and if I wasn't sure that you would say: "Don't cry, Mariana, please, don't cry," if it wasn't for that, I would feel the same revulsion I felt last night for the pile of papers I'm now feverishly adding to, out of pure habit, while I await the miracle of your phone call.

Viewed from another angle, though, this whole tirade could also be seen as another case of split personality to be added to the many already noted down by Dr León, scattered amongst a plethora of dog-eared index cards, papers and notebooks rejected as useless and then re-read yet again. Why, I ask myself, does she need so many examples? It seems that they're all useful to her, she gets something out of all of them and she squeezes them dry, not wanting to waste one drop of their health-giving juice which she adds to her thesis, a special glue, a new brand, with which to stick together this pile of fragments classified by size. And for what? I ask again. For once they're carefully glued together – so carefully that, at times, you can't even see the join – when you look closely at all the resulting stories of this makeshift composition, they are so similar, they lack any kind of conclusion and they still stand exposed to the storm winds of neglect.

There they are, restored, accounted for and filed away, until the next upheaval warns of another possible disintegration. Then that middle-aged lady reappears; she's slim, usually elegantly dressed and has rather gnarled hands; she approaches the couch. Josefina Carreras has usually given me the file beforehand so that I can address the woman by her name, otherwise I might have forgotten it or confused her with another. All of them have a vaguely artistic bent which they don't quite know how to channel, which brings them no consolation, and all are eager to prove that they are different, to present their case as quite distinct from any other, and all have a certain curl of the lips that indicates a farewell to any hope of ever being kissed again with passion, and I say her name, what brings her here?, nothing, the usual, only slightly worse; they're

302

like Señora Acosta's recurrent appearances at your front door, come downstairs and have a look, it's a plumbing problem, the usual thing.

Of all the files on the table here, the fattest one is a file labelled "Female loneliness", where almost all the notes I don't quite know what to do with end up.

Yesterday evening, before going down to the bar on the beach where I'd arranged to meet Manolo, I was going over some of those notes, as if I were preparing for an examination, trying to memorize some of the fundamental conclusions while I was having a shower; it was like half-heartedly injecting myself with a vaccine against an illness that's already incubating inside me. Through the lines of words, some neatly typed, others broken up by ragged handwriting, flow the unseasonable waters of a thousand rivers which, before, were streams and trickles all from different sources that carved out a path amongst tree trunks and stones, over abrupt precipices, each one growing in volume, forming pools, singing the song that distinguished them from the others and guided them on their way, until the day, without knowing how, they flow unstoppably into the heavy swell of solitude, that common grave dominated by a constant unanimous rumble, where all the waters that found an accompanying echo along the way finally come together – all the lonelier for being closer, all the lonelier because they all complain of the same thing, a uniform complaint that does its best to sound – to continue sounding – exceptional. Other people bore me, they don't understand me, they don't listen to me, they're always complaining about the same things, making mountains out of molehills, Doctor, if they had to go through what I'm going through ... and the worst thing is that I haven't got anyone to talk to, I mean it, it gets more and more difficult every day, people are only interested in themselves and no one else.

When you consider how much thought you've given to this subject, Mariana – I said yesterday evening to the woman looking back at me from the rather steamed-up mirror in the bathroom – how often you've gone over it, given advice and lectures on it, you'd think, by this stage, that you'd be an expert on it. Surely you can make some use of it, sister, take note, concentrate and see what sense you can make of it all. I was enjoying watching my hair flying about, blown by a warm current of air, not, as at first sight appeared, from a hairdryer, but blowing in from the east, rippling through fields of sunflowers, filling sails, shaking the clothes hung out to air on the flat roofs of white villages that suddenly, before my astonished eyes, were raised aloft at the very sound of their names, Arcos de la Frontera, Veger, Ubrique, Zahara de los Atunes, Ronda, Alcalá de Guadaira, Lebrija, Medinasidonia, Osuna, Jimena, Antequera, and the frame of the mirror became the open window of a Fiat Uno with the mountains of Grazalema in the background and mother-of-pearl clouds tumbling southwards towards Tarifa across the Straits of Gibraltar. Your startled eyes, Mariana, saw those clouds, villages, mountains and beaches, they saw it all. Remember it, rescue it from the depths where it sleeps, from the hard rock on which your solitude sits, knit it all up again to keep your heart warm now, you saw it, it was true, it still is, don't let it perish unaided as if it were a lie, for everything depends on being willing to change, you've often said so yourself, on being able to manipulate the material each of us has been given. Solitude can also be the subject of craftsmanship and manipulation: if you don't believe it, ask the poets. It's simply a question of not treating it as if it were a prison sentence and not expecting to receive anything from the depths of that black hole, apart from the opportunity to explore it. "It's better to see blackness than to see nothing at all," that's what Machado said: he meant that it's the very persistence of our gaze that finally strikes diamantine sparks from the depths of the coal mine and allows us to paint a picture which is not necessarily either sombre or uniform. After all, there are many different shades of black; it takes a while to distinguish them, it's true, until your eyes grow accustomed to the dark; it's the same with any colour, even clouds aren't easy to paint. Manolo used to say that they were the most difficult thing of all, that you needed to spend hours looking at them. It always takes a long time to see anything of value, it takes sheer hard work, but there's no reason why anyone need know how difficult or easy it was to achieve. You just put up with it quietly, impassively: just remember that what will be will be, don't worry. The secret is not to lose your cool, the secret is in the alchemy that allows you to distil out of our kingdom of shadows a dreamy, absent look, verging on the immaterial, just like the look that rises up from your memories and that the mirror reflects back at you now, an impenetrable look that is yours alone, that only just breaks the surface, that drives away all excess and invites others to decipher it; see if you can keep it up all evening, Mariana.

However, while I was rehearsing that controlled, remote smile, concentrating more on the effect it would have on Manolo than on endowing it with any appropriate inner discourse, I realized that the very fact that I was investing time and energy in these machinations was a sign of my insecurity. Before, when we arranged to meet, I would of course look in the mirror, but not in order to practise phoney expressions nor to find out anything I wasn't sure of already – a touch of lipstick, and I'd be off, it was an exam I passed instantly and with top marks. The most important thing was not to keep him waiting, because he got impatient. He used to say that it always seemed like a miracle to see me again.

My hair looked good, loose and slightly curly at the ends, the way he liked it, especially when we went out in that car of his which ended up being my car too in a way, when I would lean out of the open window and drink in the landscape, the mixture of smells, speed and light, always aware at the same time that he was looking at me out of the corner of his eye, watching how the wind tousled my hair.

"You must never tie it back. Your hair is made for the wind to play with, to blow about. Just leave it free to do its own thing."

Now I wear it a bit shorter than I did that summer – I was thinking – I don't know if he'll like it and I don't know what will have happened to the Centaur, that metallic-blue Fiat Uno in which we drove through so many villages, from which we saw so many sunsets and moonrises, and which I became as attached to as if it were a house; I named it after the notebooks I usually use, ringbound with blue covers, I'm sure you know the ones I mean. The car had two dents on the right side, another at the back, and which, according to Manolo, guaranteed its survival; who would ever bother stealing it? He always left it unlocked.

"No self-respecting thief would want it," he used to say, "but if God

305

wants someone to steal it from us, then fine, don't you worry, we'll know better next time."

He used the plural, as if the car belonged to us both.

"Of course it belongs to us both. I put petrol in it and I drive it and if there's a puncture I change the wheel. But you're its godmother, the one who baptized it. Besides, it was waiting for you, it's the first time I've spent so much time in it with one person."

"Liar!"

"No, really, I usually make these trips to villages on my own."

Then I would smile.

"I hope I disappear before you get fed up with me. I never like people to have too much of me; always too little."

"What do you mean? With you, I wouldn't get tired of the Centaur or anything else. And don't threaten me with goodbyes. For your information, my love, we're only just beginning! There are still walks to be taken, glasses of wine to be drunk, songs to be sung and journeys to be made."

"And secrets to be told?"

"Oh no, the secrets you've told me will go with me to the grave, but the secrets we have from each other, that's another matter, we're free agents, all right? That way we'll always see each other as if for the first time, with no baggage."

"'Always' is a long time, don't you think?"

"It doesn't matter, you have my word and I'm the one in charge of this contract with no signatures, no seals and no notary. I give you my oath and that's enough, it will always be like this. Every time I see you, I'll feel exactly as I felt the first time, that I want to be with you that day and the next day and the next."

I knew that wasn't true, that it was impossible. I almost wanted it to be over once and for all so that I could go back to my usual routine, to my refuge of common sense. God, what a summer!

Two hours before the appointment, when I'd given final approval to my physical appearance, I started inventing an ideal dialogue in order to kill time and so as not to get too nervous. It was so good that I memorized whole chunks and I even wrote down some of my more inspired, amusing replies in a pocket Centaur notebook, afraid I might forget them. Then out fell the recent photo of Manolo that I'd taken from the newspaper and slipped inside; I saw a spark of mockery dancing in his eyes, like when he used to say to me: "Stop explaining my own soul to me, even I don't understand it"; and then I realized that my speech was leaving out anything he might have to say, that I wasn't going to meet a ghost, still less a weak, vulnerable patient whose file Josefina Carreras had just passed to me, but a man about whom I know almost nothing now, and who, moreover, hadn't even phoned to confirm that he'd be coming to the bar on the beach, but who, if he came, would have his own ideas about what to say. He wasn't someone to let himself be bossed around and, of course, he wasn't going to ask me the anxious, passionate questions implicit in my questionnaire and which would leave him at my mercy; he would ask others that occurred to him on the spur of the moment, God knows what, perhaps none at all. So all my felicitous phrases, once they lost the sustenance that gave them support, sank like stones to the bottom, dissolved like sugarlumps in water, leaving me helpless, stripped of my armour.

There was another adverse factor that considerably diminished my ability for taking the initiative with someone who, moreover, had always been the first to do so: I refer to my lack of training. I realized that the time I'd spent in cultivating my ego and voluntarily excluding myself from any dealings with other people had diminished the verbal agility that comes with practice, a fact that rather – indeed greatly – militated against me. I'd spent too long without talking to anyone, almost since I left Madrid (because my encounter with Silvia hadn't provided a dialogue worthy of the name, it had simply made me build the wall around me higher). Inevitably, my organism had begun to notice that grave lack of vitamins – how could it not? I was becoming defenceless; it was best to recognize it now. A long time had passed since I escaped from Raimundo's house clutching a bunch of lilacs. Where was the nostalgic perfume of recent company? I'd spent days without phoning anyone, without looking anyone in the eye, days fleeing other people's company, looking at them as if through a smoked glass window that made them seem more distant, days spent talking to myself, going for walks on my own, eating alone, taking absurd decisions on my own and, of course, sleeping alone. Sometimes I idealized that solitude and at others I hated it, but I was unable to stop its tenacious, progressive invasion, inventing beginnings for an epistolary novel addressed to someone about whom I also know almost nothing, who will meanwhile have been ploughing their own furrow – a mere framework on which to hang an egocentric stream of consciousness whose sole aim was to explore the gradual process of deterioration which is of interest only to the person who is partly experiencing it and partly provoking it; she's the only one who would think it worthy of a novel, worthy of being read with interest by the presumed reader of these letters, a vague figure whose name, Sofía, coincides with yours, a nebulous dream, a memory, until this morning when Consuelo's garbled story, by imposing itself on mine and thus nullifying it, released you from the spell I had cast on you, and freed you from being some kind of plaster-of-Paris support and turned you into a flesh-and-blood friend who invents words for songs and also sleeps alone, who has perhaps, without my knowing it, been in need of my voice and my help throughout this long, indefinite period of time during which a horribly familiar virus was taking hold of my organism, a virus I have so often examined under the microscope.

I realized that in the present case it wasn't a matter of advising patience, determination, astuteness or serenity to one of those opaque women with faded names who come to my consulting room complaining of some indefinable malaise and whom I have deceitfully struggled to provide with a light they did not have, it was a matter of accepting something which was as disturbing as it was self-evident: that, at that moment, four o'clock yesterday afternoon, sitting on the little terrace of a bar with my hair newly-washed, watching the capricious clouds of a disquieting afternoon unravel themselves above the sea, waiting for the hypothetical appearance of a no less hypothetical lover, I could have been any one of those women.

***

I couldn't stand being in my room and so I went off to the beach. I went down the steps at the end of the swimming pool and, feeling very low and acutely lonely, feeling that nothing mattered any more, I started walking towards the left, away from the bar. What was it that grumpy old French teacher who taught us in the fifth year, M. Dupoint, used to say, do you remember? "Encore un peu de patience et tout finira mal." At any rate, I had ceased to be in control of events.

The tide was out and I walked mechanically along, gazing into the distance, as if I were expecting some signal or some marvellous presence, the sort that turn up in fairy tales to guide the steps of those who have lost their way. This scene, I realize now, is what must have fuelled the confusing story of espionage that slipped into this morning's dream and ended with your appearance, the dream that provoked my phone call to Madrid to ask for help.

It was a feeling of being lost and helpless, like the feeling you get moments before an exam, when you can't seem to remember anything and you're sure that the subject they're going to ask you about wasn't even in the notes you've been feverishly revising, or else they'll ask questions about one of those peculiar lessons you had right at the beginning of term, what was it about now? a battle or a council perhaps, something very ancient – anyway, it's bound to be that; and a sticky paste of certainty and forgetting stifles your breathing and stops you thinking about anything else.

That anxiety, added to that provoked by my conjectures about whether or not Manolo would turn up, attached itself now to the blurred image of Raimundo talking in a low voice on the phone so that I couldn't hear and to the memory of my escape – clutching a bunch of lilacs – half-buried sequences which, once revived, only served to make the present situation more complex. I felt incapable of giving any coherent answers on the subject, I didn't have a clue. Raimundo? What Raimundo? I was sure to fail, my mind was a blank. Were you crying over Raimundo a few days ago? How many days ago? His family name was Ercilla, you must remember something, did you sleep together? What were your intentions? Tell us about the promises you exchanged with him, about your dreams of being a young bride prepared to dedicate the rest of her life to her beloved. Do you, Mariana León Jimeno, take Raimundo Ercilla del Río to be your lawful wedded husband, for better for worse, in sickness and in health, till death do you part? Wait a moment, Father, I don't even know who this Raimundo is, I can't even remember the sound of his voice, just give me a moment to think, to find out at least if I'm dreaming or not. What's wrong, Mariana? You're very pale; it must be the excitement: that, I would remind you, is how all those happy-ever-after love stories hidden in the folds of your subconscious end up; wasn't that the conclusion you wanted? Didn't you want to have me always with you, my head on your pillow, forever removed from dangerous, ambiguous friendships? I give you these coins and this bunch of lilacs as a sign of marriage; the bride and bridegroom should join hands. Now you know, Mariana, the priest has just told you so, we're joined together in sickness and in health, in boredom too, he forgot to mention that, together in Calle de Covarrubias until death do us part, until I get tempted to commit suicide again, unless you can do something about it, but you will do something, won't you? I trust in your abnegation and vigilance. In the name of the Father, the Son and the Holy Ghost, I declare you man and wife. Say a rosary as you kneel next to Mrs Dean in Calle de la Amargura and, after the Litany, pay heed to her wise warning: "If, from this day forth, either of the two contracting parties should participate in a clandestine meeting with an Andalusian painter now resident in Manhattan, she will be committing the sin of adultery, *ora pro nobis*."

I felt as if I were going to faint, my knees buckled and I had to stop walking and sit down on a small mound that I later identified as the remains of a huge sandcastle complete with turrets, moat and passageways. The probable builders of the castle, some children who were now shouting and running barefoot along the shore, had left a plastic orange rake next to the moat. I picked it up and started drawing spirals and crisscrossing lines on the sand, while I sang an old song of Gracia de Triana's which was on the tape that Manolo liked to play when we travelled in the Fiat Centauro of blessed memory, invulnerable to theft:

> I have a sandcastle
> built out of thoughts,
> the towers are sighs,
> the foundations jealousy.
> Ah, the castles of desire
> that all of us build,
> then watch as they fall!

I stayed there for a while letting myself be lulled by that song which finally dislodged Raimundo's name from my confused brain; I saw it come snaking out, the big R followed by the four vowels and three consonants, rolling along the sand ahead of me; it reached the seashore all in one piece and then the waves swallowed it letter by letter until it had disintegrated completely: Aimundo, Imundo, Mundo, Undo, Ndo, Do, O. Before plunging into the water, an H attached itself to the O, waving like a little flag, calling to you, Oh Sofía, to our childhood games; how I'd like to play with you by the seashore inventing stories, pulling the petals off words as if they were daisies, giving them wings in order to hunt them down and later set them free, like in that drawing of the butterfly catcher, do you remember? "Never stop playing with words, Señorita Montalvo." Don Pedro Larroque was right, it's the only game that serves as both distraction and consolation. To me, too, as you see; I wish you were here by my side, looking out at the immense sea, so that I could play word games with you.

Filled by a strange torpor, I'd forgotten about the time and about myself. I occasionally looked up from the hieroglyphic I was indolently tracing in the sand and saw the small architects of the ruined castle silhouetted against the sky, haloed with foam. They ran back and forth, dived into the sea, waved their arms about calling each other by names that, one day, will be swept away by the implacable and redeeming tide of forgetting. I wasn't thinking about anything. I would have liked to lie down and go to sleep there on the ruins of the sandcastle, lulled by the murmur of those happy, distant voices.

At one point, I noticed that the clouds that had been chasing each other and unravelling over the sea had come to a halt and were beginning to be tinged with the colour that used to be Manolo's favourite when he wanted to get a sense of the transience of evening in the watercolours he painted: a cocktail of ivory, ash-grey and mauve, the colour of goodbye he used to call it, which could easily go to your head. I got up, brushed the sand from my skirt and retraced my steps back to the bar.

The bar is on the far side of the hotel, at the end of the beach. Beyond it there is only a promontory of abrupt rocks on which the lighthouse stands.

As I approached, that fear of the unknown resurfaced, a feeling that my daydreams had anaesthetized and turned into a platform for levitation; so intense was it that every step forwards felt like two steps back down the slope towards my initial obsessions, a narrow, slippery path. "Not that way, Mariana, grab hold of something and if there's nothing there, invent something, but don't go down there, please, don't fall into that cave again, climb out. Surprise is a hare, defy the light of the unexpected. Do you remember when you wanted to be a grown up? Well, you are, live for the moment, don't let life get to you," a tenuous, weightless voice seemed to be saying to me from afar, from those clouds the colour of goodbye, perhaps the same voice which once, watching a similar sunset, tried to sweeten my painful longing to grow up and teach me to savour the juice of the present moment, the touch of the air "full of angels" drifting in through the open window of a train.

But you weren't with me, Sofía, as you were on our way back from that trip to Ávila, and I couldn't put your advice into practice. I didn't know how to unblock the rubbish in the pipes through which our friendship once flowed, I still don't know how to do it, and your words, of course, when they found the access route to my lair-cum-bunker blocked, simply scattered their luminous energy into the air and swung out over the sea, enriching the beauty of the sunset – "Energy isn't created or destroyed, it's merely transformed" – a gift of light that slowly faded as I continued to regress, however much I pretended to move forwards, neurotically rejecting the hand you held out to me: "But something really nice is going to happen to you, Mariana, a reunion.

Don't you remember how we used to love stories about reunions, even if it was only so that we could sing 'What might have been and never was'? Think of it as a romantic adventure; it's up to you, you're walking towards the unknown and the unknown is always enjoyable." Enjoyable, njoyable, oyable, yable, able, ble ... The last syllable fleetingly filled with air like a balloon and then dissolved into the tail of a pearl-grey cloud.

The bar isn't set on the beach itself, but slightly higher up, separated from it by thirty steps carved into a rough spiral. I counted them the other day. Manolo was up there talking to Rafa, the waiter. Although my long sight isn't very good without my glasses, I spotted him at once – his unmistakable silhouette – and my heart turned over when I realized that he must also have seen me. If he still had his lynx-sharp vision and that talent for not missing a single detail, even when he didn't seem to be looking at anything in particular, he would immediately have noticed how hesitantly I approached and might even have guessed how I longed to throw in the towel and run away. He had the advantage, like troops ensconced in a castle watching for the approach of the enemy hosts; I feel ashamed to write down that warlike metaphor, but it was, I confess, what first came to mind. What would my patients say if they knew? I've always tried to wean them off the idea that there's a parallel between battles in love and strategies in war; it's the root of all evils. Realizing that I had fallen into that same pernicious rhetoric frightened me even more. As I approached, though, there was nothing in his attitude that suggested he might be feeling either concerned or unconcerned about any possible invasion of his territory, and since he made no gesture in my direction – not even the wave of a handkerchief – I decided to keep my eyes fixed on the ground and to concentrate on keeping control of my breathing and not falling over. Assuming his indifference was not just a pose, what point was there in catching him unawares if I was defenceless and already beating a retreat?

When I reached the top of the steps – the ascent had been the most gruelling part – I had no option but to look up, and, worse, continue to advance. They were the only two at the bar, not surprising since the afternoon had grown very cool. That realization coincided with a shiver that ran through me, reminding me of yet another mistake on my part. In my hurry to leave the hotel, I hadn't thought to bring anything warm to wear and it was windy up there and there was no shelter. The two men didn't seem to notice the cold. They were sitting at one of the tables towards the rear, close to the bar. Manolo had his back to me, he was in shirtsleeves, his jacket draped over the back of the folding chair. They were engaged in a lively conversation, unhurriedly sipping their drinks as if they weren't expecting anyone at all. I had heard them laughing while I was walking up the steps, eyes lowered; Manolo's was the predominant voice and I felt it pierce me like the first poisoned arrow. They were talking about New York.

Rafa saw me first and indicated my presence with a gesture to his companion. Manolo must have told him I was coming. But what words would he have used? In what terms would he have alluded to this woman who had arranged to meet him after so long without seeing each other and when she had been the one who had rejected a much deeper, longer-lasting relationship? What does she want now? There's no understanding women, Rafa. I became aware that I was talking to myself again and in those few, brief seconds, conscious of my inability to guess Manolo's state of mind as he waited for me to arrive, I realized that a look of ill humour must be darkening my face, while all my sentimental conjectures were fading fast, leaving me sticky with the grease they left behind them.

Manolo only turned round and stood up when I'd almost reached their table; I was determined to behave naturally, though I was feeling more dead than alive. Suddenly he was kissing me:

"Marianilla, it's great to see you!"

My eyes slid away, defeated, fearful to look into the face that had uttered that banal phrase. I, who had arranged to meet him there for a session of gazing into each other's eyes, knew then that the experiment would not take place, that I myself had decided to cancel it. I did so out of fear and out of anger at myself for feeling that fear, whilst during that first fleeting embrace I breathed in the artificial fragrance emanating

314

from his face and body, Herrera for Men; I recognized it because it's the cologne Raimundo has taken to using. I was in such a state that I kissed Rafa too, although I'd never done so before, as if inviting him to stay with us, thus implicating him in the events of that ceremony doomed to failure.

He did in fact stay with us for quite a while because Manolo encouraged him to, and when he protested that we must have things to talk about, I made a gesture with my hand as if to brush that aside, while I gazed out to sea.

"You two have things to talk about as well," I said.

"You see, the reply of a fine woman," said Rafa approvingly, obviously satisfied.

After my remark, they resumed the conversation that my arrival had interrupted. They were talking about some friends from Chiclana, mutual friends, who had opened a bar on the south side of Manhattan. They were enterprising people, Manolo often dropped by there and he said they were doing really well.

"Sure, because they had the money to buy the place," said Rafa from the bar where he'd gone to prepare a gin and tonic for me, "or else, like you, they were lucky enough to meet someone influential. Everyone needs a fairy godmother, if not, forget it."

"I wouldn't go that far, Rafa; you have to make your own luck. Besides, Sheila isn't influential because of her family, you know, she's had to take chances to get where she is, and you know what they say, nothing ventured nothing gained."

"I only thought because of what you were saying about her earlier on …," said Rafa, shrugging his shoulders.

So before I arrived they'd already been talking about that person whose name I didn't even want to think about and which, nevertheless, erupted from then on like the chorus of some hard rock song, Sheila-Sheila-Sheila, and however hard I tried to break it up, "eila, ila, la, lalala, lalala, lalala", the final vowel refused to be drowned in the sea or swallowed by the clouds, it re-emerged, grabbed hold of the tail of the initial S and the whole name would unfurl again like the Jolly Roger, waving in time to the rhythms of a piece of deafening, furious music; you would have had to shout to silence the racket it was making.

"Do not try to silence her, it's impossible to do so," Manolo had once whispered into my ear one night when we were at the Venta de Vargas listening to a gipsy friend of his, a brilliant guitarist, who was celebrating someone's birthday, "she weeps monotonously the way water weeps, the way the wind weeps", and later, in the early hours of the morning, when we were both driving back in the Fiat Centaur, drunk on sherry and the full moon, he continued quoting from García Lorca: "The wine glasses of the dawn shatter," and he stopped the car on some beach or other and we walked down to the seashore with our arms around each other and he said to me: "I was longing to kiss you back there. Sometimes, when we go to places together, I feel like everyone else is in the way. Don't you feel that too?" And I was surprised, because at the party he'd hardly paid me any attention at all, but was charming to everyone, sang, disappeared for long stretches and didn't seem to mind that I did the same, which was one of the things I liked most about him, Sofía; you never quite knew what he was going to do next. And, of course, yesterday, warmed by that sudden memory, I wondered, almost without wanting to, if perhaps the same thing would happen now, if he wasn't just stringing Rafa along in order to savour his absence later when we finally got rid of him, and my imagination ran wild: "I wonder what plans he has for tonight, we've the whole night ahead of us, it hasn't even begun yet, and he knows how much I always enjoy preliminaries; perhaps we'll go and have a dance at the hotel." Yet, in spite of everything, I still didn't dare to look at him directly, because he didn't give me any reason to, apart from saying that I'd been quite right to tell him what a fascinating city New York was. Although I couldn't remember having provided him with this abstract information, or when I did so, I hurriedly agreed and asked him if he'd seen the inside of the Chrysler Building yet and said that there was nothing to compare with the architecture of the 1920s, ascertaining, meanwhile, that I was breathing more easily and that the repetitive, hateful hard rock refrain was now fading, silenced by the weeping of the guitar and the shattered glasses of an unforgettable dawn spent by the seashore. Then Rafa, in a growing state of euphoria, was addressing me from behind the bar, asking if I had any preference as to which gin I drank, that we had to drink to Manolo's success in the city of skyscrapers, that the drinks were on him, and I said that yes, I did, I preferred Gordon's. He'd suddenly started calling me by my first name.

"Manolo was telling me earlier that you were a psychiatrist, Mariana. I was amazed. You don't look like one at all."

"No? What do I look like?"

"Like a film actress."

Manolo burst out laughing while he raised his glass and clinked it against ours. He was talking as if we'd only seen each other the day before, with a confidence bordering on impudence.

"Come off it. If you knew her better, you wouldn't say that. Film actresses are all a bunch of hysterics. Not Mariana, she always knows exactly what she wants, and if you're not careful she'll tell you what you want too and even what you're thinking; she's a very clever woman, always in control. Come on, Rafa, sit down."

They were in such a good mood! And we started talking about psychiatry, about how the patient can influence the doctor and how, according to Rafa, you need to be pretty tough to spend all day with mad people without going mad yourself. Manolo pointed to me and said: "Well, there you have someone whose head is always firmly on her shoulders." I forced a smile, my eyes fixed on my glass, feeling the wind ruffling my hair. I felt like crying; I wanted to remind him that it was he who had managed to convince me that quite the opposite was true, that he was the one who had boasted he had taught me to rebel against the rules of duty and had discovered, behind my apparent common sense, the hidden well of an insatiable thirst and a desire to quench other people's thirst too, but that the well was very deep and needed a very long rope, and the shortsighted who peered into it believed it to be dry. He came up with such nice images, Sofía, the kind of images I could only repeat to a friend like you. "No, my love, I'm sorry to contradict you, but you're not sensible at all; in fact, you're completely lacking in common sense. You're like an unbridled horse and it's just as well that

317

someone finally found you out." He was the first man to have chosen me rather than allowing himself to be chosen, just to see what would happen if he set a burning brand to my perfect papier mâché geometry, and he'd dared to do so without asking my permission, "Because you're not that sort, I just have to give you permission to do what you like, give you a push in the right direction, a bit of encouragement. I don't have to do much but, depending on the day, you like a bit of encouragement, don't you?" While we were talking about our respective jobs and trips abroad, Rafa grew ever more cordial and admiring and I felt more and more like one of the ice cubes bobbing about in my gin and tonic, unable to believe that Manolo didn't realize that at that precise moment I needed all the encouragement I could get because my spring had wound down like an old toy about to be relegated to the rubbish bin. He had the key in his pocket and all he had to do was give it a half-turn. Anything would have done, as long as it warmed my heart or my instincts: a compliment, an insult, a howl, a challenge, a sigh, a reproach, or even a slap in the face, anything that would have cut through that fog of banalities and given me a chance to respond to him, to answer back and dispel that strange apathy, to throw off the restraint that prevented me from looking into his eyes and asking him if he remembered what he'd said about the well and my thirst and the burning brand, because if he didn't, I thought I might go mad, I might believe I'd just invented it all like the letter to the hotel guest in room 204; please, he had to tell me, because without the support of that other memory, I'd be lost in my own memory as in a labyrinthine dream from which you wake up feeling numb. I was almost trembling with cold by the time I'd finished my gin and tonic, and Rafa had got up to pour me another and to serve a group of young people who'd just arrived.

"You seem odd, Mariana, what's wrong?"

"Nothing. I'm just cold. Don't you feel cold?"

"No, I'm fine. Here, put my jacket on if you want."

He got up, took his jacket off the back of the chair and put it round my shoulders. I fleetingly noticed the smell of his cologne, but by then he was sitting down opposite me again.

318

"Better?" he said, smiling.

"Yes, much better, thank you," I replied, putting my arms in the sleeves. "I went for a walk earlier and I forgot to bring anything warm to wear."

It was a beige wool jacket. It was his, it smelt of him and it consoled me to have it on. The clouds had darkened.

"Are you staying here long?" he asked, after a brief pause.

"No, not long. I might leave tomorrow. In fact I came to visit a patient of mine who lives in Puerto Real and then I fancied the idea of staying here, one of those spur-of-the-moment decisions, because I've got some lectures to prepare and I needed a rest. I don't have time for anything in Madrid, I never stop."

"So I remember," he said.

He said it in a voice that attempted to be neutral, but for the first time it touched on our secret code, as when you furtively stroke someone's skin. He had grown thoughtful, looking out at the bruised clouds growing dark over the sea. There was a circular ornament at the top of the steps behind him that framed his head. I couldn't stand the silence any longer.

"Manolo."

"What?"

"Why did you say 'So I remember'? What do you remember?"

"I remember how little notice you took of me in Madrid when I went to see you that autumn, I remember what an awful time I had. I don't usually regret anything, but I do regret that trip. I still have nightmares about it. You should have told me not to come, that our relationship couldn't last. I behaved like an adolescent, like a real idiot."

Rafa came back, but he didn't sit down. I took a long sip of my new gin and tonic and got up to go to the toilets. I was feeling so confused that I needed to be alone for a while. The tiny mirror hanging in that small room reflected back at me the tense face of a Dr León who didn't even extend a hand to pull me out of that hole because she couldn't, because she too was implicated in that inquiry into my defects. She accused me of having a very selective memory, of being in the

319

bad habit of omitting any memories from which I didn't emerge smelling of roses, of tearing them up the way ageing movie stars tear up unflattering photos of themselves; and she imposed a penance on me, making me hold that cold, severe gaze until the tears welled up in her eyes. The crying did not improve my looks, because the memory that provoked the tears was not a pretty one either – a conversation with Josefina Carreras during Manolo's brief stay in Madrid that autumn, so long ago now. We were both in my office and I started talking about him – he'd just kept me on the phone for a quarter of an hour – as if he were some importunate visitor who was taking up a lot of time and demanding too much attention. Even then, Josefina's half-understanding, half-officious remarks – she was prepared to offer me unconditional support if it gave her a chance to be involved in my life – aroused an immediate feeling of repugnance in me, much as St Peter must have felt when he denied Christ three times before cock crow, and I then buried the scene in my trunk of unmentionable causes of remorse. Those words exchanged by Dr Carreras and Dr León, erased from my memory for two and a half years, sprang starkly back into life in the cheap glass of that small, round mirror, foiling any of my attempts to make reality jump through the hoop of some distorting fantasy. It was very hard for me to lose my illusions, to abandon my lies.

It's a well-known fact that lovers harbour and nurture mutual inexactitudes, that they are accomplices in the state of perpetual misunderstanding fomented by any confession of love. They take refuge in the flow of a dialogue untouched by reality, but later, when they continue the conversation on their own and discover their own deficiencies, the lie erected between the two of them grows bigger and the hooks that catch at them grow sharper. These are things, however, that we prefer to forget.

I splashed some water on my face which stood no chance now of appearing seductive or provocative; it dispelled any hopes I might have had of something extraordinary occurring. When I emerged from the toilet, the sun had just set. Manolo was still looking out to sea and Rafa was no longer with him. I took another long sip of my gin and tonic, but I didn't sit down.

"Shall we go?" I asked.

Manolo finished his drink and got up.

"Whatever you want. It is a bit chilly now. It looks like it's going to rain."

We said goodbye to Rafa at the bar and Manolo promised that he'd come back. Rafa didn't want to take our money. I didn't promise him anything, but I gave him a kiss.

"Have fun you two. It's great to see you together again."

We left by the front door, the one that leads to the road to the hotel. We were walking side by side, but keeping a safe distance. We were silent. He looked at his watch, a slim, modern watch he didn't have before.

"What shall we do?" he said. "I've got my car over there. I thought you might like to come and have supper with us in Cádiz. Sheila wants to meet you."

"Thanks, but I'd rather not. I'm sure you understand."

"No, I can't say I do, but it doesn't matter."

We'd reached a rather expensive red car. It wasn't the Centaur. I took off his jacket and gave it to him.

"Goodbye, Manolo," I said. "Good luck."

"Get in. I'll take you to your hotel."

"It's only a few hundred yards away."

"Yes, but I thought you were cold."

I got in, and that journey, as brief as it was silent, seemed to last an eternity. As soon as he stopped, before he could say anything, I gave him a kiss.

"Goodbye, Manolo."

"You're suddenly in a great hurry to get rid of me!"

"Yes, I am. There aren't many things I regret either, but I do regret writing to you the other day. Now we're quits."

He stroked my hair.

"But we haven't looked into each other's eyes yet," he said with sudden tenderness.

I bent my head and realized in despair that I could no longer hold back my tears. He tried to raise my chin to make me look at him, but I hid my face against his shoulder and broke into sobs.

"No, please don't! Just leave it, will you, leave it!"

He put an arm round my shoulders and held me against him.

"Come on, Mariana, what's wrong? Calm down."

"How could you possibly ask me to meet her? How could you?" I kept repeating between sobs. "Ask me anything you like, anything you like, but not that!"

"I'm not asking you to do that. What do you want me to ask you? Tell me, but don't cry. Shall I park a bit further along?"

"No, it doesn't matter. I'm going now anyway."

The pressure of his arm had eased. He held out a Kleenex to me that he got out of the glove compartment. He seemed rather embarrassed.

"Come on, dry your eyes. What do you want me to ask you?"

I breathed in the smell impregnating his shirt one last time and then moved away from him.

"Nothing. I don't need you to ask me anything. If you want to ask somebody something, I'm sure you're not short of candidates."

On the other side of the window, I could see the receptionist with the toothpaste smile; he was just leaving the hotel with some guests. I saw that he was looking at us with some curiosity, but then quickly looked away. In a brilliant flash illuminating every detail, I suddenly remembered the lover's quarrel at the restaurant of the one-eyed sea-gull. I angrily dried my eyes and made to get out of the car. I was trembling.

"Goodbye, Manolo," I said in as firm a voice as I could manage. "And forgive me, all right?"

"Don't talk nonsense. Don't go yet, don't go like this. You're trembling. I'll call Sheila and tell her I'll be late, and I'll come up to your room for a while, until you feel a bit calmer."

"Don't mention her name!" I screamed, completely beside myself now. "Don't mention her name! Do you understand? Never, never again!"

I got out of the car, slammed the door shut and ran towards the hotel without looking back.

PS It's midnight, Sofía. You'll have been in the train for a while now, in the train bringing you south, lying in your bunk bed or having supper in the restaurant car, perhaps writing, a healthy habit which I'm glad to hear you haven't lost. What I do know is that, like me, you'll be looking at the moon.

The story continues. When I show you the letters that I didn't send you – which I've just been putting in order in a file – you'll see that the first letter is the fruit of my sleepless night in that same train while Noc's words slipped in through the window. There's quite a pile of them, more than a hundred pages. I realize that since I left Madrid, I've done nothing but write to you, and that's what has kept me alive and why this absurd journey has not been wasted. My greatest joy at the moment is knowing that you didn't stop doing your homework either and that you're bringing me a present of several notebooks. It could be a wonderful swap, don't you think, your notebooks for my letters, because, now that I think about it, we're bound occasionally to have touched on the same subjects but from a different perspective. I don't know if you ever saw *Rashomon*, that Japanese film that told the same story from the viewpoints of three different witnesses; I like the idea of multiple versions. I keep thinking that if we just sorted it out a bit, or even if we didn't, we could probably make a wonderful novel out of what you're bringing with you and what I've got here. I can't wait to see you, to read your notebooks and to find out what you think about the idea. I can guarantee that what you've written is good, even though I haven't read it all; your first letter about the plumbing problems was enough for me to judge. But my letters have a certain something too, at least I like them when I re-read them. I think you'd have to help me to prune them a bit because I may repeat myself too much. Well, I don't know, I'll leave it up to you; you might think we should change the names too. I love the idea of adding my letters to yours and editing the whole thing together, with you having the final say, of course. It's not a bad idea, is it? I would leave psychiatry and you would

323

leave your husband. Call me mad, but I suddenly found myself remembering that when I lived in Barcelona I knew some of the publishers who are making a name for themselves now, for example, Jorge Herralde, who has a reputation for discovering new writers and having the courage to publish them; he was studying to be an engineer then, I think; he moved in more or less the same circles as I did. I've had to give myself completely different advice from the advice I gave myself yesterday evening, I no longer need to instil myself with courage and have more confidence in myself; on the contrary, I need to rein in an enthusiasm that borders on madness. I've been so excited since you told me that you're coming that the drowsiness I was feeling when you called has disappeared completely; logical, don't you think, seeing that I haven't had a thing to eat all day together with the exhaustion of a sleepless night, a lover's tiff and then worrying about whether the phone would ring or not and wanting to know what had happened to you which, by the way, you've only told me about very superficially. So, you see, instead of going to bed, I'm still scribbling and, as if that wasn't enough, I now nurse the ambition to be to you what Ramalho Ortigão was to Eça de Queiroz in *The Mystery of the Road to Sintra*. In short, the postscript threatens to be longer than the letter, as my father used to say about guests who didn't know when to leave.

I love you so much, Sofía. It seems impossible that in a few short hours, I'll see you again. What I most admire about you is the way you just jump straight in. I say to you in discouraged tones: "I just seem incapable of making a decision. I'd love to have you here with me, that would be my one consolation," and you say: "What time's the next train? I shouldn't think there'd be any problem getting a ticket. Come to Cádiz to meet me. If I don't call again, it means I'll be on that train, the night train. No, don't worry, I've got bags of time. Okay, okay, you can tell me all that later, I've got loads of things to tell you too. I'm going to hang up now, so stop talking. I'll see you tomorrow." And since midnight, that tomorrow is today, and I'm going to see you today! How can you expect me to sleep?

And then, Sofía, not long after I'd hung up, not more than half an hour later, reception phoned me. I thought it must be you again to tell me that you hadn't been able to get a ticket or that there'd been some problem with your husband, I don't know. Anyway, you can imagine my surprise when the receptionist told me that someone had left a package for me and did I want the bellboy to bring it up. I said no, I'd rather come down, although he warned me it was big. I raced down there, as you can imagine, it must have been about six o'clock or thereabouts, more or less twenty-four hours after my meeting with Manolo, I don't know if he did that on purpose, it would be just like him, and there I was looking round to see if I could see him, and I said to the receptionist who handed me a flat package wrapped in creamy beige paper: "Who brought it? Didn't they leave a message or anything?" and he said: "No, Madam, they told me the card was inside," and I said: "Who told you? (my voice betrayed my eagerness) Who brought the package? Was it a dark young man, quite tall?" and then he leaned a little over the counter and with a smile of assent and complicity far more sympathetic than the nickname I gave him would lead you to expect, he said to me in confidential tones: "I think, Madam, if you'll forgive the indiscretion, that it was the same gentleman to whom you were saying goodbye last night, he was in a red Volkswagen. He asked me if you were still in the hotel. He seemed to be in a hurry." I felt like telling him that in my novel, he had just been promoted from a minor character to a figure of some importance, but instead I merely returned his smile and held out my hand which he shook effusively. I couldn't hide the happiness suddenly flooding through me, I needed to share it with someone: "No, really, you're not being in the least indiscreet. Thank you very much, Arturo, that is your name, isn't it?" "Yes," he said, "at your service. And don't thank me, Madam. It's about time something arrived for you, considering how long you've been waiting." Once back in my room, I nervously opened the package; I could see from the size and shape that it was a painting and, miracle of miracles, as I'm writing to you now, I can look up every so often and see it hanging in front of me; it's replaced the horrible engraving of icebergs which has been relegated to the cupboard. It bears no resemblance whatsoever to Gregorio Termes' fried eggs. It's a watercolour measuring fifty-five centimetres by forty centimetres and it's entitled *Farewell Clouds*. Manolo had it hanging in his studio; he'd never exhibited it because he didn't want to sell it and I often told him that I felt tempted to steal it, that it was my favourite of all his paintings. "It's mine too," he said. "Ask me for anything you like, but don't ask me for that water-colour." It's a painting of evening clouds over the sea and in the distance there's a boat and a blurred female figure standing on a cliff, waving goodbye. It's beautiful, you'll see it when you come. He sent it to me exactly as it was, in the same frame and even with a little of its old dust. He must suddenly have decided to go over to his old studio – assuming he's kept it on – taken it down, wrapped it up and rushed back here to deliver it to me. All very clandestine, I'm sure, as an affair of the heart should be. I realize now that Manolo has never seen me cry; it must have been a shock for him to see me hysterical, unmasked, even though he didn't know how to react at the time. Perhaps he'd already started planning this when he was driving back alone to Cádiz in the dark; he must have remembered a lot of things on that journey, he probably hasn't stopped thinking about me since then, all the time I've been shut up here feeling like an utter worm; and of course he would have had to think up some excuse to get away from Sheila that evening without her noticing that it was an urgent matter that took him from her side. She may not even know the watercolour of the lover waving goodbye and she probably wouldn't know how to appreciate it if she did, since she's the inspiration behind all those daubs that have transformed Manolo Reina into a Lexington Avenue-type avant-garde artist. She would have even more difficulty understanding why he was giving it to me. Private business, my friend, this is a matter between your boyfriend and me and has nothing to do with you; he lied to you today, he didn't tell you where he was going. I'm sorry, but you're completely excluded from this particular love story with a bittersweet ending. I don't need to go and ask Arturo if the gentleman in the red Volkswagen was alone or with a woman. Inside the package, stuck to the frame with Sellotape, was a card with this brief message: "We already share a garden which is ours alone: the garden of the lost past. Look after it for me."

I'm getting sleepy, Sofía, and we've got a heavy day ahead of us. I've just put the alarm clock on for seven o'clock because at a quarter past the taxi's coming to pick me up and drive me to Cádiz to meet you. I feel like a different woman today, I can't believe how happy I feel. But I'm exhausted too. I'm going to see if I can sleep for a few hours and be in good shape to meet you. See you later, Per Abat. Your friend,

Mariana.

XVII

The persistence of memory

I woke up around dawn. I had a terrible headache, was shivering all over and my mouth was dry. I think it was thirst, a raging thirst, that woke me up. There was no one with me and I didn't know where I was, but a shred of intuition, perhaps the epilogue of an interrupted dream, led me to think, when I got out of bed in the dark, that I was not on enemy territory. Except it isn't a bed I've got out of, but a boat I was earlier forced into — it's nice, despite the feeling of danger, to have suddenly learned to swim with such precision and making no noise at all — it's night, I'm drenched to the skin and shivering with cold when I reach this unknown shore. I was swimming with my head under the water, but I could hear the "chop chop" of the long oar entering and leaving the water, rhythmically propelling the boat along, away from me, a square, solid boat with the oarsman standing up on the prow, inscrutable, all dressed in black, in rough clothes made out of coarse wool. He didn't hear me escape or else he pretended that he didn't.

I feel my way along the walls, I advance cautiously and I come upon a vaguely familiar surface, something that feels like wood, turned wooden bars with knobs on top. It doesn't reach the floor, it contains books, protruding bits of paper and other disparate objects collected together at the front, almost on the very edge. One of those objects has just fallen off after I brushed it with my hand, it shattered on the tiles, the noise of broken glass, perhaps an inkwell. I wonder if I woke anyone up? I can't find the light switch, there isn't one, how odd, or rather it isn't where I expected it to be, an automatic gesture guided by the experience of infinite repetitions.

I go out into the dark corridor. I count the steps to the next door, then from that door to the next, and then on to the next. The distances coincide with the approximate geography of touch that is evolving inside me, like a map with corrections superimposed on it. The thing I thought infallible fails, the first thing that God invented when he made the world so that people would be able to see the things he had in mind to invent later on: *fiat lux*. Sometimes, when I was a child, I used to wonder if that divine order was accompanied by the mechanical gesture I now make in vain: I mean, were there switches or something similar in the time of Genesis; there don't seem to be any here, although nothing is clear when you can't see. Could I be in the wrong house?

After the third door I can't go any further, there's a wall. Of course, that's the wall that was built to divide the apartment in two, thus returning it to its former state, the way it was when my in-laws were alive, albeit with certain changes of physiognomy, an entity divided into right and left. "Don't worry about it, Mama, it's better to accept this simple division rather than turn into a schizophrenic," my son Santi used to say as a joke. He got over his communism, thank God, the way children get over measles. He was the one who came over from Houston when his father died and took charge of everything (What did I want with an apartment that big now anyway?), the one who organized all the building work and restored life to those half-neglected rooms that were separated off from the other rooms by a heavy curtain. There was quite a lot of wasted space – about ninety square metres according to Santi – a magnet for cockroaches and sundry accumulated junk: the ancient kitchen with a kind of pantry attached, the coal bunker, the larder, and the bathroom (the bath had clawed feet like the ones you see in horror films), where he sometimes used to develop photographs as a young man. "The Kingdom of the Murds" his sister used to call it when she was a child, and she'd simply shrug her shoulders when her father and I asked who the Murds were; she'd make a vague gesture up at the flaking ceiling, her fingers fluttering. "Well, the Kingdom of the Murds is no more, Mama; it'll be a lovely apartment, you'll see, the whole of what used to be 4b according to the plans, and you don't have to worry about a thing, just leave it to me, you won't have to lift a finger." I said he should consult his sister, but she wasn't interested. "Removing old things and adding new ones, that's all it amounts to, it's a waste of time," she said with that distant smile of hers, as if she were above such worldly matters: "We spend our whole lives removing and adding, and what for?" Her children are the same: it's no good asking her children's opinion about anything. They were part of the protest generation, especially the two older ones, always dreaming up alternative adventures, rejecting the consumer society, and with a father who was beginning to earn money by the fistful, and who, if truth be told, kept well out of it, an apartment in Calle Lagasca?, not my problem. "Besides, Mama," said Santi, "since I haven't got any children and don't intend to have any, not with the state the world's in now, you can do what you like with 4a, just leave it in your will to Sofia's children and forget about it. But 4b is mine." He took care of everything, he modernized the Kingdom of the Murds, the study, the big bedroom and the "screen room". He had the wall that used to separate the two flats rebuilt and he sold 4b for a good price, investing the proceeds at very advantageous rates so that I wouldn't have any money worries. "Not that you need to worry about that, anyway, Mama, not while I'm alive," he used to say in the letters he sent me from America, "I'll pay your air fare any time you want to come over and see me." But I've always been lazy; I kept putting it off from one year to the next. "I don't want you to die without seeing America," he said. Well he'd just have to lump it: what did America have to offer me? "If you get married, fine, I promise I'll come to the wedding," I used to say to him in letters and over the phone, because, in the end, I was more or less resigned to the fact that he'd end up marrying some Yankee, even if she was Russian or Jewish. And he'd always say, what has that got to do with anything, it was emotional blackmail. I wonder if he's got married yet; he had a high-flying career as a biologist, he was wanted by all the best universities, always getting grants and he was so good-looking; some things I'll never understand.

My main regret about dividing the apartment in two and selling off the other half was the loss of the "screen room". "What use is it, if you never have any visitors now?" and he was right about that, as well as about everything being handier and easier to clean. I don't know, though: I was fond of that room, it was always so nice and bright, I u to enjoy spying on the people hurrying down the cold street, with their griefs and their packages, and there I'd be, sitting at the table, sitting sewing on a balcony, safe from problems that would never touch me or involve me; it was like going to the theatre. I was never a sociable person like my husband. He and Santi were the ones who brought friends home, she less so. I don't know if it was because, deep down, she was more like me than she thinks or because she was afraid I might pass judgement on her friends, which, knowing me, was only natural; the only one who came was that pretty girl, Dr León's daughter, but then they quarrelled: I can't remember why. There wasn't time for her or me to change, for us to break the ice between us: she got married so young, too young. Well, what's past is past. And then we didn't agree about how to bring up the children either; I talked to her husband about it. She gave them too much freedom.

I know nothing about life beyond these walls and I don't want to. I never cared to meet the people who bought the other apartment, a foreign couple with a little boy. I sometimes used to meet them in the lift and we'd exchange brief greetings, though never enough to encourage familiarity, I've never liked being on familiar terms with strangers. "How are you ever going to get to know anyone?" she used to say, "You'll spend your entire life amongst strangers." They bought some furniture from us too; they may not be the same people there now, they may have resold the flat, I can't say it matters to me. What does matter is having to leave here without knowing who now lives in 4a.

I feel my way along the wall, then turn round and follow it back along the other side, as if I were changing pavements to explore the shop windows opposite. A small recess and an unmistakable detail: the double door that you push open with your foot, no latch; through it you enter the rooms belonging to the kingdom I always felt was almost exclusively mine perhaps because everyone encouraged me to think that: the kingdom of the kitchen and environs. I walk straight past it, a taste like ashes in my mouth; all that makes me feel bitter, very bitter indeed, who would have thought it? I imagine myself buried beneath an avalanche of birthdays, first communions, Sunday lunches and high teas

t of his, the sort of meal you don't know whether to serve

oom with a lace table cloth and the best china – a sit-down

o things more informally, a style that gradually became the
norm, where everyone serves themselves with what they want and then
eat sitting down or standing up, as they choose; I actually found that
harder work, it was more difficult to control. "You choose," he used to
say. In his later years he grew more and more distracted, more indifferent
to the difficulties I experienced socially: "Whatever you do will be fine,
Encarna, just do as you like," as if taking for granted that I would find
some pleasure or excitement in spending the whole day in the kitchen and
then getting dressed up just in time to sally forth and smile at all those
faceless couples and thank them if they brought us a bottle of wine or a
box of chocolates, and then, as I was handing round trays and filling
glasses, while the men talked business, I would have no option but to
exchange banalities with the wives, wives who left no impression on me,
just as I left no impression on them when I went to their houses with my
bottle of wine or my box of chocolates, wives for whom I never felt any
liking, pity or curiosity, just as they felt none for me: I was just another
resentful, lonely wife. Once, when I was talking to my eldest niece about
egotism, she told me that, despite what people have always thought, the
worst thing about the egotist is that he doesn't really like himself at all,
which is why he's incapable of loving anyone else, because nothing
comes of nothing. She brought me a few psychology books on the topic,
but I much preferred it when she explained it to me herself; I understood
things better then. Adela used to say: "She's the apple of your eye,
Señora," and of course she was. No one else has ever talked to me like
that, looking me straight in the eye, and in that gentle voice, persuasive
and sincere, that went straight to my heart – and that's no easy task; I
never loved anyone the way I loved little Encarna, not even my own children, and I missed her when she didn't come to visit me, spontaneously I
mean, without warning, just because she was passing and fancied coming
up for a natter, not just because it was marked down on the calendar,
something she used to complain about to me later. "But you're the one

who says we have to keep to the calendar, Grandma; you're the one who insists we keep to it as strictly as if it were the law. If Amelia or Lorenzo or I miss one of your wretched Sunday lunches, you get all offended, don't you?" I had to agree, what else could I do, I even found myself agreeing with Sartre, though I've never liked anything that came out of France, least of all existentialism. However, I learned by heart that phrase of his that Encarnita was always quoting: "We are all the semi-victims and semi-accomplices of what happens to us," for he was absolutely right there, I can't deny it, even if he was a horrible, cross-eyed little atheist – not exactly one of my favourites. He and his fancy woman were friends of the other Sofía Montalvo, that cousin of mine; she was a bad lot – may she rest in peace, though I doubt if she does, I never did like her. So, yes, I was a semi-accomplice in all that, but I couldn't do anything about it. As the years passed, I made martyrs of them all with those Sunday lunches, but Sofía was more of a martyr than her children, because she never really stood up to me and my desire to keep tabs on everyone, even though I only did so from a distance. I made her feel guilty with my sighs and my constant glances at the clock whenever the children were late arriving or weren't hungry because they'd already had something to eat with friends beforehand or when they rang up at the last moment with an excuse; only natural really, they were being forced to come and so they wanted to escape and sometimes they didn't even stay for coffee; I bored them with my endless complaints, the rice is over-cooked, you might have told me sooner, you and your friends, will *they* feed you?, anyone would think you were being invited to the gallows not Sunday lunch, and she was even more bored than they were, always having to smooth things over, having to stick up for them, feeling I was blaming her, putting up with my eternal bitterness, with my slavish devotion to the clock and to dates, she was the one who suffered most. I knew that and she knew I knew, but she carried on lying and trying to smile, she even resorted to clichés – which she'd always loathed ever since she was a child – to desperate remarks about the weather or some event that had been reported in the newspapers or to domestic problems – especially plumbing problems, the poor woman was always being pestered by plumbers – things she said to fill the void, words that could as easily have been left unsaid. When I looked at her, I felt gripped by a sort of remorse, which I declined to analyze because it was too intermingled with the pleasure of having her exactly where I wanted her and that, I knew, was what stopped me opening my arms to her, from melting the ice of old resentments: perhaps it was too late for that. The fact is that she didn't do anything either, she made no effort to bring us closer together. Latterly she looked quite ill, always tense, distracted, on the defensive, unable to hide her sense of failure, apart, that is, from the last time I saw her, when she'd just got back from London: she looked really pretty then, almost rejuvenated.

More doors, three more and then the front door, lined with damask, the first door I've come across that's closed, because the others were open or half-open, apart from the double door, of course, which is a swing door. And I said to myself in passing: whoever these people are living here, they're obviously the sort who don't shut doors: as my grandfather used to say: "Where were you born, in a field?", an anti-quated phrase that nobody finds funny. Even we didn't find it funny when he said it then; it was just that if the adult saying the phrase started laughing, the children would simply follow suit, without much convic-tion, out of pure contagion and duty. Nevertheless, expressions like that stick with you throughout your life and even beyond, they cling to your brain like limpets, they live on, spinning round and round inside your skull. I'd like to sweep away all those banal phrases, like so many dead, November leaves, pile them all up on a truck and set fire to them, even though half my own history would be go up in smoke with them; it's not possible though. Honestly, even the bathroom door is ajar! They obvi-ously *were* born in a field. I pause outside one of the doors, listening, sniffing the air, wanting to go in, but I can't quite decide, something holds me back, a kind of unease: I might find something I don't like. "You don't like it because it's strange, different, and for you, different means bad or worse. Honestly, Mama, you've spent your entire life expecting the worst, always absolutely convinced of your own opinions, never trusting anyone who didn't think exactly the same as you." Well, yes, that's absolutely right; I resisted making new friends and did nothing to win back old friendships that were lost gradually, and so I reached the end of my life utterly alone; I regret that now, Sofía, but that's how I am. All I want at this moment is for you to be able to hear me, not so that you can forgive me but so that you could look into this dim mirror and decide once and for all to do whatever was necessary not to end up like me, for as the years go by, you inevitably end up resembling your parents, and more in their defects than in their good points. But what I'd like more than anything is to be able to wipe away your regrets, if you have any.

I'd like to go now, go back to the boat, because I don't understand what I'm doing here, nor what any of this has to do with me. It is odd, though, that all the doors I've come across have been open or half-open, even though it appears to be night. Maybe I'm a bit obsessive, but I wouldn't want to go without finding out something. It smells odd in here, a strong smell that almost makes me dizzy; it smells rather dirty too, like a provincial boarding house. From one of the rooms, from the study I think, I heard the whisper of unfamiliar voices, two men I think, and muffled sighs. It would be best just to leave.

I stand in the hall and press my ear against the damask lining of the door. The lining's a bit shabby now and I can't remember the name of the man who lined it for me, but it must be in my green address book, if you haven't thrown it out, under U for Upholsterer; his address will be there too, he used to live near Calle Legazpi. I can't do anything about it, I'm poking my nose in where it isn't wanted; what does it matter whether a bit of upholstery lasts or not or whether it gets dirty? I can't believe that I still haven't got into my head what the Bible says about "dust thou art", even though I always used to repeat it to myself at funerals, and I attended quite a few. "Now, Encarna, don't take all that ironing and polishing and stain-removing so seriously, you see how it all ends," but it was only a fleeting thought, that only lasted as long as the *dies irae*, the organ music and the time it took to file past the family members to pay my respects. Just as well too, because if you spent all day thinking, "dust thou art and unto dust thou shalt return", you wouldn't even be able to enjoy tucking into a good paella.

335

I grab the bolt intending to slide it open and escape down the stairs, but I stop because I think I hear the lift which sounds different now, more metallic since they got rid of the mahogany cabin with its frosted glass doors and the little red velvet bench. I don't want anyone coming in here and finding me turned into a ghost, which is what I am; I wouldn't know what to say. They probably wouldn't be able to see me because ghosts can see without being seen, at least that's how it is in the films. I remember seeing a very funny film once, starring Myrna Loy and William Powell, *The Thin Man* it was called, in black and white, although I'm not sure if they were playing ghosts exactly, but they were so good, they seemed so modern to me; they're probably both dead by now. We all end up the same, it's stupid to think otherwise, deluding yourself that you might be the exception and hang around for ever; besides, it would be awfully boring, not knowing anyone any more and getting in everyone's way.

I turn round and carefully feel my way back to the place where I think I started. Yes, I can feel that shelf with its bars and wooden knobs. I'll be more careful this time, I don't want to knock anything else over. I've closed the door now and I advance with my hands held out in front of me so as not to bump into anything, as if I were playing blind man's buff, for I came in here drawn by the certainty that the key to what I've been thinking about and to what I still don't understand could be in this room. My feet feel like lead as I walk forwards, trying, at the same time, to remember what I was doing here before, where and how I got in.

I feel for the wall, press myself against it and immediately my feet touch something which I crouch down to feel with my hands. It's a soft surface, a divan or a sofa; I stretch out my fingers to explore it and, underneath the soft blanket, there's a human shape that I immediately recognize, a body curled up in a ball, face to the wall, with one foot out and the head almost covered. That's how she always used to sleep, ever since she was a child. "Just look at you! You always make the top of the sheet all creased. What kind of a way is that to sleep, child! It looks more like a gypsy's bed than a young lady's," and she'd say why couldn't I just leave her alone, what right did I have to come into her room without knocking, everyone has their own way of sleeping, did she criticize mine?, and anyway she was fed up with all that racist talk about gypsies, they probably slept impeccably or at least their mothers allowed them to sleep, she would grumble, covering her eyes with one arm as if the sunlight were a poisoned arrow, "and I was having such a lovely dream." When she was very small, she used to cry with unhappiness whenever I'd spoiled some marvellous dream of hers, and I found that odd, because she seemed absolutely serious; she felt the same as I would if a maid broke one of my good crystal glasses; I would look at her as if she were some kind of strange beast. "Of course, *you* can't understand, because you never dream about anything anyway." Her most bitter complaint, however, despite all the years we'd lived together, was that I had never found a way of waking her up gently, rather than army-fashion, flinging open the shutters, crash, just like that, and then immediately launching into a discussion of some tedious subject belonging to the pitiless world of daylight, for which the mind of the sleeping person is not yet prepared – "Don't forget this … don't forget that … and don't forget to …", a hail of warnings with no transitional stage like a caress, a cup of coffee, or a gentle back rub, nothing.

I stumble over several books thrown untidily on to the floor, along with a cushion and a pair of shoes. It's her all right. I pick up two or three that are lying open, close them and feel for an empty space for them on a shelf, a table or an empty ledge. I touch a cold surface, like marble, and when I put the books down on it, I notice a table lamp, I feel hopefully for a switch, it's not on the wire or on the base either … but if I pull this little chain, at last, *fiat lux*! It's a rather dim light but such a relief! Despite the changes made, I can still recognize my old sewing room. The wardrobe with its three full-length mirrors, for example, has vanished as if by magic. I don't know how they managed to dismantle it, because it was a fair old size.

What I don't understand is what she's doing sleeping here, apparently on a temporary basis, because she has no sheets and no companion. I kneel down on the floor to pull the blanket over her again and cover up the one bare foot that emerges from the bottom of her corduroy trousers, and I suddenly realize that she *isn't* alone. There's a cat sleeping at the foot of the sofa bed, because that's what it is, a sofa bed. It did give me a fright! We never had cats in the apartment, this one seems very affectionate, almost a kitten, a very pretty tabby; it purred and changed position when I touched it. She, on the other hand, hasn't moved, not even when I switched on the light or covered up her foot to stop it getting cold, even now when I said out loud: "Good grief, a cat!", well, at least I think I said it out loud, who knows?

I sit on the floor by her side, prepared to do my best not to give her a cruel awakening. The carpet is the same one as before, a dirty pink, and it really *is* dirty, they've ruined it, there are even cigarette burns on it; I think that upholsterer in Lagazpi also laid carpets and linoleum, well, what people call vinyl these days. I lean back against one of the cushions on the floor, which is large and very soft, and I take a deep breath. The other thing I can't see is my sewing machine, a Singer manual, that belonged to my mother, it was one of the first. According to Santi they're worth quite a lot now. They probably sold it in the Rastro.

"Sofía," I say softly, whilst, almost fearfully, I stroke the hair sticking up above the blanket. "Sofía, wake up. What are you doing here? Why are you sleeping with your clothes on? Is something wrong?"

She lets out a slight groan, like that of a feverish child, and kicks the cat who merely moves and snuggles up instead against the curve of her belly, and the two of them lie there curled in a semi-circle facing the wall.

There used to be lots of family portraits on this wall ranged in rows at varying heights; "the tunnel of time" Santi used to call it jokingly, photos of my wedding, my first communion, of the two of them when they were children playing in the park with that ugly English governess Sofía christened "Miss Nelly" after the governess in *What Celia Says*, several colour photos of Sofía with her children at various ages, my father in military uniform, and another, very romantic portrait of myself which I would be sorry to have lost. I used to love looking at it every now and then and see myself there looking so happy. It was a snapshot taken by the brother of a friend of mine when I'd just turned sixteen. I was leaning against a peeling wall, by a door, looking into the distance, and there was a horse standing next to me. It was a stable door, the sort where the two halves open separately. Anyway, out of the top half leaned the white head of a horse, almost brushing mine; I wore my hair parted in the middle and I was still all in black, in mourning for my Grandmother Carmen. "Poor thing, let her come and spend a few days with us," my friend's mother had said to Mama. "She might cheer up a bit." I had found grandmother Carmen dead in her armchair with her crochet work still in her lap, and it wasn't until I went over and gave her a kiss and noticed how cold her face was that I realized she was dead and ran screaming out of the room. I went from bad to worse after that; I was feverish for several days and my period started. It was my first encounter with a dead person. Now, I've lost count. Anyway, my parents accepted the invitation. My friend was called Herminia and we were staying on a farm her parents owned in the province of Salamanca and we were driven there by their chauffeur in an old, very tall, black Buick — they had a lot of money; Herminia's brother was older than us, he was studying medicine and he was in love with me. No one knew it, not even Herminia I think, and I don't even remember how *I* found out, but at that age you guessed at rather than knew such things. And I guessed it at the very moment he took the photo. It was a summer evening, the sun was going down and I was leaning against that white wall, standing very still next to the horse; I was feeling very excited, my eyes fixed on the sunset, think-ing that soon the crickets would start to sing and night would fall. "Don't move," he said, "I'm going to take a snapshot of you," and my dreamy look is the sort of look a young woman wears knowing that it makes her more beautiful and that someone you're not even looking at is looking at you. The men were working on the threshing machine and I could hear them singing something about furrows and labourers, "If you plough the furrow right up to my window, tomorrow you'll be my father's man," and Lucas, for that was his name, said that the song referred to the daughter of the previous owner of the farm who had fallen in love with a labourer, someone of lower social status than her; at the time the theme of the social inequality of two lovers was a popular one in songs and novels: the young lady and the bullfighter, the governess and the marquis, and it was all terribly exciting, because the family would set almost impossible obstacles in their path. Those taboos are almost gone now, Eduardo's family, for example, were very undistinguished, from some back-of-beyond town in Teruel, and no one said a word, but then in the circumstances ... The sky was red, and then the first star came out; we stood there for a while alone together, not saying anything, just listening to the sound of the threshing machine, and Lucas said: "Look, Encarna, the first star," and I said: "Yes I saw it, it's the evening star, we have to make a wish." "All right," he said, "but wish for something for us both," and my heart was in my mouth. And I started saying very softly, almost as if I were praying: "Star light, star bright, first star I see tonight, wish I may, wish I might have the wish I wish tonight." I'm the only one who remembers that evening that was never repeated and never will be; I carried it with me to the kingdom of shadows: now not even the photo remains.

On this wall now there's a large reproduction of a rather ugly painting framed in grey *passe-partout*. Well, when I look at it, it's not so much ugly as bizarre and a bit frightening too. The truth is, though, that my eyes are drawn to it and I can't look away from the scene it depicts, if you can call it a scene; it's more like a still life, but it's not that either. In the background there's a kind of cubist cliff or mountain and in the foreground, set against a dark backdrop, is a series of melting clocks hung out to dry, one on the bare branches of a tree, another on the edge of a kind of table, another on top of a giant snail, they look like molluscs, there's only one normal one, with the lid closed, but what am I saying, "normal"? When you look at it closely, it turns out that what you thought were jewels encrusting the lid are, in fact, ants: it's horrible, *very* strange. I sit for a while looking at it and find it so disturbing that I stand up to have a better look. Underneath, in small letters, it says "Salvador Dalí, *The Persistence of Memory*, 1931, Museum of Modern Art, New York". I wonder if that bizarre memory is the one that will persist, Sofía; have you thought that too? It's not my memory, or yours either, just one of that madman Dalí's inventions, and he must have meant something by it, perhaps that clocks are an illusion, that they serve no useful purpose, apart from measuring the obligatory, trivial time of colds and visits and Sunday lunches and rent days, the time for giving orders, for waiting until it grew dark in order to switch on the lights, for ironing the sheets that you had creased and for complaining because there was a stain on the carpet and for calling in the upholsterer, but they have nothing to do with the time of that summer afternoon when my Grandmother Carmen died; like tonight, the passing of time then was doubtless ruled by different laws; perhaps that explains why the clocks in the picture are melting. If they didn't melt, if they preserved their rustproof certainty, I wouldn't be sitting here now watching over your sleep and that of the tabby kitten, wondering what Dalí meant by his painting about the persistence of memory. Can you imagine, Sofía, even remotely, what kind of memories your children will have when you disappear? Of course not, we'll never know. I don't know what you remember and what you don't, nor how you order or explain those memories inside your head, nor which memories you've discarded with the rubbish, I've no idea. Look, I'm going to say just one thing: don't go making inventories like I did; if something causes you pain, get rid of it.

I sit down on a sofa, put my arms around your body and start to stroke your head, crying and remembering – why I don't know – when I first taught you how to tie your shoelaces and to button up your own overcoat and how to open and close a safety pin without pricking yourself and how to unscrew the tops of jam jars and how to brush your teeth; and I remember a day when you had such a high fever you were delirious and kept saying that you were sure you must want to be a bad girl because you couldn't stop thinking up wicked things to do, for example, sleeping with a dirty gypsy in an unmade bed, everything I'd told you not to do, and that you wanted to disappear and forget about this house for ever, and about cities and about people, that you wanted to fly and fly as high as the eagles to places where there's no air and where people die of cold.

"Sofía," I call, "Sofía."

I realize that I'm going to disappear at any moment, that I'm already forgetting the message I wanted to give you, I don't know what it was now.

"Sofía, give me a kiss. Now I'm going to fly like an eagle too, and I can imagine the house from high up, spinning in the darkness like a blind planet, adrift in space; it was some question about clocks and watches I wanted to ask you, I can't remember now where I put the jewels nor where I put the paper where I said how you should share them out; I'm especially sorry about Papa's watch, but it doesn't matter; tell me what's wrong, because that's what matters and there's no time for anything else, you won't be able to see me now, I'm disappearing, wake up, can you hear me? What are you doing there with that cat, with those soft, flattened clocks, with that foot you've stuck outside the blanket again, what are you dreaming about? Has something bad happened?"

She stirs and moans, she's probably having a nightmare, she turns towards me, waves one arm, uncovers her face and although she's still got her eyes closed, I see that face is contorted, anxious, as if she wanted to cry out and couldn't, I shake her, but I've almost no strength left now.

"Sofía, Sofía, I'm here with you now, but I won't be here for long, wake up, don't be afraid, it's just a dream, it was just a dream, a bad dream, I've got to go now, I'm going back to the boat. Sofía, don't forget what I said to you, don't suffer any more, never again, goodbye Sofía."

"What's going on, please, tell me, what's going on? What time is it? Where are all the clocks?"

I woke up with a start. I had a terrible headache, I was shivering all over and my mouth was dry. I think it was thirst, a raging thirst, that woke me up. And I was having a dream about clocks. Mama hadn't died, she was here with me, *I* was Mama. I'm sitting on a bed, but I don't know whose bed it is and it takes me a while to recognize the room, even though I can see it, since it seems I went to sleep with the light on.

Next to the lamp is a glass of water. I gulp it down. It's lukewarm and has an odd taste to it. Or is it my mouth that tastes odd? Then, after having a good look around me to orient myself, I finally recognize one bit of furniture, the bookshelves with the wooden knobs. However, recognizing it doesn't mean a gentle landing back in time, more of a stagger that leads me to throw back the blanket covering me, stand up and start walking round this enclosed space, a brief voyage of discovery in search of a large wardrobe with three full-length mirrors which, of course, isn't here.

I'm barefoot. I touch my own body, I'm wearing a pair of corduroy trousers and a light sweater. I went to sleep with my clothes on, like on that rainy September night in Mama's armchair, a heavy wing chair that has also disappeared; we used to call it the "camphornium". Perhaps Santi carried it off along with other old relics to his house in America on one of those feverish, crazy impulses he gets from time to time after a brief spell of nostalgia. It used to stand by the balcony, near the sewing table and the telephone table. It was the chair she always sat in, where she used to read the paper, sew or knit or do crossword puzzles, the chair from which she used to call us to ask if we would be coming to lunch that Sunday and from where she would watch the street with her clouded, cowardly widow's eyes, the mustard-coloured chair where, with no escape route possible, she was struck down by the fulminating ray of a heart attack.

I went to see her the afternoon before, just after I'd got back from Brighton. We talked for quite a while and it was nice, because I'd come back from that extraordinary trip – like something out of a novel – in a mood for compromise, and she said to me then that she'd have to call in Tomás the upholsterer because that pale mustard colour – she said, touching it – was really getting beyond the pale now, and she laughed at her own joke. When things got beyond a certain point or some situation reached rock bottom, she would always say that things were getting beyond the pale, an expression it seems her grandmother often used, and she never forgot to mention the source, like someone adding a footnote. "Did I tell you that I've bought a new TV? I came to a decision the other day, I said to myself: 'It's now or never', if I don't act today the problem will stay unresolved until the crack of doom." I asked her if that was something else her grandmother used to say. "No, that comes from your late Uncle Luciano, credit where credit's due." Then she got up because she wanted to show me the new fabric for the

343

"camphornium", and she smiled when she said that too, because she only called the chair by that name when she was in a good mood, otherwise she considered it an insult. She took the package out of the wardrobe, we went over to the light and I helped her to unroll the fabric from its cardboard tube (it was the end of a roll); it was a print in reds and blues. She asked me for my opinion and said that she thought it was more hard-wearing than the present fabric, the term "hard-wearing" being a guarantee of quality for her, perhaps because she connected it in her mind with "long-suffering", a quality she admired in people. "I don't know about hard-wearing, but it's certainly cheerier, and that's the main thing." She refused to enter into any discussion on the respective merits of being hard-wearing or cheery, which might perhaps have led us into dangerous territory, and brazenly changed the subject. "Would you mind phoning Tomás for me, because since both of us are a bit deaf and Adela's the same, our conversations are a bit like something out of a comedy by Arniches." She laughed again, remembering how funny Valeriano León had been in the role of a deaf man who, when told he was to hear a Mass by someone or other, replied, with his ear trumpet to his ear: "Hear a mouse? Well, if it speaks up, I'll do my best." She said how wonderful Spanish theatre had been when it was dominated by those distinguished theatrical couples: Valeriano León and Aurora Redondo, Vico and La Carbonell, Loreto Prado and Perico Chicote, López Heredia and Asquerino, they were so elegant. You should have seen the way Mariano Asquerino put his gloves on. Just knowing that they would be on stage meant that you were guaranteed a good time when you went to the theatre, whatever they were putting on. "Well, Mama, the idols may change, but it's just the same nowadays." She pulled a face, dismissive, categorical, a look that presaged trouble: "Honestly, there's no comparison!" And I fell silent, because I knew that even an argument as silly as, or sillier than, that one, could put Mama in a bad mood for the rest of the evening or for two whole days, and that a vein of bitterness would surface in her, bitterness against the cosmos as a whole, which clouded everything else and made it impossible for her to see the pleasant side of things which only a moment before

344

she'd found so amusing and which had made her laugh. It was just as if a fuse had blown, her capacity for enjoying herself had simply switched off and there was no way of getting her back into a good mood; I didn't even try. What I'd learned was to sense when those strange moods of hers were coming and to fear them. To test her mood, I knelt down on the floor to roll the material up again. "Do you think it would be better to take the tube out, Mama? It would take up less room." She put up a bit of a struggle: what did I have against the tube?, why did I want to take it out? "Give it here," she said and, muttering to herself, she leaned it in one corner of the room. She was a great one for keeping useless objects which, later on, when they *were* needed, she would be unable to find; she's like my daughter Encarna in that respect. Then she looked me straight in the eye, one of those looks that says "You caught me out!", because you could see that she was reading your mind, and she said: "We're so different, you and me, it's incredible, a classic casebook study," but she said it with an understanding smile which signalled that the clouds had lifted. Then, without further ado, apropos of nothing, she added: "You've come back from England looking extremely pretty, my girl. What did they do to you there?" I had to look away because I realized I was turning red as a tomato. Now I think I was silly; I should have told her about my recent adventure with Guillermo, leaving out the more shocking details, presenting it to her as a kind of romantic novel. She might have understood, who knows? Later on, it occurred to me that she could probably see it in my face, after that penetrating look of hers, the last she ever gave me and which I was incapable of meeting. She must have noticed that I turned bright red, but she didn't say anything. And we put the package, a remnant of two and a half yards, double width, back in the wardrobe. I thought that however large the chair, she had still bought too much material. "I got it very cheap," she said, "anyway, it's always better to have too much than too little. I can have some cushions made later on."

Two and half yards would be more than enough for that. I think I was looking up Tomás's phone number, or thinking about looking it up, the following evening, when Adela, my mother's maid called me. I raced over here in a taxi along with Encarna and Daría who happened to be with me at home, but we didn't get here in time.

She left instructions that they shouldn't move her from the sewing room: she had insisted on that, according to Adela. She wanted to be left there: you should stay where Fate had found you. Her Grandmother Carmen had been taken while she was sewing too. "Don't move me from here," she said and that, it seems, was the last thing she did say. "Surely she didn't mean that she should be laid out here." "Yes she did, Señorita Sofía, I can assure you she did, that's exactly what she meant, that's what she wanted. She could hardly even speak by then, she could only make gestures, and she made a long, sweeping gesture, like this, with her hand, moving her chin too, and her eyes were sort of blank but anxious too, as if she wanted to make sure that I'd understood. When I said that I had, she calmed down again, she died like a saint, her head just slumped on to her chest. It was obvious what she meant."

So there she stayed, in the sewing room, this room, I've just realized; it looked bigger then because of the three mirrors on the wardrobe. I watched over her body and fell asleep curled up in the mustard chair, the camphornium which it seems Santi must have taken with him on one of his Baroque removals to the other continent. I've no idea where the package with the new fabric ended up, what with the chaos that ensued shortly afterwards. This is the first time I've been in this room since, and I've no idea what I'm doing here. I stand absorbed, my eyes fixed on the centre of the room where they set up the black rectangular box surrounded by fat candles with her lying inside on a layer of mauve velvet. I looked at her from my chair, or rather, her chair, not directly, but at our reflections in the three mirrors that took up almost the whole of the opposite wall. An oblique view that distorted the scene and fomented daydreams that removed me from it all and made it seem unreal, like when you go to the theatre and your thoughts drift off to your own problems because what the actors are saying doesn't hold your attention – you don't believe it – well, that was what happened then. I was watching the scene, but I wasn't thinking about Mama nor about what would happen to the apartment, nor about whether Santi, who was at a conference in

Atlanta, would arrive in time for the funeral or not, nor about who the echoing voices and footsteps belonged to that drifted in through the gap under the door, nor who had drunk the coffee whose grounds remained in the bottom of a cup on the little table, probably the last person who had kept me company, yes, someone who had placed a blanket over my legs and stroked my hair. "We'll leave you alone for a while, poor thing, shall we turn out the light?" And I said no, thanks, I was fine like that. I was glad to see that it was starting to rain. Then I fell asleep.

I woke up suddenly, alone, in the middle of the night, with her lying in her coffin and the rain beating down outside. Above the open coffin and her folded, motionless hands holding the rosary, the mirror on the other bank reflected back at me an absorbed, sensual smile, the remnants of an unmentionable but reassuring evocation, proof against the rust of guilt. The stories I used to invent about the ragged gypsy when I was an adolescent and wanted to enrage Mama had been far more perverse and twisted than the present one, distant resentments never acted upon; no, the present story wasn't something I'd just cooked up, but a new story, real and unexpected, like a hare suddenly springing up in a field, and only a week had passed since it began, that was why my smile, still bearing the traces of that recent, unexpected injection of vitamins, was at once innocent, bold and secretive, and its reflection in the mirror gave off the iridescent rainbow of the sorrows of love. As I sat by my mother's coffin, I relived again and again every detail of a far more passionate night, the last night I spent with Guillermo in a room in a bed and breakfast in London that had also been furnished with a wardrobe with a mirror that caught the changing contours of our entwined bodies – everything is an infinite game of mirrors – a room papered in blue where he had begged me in tears not to leave him again, as if it had been me, and not his wife, who had abandoned him, a plea followed by a dense silence in which irreconcilable memories and intentions did battle together, a silence I at last broke with my words. "No, Guillermo. I don't want to end up like Anna Karenina," I said in a firm voice, but at the same time feeling as if I'd been touched by the unreal hand of Greta Garbo who changed me for a few moments into Tolstoy's tempting

347

seductress only to make me immediately foreswear her sordid destiny, amidst sighs and tears as fantastic as they were true, decanted from her fiction into mine. "Don't see your own reflection in this mirror," she seemed to be saying to me, "that's why I'm showing it to you," another game of superimposed mirrors; no I wouldn't accept that image of ruin and misfortune, I definitely didn't want to end up like Anna Karenina. It was above all that final sentence in my novel that illuminated the mouth of the tunnel leading back to reality, a tunnel I didn't dare go through yet and which I imagined would be interminable. Outside the rain was falling endlessly: 'Oh, le chant de la pluie!' I savoured those words, like a text you know by heart but which still moves you when you re-read it; they flew over the room like birds of fire, they fluttered over my mother's slightly rounded belly, beat down outside with the rain, no, not like Anna Karenina, but spoken amidst kisses, a symphony of passionate farewells with touches of Eros and Thanatos. It had been a troubling, bittersweet farewell to the affair of the grey-blond wolf, to what might have been and wasn't – my love will be with you for all eternity – a suitable ending for a sad love song.

I'm still extremely thirsty. I hear a low miaow and feel something soft brushing against my bare feet. A small grey kitten is rubbing against them, it grabs the bottom of my trousers and looks at me as if asking permission to climb up. I crouch down and stroke it while I look for my shoes half-hidden by a cushion, and he starts playing with a tube that's rolling about on the carpet. He chases it, giving little leaps. It's an empty tube of pills.

"Where have you come from, pussycat? Now keep still, come on. What do you want? I'll be with you in a moment, just wait a bit. Are you hungry or do you want to play, or both? You're certainly not sleepy, I can see that. Neither am I, but I can't remember what I'm doing here. Come with me. Ah, aren't you soft. Let's go and see what's happening in the outside world, shall we? We can share whatever we find. We're bound to come across a few surprises."

The cat purrs and allows itself to be picked up in my arms, closing its

348

eyes voluptuously. We sally forth into the corridor together in search of new adventures. I hope we find something less imaginary, although that might be asking too much.

The first thing I do is to go into the kitchen to drink some more water and to see if there's any food for this unexpected friend, and while I gently scratch his head, it occurs to me what a terrible lack of affection there is in my life and, worse, that I've got so used to it, I haven't even realized it until now. It takes a little animal like this for me to do so. Ever since Mama died, I've become more and more locked up in myself, just like her, something I always reproached her with: "Why don't you phone a friend? Well, of course you haven't got any if you never call them. It's just like your plants, if you don't water them, they dry up." She would tell me to leave her alone, she couldn't be bothered. It's bad to isolate yourself like that. Soledad said the same to me when she was talking about her mother who it seems either gets eaten up inside about something and doesn't breathe a word to anyone or else pours out all the venom on her children. That's no good either. I don't want to end up like her or like poor Mama, lonely and resentful, someone who'd rather die than ask for help or a bit of affection. Keep yourself to yourself, she used to say, but then she was always waiting for someone to come to her; there was never anyone there when she felt like confiding in a friend or having a good time, I don't know, a friend of her own age and with similar tastes; once your kids grow up they start broadcasting on a different wavelength altogether, they have a strange way of talking and you can never tell what they think about you. On the other hand, with your own friends you can talk freely and say how awful life is, but you can also laugh and then the problems of youth don't seem so important, and you can remember past summers and song lyrics and films, there's a genuine interchange. If you don't do that, you go mad, you lose your sense of humour. My thoughts naturally go to Mariana; her figure cuts a swathe through the mist of all that is false, she shines bright as the midday sun, I want to feel her warmth, I miss her terribly, with sweet, sad longing, with *saudade*, yes, only the Portuguese word will do. I can't wait any longer, I need to stop scribbling in notebooks and deliver them to Mariana, because writing is just an excuse to be able to see her again; I want to see her now, tomorrow if possible, my friend Mariana León Jimeno. Jimeno was her second name, I just remembered it as I was taking a bottle of mineral water out of the fridge, just as I'm trying to find an empty space for it on the marble table. León Jimeno, tell us about arthropods. And I smile.

At that moment, I realize that someone is looking at me. He's a thin young man with tangled hair and wearing small glasses. He has an earring in one ear. He's just come out of the toilet and is zipping up his jeans.

"Aha!" he says, "So Pussy was with you, was she! No wonder we couldn't find her. Do you know, Raimundo thought that you'd probably gone off together; he said it was just like you to go off with a cat. He really picks up on things like that. Come with me, Pussy. I was looking for you in the wardrobe! Have you given her anything to eat?"

The cat leaps out of my arms on to the table and nimbly steps around the different shapes that make up the relief map of its intricate geography. It sniffs at a white puddle and arches its back.

"Something to eat? No, I haven't. We've only just met," I say, while I look in vain for a clean glass amongst the mountain of dirty dishes still with bits of food clinging to them, greasy cups and overflowing ashtrays that fill the sink and spill over on to the draining board. "He just turned up, as he'll tell you himself, right in the middle of another scene entirely, like the Virgin at Lourdes. He wasn't in the original script."

The young man has picked Pussy up in his arms, but he stays where he is, giving no sign that he's going to do anything, not taking his eyes off me.

"He wasn't in the original script," he repeats with an absorbed smile. "Far out, man! But I've no idea what you're talking about."

"It doesn't matter. Do you know where I could find some glasses? Clean ones, I mean."

"There might be some in the living room. A few got broken during the party last night. Drink it straight from the bottle. By the way, are you feeling better?"

I sit down on a stool. Then, while he watches me with bemused amusement, I unscrew the top of the plastic bottle and drink the whole lot.

"Better than when? Better than before I had a drink of water?"

"If you like. You're a woman after my own heart. Why go back any further? That's the trouble with Raimundo sometimes, he likes delving around in ancient history."

"Well, since you ask, I'm feeling much better actually. Listen, would you mind closing the toilet door and switching off the light on your way out; it's not the most scenic of views, you know. Or are you one of those people who was born in a field?"

He obeys, choking with laughter.

"Born in a field! You're too much," he says, "far out."

"Do you think so? Well I don't know, I wouldn't say I was that far out. By the way, what's your name?"

He says his name is Antonio and that's all I can get out of him because then he laughs so uproariously that he almost chokes. He repeats, emphasizing his refrain with a gesture of his hand, that really, I'm far out, out of sight. The cat escapes from his arms, pushes open the swing door and goes out into the corridor miaowing. The boy stumbles, leans against a wall and I notice that his eyes look somehow clouded. I get up and place a hand on his shoulder. He's gone deathly pale.

"Antonio, aren't you well? What's wrong, Antonio?"

He lets me lead him to the table. I pull up a chair. He sits down gripping the back, throws his head back and breathes deeply, his eyes closed.

"It's nothing," he says between clenched teeth, in a voice that sounds suddenly vulnerable, "I'm just coming down."

"Wait, I'll get you some water."

There's no more water left in the fridge or wine or cola or beer, nothing at all apart from half a mouldy tomato displayed like a surrealist still life on a chipped hors-d'oeuvre tray painted with butterflies which was part of the old dinner service when the house belonged to their grandparents. I turn the tap on in the sink but realize that it's splashing too much and that I'll get drenched if I don't remove the first layer of dirty dishes and pots blocking the flow of the water. I start a provisional clearing of obstacles, although I know from experience that when things reach this grave state, there are no half measures: you start by just clearing the worst of it, but you end up doing the whole thing. Good grief, this is definitely beyond the pale: there are even cigarette ends floating around inside the blender. And he says there's more stuff in the living room too. This is a fine mess we're in.

Sure enough, after a first emergency drainage of the sink, during which I manage to create a channel so that the water can flow freely, disinter a glass, wash it thoroughly and fill it with water from the cold tap, by the time I turn round and set it on the table before Antonio, I'm already tying on a Donald Duck apron I found hanging on a hook and have decided on my short-term plan. It's a familiar feeling and sometimes – although not often – it's not an unpleasant one either: it's like regaining control of an extremely routine, banal matter, but one at which you could defeat the most skilled of champions. It's a doddle, as my children would say.

"Come on, don't just sit there as if you'd had a shock. Aren't you thirsty?"

Antonio shakes his head, without opening his eyes. Instead he feels for my hand and kisses it.

"It doesn't matter, come on, drink. Water always does you good. There it is on the table, look."

As if it were a tremendous effort, he opens his eyes and reaches out to pick up the glass. His hands tremble slightly.

"Ah yes, the water, thanks."

While he drinks, I stand by his side and lightly stroke his rough, ringleted hair, dirty blond in colour. His response is an almost imperceptible groan of pleasure, feline, such a funny, faithful imitation of Pussy's purr that I can't help but laugh. Then, having checked with him first, I stand behind him and very gently start to massage his shoulder blades and the back of his neck through his shirt; he says it would be better if he took it off. He does so with a speed not at all in keeping with his apparent crisis of lethargy, throwing it gaily into the air – "*allez hop!*" – and then leaning forward to rest his head and arms on the edge of the table. I push a few bits and pieces to one side so that he's more comfortable. How wonderful, a massage, there's nothing like it for clearing your head, Raimundo goes to that Villamagna place twice a week, and to the sauna, he's really got it sorted, I'm a real star, he says, Raimundo said so too, that I was really great. He smells slightly of sweat. His T-shirt has fallen on top of an empty litre bottle of beer and it hangs there like an anachronistic flag, sending out impossible orders. I manage to read amongst its folds the words: "and your body", the rest remains hidden. Messages on T-shirts get more and more complicated, they have more words on them than an advertisement in the *New York Times*.

This boy must eat badly, you can see his ribs. But his skin is very smooth, no red marks or spots, like a child's. The only thing I notice is a very pronounced mark underneath his right shoulder blade: it's coffee-coloured and looks vaguely like a map of Italy. I tell him and he laughs, but differently from before, he sounds more trusting, more tender, even slightly sensual, "You really know how to communicate; you women are the most. Great vibrations!" And he says that it's a birth mark, a souvenir from his mother, who probably saw *La dolce vita* on telly when she was pregnant, poor thing, not that she would know the first thing about having an easy life.

Suddenly, unexpectedly, he turns round and, still sitting on the chair, puts his arms around me, weeping, and I hear a string of suppressed moans uttered at about stomach level, just near Donald Duck's head, who thus becomes a kind of improvised confessor; he says Madrid is awful, a terrible disappointment, why didn't he stay in Pola de Langreo helping his mother in the bakery instead of moving around all the time, living off other people and off stupid dreams, caught up in other people's problems, disposable friends, ready for anything, up to no good, his home town might be a hole, but at least it was his. By now he would probably be married to Nines and have given his mother a grandson instead of one worry after another, not to mention lies, damn it, and she was always on about wanting a grandson. He's suddenly talking with a very marked Asturian accent and throws in the occasional country expression. He gradually calms down and releases the pressure of his bare arms round my waist; he asks me to forgive him, something just came over him, it does sometimes.

"Don't worry, you don't have to apologize," I say. "How old are you?"

"I'll be thirty on the first of the month, in August."

He's pulled away from me now, he drinks a little more water, picks up his T-shirt and, before putting it on, wipes away his tears with it. It seems to have done him good to have had a cry, it never fails.

I walk over to the sink area again and continue the conversation from there, whilst I carry out my task with all possible care and efficiency, conscious that the harmony of my gestures communicates itself to the serene voice with which I try to pacify this lost soul of the big city. I tell him he's still very young, that he's got plenty of time to have children with Nines or whoever, and that anyway you shouldn't have children just to please your mother nor even to please the mother of the child. What you do have to think about is the child itself, because if you view your children, even before they're born, as a source of personal satisfaction or as territory to be colonized rather than as independent beings, then you might as well forget it. "Perhaps I'm going on a bit," I think at one point and I turn round to see if my lecture has sent him to sleep. He's looking at the door to the little corridor that leads to the service entrance and what was Adela's room. There's a look of confused absorption on his face, and he says yes, of course, but that's not what the problem is, it's got nothing to do with that.

"Well, it must have something to do with that," I reply, a little disconcerted, noting for the nth time in my life how quickly piles of plates go down once you've got rid of the bits of leftover food and any interposing knives and forks.

He keeps saying no, his problem is more complicated than that. I decide not to say anything further and to see if that gives him a chance to untangle the knots of the obsession that has suddenly made his voice

354

sound so sombre. Then I realize that listening to him will not only help put his jigsaw puzzle back together, it will also help me find some of the missing pieces in my own. He said he was as surprised as everyone else to find out, after I went to bed, that I was Lorenzo's mother. Raimundo was the only one who had known, but then he's older than the others. "Or perhaps you told him, because you were talking to him for quite a while on your own." And suddenly the "tú" he uses to address me sounds more timid, as if the ghost of his own mother, the baker from Pola de Langreo, stood between the woman who had appeared with the cat in her arms and the woman now washing the dishes and he was exploring my ability to accept his confession sympathetically, a confession that soon emerges, not that it was really necessary, because long before I got stuck into the cups and the glasses, I realized that the only reliable method for giving that lady a grandson was not amongst those practised by Antonio. I wonder if Mama died without suspecting that it was the same with Santi. As for Lorenzo, I don't really know. He likes girls a lot, he was with one today I think, but, according to Encarna, bisexuals are pretty thick on the ground these days. While I rinse the glasses and put them to one side, I give myself a mental order, from this moment on, not to let a kind of Miss Marple quality adulterate the attention I'm paying to what Antonio is saying.

His speech is clumsy and fragmentary, its flow obstructed by endless asides. I learn that he works as a photographer, although he also mends household appliances and drives the estate van of a colleague who owns a nursery, someone he used to live with before in Costanilla de los Ángeles, he's lost count of all the places in Madrid he's slept, and always for free but only until you start to feel that you're in the way, finding somewhere to live is really hard. I learn too that Lorenzo has helped him a great deal, because he's a terrific guy, always ready to help anyone if he can, Raimundo could learn a thing or two from him, and that they're writing a book together about roof gardens in Madrid, they've asked for a grant from the city council, and that he's been staying in the house for two months now.

"I've got a room of my own over there," he says indicating with his chin the direction of his gaze, "it's great here, but only temporary, of course, I'm not going to stay here for ever."

I'm tempted to tell him that no one stays anywhere for ever and then I'm suddenly gripped by fear because I think I might see Adela emerge from that doorway all dressed in black and I close my eyes, feeling as if I were about to faint. "No," I say to myself, while I continue dreamily listening to Antonio, "just keep calm and hang on to the present moment, you're in the refuge, the refuge for tortoises to give it its full name, and this boy to whom Lorenzo has given asylum must be the blond boy the vases were meant for, the ones that Cayetano Trueba delivered, sent by someone in Calle Covarrubias, who is, unless I'm very much mistaken, the same Raimundo fellow this refuge refugee keeps mentioning and who he is now describing as someone who only ever thinks about himself, an out-and-out egotist. I haven't noticed the vases, even though Consuelo said they were huge, but I immediately abandon my search for them. I've got enough loose ends to tie up as it is and besides I haven't quite got over my fear that Adela might suddenly appear all dressed in black. There was a moment when I had to hold on to the sink because I thought my legs were about to give way.

"Of course, when new people turn up," Antonio says, "he really turns on the charm. If Michael Jackson came through that door, he'd have him eating out of his hand in no time, because he can do it, because the guy's a genius. You saw what he was like today, such a smooth talker. But that's as far as it goes. When it comes to doing a favour for friends and we really need his help, he won't move a muscle, it's just 'me me me' all the time. And it's a bit much that, don't you think, just slamming the door in someone's face like that? He could easily have me to stay at his apartment, which is hardly pokey, he's got more reason to than anyone, but he's never even suggested it, never. He only calls you when he's bored or when he's in a state, that's what I told him when we were in the living room just now, I'm sick of it, because you do get sick of it, as if the rest of us never got in a state, but you can't tell him anything, you should see the way he reacts, he just goes into a terrific sulk. As soon as he no longer

356

has an audience, of course. He's suddenly got really low, he sees everything black, and he doesn't want to go home. I don't know what to do because Lorenzo's gone to bed already. Could you have a go, use your charisma on him?"

Suddenly I don't know what to do, my eyes slide over meaningless surfaces and I seem to perceive a kind of threat, as if the whole house were about to disintegrate along with all the ghosts it contains – a blind planet spinning in the void – unless some link can connect it up with life again. I've just found that link. Noc. The garden in the house at Suances.

"Where's Encarna?" I ask. "Didn't she come home last night?"

"Not as far as I know. But she called earlier, I think."

"And who did she speak to?"

Saying Encarna's name is like taking in air, taking steps, taking stock, injecting serum into the veins. Leaving the bell jar. She lives in this house. I'm in the refuge that she prepared for me with windows that look out to the sea, she's my captain. She will come.

"Raimundo spoke to her, I think," says Antonio. "But she can't sort anything out, even if she does come. They don't get on at all. Raimundo's been asking for you. Loads of times."

"For me? I'm sorry, could you go a bit more slowly, then perhaps I'll understand."

"Yeah, everyone was really tripping out, but as soon as you went to bed, the happening stopped happening and we all got bored. And he started drinking and writing boring poems and getting angry because I wouldn't say they were wonderful. He says you're the only one who could understand them. You just blew his mind, you inspire him. Well, it works both ways, you're on the same wavelength, you could see it the moment you came in the door; I thought you must have known each other all your lives."

I take off the Donald Duck apron, hang it back on its hook, and out of the fog of my brain, very slowly, like a Polaroid photo, there emerges the figure of a gentleman with white hair and a very nice voice who was speaking on the intercom downstairs when I got to the house, having escaped from mine. I liked his half-pompous, half-delicate gesture when he ushered me in ahead of him through the door and we came up together in the lift, chatting with a kind of instant intimacy as soon as we learned we were coming to the same apartment. He gave me the support I needed, I saw that at once, although it seems odd that I should need the support of a stranger to come here; who would have thought it, as Mama used to say. But there was no one here that I knew, they didn't care whether I came in or not, and I'd already spent a while wandering alone around the streets nearby. I had a drink in a couple of bars, uncertain what to do, I might get here and be in the way, and I didn't know what to say, I felt horribly like crying. In a bar, I'd just heard the voice of Ana Belén singing: "Am I really back on the road to hell again?" and if Raimundo hadn't been at the door I might well have walked straight by, straight down the road to hell, caught up in that *Fleurs du mal* rhetoric that has done so much damage ever since the day Baudelaire wrote them. It was just lucky that he paid me so much attention right from the start, like a rather bizarre host, because he says the most extravagant things, but I enjoyed plunging with him into that soothing fiction that took my mind off my problems. Yes, maybe we are on the same wavelength. We were talking about literature, about Pessoa I think. He was saying that I should split myself into two people, that I should build a dream version of the streets of my new country, and all the houses too, brick by brick. He'd realized that I was sad and lost, and, gradually, I stopped being sad and lost because he created a little homeland of words for me, a temporary refuge.

Then Lorenzo arrived with more people and took me to his room for a while; he was very sweet, saying that I could stay there as long as I liked, of course I could, I had more right to be there than anyone. I should slam the door in the faces of Eduardo and that Magdalena woman; he obviously knew the name already. These things happen and that's all there is to it, Mama, just forget about it. He didn't want me to cry, I was as tough as they come, the queen of the refuge: Encarna would say just the same. But it had been the white-haired host who had been the first to lend me a hand. Then we went out into the living room again and things got complicated.

"That was when you started to imitate the parties that posh people go to," Antonio was saying, "You were like a comedy duo, just fantastic, you couldn't have done better if you'd rehearsed, but don't get me wrong, you were the star turn. I thought you must be an actress, because he goes round with a lot of theatre people, but no, you're different. Everyone just flipped out, you're really too much. And Lorenzo told me you were in a bit of state at the moment. I'd never have known it."

I've just tidied up the table and wiped down the marble top. It looks completely different now. I think I'll go and look for a reading lamp, there must be one in the living room, then I'm going to come back here and write, because my brain's bursting with things I need to get down on paper. I've got a huge backlog of things to write about.

Antonio is smiling.

"The kitchen looks cool! Consuelo doesn't work hard like you do, she's always skiving off."

"Tell me about it. I've known her for years. What you need in this house is some food. Perhaps we can put that right tomorrow. Meanwhile, we can go and see Raimundo if you like, only briefly, mind. Then I've got things to do."

He tells me again that I'm really far out, then kicks open the swing door and we go out into the corridor together.

There's a light on. A girl crosses from the bathroom to Lorenzo's room, the door of which stands open. She closes it behind her. She is barefoot. She is wearing a pair of satin knickers and nothing else. Neither Antonio nor I make any comment.

Raimundo is in the living room lying limply on the floor, with a half-empty bottle of whisky by his side. He's writhing about a bit and moaning as if he had a fever or was in pain. He's nothing like the man I saw before, so particular about his appearance and his every gesture. Fortunately, he doesn't at first show any signs of recognizing me. On the other hand, he immediately addresses Antonio and starts reproaching him in a loud voice for having been away so long, as well as for other less obvious, more absurd things. He calls him Zajar.

"I'm going to have to dismiss you, Zajar, you're simply too real and too useless. You're no use to me whatsoever. Trying to lead a normal life is just impossible."

Antonio doesn't seem the same person either. He gets aggressive and says that he'd better call him by his real name – or else – he won't put up with any more crap, he's had enough, he's leaving. He kicks him, stumbles and falls on the floor on top of him. I step in to separate them.

"Come on," I say with a conciliatory voice, "you're like two little boys. You're fighting over nothing."

Raimundo crawls over and sits leaning against the edge of the sofa. He looks at me with sad eyes. In them I see the effort he makes to disguise beneath a theatrical mask his sudden recognition of my identity. He puts on a slightly affected voice.

"Zajar is a constant torment to me," he says in a whisper, "he follows me round like a dog that I sometimes shoo away. Give me a ciggie, Zajar. I've no idea how long I've been alone in this dark dungeon. I don't know whether this is coming to an end or if it's over already. Shadows of shadows. Pour the Baroness a drink."

"I don't follow you round like a dog," protests Antonio, "I don't need you at all. You bore me to death anyway, and everyone else, if you must know; no one finds you funny, no one, people avoid you."

"Shut up, you worm! We must ask the Baroness's forgiveness. Neither of us can claim that this has been one of our better nights. I see you have nothing to say. Let us allow our classic writers to illumine us on a night like this."

And while I look exploratively around me in search of a lamp which I can't see amongst the surrounding chaos, I hear him recite something which sounds like Shakespeare:

"On such a night as this, Thisbe, coming first by night, did scare away, or rather did afright, the shadow of a lion."

Antonio bows and starts applauding wildly like a fool, while Raimundo looks at me with eyes that are simultaneously servile and imploring.

"Tell me, noble lady, what is it that you seek?"

"Perhaps a notebook in excess to your needs, or some other such writing material. I desire to be your chronicler," I say, trying to play him at his own game.

His eyes light up and he holds out his hand so that I can help him to his feet. He can barely stand.

"That is indeed a fine request," he says, "worthy of someone like yourself, my lady, who has set her standard amongst the clouds."

He weaves his way over to a small table full of books and papers. There are a lot of newspapers piled up there too.

Antonio has come over to me now and is following his friend's movements with an expression which is suddenly tender and astonished.

"Didn't I tell you?" he tells me, almost whispering in my ear. "Didn't I tell you that you inspire him? And he's completely gone, stoned out of his mind. But you've tamed him, you see. Everything under control."

Raimundo turns round and looks at us. He holds out a black notebook with oilcloth covers which he's previously inspected and from which he's torn out the first few pages.

"Do not plot behind my back," he says, "for it is finished. Unable to confront the enemy hosts alone, a defeated man surrenders. Weep for the knight Raimundo de Ercilla!"

He covers his face with his hands and slumps back against the sofa crying. At first, I think he's still acting, but then I don't know what to think. I kneel by his side, while Antonio calmly rolls a reefer.

And suddenly I know with absolute certainty who this man is staring into space and saying with a voice thick with tears:

"I don't want to go back to the intensive care unit! But alas, I can't go back to the depths of the cellar either with my candle lit. Antonio, please, call Dr León, it's urgent. Where's that bitch got to? Mariana!"

Antonio inhales deeply from the newly lit reefer.

"Bloody hell, here we go again," he says. "All right!"

I get up and disappear almost on tiptoe without saying a word, without anyone stopping me. Once out in the corridor, I hurry back to the kitchen with the black notebook clutched to my chest. I can't wait any longer. There are too many things. I can't keep them in any longer.

I don't know how long I can have been sitting here writing furiously, without looking up, but it must be nearly morning when the latchkey turns in the back door and I hear unmistakable footsteps coming down the corridor. I take off my glasses, fix my eyes on that spot and await her appearance like someone watching for the sun to come out after an endless night. She comes in, stops and we look at each other for a long time with no surprise, no fear, no ulterior motives, the most natural thing in the world, like drinking water or eating bread, but it's also the most extraordinary thing, a food whose value we only appreciate when we don't have it.

She's wearing a miniskirt, flat shoes and a man's jacket.

"Hello there," she says, smiling.

She doesn't ask me what I'm doing here at this time. She's always boasted of her imperturbability, of being ready to cope with anything, with no questions asked, no fuss, "not even if Charlemagne got into the same lift as me dressed as a bullfighter". That's her motto.

I can see she's in ebullient mood though and is still ruminating some recent pleasure. She'll tell me about it eventually, if she wants to. And if not, it doesn't matter. It's enough to see her, hear her, feel her touch. She comes over and gives me a kiss; I put my arms round her waist and stay there for a few moments with my head pressed against her young belly, in which the continuation of these memoirs may one day build its nest. The image of the baker in Pola de Langreo suddenly reappears, but I close the door on her immediately, because if any more of these minor characters come in, the kitchen will end up like the Marx Brothers' dressing room.

I know it would make us both laugh if I told Encarna what I was thinking, but it would require too long a preamble and there are a host of other more important subjects queuing up to be discussed. That always happens when I see her again. I just don't know where to begin.

With pleasure I notice her fingers playing silently with my hair.

"What a relief to see the kitchen looking so tidy when you get back late!" she says. "It's like a miracle, as if Granny had come back."

I feel a lump in my throat that stops me talking. Encarna moves away

362

from me and places a red and black plastic bag on the table. From it she produces yoghurts, beer, sliced bread, milk, biscuits, things wrapped up in aluminium foil and a few tins.

"I dropped in at the supermarket," she says, "because one thing that definitely isn't the same as it was in Grandma's time is the fridge. I don't even need to open it to know that. And I bought some food for the cat too, because it's always Pussy this and Pussy that, but if it wasn't for me, the poor creature would be on a starvation diet. But what's wrong? Have you lost your voice?"

"No, I just can't cope with so many things in my head all at once. As you used to say when you were a little girl it's all the little bits, all the bits and pieces. Don't you remember?"

She bursts out laughing.

"Of course I do. I said it in Suances, didn't I?"

I look at the black notebook, at my still fresh handwriting.

"Yes, and you said it only a moment ago too. I was writing down things about that summer in order to pick up the thread of my arrival here tonight. These, as you see, are all the little bits of a very long story."

She's taken out some cheese from one of the packages and is making a sandwich for herself. She opens a can of beer and sits down opposite me.

"What bit of the story are you referring to exactly? Don't go all mysterious on me. What are you thinking about now, for example, at this very moment? Just like that. And no tricks. I give you fifteen seconds."

"About Grandma. About how strange it seems to me that you should mention her as soon as you came through that door, that you should have said: 'It's as if Granny had come back.' I'm not trying to be mysterious or odd or anything. It's just that she really has come back. Grandma did come back last night, I swear she did, Encarna. Don't laugh."

She looks at me very seriously, the way I did when she explained to me about the universes.

"What on earth makes you think I'm going to laugh? The dead do sometimes return to the place where they used to live, especially when you leave them free to do so, when you don't hem them in; they visit us in our dreams. Did you dream about her?"

"No, it was something much more powerful than that. I was walking along the corridor as if I were her. Yes, I've just remembered, part of me split off into her, I *was* her! She was looking round this flat and she didn't recognize it, and then, oh, I don't know, a lot of other things too. It's never happened to me before with Mama, it was almost as if I'd given birth to her, really, it was incredible. And I was thinking with her words and reliving her memories. Some I've forgotten, but not others. That's why I started writing, so that I wouldn't forget what I have managed to retain, in order to retrieve it."

"Well," says Encarna, "we always write for the same reason, don't we, salvaging what we can from the wreckage?"

There was a silence. She takes a sip of beer. She's looking at me differently now, she's laughing, but she's got her detective face on. Sometimes I think she looks a bit like Mariana.

"Have you been here long?" she asks.

"I don't know, I really can't remember; that's another reason why I was writing: to come to terms with time which sometimes has a very strange way of presenting us with the bill."

She looks at the notebook and for the first time since she came in, she looks upset. She picks it up and looks at the first page.

"This is my notebook! Where did you get it? Wait … Sorry, I'm not checking up on you! But do you see, here at the beginning you can see my writing. I'd written more than that though. Did you tear out any pages?"

"No, I didn't even know it was yours. It was Raimundo who gave it to me, a friend of yours who's in the living room, he was the one who tore out the pages."

"He's no friend of mine, he's a friend of the lodger's, you mean. You know I'd really like to have an apartment to myself. That guy really is the limit; now, he's even doling out my notebooks to people. He's got his own home, you know, and more than enough money."

"I'm so sorry," I say penitently, as if I had been the cause of the mess. "Anyway the other bits are in the living room. I don't think he's thrown them away."

I was about to add: "We can stick it back together again," like I did as

364

a child when I'd broken some valuable object and my mother found out; for her all objects were valuable. I look up and her granddaughter, who has not turned out like her at all in that respect, is smiling again and making a gesture very typical of her, as if she were erasing some incorrect formulae from the blackboard.

"It's okay, don't worry, I don't want to spoil your night, not now you're here. Anyway it doesn't matter, I'll have written it out properly somewhere else. Come on, stop looking like a frightened child. I only want to make it absolutely clear that the notebook," she adds, replacing it on the table, "is a present from me, not from Raimundo, from me! And it's rather an appropriate quotation too. Have you read it?"

I say I haven't and I look at the first page. "You can climb out of any hole you want to" – I read – "if you're curious enough to know what's going on outside while you're drowning." I look up. She's making a ham sandwich now.

"That's really nice!" I say. "Whose is it?"

"Mine, but you can have it. By the way, have you met Raimundo before?"

"No, I met him here for the first time last night. He strikes me as someone who's having a hard time, but he's very intelligent. I don't know, perhaps he's having a hard time precisely because he is intelligent."

"Everyone's having a hard time, Mama. Who doesn't have it hard these days? And no one's saying Raimundo isn't intelligent. He gets his kicks out of charming people, playing Pygmalion, because that's what he loves doing, make no mistake about it, but he's got his own apartment to do that in, hasn't he? That's all I'm saying, and lately he's become a bit of a drag – he goes too far, really he does. He goes on about his pain and his fear of being alone, and we can't get him out of here for love nor money. And of course, Lorenzo feels sorry for him. It's just that a few weeks ago, he tried to commit suicide, did you know that?"

"Yes, I did."

"From the newspapers?"

"No, it's one of the little bits and pieces. But that's not important now, let's get back to Grandma. What were you saying about her?"

She sits thinking for a while. The detective look reappears on her face.

"Oh, right. No ... I was asking what time you arrived and if there were other people here, just to find out if you'd smoked any hash or not."

"Yes, I think I did. I can't remember. Lorenzo must have taken me to the sewing room because he saw I was getting dizzy. And I'd drunk quite a lot too."

"Say no more. That business of thinking you're someone else is quite common if you're not used to smoking hash: it's fairly typical in fact. It's happened to me sometimes too. What it does do, though, is really set you up to write. The two planes of dream and interpretation fit together fantastically well. Anyway, we know what you're like. You don't need to smoke hash, you could get high on a packet of peanuts, given half a chance."

And suddenly we're talking about the problems of writing fiction, about coincidences, metaphors, beginnings and endings, constantly interrupting one another, with the enthusiasm of someone with a long-standing thirst for something. It was as if we'd never talked about anything else in our lives. Indeed, taking advantage of one of the few pauses that arise, I remark on this and she responds very seriously, of course. Why was I surprised? Have we ever talked about anything else? Not to complicate the argument with new adornments, I need only recall the summer in Suances ("mentioned above" she adds smiling and pointing to the black notebook), were those not rigorous discussions about literature?

"I'm feeling very happy," she says suddenly, "because I'm going to have a book of my short stories published."

"Really? How come you didn't tell me before?"

She bursts out laughing. She waves her hands about in the air and shrugs her shoulders comically as if she were scaring off a cloud of mosquitos or trying to remove something that had got stuck to her clothes.

"You've got a cheek demanding a 'before' and an 'after' from me, Mama, with all those bits and pieces in the air and on the floor! Though they're more like remnants really, don't you think? Threads, buttons, safety pins and empty cotton reels, "the bits and bobs of sewing", that's what Grandma used to call them, because it all comes down to sewing things together. I told you when it was the right moment. Quite apart from the fact that I didn't know for sure until tonight."

She tells me that she's been having supper at the house of a young publisher who is very enthusiastic about her book; he invited her to supper in order to tell her that and also to say that they were going to publish it. Then she starts telling me about this publisher, about how and where she met him and she says that he's lovely, that she's never known such a nice man, and that he didn't invite her just because of the book.

"He ambushed me, you know, but in the nicest possible way. He's not at all the wham-bam-and-thank-you-mam type. I'm fed up with that kind of guy. As you always say: 'The play is short and the interval's very long'."

She looks so pretty, so excited, radiating so much light that the sombre story she wrote when she was much younger and which, some hours ago, had provoked my decision to turn up at the refuge, disappears as quickly as a bat put to flight by the first glimmers of dawn. After that "exile with no return", or with no apparent return, my daughter and I have found each other again here. I'm sure she doesn't write such sad stories now. She wouldn't look the way she does.

"It's lovely to see you looking so happy! It does my heart good, as Grandma would say. I haven't seen you looking so pretty in ages."

"I know," she says, "I seem to be flying tonight. That's why I wasn't even surprised to find you here, nor that she should have decided to make a tour of inspection of the corridors. I take all marvels in my stride."

I ask her about the title of her book and she says that it's had several, but that, after discussing it with Nacho Egido, the name of her publisher-boyfriend, they both decided that the best title was *The Persistence of Memory*, and they thought that the cover could be a reproduction of the Dalí painting.

"You know the Dalí painting, the one with the over-ripe watches," she says. "We've got a big poster of it in the old sewing room. Lorenzo bought it in New York. If you slept there, you must have seen it."

I think for a moment.

"I have seen it, yes. *The Persistence of Memory*. But listen, I'm sorry, I was thinking before – because I've been shifting endless bits of furniture and other objects around in my head – what happened to the photos that Grandma had pinned up on that wall?"

"What photos?"

"I don't know, there were lots of them. But there was one in particular that I can't get out of my mind; God knows where it's gone."

"But which one? If you tell me which one ..."

"You probably don't remember it. It's a photo of Grandma when she was young, with a horse."

I look at her. She's smiling. She reaches into her bag which has been left on the floor, rummages around in it and very carefully, like someone preparing a surprise effect, produces a photo of my mother from an embossed Morocco leather purse. She puts it on the table and reorders the others in the same bundle.

"Do you mean this one?"

"Of course. How come you've got it?"

"Because I always liked it. I made off with it when she died. Besides, it's a photo with a story."

"What story?"

"A love story. But that's a secret between Grandma and me, if you don't mind. I had my secrets with Grandma too, you know."

Only at the end, when we're both almost falling asleep, does she ask if I've come to stay because something bad has happened.

That last part of the conversation, the shortest part, has as its backdrop the old sewing room, where she's taken me to view the Dalí reproduction, with me lying on the bed and her sitting on the carpet, both of us barely managing to stifle our yawns.

I speak as lightly as possible about the redhead and my decision to disappear from the house, at least for a few days. At the end, though, my voice falters.

"What do you mean 'for a few days', Mama. What you have to do is leave for good. You haven't belonged there for ages, not at all. Come on, please, don't start crying now. That's all we need. Let him have his fancy piece. Forget about them. And forget about Aunt Desi too. Who cares about them?"

"Yes, but what am I going to do?"

She holds out a handkerchief to me.

"For the moment, you're not going to cry, all right? And then you can do whatever you like, whatever comes into your head. Let's see, what would you like to do, where would you like to be at this very moment? I'll give you fifteen seconds."

"I don't know where," I say, drying my eyes, "but I know who with. With a friend of mine, Mariana León. Do you remember Noc?"

I catch a slight note of impatience in her voice.

"Yes, Mama, but don't get any more bits and pieces out until tomorrow, I'm dead tired. Let's get to the point. This Mariana León – who is she, where is she?"

"That's what I'd like to know. She went on a trip, but I've no idea where."

"Well, for the moment, go to sleep. Tomorrow we'll find out, I promise. I'll disguise myself as a policewoman and accompany you in your search; we'll leave no stone unturned. Now, go to sleep, we're both exhausted. And by the way," she adds while she bends over to kiss me, "I must give you the name and brand of a firming cream made out of royal jelly; it's supposed to be really good. Raimundo uses it. You haven't been taking care of your skin."

"I know, I've got out of the habit of taking care of myself."

"Well, that's another of the many first things we'll have to put right. One very important bit. Now, though, you've got to switch off. Tomorrow's another day. I'll turn out the light, okay?"

"Yes, love, goodnight and thanks for everything," I say, when the lights are out, trying to hold her a few moments longer in my arms. "But tell me just one thing, one last thing, you do remember Noc, don't you?"

"Of course I do. He's here with us now," she says in a whisper.

"Don't frighten him away. You know he only likes to visit when it's dark."

Consuelo woke me up in the early afternoon. There was no one else in the refuge. She didn't want to be indiscreet, but she'd just popped in to tell me that a friend of mine had called from a hotel in Cádiz. It seemed to be urgent. My friend Mariana León.

EPILOGUE

Rafael Heredia, the waiter at La Caracola, was wiping down the table just vacated by an oldish German couple. He collected up the bottles, glasses and the saucer containing a tip and placed them on a tray, then, back at the bar, protected from the weather by a precarious structure of aluminium, glass and asbestos, he leaned on the counter, poured himself a whisky and stood staring with an inquisitive, expert eye at the whirl of ominously black clouds on the horizon that were marring the ceremonious setting of the sun. With a lift of his chin he indicated the far end of the railing that circled the terrace.

"Those two are going to get wet if they're not careful," he said to his nephew and temporary assistant, a dark-haired young boy of fifteen with the face of an intelligent mouse. "They can't say they haven't been warned. The forecasters said as much on the radio and on the telly."

The boy finished rinsing some glasses.

"What did they say?" he asked without much interest.

"Cloud variable with occasional showers over the whole of the southeast," said Rafa, after savouring the first sip of whisky. "It's blowing in from Africa."

"Hmm," said the boy. "There's definitely a storm brewing. And it was really sunny this morning."

He began humming a recent pop song.

As the light faded, a strong, damp wind began to blow, catching up plastic bags, wrappers, a torn newspaper and empty cigarette packets from the beach down below. Like a face flushed with fever, the sun occasionally managed to break through the clouds which were now dark red verging on black.

The two women sitting opposite each other and looking out to sea, at a table at the far end of the railing, seemed unaware of the imminent arrival of rain or night. Theirs was the only table outside still occupied, although, to tell the truth, they were actually taking up two tables. On one they had their drinks, cigarettes and the odd sheet of paper or notebook, but it was the other, larger table, which they'd pulled up to join theirs, piled high with papers, notebooks and files, that they kept consulting. They'd taken the precaution of placing stones and a heavy glass ashtray on the pile of papers as improvised paperweights, but that seemed to have been their only response to the gathering storm. Completely absorbed in their work of reading the sheets of paper and occasionally scribbling something in the margins, they only interrupted their work to exchange comments that usually ended in laughter. If one of them was sitting silent, looking pensively out to sea, the other would soon break that silence by gesturing expressively or handing them the sheet of paper they were reading, indicating one particular paragraph. They were leaning towards each other across the folding table. Their cheeks were flushed and in their right hand they each wielded a fountain pen with a fat nib: one black pen and one green. The air, growing ever wilder, tousled their hair and tugged at their clothes.

"If only they'd come and sit at one of the tables inside, they'd be safer," said Rafa. "Besides, soon they won't be able to see a thing."

The boy interrupted his melodic litany, in which he complained repeatedly that someone was a stone in his path and the cross of his destiny, to reply dully:

"Well, say something to them, then. You seem to know the taller one, at least that's what I thought you said yesterday."

"Yes, she's a psychiatrist. She's been staying up at the hotel for quite some time now. I don't know the other one. She suddenly turned up three days ago. I don't know – she must be a friend of hers. And there they are, as you see."

The boy pulled a face of comic surprise.

"What do I see? I don't see anything. Don't go on about them, Uncle. Leave them in peace."

Without taking his eyes off them, Rafa took another sip of whisky, then he shrugged.

"They can stay there for all I care. What I don't understand is exactly what they're up to. You might say it's obviously some kind of work, all right, fine, but you don't joke all the time when you're working, as if you were at the cinema watching a film. Besides, when they've got a fantastic hotel room – because it's a good hotel as you know – why on earth do they come down here instead and use this as an office and ask me to turn the music down? Can *you* understand that? They've spent three whole afternoons here and today, Paquito, they're going to get wet."

"Fine, then let them. They must like the open air. You know what the rich are like. I bet she makes a fortune looking after all those mad people."

The only reply Rafa gave was a sudden glance up at the horizon and a huge snaking flash of lightning, brilliant against the blackness of a now entirely overcast sky. He completed his look with a shake of his index finger and the complacent smile of someone who knows he is right.

"Dear God!" murmured Paquito, covering his ears against the crash of thunder that followed and whose echoes immediately gave way to a shower of plump drops of rain that soon grew heavier.

"Didn't I tell you?" said his uncle. "It's always the same, people only turn to religion when it thunders. But that's the way the country's going these days. Let's go and give those two a hand, come on, they're going to need it. Good grief! They've got everything there but the kitchen sink."

The two women had stood up, and, while still maintaining their calm, were rapidly gathering their notebooks and files together and sticking them into a large canvas bag. Not even now, though, when the rain was beginning to pour down their faces, did they show any sign of tiredness, irritation or haste; they seemed lit up from within by a glow of serenity.

They greeted the arrival of the two volunteers with affectionate cheerfulness and between the four of them they quickly cleared the tables and raced back to the covered area of the bar. Their jackets pulled over their heads to protect them from the rain, the two women went first, smiling, concentrating on the bundles they were carrying.

A piece of paper escaped from one of the files that wasn't closed properly and was whisked away. Paquito, who was escorting the women, put down the tray laden with cups and glasses that he was carrying and raced off down the stairs to the beach in pursuit of that fugitive bit of paper whirled about by the rain.

He caught it, already rather dirty and soggy, at the edge of the last step, after two failed attempts to trap it with his foot.

It was freshly written and the ink had run on one of the words written in capital letters. There were only two words altogether. The second word, CLOUD, was almost illegible.

MADRID, April 1984–January 1992